CIRCLE OF DECEIT

CIRCLE OF DECEIT

Callum Gunn

DIADEM BOOKS

Circle of Deceit
All Rights Reserved. Copyright © 2015 **Callum Gunn**

Published by Diadem Books
For information, please contact:

Diadem Books
16 Lethen View
Tullibody
Alloa
FK10 2GE UK

www.diadembooks.com

ISBN-13: 978-1-908026-64-4

At seventeen he falls in love quite madly
with eyes of tender blue,
At twenty-four he gets it rather badly
with eyes of a different hue.
At thirty-five you'll find him flirting madly
with two or three or more;
And when at last he thinks he's past love,
it is then he meets his last love,
and he loves her like he's never loved before.

'Maid of the Mountains'
Lyrics by Harry Graham.
Music by Harold Fraser-Simpson.

(And by that destiny) to perform an act
Whereof what's past is prologue; what to come,
In yours and my discharge.

The Tempest Act 2, scene 1, 245–254

PROLOGUE

What's Future is Prologue

THE DAWN LIGHT filtered through the curtains and his eyes opened, the dream of a provocative Scots girl still with him. The pressure in his bladder reminded him of the need to visit the toilet. He slid out of bed and lifted himself up, for a moment befuddled as his eyes focussed on the familiar walls of the room. He felt disoriented, slightly dizzy and steadied himself on the door handle to the en suite bathroom beside his bed. Why did he feel confused, as though the bathroom was in a different place, beyond the foot of the bed? He opened the bathroom door and, slipping down his pyjama pants, slumped down on the toilet seat. While the thin stream between his legs trickled into the pan below, his half-awake mind tried to grasp the retreating vestiges of his dream. It was such a weird dream—of a woman, a vital, vibrant Scots girl that laughed and teased him, and seemed so real, yet a woman he could not for the life of him place or recall. Dreams could be like that, he thought, and it was amazing how the unconscious mind can be creative, conjuring up people you have never met yet think you know.

He stood up and flushed the toilet. He liked the comfort of his en suite bathroom, just next to his bed. He liked the way he could just swing out of bed and put his hand on the handle of the bathroom door. At his age, he liked his comfort, and somehow felt especially relieved this morning that he had this comfort. He climbed back into bed and saw that Sylvia had woken, too. She stretched her arm out, resting her hand on his shoulder. It was not often that she touched him, but he liked it when he felt the contact.

"It's time to get up, darling," she yawned. "You said you wanted to go over your part of the sermon the minister gave you to read."

Memory flooded back and clutched his stomach with alarm. "I…," he began. "I can't explain it, but I don't think I should go."

She frowned. "You can't let the minister down—you said you would read your part."

"I'll phone Sadie—she'll read my part," he said. "She a deaconess… she has a copy of the extract in case something happens to me… I'll say I have a stomach ache."

"That would be a fib!" she laughed. "You're acting out of character. I thought you said the Lord put you in Kennoway because he meant you to go to the nearest church!"

"I just have a feeling… I shouldn't go. I'll come with you this morning—to your happy-clappy church in Kirkcaldy. We should really worship together, you know." He grinned. "It's time I got another hug from Huggy Peter!"

"Well, that would be nice," Sylvia smiled. "We *should* worship together. What God has joined together, you know… Nevertheless, you can't shirk your responsibilities. Go to the Church of Scotland this one last time, then next week we'll go back to the routine of worshipping together at the Kirkcaldy Full Gospel Church."

"Okay," he said. He felt uneasy—but then succumbed to an overwhelming sense of comfort.

It was right that he and Sylvia should do things together. After all, they belonged to each other, like a comfortable pair of slippers.

He got out of bed to go to his study and practice the sermon extract he had agreed to read. Just then a disquieting thought crossed his mind. "Did you have that annual cancer scan at the hospital?" he asked.

"Yes, darling," she smiled, sitting up. "I've been given the all clear—nothing to worry about."

PART ONE

CHAPTER ONE

Lynsey Anne McCann

CHARLES never forgot the first time he saw her. He had participated in the morning service by reading an extract from the pre-prepared sermon the minister had printed out to be read by volunteers in his absence. After the final hymn and prayer, followed by the long drawn-out three-fold 'Amen' sung by the congregation, the various readers had lined up at the church door to shake the hands of the congregation as they filed out. He had never seen her before, but she engaged his attention the minute she appeared before him and grasped his hand. He thought afterwards, in her bright floral dress she was like a red rose amidst the mundane black and grey outfits of the other worshippers. Also, she was effusive in her thanks, which surprised him since he'd only read one piece: one would think he had given a whole, original sermon that had gone straight to her heart. Her lucid brown, slightly slanted almond eyes smiled at him in a lavishly made up face, yet he was very conscious of a creamy cleavage that suggested supple liquid breasts. "You're welcome," he smiled. "I hope you might join our little prayer circle on Wednesday evenings." And he let go her hand.

But she did not let go of *his* hand. His hand had gone limp, signalling the end of the handshake, but since she continued to grasp his firmly beyond the time normally allotted to a handshake, he felt obliged to re-tighten his grasp.

"Och, I weel," she said with a laugh. "I worked fur a meenister once, and it's time I came back to the kirk!"

Her Scottish accent was very local—an accent that usually grated in his southern ears—but somehow, coming from her, it was musical, like the twitter of an exotic songbird.

She let go his hand and moved on to the next handshaker in the line. Before long everyone had passed onto the green lawn outside, but he was still aware of her musical twitter as various members of the congregation thronged around her.

She was effusive, almost over-friendly, while others looked slightly embarrassed, some staring at her, even shaking their heads. Then it occurred to him—this brightly coloured, effusive and fluttering songbird was quite drunk.

The church was situated between a new development of smart estate houses, where Charles lived, and a medley of sombre terraced council houses, where many of the congregation lived. It was typical of the sprawling industrial towns of Fife, where the town planners, in their wisdom, thought it a good strategy that poor housing should be cheek-by-jowl next to new executive commuter estates. It was a form of civic integration, or, if you like, care in the community. Charles was pleased with his acquisition of two modern 4-bedroomed houses, one in which he and his wife Sylvia had now lived for three years, the other being an investment property they used for rental income. Their house overlooked an industrial whisky storage plant, but also the Lomond Hills that rose steeply up to the horizon beyond the storage plant. He firmly believed the Lord had placed him in this location—and he took comfort from Psalm 121 which assured him that where he was he could lift up his eyes unto the hills—and unto the Lord who made heaven and earth, and for that reason his 'foot shall not be moved', as the psalm promised.

And if the Lord had put him here, then it stood to reason that he was to worship at the nearest church—which in fact was only fifteen minutes' walk away. He later thought, had the Lord not put him here, close to this small Church of Scotland in this town in the Kingdom of Fife, he would never have met Lynsey Anne McCann.

CHAPTER TWO

NOT THAT CHARLES particularly chose to attend the local Church of Scotland in the first place. Because it was the nearest church, he went there to begin with. The church was beautifully decorated with Christmas tree and flowers—it was just before Christmas. There must be a lot of love here, he thought, with such evidence of loving care bestowed upon the decorations. But no-one spoke to him or his wife Sylvia. Even the minister, after his third visit, asked him, as he had done on the last two occasions, if he was a visitor to the area. It seemed to him that the very local Scottish congregation were very parochial and spoke only amongst themselves.

He was used to a more evangelical form of worship, with a more evangelical outreach, in any case. Before he and Sylvia came to the area they had enjoyed the warm fellowship of the small Baptist Church in Hull. Here there was no Baptist Church nearby, but there was a Full Gospel Church in nearby Kirkcaldy that he and Sylvia felt obliged to try out after the very indifferent welcome they had received from the local Church of Scotland. It meant a drive of some twenty minutes. Certainly, they were warmly welcomed there. For one thing, they were great huggers there. In fact, Portly Peter, the doorman, was inescapable, and he would wrap his arms around Charles and compress him to his beefy chest—awkward, because Portly Peter (or Huggy Peter, as Charles came to call him) always had his spectacles dangling on two pieces of cord against his very convex chest—and being squashed against the fragile obstacles that might break required an awkward resistance to being pulled up against them. Hugs from the few middle-aged women were more tolerable—most of the women there were young, mind you—but what really went against Charles's starchy grain was the universal raising of arms and waving of hands as they worshipped—eyes shut as they repeated, again and again, the same worshipful lines of love and adoration. It all sounded very good and Charles enjoyed singing—but could not get the hang of singing over and over again, *ad nausea*, the same trite phrases. It was like a mantra. 'Yes, I'm sure the Lord heard those words the first time,' he thought, and at length, deflated, he would sag down to his seat while everyone else continued to stand, hands and faces lifted up in worshipful adoration, faces with eyes shut in rapt ecstasy. At length they got themselves so worked up, it seemed, that they began to break out in babbling tongues that, to Charles's conservative ears, sounded nonsensical. One dear Scottish lady hugged him, the tears in her eyes confirming her sincerity, saying that in time the spirit would move him, too, to praying in tongues. She presented him with a book on the Holy Spirit, saying he should read it and try practicing praying in the Spirit.

So he did. He went for long walks praying aloud, allowing his tongue to waggle, his brain in neutral. No warm feelings of the Spirit suffused him. Nothing changed even by the occasional introduction of the name 'Jesu' into the pseudo African-sounding tongue he managed to produce. No, he decided, those huggy Full Gospel folk were not the Lord's chosen mission field for him. It suited his wife Sylvia, however, and soon she had agreed to give a lift to two elderly folk on a regular basis, picking them up from the local council estate and taking them to the church every Sunday morning. Charles had nothing against this church—which he thought of as a 'happy-clappy' congregation; it was okay for them, but not for him. Apart from the few middle-aged folk there, the congregation was largely made up of young married couples, full of the enthusiasm and the energy of youth—of the upwardly mobile. No, he decided, he would return to the lukewarm indifferent working folk of the local Church of Scotland just down the road from his house—it was, after all, his closest church, which the Lord must have intended as his spiritual home. He recalled the words of a lady preacher in Hull, who was a cook, that 'the Lord puts you where he wants you'. In any case, he argued, why should the Spirit be poured out in the Full Gospel gathering in Kirkcaldy and not in the working-class congregation of Kennoway where most of its members came from the poor council dwellings—where, he was told, drug addiction, and alcoholism too, was rife, as it was in Hull around the struggling Baptist church. Why should not the Spirit be poured out in such places, too? It just wasn't fair! Surely the indifferent, the sinners, like him, deserved to be saved, too? Did not Jesus seek out the sinners—the prostitutes, the drunks, the poor in Spirit?

So he persevered and went back to the local Church of Scotland while his wife Sylvia routinely worshipped at the evangelical church in Kirkcaldy with its fervent born-again people. He enjoyed the traditional hymns and sang out with enthusiasm in his local church—there were no vain repetitions of inane phrases. The words were projected on the ceiling of the nave in front so you could look up and sing with open eyes. The organist hammered the organ until it hummed with a fervour that brought tears to his eyes. But as before, no-one spoke to him, though the minister, when he shook his hand at the door, thought he might have seen him before.

He looked at the printed intimations in the order of service when he got home and noticed there was a Bible Study and Prayer Circle that met on Wednesday evenings. 'I'll try that,' he thought. 'Perhaps someone will speak to me there.' He asked Sylvia: "Would you come with me to the prayer circle at the Church of Scotland? At least it won't clash with your church in Kirkcaldy." Cautiously she said, "We'll see." They were contented with each other, having been a married couple for thirty-five years. The passion of their early years together had long since evaporated, but, he felt, Sylvia was comfortable with him, as one would be comfortable with an old pair of slippers.

CHAPTER THREE

CHARLES WAS ALONE when he walked down to the prayer meeting on Wednesday evening. When he entered the church hall he was taken aback by the resounding burst of applause that greeted his entry. There were only eleven members of the Prayer Circle that were already seated around a table. The smiles were warm and genuine—clearly they were delighted that a new person had ventured into their midst. He took a seat amongst them, flashing a self-conscious smile. Apart from one younger man and the minister, a well-built avuncular man who, it turned out, was on the brink of retirement, all were, like Charles, in the twilight years of their lives.

Bibles were open in front of each member, as was one which lay open in front of Charles. He was invited to introduce himself, and the minister followed up by introducing himself and each member. "This is Fiona," the minister said, indicating a white-haired lady who gave him a sweet smile. "We call her Fiona the Ferocious, because she's the fighter amongst us." A thick set man roared with laughter and gave vent to a stream of words that Charles found impossible to decipher. The minster nodded towards the man. "Nimrod is our timekeeper—he lets us know when it's time for tea." Another loud guffaw from Nimrod was followed by another stream of undecipherable information. The minister indicated another lady, swarthy complexioned, thin, wreathed in wrinkles and smiles. "This is Maggie," he said. "She runs the Women's Guild." Maggie added another wreathe around her drawn mouth as she gave Charles the benefit of a warm smile.

The evening proceeded as Bert, the leader of the group, opened in prayer and read from a book on the psalms. Psalm 2 was read out, followed by questions raised in the book, which generated a few enthusiastic answers from the group. The minister explained that Psalm 2 was a Messianic psalm—a psalm which anticipated the coming of Jesus as a King, to suppress the wicked nations and assert divine rule, not as the meek and mild figure that most children thought of him as. And yet, the minister went on to explain, Jesus was the Lamb of God who, because he loved us all, allowed his blood to be shed for all of us as an atonement for our sins so that we might have eternal life in the Kingdom. This was followed by discussion about how one worshipped a God that was both to be feared—or respected—and loved. Charles took the opportunity to say he was a square peg in a round hole, as proved to be the case when he attended another church where worship was amplified through the speaking of tongues. Fiona took the bait immediately. "I am not a second class Christian because I don't speak in tongues! Some of these people make me feel like that because I worship in a respectful, old-fashioned way. I agree with Charles—God is love, but the fear of God is also the beginning of wisdom." Bless her, Charles thought, warming towards her. He felt much happier amongst these second class Christians.

When Nimrod indicated it was time for the tea break by tapping his watch, Bert gave a concluding prayer. The ladies brought in tea and coffee, while the minister unwrapped a special cake he had acquired from the Asda supermarket the day before. Soon the party was enveloped in conversation that wrapped around Charles in Scottish accents that were alien to his ears. "Pardon?" he kept repeating as different members asked him questions about himself. He found he could understand them if they spoke directly to him, slowly—but when they spoke to each other they might as well be speaking in tongues. As for Nimrod, apart from his guffaws, his speech was totally indecipherable. It turned out, as Maggie later explained to Charles, that Nimrod was the result of a casual relationship between his mother and a Canadian airman during the war. His mother had been "simple-minded" and the airman took advantage of her vulnerable condition.

After the tea break Bert called for order. "Aye, we better make a wee start then." Bert conducted the prayer meeting with loving humility and total absence of any sense of importance. He asked for names to be prayed for, and most members of the group mentioned folk who had been ill, were about to be operated on, who had recently been bereaved, and some who had fallen prey to drugs and alcohol. Having written down the names in a list, Bert opened the prayer: "Well, Lord, as yer c'n see, we have as usual this long list to bring before ye…" He prayed for each name, each time ending by saying, "We ask this in Jesus' name." Before he concluded his prayer he thanked the Lord for prayers answered. It was not mandatory for members of the group to pray, but most always did, and a silence after a prayer was soon broken by another volunteer. Charles felt moved to pray, too, and followed a silence after another's prayer by asking that the Holy Spirit be poured out in Kennoway. As he was speaking there was a loud bang on the metal door to the side of the hall. There were some jeers followed by another two loud thuds and he hastened to end the prayer with a quick Amen. The minister at once got up and in his rapid rolling walk made his way to the door and opened it. Charles, alarmed, got up and followed him, as did Bert.

Three young boys ran away as the three men emerged. Another two boys, barely 12, were sitting on the wall of the adjacent cemetery, shamelessly smoking. One of them was still clutching a stone. This proved to be a common occurrence, and happened on most prayer nights when the weather was dry and warm. In subsequent meetings Charles found it was a good idea to bring with him his small camera. If the boys could see one taking a photo they would melt away with a will. On another occasion the hail of stones upon the doors and roof was particularly bad and Maggie in the prayer circle felt obliged to phone the police on her mobile phone. When the police eventually arrived the boys had long since dispersed. It was all too familiar to Charles, who had lived in a house near the Baptist Church in Hull. The youngsters would prowl the area like vermin and trash any empty house they could find. Charles's own house in Hull had been trashed in his absence, the windows broken and the walls torn apart inside, the carpets soaked in urine. This was why he and Sylvia had uprooted in Hull and come to Kennoway. He had searched the country by means of the Internet for the most affordable housing estate in a respectable area. After a life as a university professor of English and then working for the British Council in Africa and other third world countries, he had limited funds to invest in property but managed to stretch to two houses, one to live in and the other to generate rental income. His modern four-bedroomed house in Kennoway was a haven after the nightmare of the terraced housing in Hull, where the women were tattooed and sprouted metal piercings, and where the men argued in the streets, the most descriptive adjective they could come up with being 'fooking' this or that. At least this time he and Sylvia were living in the civilised part of the divide between rich and poor.

He now understood why the prayer circle was so small. It took courage to attend.

Peace restored, that first prayer meeting ended—and as they said the final prayer, they all stood up around the table holding hands. Aloud, they said the same strange words: "Bless us, Lord, as we go our ways, to infect others for Jesus!" When they said Amen, each squeezed the hand of the man or woman on either side. At that moment Charles felt a rush of love for the entire group in the circle. Like John Wesley, his heart felt strangely warmed. He had found his group. This was where the Lord wanted him. There were lambs here to feed, and to save.

CHAPTER FOUR

TWO YEARS had gone by since that first meeting with the prayer circle and Charles had become a well-integrated member of the coterie that met faithfully every Wednesday evening. The minister had retired and an elderly locum minister, who did not attend the prayer circle, was taking the church services until a new minister could be found. The prayer circle soldiered on under the competent and unassuming leadership of Bert. One Wednesday in August the meeting was held with a difference, for an African medical doctor had been invited to address the group on his work in Ghana. The seats, instead of being placed as usual in a circle around a large table, were arranged in rows so that everyone could face the speaker at the front.

When Charles arrived the speaker was already seated at the front desk with a few members of the group in the chairs that faced him. He was surprised to see, seated in the front row, the same flamboyant figure of the tipsy woman whose hand he had shaken at the church the previous Sunday morning. So, he thought with a flush of pleasure, she had taken up his invitation to join them at the prayer circle. As he took his seat in the third row from the front, the woman turned and flashed a dazzling smile at him, as though in recognition. He nodded, returned the smile, mildly curious that his pulse had quickened. It was great that she was there, for in two years the group had not expanded. Would she keep coming, though? She was dressed, as before, in a style that exuded glamour: her face was made up with eye-shadow that matched her sweeping green iridescent dress, the bright red lipstick dramatically emphasised by her immaculately powdered face. She certainly put the rest of them in the shade, Charles thought, with their plain, if not frumpy dresses or slacks—apart from their chairperson, Sadie, who was dressed in a smart two-piece tweed suit with sensible flat shoes. It was nice that the new woman should have taken so much trouble, Charles thought, but was her attire appropriate for a prayer meeting, her low-cut dress even revealing a soft milky cleavage that his eyes found difficult to avoid. Surely she was not tipsy, as before?

The speaker was introduced by Sadie who sat next to him. She explained how Robert had lived in a poor village in Ghana and had to walk to school without any shoes. He had given his life to the Lord when he responded to a call to come forward and commit his life to His service. Robert had been embarrassed to come forward since he had no shoes. He played a drum in the church band but was able to hide his feet behind the drum. Nevertheless, he overcame his pride and came forward to shake the hand that welcomed him into the brotherhood of Christ, and had never looked back. Against all odds he became a medical doctor at a university in Germany, and today worked as a doctor in England, putting aside all his savings to send money to Ghana to be used for the building of a new hospital for poor people who could not afford medical treatment—a hospital to be called Christ the King Hospital. This was his vision—his dream that he wished to fulfil.

When the speaker resumed his seat Sadie expressed the group's appreciation for his talk and invited questions. Just about everyone wanted to say how he or she admired his commitment and wanted to know what had driven him forward to becoming a doctor, given that he had grown up in such a poor village. Robert smiled and spoke of a vision he had received when still a young man in Ghana, that one day as a doctor he would be talking to a friend of his in London. It was a simple visual image that remained with him, like an assurance that what he saw would be realised in the future. It was a matter of faith, he explained, and he quoted the first verse of Hebrews 11: "Faith is the substance of things hoped for, the evidence of things not seen." He said: "Just as the Holy Spirit gives you an assurance of your salvation, so He also sometimes prompts you with a vision to realise a goal that He has implanted in you."

Next, the hand of the flamboyant woman shot up. Not waiting for Sadie's acknowledgement, she blurted out, quite loudly: "I want to raise the question of the speaker's colour! Does he find he has a problem being black in this country, eh?"

There was an awkward silence. No one felt it was polite to draw attention to the colour of Robert's skin.

"I don't think that's relevant," Fiona said, crossly.

"Oh, but I'm sorry, I think it is!" the flamboyant woman insisted loudly and with conviction. She turned round and flashed a smile at Charles, as if seeking support from him. Charles squirmed at the unwelcome attention. "Do you no' find you have a problem with people here, eh?" she went on, addressing the speaker directly. "Your patients, are they no' put oot being looked after by a black doctor, eh?"

"I dinna think this is a relevant question!" Fiona objected. She was a dear, sweet lady, Charles thought, and looked very uncomfortable that the speaker should be subjected to this unwanted attention.

"I really don't mind," Robert said with a relaxed smile. He was a short man with a round moon face. Charles couldn't imagine anyone taking exception to him, regardless of his colour. "Most of my work is done in prisons, as a prison doctor. Many of my patients are addicted to alcohol and drugs—no-one seems to mind my colour."

"But do ye no' come up against rubbish people that canna accept you?" the woman insisted, turning round again to elicit Charles's support.

Charles avoided her eyes, but felt drawn in to say something. Reluctantly, he said, "We are all equal in Jesus. Paul himself said there is no Jew, or Greek, slave or freeman, not even male and female, in the Kingdom of God—we are all one in Christ Jesus. The world does not always appreciate this, of course, so—I suppose—the... the lady's observation is relevant in that sense." He realised he didn't know the lady's name.

"Thank you!" she said volubly, smiling and still trying to catch Charles's eyes—which he assiduously avoided. He asked himself, why does she keep turning around to look at *me*!

"Well, moving on!" Sadie said quickly. "If anyone should feel moved to support Robert's vision, he has left copies of his card on the table here... He will welcome anyone wishing to keep in touch..."

They didn't break for tea this time—they would have refreshments at the close of the meeting—and after a few prayer requests went straight into prayer. Various people in need of succour were mentioned, and the Lord was asked to bless Robert's work in the prison and his mission to found the Christ the King Hospital in Ghana. Each prayer was followed by an approving "Amen". Then, to the surprise of all present, the drunken woman said a prayer—for by now it was clear to most, Charles included, that the woman was indeed in her cups and was bold with Dutch courage. "Lord," she prayed, "grant me the serenity to accept the things I canna change, the courage to change the things I can, and wisdom to ken the difference!" She said it quite assertively.

Even this elicited a polite "Amen" from the group, and Charles thought it was a strange prayer to pray in the context of the meeting. The words were familiar to him—clearly she had memorised them from somewhere and now regurgitated them like a child that had learnt the words off by heart. It was as though she wanted to impress the group. Somehow, he felt there was something very sad about her and he felt a touch of embarrassment on her behalf.

Charles was surprised to see the woman again, the next Sunday. She was made up, as before, in glamorous attire and plastered face, and sat alone in a pew just in front of the door at the back of the church. He sat next to Sadie, as he usually did, in the middle of the church. As Sadie said, "We are like cows—we always take the same place in the byre!" When everyone filed out of the church after the service, he looked for the brightly clad woman but she had already left. He wondered if anyone had spoken to her. He walked home with Sadie, as he often did, for she, like him, lived in one of the "posh" houses in the new estate. They often shared notes, as they walked, about their Christian life. Once he asked her how she came to know the Lord. "Oh," she laughed, "when I was a wee lass, I lost a very precious ring on the beach, just where the sea washes over the sand. I went home very depressed. Then I asked the Lord to help me find the ring, and I said if I found it I would give my life to Him. The next day I went back to the beach—and there it was, exactly where I looked, catching the sun's light just below the water!" She laughed. "And the beach was huge, a mile long—it could have been anywhere!"

"And so you have served the Lord ever since," Charles smiled. What a lovely Christian she is, he thought, giving her a sidelong look as they walked together. She was short, freckled, and her handbag hung low, close to the ground. "It's a lovely testimony," he said.

At the crossroads they separated. She, an older woman in her mid-seventies, lived with her retired husband in the more expensive bungalows at the top of the hill. Charles branched off to his comfortable house that he shared with Sylvia who was ten years younger than him. He had lived contentedly with her ever since their marriage thirty-five years ago. The passion of their love had died down long ago, his main solace being listening to Mozart or Beethoven while he sipped a wee dram. He had authored a number of academic books in the years

19

while he was a Professor of English, and had even self-published a few of his own novels. He still channelled his creative energy as an editor working from home, editing and facilitating the publication of other people's books. Coming home after church on Sundays was his time to relax, listening to his music and partaking of a drop from a bottle of Bell's whisky. "For whom the Bell tolls," he would say, lifting the glass to his lips as he relaxed to the strains of Mozart's clarinet concerto.

The following Wednesday evening Charles and Sylvia met up with Sadie at the crossroads, as usual, and they walked together to the church hall. Though Sylvia worshipped at the Full Gospel Church in Kirkcaldy on Sundays, she was happy to join her husband in the Church of Scotland prayer meetings. When they entered most of the group had already taken their places around the table—and Charles's eyes were immediately drawn to the tipsy woman who was there, at the near end of the table, next to Bert. Charles and Sylvia took their usual places next to Sadie at the far end of the table. By accident or on purpose, Charles could not tell which, the eyes of the woman kept meeting his—and she would smile and hold his eyes with an unwavering gaze. He was unsettled by this, for it quickened his pulse. She was as usual clad as though prepared for a party, a night at the opera. Surely, he thought, she could see that she was out of order, for everyone else wore casual, even dowdy jumpers and jeans. And she was vociferous, too, often side-tracking the discussion away from the study under scrutiny. Asked how she was, she tossed her hair and said with arched eyebrows: "I'm a verra happy gel—free as a bird, twittering at life's wee troubles, eh!" In her prayer she thanked the Lord for guiding her to this prayer circle, saying how much she appreciated being welcomed in as a new member. Charles was heartened that the small group had no qualms about having her there, but he was especially touched that she felt she had been warmly welcomed.

At the conclusion of the meeting most of the women busied themselves in the kitchen washing up the tea things. Charles was helping to put away the chairs and stopped for a moment next to the new woman and asked, "By the way, what is your name?"

"Lynsey," she smiled. "And what is your name, eh?"

"Oh, Charles," he smiled, "as in Prince Charles," and lifted the next chair which he lined up with the others next to the wall. Now he knew her name, he could pray for her, he thought. Lord knows, he found himself wondering and thinking about her in spite of his efforts to dismiss her from his mind, so he might as well turn his thoughts into positive prayer. She certainly could benefit from the Lord's intervention, especially if she was hitting the bottle.

When he and everyone else left the hall she sidled up to him, her hand on his elbow. It was dark outside and Sadie and Sylvia were already making their way along the pavement, in the opposite direction to which Lynsey was about to go, towards the drab council houses.

"Yer a verra intellectual person, aren't yer, Prince Charrels!" she said, smiling with her almond eyes. "Ye seem a braw niece man." He thought she had a cheeky come-hither look, and she was standing too close to him for comfort. Her hand crept higher, up to his shoulder, and he was suddenly terribly aware of her intoxicating perfume.

"Am I?" he said, embarrassed, conscious that the others might see them this close together. Besides, Sylvia and Sadie would be expecting him to catch up with them. "Well, I can't say for sure. You don't really know me, Lynsey." In spite of his better judgement, he placed a hand on her bare shoulder and his heart missed a beat. Her skin was as soft and smooth as silk. He had to admit, she did seem very… very kind, sweet, in spite of her inebriated state. He hadn't been touched by a woman for many years.

"I think yer verra sweet," she said softly.

"Well," he smiled, "I was just thinking the same of you." His pulse had noticeably quickened and he felt guilty, wondering what the others would think if they saw them together like this. His guilt was enhanced by an involuntary stirring in his groin. Besides, he had to catch up with Sylvia and Sadie. He would be conspicuous by his absence.

"Are you going to be safe walking home by yourself, Lynsey?" he asked. It was dark and he was concerned about her reaching her home. He half wondered if he should risk offering to walk her home. No-one else seemed to be concerned. He had no idea how far her house was.

She pulled herself up to her full imperial height and said cheekily: "I'm a big gel—I c'n look efter mesel'!"

He looked at her upright back as she walked into the night. He had to admit, she had excellent posture, tall and almost regal as she went quite steadily on her high heels, her shoulder-length auburn hair swaying alluringly as though in a TV shampoo commercial.

CHAPTER FIVE

THE NEXT SUNDAY in church there was no sign of
Lynsey Anne McCann. Charles looked in vain for her in
the empty pew near the back of the church. At the Wednesday
evening prayer meeting her seat remained unoccupied, too.
After the tea break when Bert asked for names of persons
requiring prayer, Charles asked if anyone had seen, or knew,
what had happened to Lynsey.

"Aye," Fiona responded. "She lives up the rood from me—
I noticed the lights are off and the blinds drawn shut. We
should pray fer the lassie. It's nae walk in the park fer her, her
being an alcoholic an' all. And it's no' easy for her either, her
partner being een tae."

It was as though a knife of cold steel had pierced Charles's
heart. He had tried to dismiss the woman from his mind, and
this news that she was an alcoholic and was living with an
alcoholic partner, too, did not sit comfortably with him.
Somehow he had not associated her bright flamboyant
personality with someone chained by addiction and... and a
partner! She was not, then, the happy free spirit she had
claimed to be.

"I didn't realise she's an alcoholic," Charles said quietly. "I
thought she'd just had a tipple or two too many." How did
Fiona know she was an alcoholic, anyway? It seemed to him a
very serious judgement. "Well, we should certainly add her to
our prayer list."

"Aye!" Fiona agreed.

What was it about that flamboyant tipsy woman that
fascinated him so? He had considered himself immune from
any form of feminine infection since the passion in his
marriage had evaporated—yet there was a sweetness, almost an
innocence, that he perceived behind Lynsey's façade of lavish

glamour. The group prayed for her, asking the Lord to give her the courage to resist temptation and return to their midst.

In the days that followed Charles found himself driven to pray in earnest for her. He did not know where she lived, but he walked along the dingy street past Fiona's house as he prayed, thinking she must be close, nearby. The houses were terraced or semi-detached, and looked bleak and drab with their uniform mud-coloured plastered walls. The small gardens were generally neat and tidy, often with sufficient space to park a small car in front of or beside each house. There was nothing to suggest a spirit of poverty apart from those drab walls and uniform designs. He could not imagine that bright, sparkling, flamboyant woman, albeit tipsy, living in one of these bleak houses.

Across the busy street that ran into Leven he came across a small lake, known locally as Denhead Pond, with swans and ducks, and he wondered if she ever came there. Looking back across the lake and the street, the majestic hills beyond were impressive, but marred by the intervening uniform mud-coloured houses that suggested an army barracks. The lake was surrounded by a wrought-iron fence and a path that ran around it, and two or three women were walking their dogs. The days were drawing in and the November weather added to the bleakness of the scene, the dog-walkers wrapped in baggy coats or shapeless anoraks. There was a park bench where Charles might have sat down and prayed for Lynsey, but the seeping damp had caused the planks of the bench to sweat a cold condensation of droplets. Instead he stood under the dull overhanging branches from the small adjacent wood and prayed there for her. "Dear Lord, wrap you loving arms around her—embrace her with your loving Spirit and renew her life, her energy, and place in her a strong heart's desire to resist the black hole of alcohol." He added, "I ask this in the name of Jesus of Nazareth," just to be sure the prayer was endorsed by the correct Jesus—the Messiah and the son of God! It was a funny prayer for him to pray, for he enjoyed his single malts, especially when the evenings drew in. But somehow, after one or occasionally two drinks, his mind and body were sufficiently comforted. He remembered an alcoholic colleague telling him, once, that the first thing she thought of when awakening was a drink of wine—and for that purpose she had kept a bottle of wine in easy reach under her bed. She could not come to, she said, without that first swig in the morning. Eventually she died and the autopsy revealed a liver snow-white with calcified tissue.

Week after week went by but Charles kept up his prayerful vigil, and the group regularly prayed for her on Wednesday evenings. He would often walk around the lake, and across to the nearest shopping centre where he supposed she must shop—but he never saw any sign of her. But he wondered— was his interest in her becoming an obsession, the prayers merely an excuse to divert some kind of passion for her? Surely not, he told himself, for she belonged to a totally different social class, a member of what in effect to him was an alien culture. The environment was a strange place for the Lord to put him in. Even if he had fostered an unlawful passion for her, the two of them would be incongruously incompatible. Besides, he had only known her in her tipsy state.

He thought again about that strange prayer she said, or rather, recited, on that first occasion when she attended the prayer circle. What was it again? "Lord, grant me the serenity to accept the things I cannot change, the courage to change the things I can, and wisdom to know the difference." Those were the words she used. They had a familiar ring, and when he reached home after a bout of prayer by the lake, he googled the words on his computer. What he read really shook him. It was called the Serenity Prayer, written by an America theologian, Reinhold Niebuhr, a prayer that had been adopted by

Alcoholics Anonymous—he supposed as a form of positive thinking in their therapeutic sessions. This revelation shook him because it confirmed that what Fiona had said of Lynsey must be true. She must have learnt the words in one of the AA meetings. It meant, too, that she, and perhaps her partner as well, must have attended such meetings. It meant, also, that she must at one point have actively tried to kick the habit and sought help. His heart went out to her all the more.

CHAPTER SIX

DURING THE WEEKS that went by the prayer circle took it for granted that Lynsey was no longer coming to the group. It was all the more surprising, therefore, that when Charles (this time without Sylvia who had stayed at home) walked into the hall on a Wednesday early in December, she was there, at her old place next to Bert. It was totally unexpected and his heart lurched as he saw her. She turned and smiled, a sweet soft smile, as he walked by. He fleetingly touched her fresh auburn hair and said, "So nice to see you again, Lynsey." He took his usual seat at the other end of the table, almost breathless at the shock of her presence.

Under his breath, he mumbled inaudibly, "Thank you, Lord, thank you!" The Bible lesson got under way as Bert read from Paul's letters to the Romans, and every time Charles looked up his eyes connected with hers, and she smiled. He had to breathe deeply to fuel his heart with oxygen—especially as he came to terms with the shock, not only of seeing her again, but of the way she looked. Her hair was the same laundered wavy shoulder-length mane, her eyes much the same hazel brown, but there the resemblance to her former gaudy self ended. He thought: her face! Her face had been scrubbed clean of all make-up, exposing a blotchy red surface, even marred by what looked like a rash of pimples. Apart from that, she had a worn, ravaged look. Her clothes were casual, now blending well with the plain winter dowdiness of the rest of the group. Afterwards, when everyone stood up to put on their coats after the meeting, he saw that she wore dark trousers that contrasted tastelessly with the flat white sneakers which, he had to admit, were a lot more practical than her high heels, given the distance she would have to walk home through the rain. Whether anyone had especially welcomed her after her absence he was unsure. She was unusually quiet and said nothing during the discussions, and did not offer a prayer during the prayer session.

So, he thought, this is the real, the completely sober Lynsey Anne McCann.

"Lynsey, I can't tell you how happy I am that you're back again," he said, going up to her after the meeting. She turned her face towards him. The smile was there but now he saw that the eyes had a weary sadness he hadn't noticed before. Close to her, he saw how blotched and rugged her skin looked. She was like a different woman, plain, haggard, someone he would never have ordinarily noticed if she walked past him in the streets of Kennoway. He took her hand. "Lynsey, I've been praying for you to come back. Welcome back, my dear."

She squeezed his hand. "Och," she said softly, "yer a reel niece man, Charrels."

And as he looked into her soft sad eyes, he no longer saw the blotched worn face but the precious soul of a vulnerable but lovely girl. An involuntary surge of love went out of his heart that moistened his eyes.

"Well, you two!" Sadie said brightly as she came up to them. "Can I give you a wee lift? It's raining and I'm giving Fiona and Maggie a lift back—we can squeeze you both in too!"

Sadie had picked up the elderly Fiona and Maggie in her BMW on account of the dark and the rain. Fiona, who was elderly and frail, especially needed to be protected from the weather. Charles was pleased to accept the lift, and particularly pleased that Lynsey would not have to walk home by herself in the rain. "Do you know where Lynsey lives?" he asked.

"Fiona knows—it's close to her house, she says. Fiona will sit with me in the front—it's easier for her to get in there." She laughed. "So the rest of you will have to squeeze up in the back. Don't worry, there's room for all of you."

Charles found himself in the happy situation of sitting between Lynsey and Maggie, Lynsey close against him on his right. The women were chatting away merrily apart from Lynsey who was very quiet and Charles, resisting the strong urge to hold Lynsey's hand, kept his two hands locked together between his knees. They reached Lynsey's home first—on a corner just a few houses from Fiona's. When Lynsey got out he noticed the figure of her partner inside the house, a frail older man with gaunt eyes standing by the window, waiting for her. The front door opened and a hefty Staffordshire Bull Terrier with what looked like a wide grin in his massive head barged his way out, almost stumbling down the few steps to the front garden. "Och, there's my big dug Tyson come to welcome me," Lynsey laughed. "I do love him!"

As the car drove off Charles's feelings were a mixture of delight and depression. It was a joy that his prayers had been answered, that Lynsey was back in the fold—but she was forever beyond his reach because she was of an alien culture and belonged to another, as he did. It was a strange kind of solace that he now knew where she lived. At least it would make it easier for him to pray for her.

CHAPTER SEVEN

WHEN CHARLES entered the church the following Sunday morning his heart gave a twist of happiness when he saw that Lynsey was there, alone, in her usual place against the wall in a back row immediately in front of the church entrance. He touched her long shoulder-length hair lightly as he walked by, and she turned and smiled at him. He had walked down in the company of Sadie, as usual, and paused while he collected the hymn book and church programme. Sadie walked down the aisle to her usual place, as she said before, like a cow that knows its place in the byre; he hesitated then, and glancing again at Lynsey and seeing her alone, smiling at him, on impulse he slid along the long back pew until he was able to take his place next to her.

"You look wonderful!" he whispered, and meant it. She was back to her glamorous self—yet this time with a distinct difference. Clearly she was completely sober. She looked elegant in a stylish black coat and long, flowing white silk scarf. She turned her face towards him and he was instantly lost in her limpid brown eyes. She wore makeup that perfectly hid the blemished skin beneath. The lipstick that accentuated her delicate mouth was not the garish red it was before and was neatly applied to enhance her heart-shaped lips.

"Och," she smiled, "Yer kent how to mak a gel feel good about hersel', eh!"

He dared to take her hand. "Lynsey, you're such a knockout! I can't believe we have the blessing of such a lovely woman in our midst." He felt a flush of embarrassment at his involuntary trite words. Her hand tightened on his for a moment and he was aware of her long delicate fingers, and it reminded him of that strong grip of her handshake that first time she came to the church. She had surely gripped his heart inasmuch as she had gripped his hand. Reluctantly, he let go her hand for it seemed unseemly to be holding the hand of a woman who was not his wife—especially in church! But he said: "You know, you have a lovely firm handshake, Lynsey— I remember that warm handshake when you first came to church. I let go but you continued to hold on! You can tell a person's character by their handshake."

She gave a little laugh. "Heaven knows what everyone thought of me that day, eh! I was as high as a coot!" She added: "But yer reet—some hands feel like a limp fish, not even a wriggle, eh! But the truth is, Charrels, I'm a really shy person. You may not have thought so that last time."

"Yes, I believe that," he said. "And you're very gentle— and sincere."

Their conversation was stopped by the church officer bringing in the big Bible that he carried and placed on the lectern—at which point the organ struck up and everyone stood. When they sat down the choir, a group of smartly dressed elderly women facing the congregation at the front, broke into song. Throughout the service Charles was mindful of the delicate perfume from Lynsey that enfolded him, like the subtle aura of her presence. He glanced guiltily towards the centre of the church at the empty seat next to Sadie where he had sat for the last two years. Surely she would think this deviation from tradition very strange. But, he rationalised, someone ought to sit next to the new lamb of God and make her feel welcome. Perhaps his courage to break from custom would set an example and others would sit next to her in future services. It crossed his mind that some would know of her past attendance at AA meetings and for that reason might be avoiding her. No, he thought, surely not. A church, after all, is a caring community, with a mission to care even, especially, for the lost sheep. Had the Lord himself not fraternised with such people?

When the service ended and the congregation began to file out, she turned to him with her gentle brown eyes and said, "Will ye sit with me again, Charrels, when I come to church?"

His heart missed a beat at her words. Did she mean that? "Of course—of course I will," he said, taking her hand again, "It will be a privilege!" Her warm smile was like balm to his soul.

For many weeks afterwards he tried to recall those words. Had she said, "Will you sit with me again?", or had she said, "Will you sit with me always?" For the life of him he couldn't remember which version was true but hoped it was the latter since he did not want to impose himself upon her against her will.

CHAPTER EIGHT

THE WEEKS went by and Charles was always pleased to see Lynsey was there—in church as well as present at the prayer meetings. He sat next to her in church on a regular basis—and he began to wonder whether his motivation for going to church and the prayer circle was to worship and glorify God, or whether it was for the sake of basking in the heady presence of Lynsey. In the prayer meetings she always came just as she was—not a trace of makeup and looking quite ravaged with her worn blotched skin. He looked at her, once, studying her across the table while everyone's eyes were shut in prayer, wondering what it was about this sometimes plain woman that pulled at his heartstrings so much. She was certainly no oil painting, he thought—but by gum, he told himself, she was such a beautiful canvas! Yet more than a canvas, because when the paint went on it failed to hide the inner light of her soul. When she walked she was regal, erect with superb posture, elegant, every bit a gracious lady. The DNA of inner beauty was there. No posturing, nothing pretentious or affected in her speech or behaviour. They say beauty lies in the eye of the beholder—but it went deeper than that, he was sure. Surely it was not just him? Others, surely, could see how exquisite she was, too?

Surely he could not have fallen in love with her, he argued. And yet he felt he loved her all the more, knowing how haggard she was under the veneer of makeup. During one of the prayer meetings he gave her a small Gideon's New Testament: it would fit in her handbag, he said, and she would find the references at the front encouraging if she ever found herself in trouble, depressed, despondent or discouraged. Once, before church while sitting next to her, he gave her a copy of a small book he had edited and had self-published, which was a collection of Christian testimonies. "They are testimonies of faith in God, and of His supernatural power in people's lives. You may find them encouraging." She smiled and struggled to fit the book into her handbag and he felt he had imposed on her, as though he were forcing his life on her. But apparently she was touched by his gifts, later saying how she enjoyed reading from the little New Testament before going to sleep in the evenings, and how she was moved to tears by one of the testimonies, about a young boy who died of leukaemia and how his mother had received strength to face his death in a dream. In fact when, as Christmas approached, the various members of the prayer circle gave one another Christmas cards, she handed Charles an extra-large card rimmed with gold glitter depicting the three wise men on a journey towards a great light on the horizon. In it she had written simply: "To Charles—God bless you, Lynsey." When he expressed his appreciation for such a large and beautiful card, she said, "I chose it especially because you were so kind, giving me the wee Bible and your bonny wee book!"

One day after the Sunday service he invited her to walk back with him to enjoy some soup and coffee. He didn't think Sylvia would mind. Lynsey declined sweetly, saying she had to walk back home because her partner would be waiting for her to make him "dinner", and so Charles had to content himself watching her well-dressed elegant figure walking away in the opposite direction. Of course, he was inclined to forget she had a partner, and he wondered what he was like.

The following Sunday after the church service he offered to walk part-way with her towards her home, saying he needed the exercise. She graciously accepted and so Charles had the benefit of spending a longer time in her company than the short exchanges they had in church. He felt happier than he had for a long time, listening to her sweet chatter beside him in that musical Scottish accent of hers. She responded willingly to his questions about herself and her family. She had been a Personal Assistant to a minister and an author, she said, and was good at typing and research. She had a daughter, Iona, who was in her twenties and frowned at her going to church. "Oh no!" her daughter had exclaimed in dismay, "You're not going back to *church*, are you!" She had two sisters, and her parents were still alive, living in a nearby village.

"Are your sisters as attractive as you?" he asked, and she dismissed the question with a laugh. "How about your partner?" he probed tentatively. "Does he mind you going to church? Wouldn't he like to come with you?"

She shook her head. "He canna stop me. He more or less puts up with my going. When I put up the Christmas tree the other night, he came down the stairs and telt me, 'Oh no, not that rubbish again!'" She explained that he was disabled, an ex-miner who had trouble with his lungs and breathed heavily when he went up the stairs. "I have to help him into and oot of his bath," she said, "It doesna half do my back in. He's no' verra heavy but he doesna help pull hisself oot or doon, ken."

"So in a sense you are a carer?" he said.

"Aye—you could say I'm a live-in carer. It means I have a roof over my head, ye see."

"What is his name?" Charles asked. "I would like to include him in my prayers."

"Hamish," she said. "Aye, it's niece of ye to pray fer us. You're a sweet man, Charrels." She always rolled the 'rr's' in his name, extending it into two syllables.

When they reached a road veering off to the left, Charles said, "I guess I'll turn off here—it will be a quicker way back to my house. But I have so enjoyed your company, Lynsey."

"Aye, so have I enjoyed yours, Charrels. Thank you fer comin' out of yer way."

They had stopped and he gazed, for a moment, into those limpid brown eyes. He grasped her folded gloved hands for a moment and quite without forethought said, "Gosh, Lynsey, I just can't get enough of you!"

Taken aback by what he had said, he smiled, said goodbye, turned, and made his way up the road that led away from the main road along which she would continue to walk. She called after him in a laughing voice: "Ye'll have to pray verra hard tonight after saying that, eh!"

His face flushed as he waved back. What the heck made him say that, he thought, reprimanding himself. At the next corner he unexpectedly saw the lone figure of Maggie, from the prayer circle, walking home from church to her house. For a moment he wondered if he should pretend not to have seen her—but then decided to wave and brave out the fact that he had walked home with a woman who was not his wife, and another man's partner. Maggie waved back and he hastened around the next corner, the final lap to his estate. His mind ran over Lynsey's parting words and he wondered if he had heard her rightly. Had he overstepped the mark, he asked himself, for blurting out those involuntary words about not being able to get enough of her? He chided himself, again, for his recklessness. Was his liking and concern for her getting out of hand? He sincerely hoped not.

CHAPTER NINE

A T THE NEXT MEETING of the prayer circle Lynsey prayed with great feeling, a prayer in which she thanked God for her acceptance into the prayer circle and for the strength she received from attending the church. She didn't know what she would do without this fellowship, she told the Lord, for it meant the world to her. "I dinna ken what I would do without this support, Lord, and I will make every effort to keep comin' to the meetings and the kirk. With all my heart I thank you for this fellowship." Her voice sounded so sweet and musical to Charles's ears, and he lapped it all up, so pleased for her. Then, as he listened, the hairs on his arms and neck rose for an instant as he realised she was thanking God for the kind, loving man that spoke to her in the church last Sunday, who took the trouble to ask her about herself and her family. Who was she talking about in her prayer? Walking back with Sadie afterwards, he asked her if she knew who Lynsey was referring to in her prayer. "The minister," Sadie smiled. "Yes, he is a very sweet man and notices people and cares for them." Yes, Charles thought, puzzled—the minister is indeed a very humble and kind man—but exactly when did he speak to Lynsey last Sunday? She had sat, alone, next to him. As far as he remembered he, Charles, was the only one who had spoken to her—apart from a brief moment when she shook the minister's hand at the door as she left. It gave him a warm sensation at the thought that her prayer might have been an oblique way of thanking him for talking to her and caring about her.

After church the next Sunday he dared to walk with her nearly the whole distance to her house, going out of his way on the pretext of wanting to buy a Mars Bar from the shop just a little beyond the turning to her house. It provided more opportunity for conversation with her and he began to feel that his only real moments of happiness was when he was close to her, sitting next to her in church, or walking back to her house with her. It provided a cocoon of happiness that melted away after each parting.

As so often happened when he was with her, he could not prevent his admiration for her overflowing into words, and he would say things like, "Goodness, Lynsey, you're so gorgeous! You have such lovely posture, and you're so elegant." She seemed to lap this up and laugh. "Yer know just the reet thing tae say to make an older woman feel better about herself, Charrels!"

"Older woman!" he exclaimed, daring to take her hand. "Lynsey, do you know how old I am? I am seventy-one—I could be your father!" In a sense it was true, for at 54 she was seventeen years younger than him.

"Charrels Haddington!" she said, her delicate fingers tightening on his. Again, that sidelong glance with the suggestion of a cheeky smile. He wondered what she meant by pronouncing his full name that way, almost as though chiding a naughty boy. Did it mean she was reprimanding him for thinking he was old and that she did not see him as such—or did it mean she was chiding him for overstepping the mark? He recalled her telling him that her partner was seventy-five, and as far as he could glean she lived with him because it gave her, in her words, a roof over her head.

Charles felt he was like a butterfly flapping around a bright light—if he got too close he would burn up, or at least get hurt—and even hurt the light itself, a thought that gave him much anguish. This woman fascinated him so, beyond reason—for was she not in reality a plain, ageing "older woman" bordering on alcoholism, living in a drab council house in an estate where drug addicts and drug pushers lived, and above all, who was tied to another man? In the evenings he would take a long hard look at himself in the mirror, seeing the suggestion of bags under his eyes, the face of a man in his seventies. "You pathetic idiot!" he reprimanded himself on one of these moments of truth.

He could only walk with her to the corner where the road turned towards the drab council house she shared with Hamish. He did not dare go closer to the house with her—and wondered if her partner would be watching out for her return.

He found out, on another occasion while walking home with her, that her birthday was in July—a birthday she shared with Cecil John Rhodes and Dolly the Sheep. (He established that later by looking up her date of birth on the Internet!) It seemed to fit her—she encompassed, in his eyes, the potential of a great leader, and yet in a sense she had been cloned from genetic stock that came from the common herd of Kennoway. He did not believe in star signs, and yet her sign, of Cancer the Crab, seemed appropriate, too—for had he not unwittingly allowed himself to be caught in the pincers of a crab? And to take the metaphor further, was his growing infatuation for her like a spreading cancer?

But it was a spreading cancer that was too delicious to resist, overtaking the synapses of his brain, bending his mind to dwell on her all the time—the picture of her face, immaculately made up, then drained of all paint, bleached with sadness, her sidelong amused glances, the occasional tightening of her fingers on his when he dared for a moment to take her hand, her elegant posture, her statuesque walk as she approached the church from the opposite direction to his... all images that called forth a feeling of love, care, protection, concern. However was he going to extricate this woman from his brain, from his soul? For God's sake, he had no right to reach out to her, to want her.

But instead of trying to extricate himself from her, he took steps to get closer. It occurred to him that he could establish a link—a spiritual link and therefore a perfectly legitimate one—by sharing a common book of prayerful daily readings. He asked her, while walking from church with her, if she used a book of daily readings.

"I don't have one," she said. "I did have a verra good one, but my previous partner wouldna give it back tae me."

God, he thought—so she had had a partner before the present one! This woman was like an onion—if you removed one layer, there was another one below. Here was a mystery to be explored later.

"Well," he said, recovering from that revelation, "I was wondering—I really need to use a daily guide myself—my spiritual life is in a mess and I need to walk closer to the Lord. What if I bought two copies of a good guide and gave you one? Then we could follow the same readings every day—and we could be prayer partners? It would help to give each of us a form of positive input, to uplift one…"

"Aye," she said. "Everyone needs a hug. It's a good idea—deal!" she smiled.

Charles's heart soared. "Deal!" he said in return. And before he could stop himself the words came out: "I would love to hug you!"

That sidelong look again with a glimmer of a smile as the narrowing pavement brought them, for a moment, closer together. There were other worshippers returning from church, walking ahead of them and behind them, and he had to watch himself if perchance he made a gesture that would alert others to the way he began to feel about this lost lamb. He had placed a hand on her waist to steer her away from a bus kiosk in their way and quickly removed it. He recalled an instant earlier on, as they were queuing in church to shake the minister's hand, when he had for a moment placed his hand around her waist—and how his heart had leapt when he felt for a moment her hand on his waist.

"There is another church I went to," he said, a little breathlessly, "where everyone hugs one another. There are times I wish the Church of Scotland would do that!"

"There would be a danger," she smiled, "that some hugs would last tae long—and set off the gossipers, eh!"

"Yes, quite," Charles said. Was she warning him? He found he was hanging on to her every word, replaying them in his mind afterwards, milking them, looking for any drops of affection, signs that his feelings for her were in any way reciprocated. He wondered if there would ever be an opportunity to hug her—they were always only together in public places, the street, the pavement, or in a church or church hall.

"Lynsey," he asked, "were you ever a model? I mean, I was wondering, because you have such wonderful posture, when you walk."

She laughed. "I had an offer, once, to go to London for a photo-shoot—when I was sixteen. But my parents were again' it. Mebbe they were reet. So when I finished my O-levels I studied accounting instead. I was tall and verra gawky, really— but I took ballet at school and was taught to walk and sit oop straight. Even today, I always sit oop straight, eh? I was really quite thin, and a good runner." She glanced at him. "Charrels, you're verra sweet to notice things about me—and say such niece things. It maks me feel so much better aboot mesel'."

"I can't help that, Lynsey—I think you're lovely."

That sidelong look again! Was she reprimanding him?

"How tall are you, Lynsey?" he asked, sidestepping the moment.

"I'm 5'9," she said. "In high heels I tower above most men!"

Well, Charles thought, at 6'1" he had the advantage over her in height—only just. She was tall and elegant walking

41

beside him. It was great—their eyes were on just the right level for him to receive the benefit of those sidelong glances.

"Hamish is so lucky to have you, Lynsey—does he realise this?" He wished *he* were her partner. When they reached the corner where the street branched off to her house he would have to let her go—as usual, back to her partner. She would be cooking his Sunday lunch, or 'dinner', as she called it, always a traditional dish of meat and three vegs followed by a pudding. Hamish would then have the benefit of her company for the rest of the afternoon, and evening, through the entire night... and for evermore. Lucky sod!

"You may weel ask!" she laughed. "He was a miner and like most Scotsmen, he is rough and ready—never says niece things tae me like you do."

"He's a rough diamond, then—I'm sure he must love you to bits."

"Aye, Charrels, he's verra rough! Has nae time for niceties or good manners, ye ken? Expects his meals on time and is verra crabbit at bath time. Because he is disabled I have tae help lower him and lift him oot the bath. It does my back in! When he moaned last time I asked him if he would prefer tae be put in a home. 'Never!' he said, 'Ah'm no' going tae one of them places!' 'Well then,' I telt him, 'yer better behave then!' He is so crabbit! When I started to go to church he said, 'Yer not going tae church agin'!' And when I put up the Christmas tree, he was comin' doon the stairs, and said, "It's no' time for that rubbish agin', is it!'"

"You have to be patient with him then—it must be difficult, him being disabled."

"Aye, ah ken—when he goes up the stairs he puffs and groans. It's from the mining, ye see—his lungs were damaged working underground."

"You're a blessing to him then, Lynsey." Charles was eager to learn more and more about her, building up in his mind a potted history of her life. If anything, it would mean his prayers for her would be more meaningful. He could pray intelligently—or so he told himself.

"Aye, I got him a wee mobility scooter that wurrks with batteries." She laughed. "I had some fun with it. It has a slow forward button and a fast forward button. I tried it oot and pushed the fast forward button by mistake an' took off—nearly crashed into the hedge! At least it made Hamish laugh. 'Ya silly moo!' he bawled."

"So at least he can get out—I suppose he would have to go on the pavements, not on the road?"

She nodded. "Not on the rood. Yer have tae stay on the pavements. An' you ken, you can be had up fer drunk driving on them scooters too—even though you only drive it on the pavements."

"I'm sure that's worth bearing in mind," Charles smiled. Hadn't Fiona said that Lynsey's partner was also an alcoholic? The thought made him realise that Lynsey had been sober for a long time now—at least when she was at church and in the prayer circle. He couldn't help wondering if there were times when she would slip, relapse, have a drink with Hamish after their main meal on Sundays and eventually end up in a drunken stupor through the afternoon and rest of Sunday. This was a thought that would come back to haunt him, for he only saw her twice a week—at church (prolonged by what had become a routine walk home with her) and at the Wednesday prayer circle, after which Sadie would always take her home with Fiona and Maggie in her BMW.

CHAPTER TEN

THE FOLLOWING SUNDAY Charles took with him a copy of one of his self-published novels to give to Lynsey. It was another idea he had of drawing closer to her—a way also, he argued, to help her in a new direction in life. She was after all living on benefits, or so he surmised—a life of full-time caring for her partner, dependent he supposed on an income of state benefits to supplement Hamish's state pension. What she needed was a mission—or a project, and he hoped he could direct her towards such a project.

He was relieved to see her in her usual isolated place, immaculately made-up, near the back of the church when he went in. The ten or so minutes before the service began constituted the limited time he cherished to spend with her in talk before the Church Officer brought in and placed on the pulpit what he thought of as 'the little "red" book'—a large copy of the Bible that was never 'read' but used as a symbol of God's presence amongst them. The congregation would stand up at the entrance of the Bible while the organist struck a stentorian note to announce the beginning of worship.

There would not be much time before the entrance of the Bible so he handed her the copy of his novel *The Cage and the Cross* as soon as he sat down, drawn into the fragrant embrace of her perfume. "It's a Christian novel I wrote when I was thirty," he said. "I thought you might like it. I was wondering if you had the inclination to write something like that, too."

She was clearly touched as she accepted the gift. "Och, that's reel sweet of yer, Charrels.'

He loved the way she rolled her r's when she spoke—particularly the 'r' in his name Charles. "I don't want to burden you with a reading project, but I thought it might stimulate you to write something yourself, like your life story," he said.

To his surprise his words elicited an almost raucous laugh from her that sounded strange in his ears, and she threw at him one of her characteristic mischievous sidelong glances. "Eh!" she exclaimed, "I c'n think of other ways that can stimulate me!"

Her words were like brandy in his veins and he felt himself blush. She laughed and apologised. "Sorry, Charrels—I have a weird sense of humour."

"Well, I love it," Charles smiled, resisting the impulse to take her hand in his. "I was thinking about intellectual stimulation, of course. You know, you have a very interesting story to tell—your life must have been very exciting, overcoming many difficulties. It's not difficult to write—just like writing a letter."

"Aye, I could do that, Charrels—but my life might shock you. I have been a verra, verra bad gel. But I'll do it—I want to get it just right."

"I'll help you," he smiled, for a moment taking her hand, aware of the ring on one of her slender fingers. "I'm an editor—I can even ghost write for you." Her fingers tightened on his before she let go. He noticed her studying the cover of the novel that depicted a dove and a cross in a cage. "The cover was printed in matt, this time—the last edition was in gloss," he said. "I thought I would see what it would be like in matt. I think I prefer it to gloss."

She turned to look at him. "Matt? That's what my foundation makeup is called. It protects my face, ken—and the makeup goes over it." She smiled as he once again took in her immaculately made-up face, her sincere brown eyes. "It's also protection against the weather," she said. "Keeps my skin fresh."

And, he thought involuntarily, hides the blemishes beneath the foundation—and his heart went out to her in her innocence. He wanted to take her hand again but the thought was thwarted by the loud note of the organ and the entrance of the little red book.

It was raining when they came out of church. "It's tippin' it doon!" she exclaimed and opened her umbrella. Walking back together in the rain and huddled together under her umbrella, she reaffirmed that she would write her story. She had always wanted to, she said. Asked if she had a computer or word-processor, she shook her head. Her previous partner had a computer and she used to use that, she said. She had also been a PA—a Personal Assistant—to a church minister for two years, and was a good typist. Never mind, she said, she could use the old-fashioned method and write with pen and paper. She would like to get all the facts of her story just right, going back to her childhood.

"Let me be your PA!" Charles said, and she smiled quizzically. "I'll give you one of my old laptops and you can use that. But you can use a pen in the meantime—as long as you get it all down. I'll be your ghost writer and editor—I will see that your book gets published. It's good to have a project."

"Och Charrels," she said from under the umbrella they shared, "that would be so kind of ye. But what is a ghost writer, eh?"

"Oh, one who holds your hand as you write, as it were—who fills in all the gaps for you—perhaps embroiders on your story, tidies it up, expands it where necessary. Trust me, I'll make it readable, fluent and interesting! You can start with your childhood—I'm sure that must be full of memories. I wonder what you were like at school!"

"Aye, I have a verra good memory of those years long ago. But I wasna verra happy at school. I was shy—I have always been shy—and only had two friends, Meg and Lynsey—that was another Lynsey—yet we got into trouble for things we didna do. I could niver speak up for mesel'. I got spanked once." She laughed. "And a verra strict teacher washed oot my

46

mouth with carbolic soap because I used a dirty wurrd! I can still remember the awful taste and the foam comin' oot my mouth. I tried to smile and I telt her it tasted good to let her know it wasna going to wurrk on me! When she did it again I spat it back at her, eh!"

"Oh dear," he smiled, and wondered what the dirty word might have been. Had it been an f-word? He couldn't imagine her using it, though heaven knew it was thrown about readily enough in Kennoway. "Oh, I was often caned at school myself," he said. "Caning was the order of the day in my day. Usually because I didn't do my homework, couldn't remember my tables, or failed to recite a poem accurately—only because I was so nervous about forgetting the words. I had learnt the poem over and over again, but when I was called to recite it I dried up." But Charles didn't want to talk about himself. He wanted to hear more about her. "Do you still have your parents?"

"Oh aye!" she smiled, "they abide in Buckhaven, no' far awa'."

"Are they well?" They must be getting on in years, he thought. He had certainly lost both his parents years ago.

"My mother's seventy-four, my father seventy-seven. My mother..." she laughed... "my mother is like Mrs Bucket, in the TV show, ken—prim and proper, things always have tae be just reet, everythin' in its place. I think you'll like her. She'll like you, being posh an' all! I'm sure you'll get to meet her one day."

"Oh yes," Charles said, inwardly stunned and shocked at the realisation that he was indeed nearly as old as her parents. Why did she think he would get on well with her mother? They were contemporaries, of course. If Lynsey and he were both free, and he made a bid for her, she (or her mother, anyway!) would regard him as a cradle snatcher, a dirty old man, probably. But he consoled himself with the thought that he was younger than her partner.

"What did your father do?" he asked. "I mean, he will be retired by now."

"Oh, he was a miner, too, like Hamish. He lost his leg in an underground mining accident. He was run over by an underground rail car."

"That's awful!" Charles exclaimed, horrified.

"Aye," she went on, "someone was supposed to press a red button to warn him the car was on its way—it came unexpectedly and the wheel cut off his leg. Afterwards the leg was amputated high up on the thigh. When the accident happened he was left bleeding and used his belt as a tourniquet to slow doon the blood loss while he waited to be rescued. Ever since—he was twenty-one at the time—he has had a wooden leg. Few would ken, but in the early days he didna want to go on the beach wearin' a swimsuit. He's a rough man, ken, verra proud and speaks his mind."

"Another rough diamond," Charles smiled. It seemed to him that most working-class men in Fife and Central Scotland, ex-miners anyway, were hard-drinking, rough men, bordering on the uncouth and brash with no romantic leanings. And Lynsey comes from this stock, he thought. She lives with an old miner even now—and yet she is so gorgeous and elegant. Granted, she was not sophisticated, but had a romantic and sensitive heart. He recalled that once during the tea break at the Wednesday prayer evening she confided how as a young girl her dream was to be married in a white dress in church, but her husband-to-be (long since divorced) was one of those rough diamonds, insisting that a registry office was good enough for the likes of her. How on earth did these rough uncouth men ever manage to capture a regal beauty like Lynsey? Perhaps, like the cancer-grab of her birth sign, such women seek security above all else and, claw-like, grab the first opportunity for security when they see it.

They walked on in silence, nearing the corner where she would turn to her own house. As usual Charles had developed the pretence of walking in her direction and a little beyond the corner to visit a nearby shop to buy a Mars Bar to munch on his way back to his house. She seemed to accept his explanation without question. Was she so easily taken in? Surely by now she must realise, he thought, that it was a feeble excuse to prolong her company for as long as possible and that the Mars Bar was purely mythical. He had put all his change into the church collection plate, anyway.

"Are you all right?" he asked, as he saw the corner approaching. "Are you managing okay, Lynsey? Remember, I'm always here for you, whatever you need. If you need a lift to the shops, or need a car to take Hamish anywhere... Can I take *you* anywhere?"

"Aye, I do struggle from time to time, ye ken," she said, ignoring the latter part of his question. "Some days are more difficult than others to get through. But I manage."

Charles couldn't stop himself complimenting her, on her posture, her beauty, or her stunning appearance, and as they reached the corner his feelings overflowed, almost in desperation to hang onto her. "Lynsey," he said, "you are so sweet. I'm so looking forward to reading your life story! I'll try and dig out my old laptop."

She smiled as they stopped at the corner before parting. "As I said, Charrels, ye make an older woman feel good. It means a lot tae me, your compliments."

His compliments always seemed to make her melt, elicit a warm smile and some appreciative remarks that in turn made him melt inside and want to enfold her into his arms. "Good heavens, Lynsey, you are only 54! To me you're a wee lassie— and a gorgeous one at that!"

Before walking down the street to her house, she touched his arm. "Goodbye, Charrels. I'll see ye Wednesday, eh?"

He walked on to buy his mythical Mars Bar—then turned at the entrance to the shop and walked home, disconsolately, retracing his steps and replaying their conversation in his head. Each time, at least, he had a fuller picture of her life.

CHAPTER ELEVEN

THE FOLLOWING SUNDAY after church, Charles was looking forward to walking back with Lynsey part-way to her home as usual when he found a thick-set man in a suit waiting at the door as he went out. He shook the man's hand thinking he was one of the elders, then stood aside waiting for Lynsey to appear, for she was just behind him coming out. He was surprised when she spoke to the man in the suit, then came up to Charles, saying, "A friend of Hamish's has come to give me a lift back. But I'll see you at the prayer circle Wednesday and also at the Burn's Nicht." And so she went off to the car park with the man in the suit. It crossed his mind that Hamish had sent his friend to prevent Lynsey walking home with her new friend... Had he sent his guard dog? The thought troubled him all week but the next Sunday, when they exited the church after the service and he asked her "Will your friend be here again to give you a lift?" he was relieved by the sweet words of her reply: "Och no! That was by chance that he was visiting Hamish at the time. His no' friend of mines!"

The Burns Evening was a special dinner being served by the Women's Guild on Thursday, and Charles put down his name to attend not only because he was fond of haggis, but because Lynsey had said she would be there too. (Was she going because he had told her he was going? Speculating on that question was a pleasurable pastime.) There would be no Scottish dancing, no strip the willow, because all the attendees would be geriatrics, like himself, there for the meal and the variety show that would follow it as part of the entertainment.

He arrived at the church hall at the same time as Sadie and her husband, walking in just after him. To his dismay the hall was already full, Lynsey seated at a crowded table, a broad shouldered man with a crutch leaning against the back of his chair. Clearly there was no chance of sitting next to her—and Sadie beckoned him to join her and her husband Stuart, so he reluctantly took his place next to Stuart. But he could see Lynsey at the table at the other side of the hall, facing him—and their eyes met across the crowded room. She looked as lovely as ever, in full makeup and fluffy auburn hair. He lifted his glass of orange juice to her, as if making a toast—and she smiled in acknowledgement.

Then it occurred to him with a sudden realisation: the crutch! The man must be Hamish! She had come with Hamish! He looked at the man and saw that he had rugged, handsome features. Was he the man he had seen at the window of Lynsey's house? The realisation that it might be caused his heart to sink and he reprimanded himself—after all, what did he expect! The man was her partner. At least it meant he could now meet him and put aside this ridiculous passion for the woman, an unlawful passion that seemed to have crept up on him and engulfed his heart.

Yet he needed to have the identity of the man confirmed and he bent forward to catch Sadie's eye, on the other side of Stuart. "Is that Hamish, I wonder?" he said. "The man with Lynsey?" He nodded his head towards their location at the end of the room.

Sadie shook her head. "No idea—I've never met or seen him. But I'll ask Maggie."

Maggie was making her way along the tables, checking that everyone was comfortable and welcoming each person personally. She was in charge of the Guild and had supervised the excellent meal of haggis and neaps. "Charles wants to know if the man with Lynsey is her partner," Sadie said to Maggie when she reached her chair. Maggie looked across the room quizzically. "I really couldna say, Charrels," she smiled with her many wrinkles around her eyes and mouth, looking straight at Charles. "I've niver met the man—but I think not. I'm sure her partner is a much older man, ye ken?"

Charles breathed a little easier after that. It meant he could maintain the illusion, the dream of hope procrastinated, for a little while longer. He knew the bubble had to burst sometime, but the bubble was safe for now.

Sadie and Stuart insisted they gave Charles a lift home in the BMW at the end of the evening so there was little hope of accompanying Lynsey to her home. He understood that she had been given a lift anyway. Perhaps that man with the crutch...

As he was putting on his coat at the end of the evening Charles went up to Lynsey. She was still seated and the man with the crutch was preoccupied talking to a man on his other side. Speaking softly, so the man could not hear, he said how he missed sitting next to her and had to be content with looking at her across the crowded room! He wondered at her reply:

"Well, it was probably just as weell!" she said, looking up at him. What did she mean by that, he wondered?

"Well," he laughed politely, "I thought this good-looking chap next to you, with the crutch, was your Hamish."

"Och him?" she said, with surprise almost approaching alarm, "I swear I niver seen him before in ma life!" It was as though she was assuaging his spark of involuntary jealousy by putting his mind at rest that he had no rival—apart from Hamish, of course.

Wednesday evenings at the prayer meetings gave him little opportunity to speak to her, for all he could do then was gaze surreptitiously at her across the table, taking in her almost craggy and tired features, as they appeared without the layers of her foundation matt and gloss covering. Wednesday evenings were mere interludes, or small oases in the desert of his week, until he arrived, yet again, at the bigger waterhole of the Sunday morning service, to drink in the brightness of her presence in all her plumage and paintwork. He had reached the church before her, on this occasion, and took a seat alone where she normally sat, his heart tight with concern that she might not appear. As each person entered through the open door behind him, he glanced sideways hoping to detect her. Then, all at once, she was there, a tall elegant figure in smart black coat, her smile shy yet radiant as she entered the varnished pew and slid up next to him. He was simultaneously enveloped by her perfume and the joy of relief that surged up from his heart.

After the service he walked her home again—as far as the usual corner. This time they found themselves walking together with Maggie and Nimrod who, overweight as he was, walked haltingly with a stick. Charles could not help but wonder what Maggie would make of him, always walking home with Lynsey, and in the opposite direction to his own home. But if Maggie wondered about it, she said nothing. Nimrod walked in silence apart from a few guttural indecipherable grunts that Maggie appeared to understand perfectly. It occurred to Charles that he had his small camera in his pocket—and here was a perfect opportunity to capture Lynsey on film! When the pavement widened around the first corner, he said to the three of them: "You know what! I have my camera with me, and it would be nice to have a picture of the three of you together. Would you mind?"

"No," smiled Maggie, her surprise multiplying the many benevolent creases of her face, but Nimrod plodded on, unaware that the others had stopped. Charles called him back and he retuned slowly, taking a place between the two women. "Ah, the rose between the thorns!" Charles joked, bringing a smile to the faces of the two women. They both looked smart next to the portly and grumpy face of Nimrod that registered an air of incomprehension as to why anyone would want to take a photograph of him. Later Charles was able to put the picture on his laptop desktop and enlarge it by zooming in on Lynsey's face. Thus he would gaze at her, repeatedly, believing he could see love just round the edges of her gentle eyes that stared at him, bemused and unblinking, from the screen. He would take in her elegance—her patterned black and white dress, black coat with imitation black fur edging at the top, the black silk scarf with red wide petals, and then, the *pièce de résistance,* that soft beautiful, gentle face and the crowning glory, her flowing laundered hair.

He thought, looking at this picture, how often he saw her with a different scarf. There would be her flowing white scarf, the one that he first admired and received thanks for noticing. Its soft white texture contrasted effectively with her dark coat. At other times she wore a red scarf. ("My mother gave it to me.") She would wear black leather gloves, and on other occasions red leather gloves—which her mother had also given to her. When on one occasion Charles came to church wearing a red tartan Stuart scarf, she said mischievously: "Red for danger!" He replied, "So are you!"—pointing out her scarf that had red petals embroidered into a black background.

Looking at the picture, again, he took in her hands, in the red leather gloves, that were holding, in front of her, the small cylindrical umbrella in its black cover, her black handbag under her right arm. But what he noticed for the first time, then, were the two delicate pearl earrings hanging like white teardrops just below the lobes of her ears, nearly concealed by the silky texture of her hair. He was intrigued: she projected such an alluring aura of loveliness and, looking at the photograph, he wondered if that aura was made up of all those charming components that were visible in the photograph, even to the two small earrings that worked so well together for good, a good that had so effectively captivated him. Above all, her bright splendour stood out so effectively, foregrounded against the dull grey background of a Kennoway street with its grey unpainted council buildings and damp cracked paving stones.

CHAPTER TWELVE

WHEN CHARLES went to the next meeting of the prayer circle he was eager to tell Lynsey that he had unearthed his old laptop from the attic and had managed to delete all his old data by restoring the operating system to its original factory settings. It was only at the conclusion of the meeting when everyone was putting on their coats that he managed to approach her and tell her about the laptop. She looked at him with grateful eyes. "I am so glad, Charrels," she said, "I have so missed having a computer, eh." She said this unsmiling, and with her eyes locked to his—and he knew her thanks were genuine and sincere. It made him feel really good.

"How do I get the computer to your house?" he asked. "I'll need to show you how it works—in case you've forgotten. Best if you come to my house, I think?" It was a statement rather than a question, for he could not imagine sitting down with her in front of the laptop in the presence of her partner. "I can pick you up and take you back—or you can walk over to my place."

"Okay," she said.

"Can I phone you to arrange a time? Do you have a telephone number?"

"Oh aye!" she said. And she told him her number which he wrote down on the prayer sheet. His hand was not quite steady for his heart had accelerated with excitement—now he had her phone number! Until then he did not even know if she had a landline.

As they were walking out of the door he said, "I'll phone you then, Lynsey," and added, "I'm here in my car tonight— can I give you a lift back?"

She shook her head. "Sadie picked me up in her car—so I better go back with her." And so she walked away to join the small group of ladies climbing into Sadie's BMW.

It seemed that his life was made up of partings from her. But this time his bubble of hope was suffused with new rainbow colourings as it drifted and floated around him. My God, he thought, Lynsey Anne McCann was coming to his house! She would actually be inside his house, sitting next to him in his own study while he explained to her the workings of his old laptop! It was the nearest he had come to happiness for a long time.

He thought he'd better not appear too keen and waited a good twenty-four hours before he phoned her. He chose a moment when Sylvia was not in the house. He had to take a deep breath before he dialled her number—and it was her voice that answered the call. He thought his heart would stop! It was strange, hearing that tangy Scottish accent divorced, disembodied from the physical body of the woman that had so captured his imagination. The voice floated through his brain and quickened his synapses, like a drug. "I can come on Saturday," she said, "Would 11 o'clock be okay, Charrels?"

Saturday suited him fine. It would be a day when Sylvia would be out shopping, taking the car, and he later told Sylvia that he was giving his old laptop to a member of the prayer circle.

"You have my address," he said to Lynsey. He had given her one of his cards with his telephone number a while ago. "Will you be able to find my house? It's exactly ten minutes' walk from yours." He could have bitten off his tongue! He knew the exact time for he had walked it himself, many times, just to stand for a while in the shadows across the street where she lived.

"Well, I'm a big gel, Charrels, and I'm sure I c'n manage." He could detect the smile in her voice. He smiled too, remembering the last time she had used that phrase.

The night before he had trouble sleeping, he was so excited, knowing that the next day he would see her—not just in a new context, but in his house! He kept waking, hugging the pillow, breathing deeply and asking the Lord to take care of Lynsey, and to ensure that nothing but good would come from his friendship with her—or, indeed, that she and no-one else would be hurt by his love for her. For he was no longer in any form of denial—he admitted it to himself, and to the Lord, that he was in love with Lynsey. "Dear Lord," he prayed, "bless Lynsey and help me to come to terms with this burden of love that I have for her."

He could not understand how this burden of love had developed for another man's woman, and a woman that belonged to a poor social class, one who was entrammeled by a lifestyle of alcoholism and state benefits. Had the Lord Himself, for some purpose unknown to him, placed this burden in his heart? What kind of joke would that be! It's the sort of thing those Greek pagan gods might have done, for they made humans their playthings, the victims of their cruel cat-and-mouse games. Then he recalled the words of a hymn that he used to sing with the congregation, in the Baptist church in Hull before he moved to Kennoway: "I will make the darkness bright. / Who will bear My light to them? /Whom shall I send?" And then the chorus which he particularly enjoyed singing... something about sending him, or her, to save the Lord's people. He could not sleep so went to his study and turned on his computer and entered the words he could remember into the search engine. For some reason he felt it was urgent to read again the words of that chorus. In singing that hymn in Hull, had he inadvertently activated some kind of contract with God? The words came up on the screen and he read them with apprehension:

Here I am Lord, is it I Lord?
I have heard You calling in the night.
I will go Lord, if You lead me
I will hold Your people in my heart.

"Oh my God!" he exclaimed aloud. The words struck him in the solar plexus and he fell upon his knees, weeping uncontrollably. When he sang those words he meant it—not thinking though that the Lord would seriously send him on a mission. He did not like the drinking, swearing working classes—he was proud of his status as a retired university professor and editor, and he despised the Kennoway youths that threw stones at the doors of the church hall when they were praying. People like that were vermin, and as for people on benefits, they should pull themselves together and find jobs and not fall prey to booze and drugs. Academically, of course, he was happy to pray for them, but…

"You've made me love these people, Lord," he cried out, "by putting in my heart an overwhelming love for one of them! That's so unfair, Lord! That's so unfair! You know my hands are tied and that I can never express my love as my heart leads me… I would be hurting her and others, especially Sylvia, and it would mean breaking your commandments…"

He controlled himself and got up and wiped his eyes. For goodness sake, he told himself, this is nonsense! It certainly was the only logical explanation for his feelings, but that was nonsense… he was succumbing to the same lack of control these alcoholics and drug addicts were subject to.

He made his way to the kitchen and poured himself a strong drink of coffee—but not before lacing it heavily with a double measure of whisky. He looked at the time—4 a.m. Great! Just seven hours and Lynsey would be here! He wondered if at last he would be able to give her a hug. It would be wonderful, to hold her in his arms—just once. And to hell with some imagined mission from God!

That morning, after a breakfast of porridge oats, he prepared the old laptop for Lynsey's inspection, open on the desk of his study. He created a few blank documents in readiness for her to write in, and as a means of demonstrating to her how to create documents and save them. He prepared a memory stick which she could use for saving documents, which she could then return to him for editing. Finally, he transferred a poem about 'liking' turning to 'love' into Lynsey's 'new' computer into a folder that he named 'Lynsey's Briefcase'. It was a poem written by Beth Richards, a member of a writing class he had once attended—a poem he thought was particularly apt and which seemed to express his feelings for Lynsey. He would not tell her the poem was there and she may not even come across it—but it gave him a frisson of pleasure at the thought that she might, and if so he wondered what she would make of it.

He read the poem again, wondering if indeed it was the proper thing to include:

When does 'I like you'
change to 'I love you'?
There's a fine line between,
But, there's no turning back,
no matter how hard you try,
the answer is,
just like a dripping tap,
that cannot be turned off!

Love can strike at any age!
Just as he feels confusion
he resents the intrusion
into his *very* organised life!

His resistance is futile!
Just as a moth cannot resist
the flickering candlelight,
that draws him towards his demise!

Will, 'I like you'
change to 'I love you'?
Only time will tell!

His love for Lynsey certainly felt like a dripping tap for it had been gradual but unstoppable—and the writer was on the money, saying 'there's no turning back'! Somehow he was going to have to deal with these feelings, whether installed by God or allowed to fester through his own perverse indulgence of thinking about Lynsey.

Finally, he installed the picture he had taken of Lynsey in the company of Maggie and Nimrod, as well as a few pictures around the lake where she said she walked her dog. There were a nice couple of shots of the swans, and one across the lake in which you could just make out her house in the council estate across the Leven road.

Whether by chance or providence, the two copies he had ordered of the daily reading guide arrived in the post at 9:30 a.m. The guide was *God Calling by Two Listeners*, and he immediately looked up the reading for the day—and was struck by the amazing aptness of the message based on the text "Wait on the Lord" in Psalm 27:14: "I am thy shield. You must know that 'All is well.' I will never let anyone do to you both, other than My Will for you... Never fear, whatever may happen. You are both being led. Do not try to plan. I have planned. You are the builder, *not* the architect..." Oh my dear God, he thought, the reading even referred to 'both' of them... the two listeners, he supposed, yet it seemed so relevant, applying to 'both' him and Lynsey. If she were to be his prayer partner, then they were united just like the two listeners. Had his love for her indeed been implanted by God, or was that wishful thinking, a form of rationalising his love? But he liked the message—it gave him an uncanny peace, especially at the thought of taking one day at a time, relying on God's leading according to his plan. He had to trust that there *was* a plan. After all, Paul said in the Book of Romans that all things work together for good for those who love the Lord—for those who have been chosen according to his purpose.

By 10 a.m. Sylvia had left for the supermarket and Charles settled down in a chair in the sitting room to listen to some music, to compose himself. Everything was ready for Lynsey's arrival at 11 a.m. He took a deep breath and closed his eyes as the gentle strains of Jonathan Wood playing Purcell on the harpsichord wafted over his ears. At 10:30 he could hear the voices of two women speaking just outside the front door. He got up to investigate, but stopped at the door, recognising the local Scottish accents of the women. One was that of his neighbour, the other—was it Lynsey? Though he knew it was her, her voice sounded for a moment like any other Kennoway housewife, to his ears common and local, but when he opened the door and set eyes on her his heart missed a beat and his ears retuned her voice to a new register of sweet and captivating. She was wearing a mauve flowery silk top under her heavy black coat with a band of beads around her neck—beads that were artistically large and oversized in front, becoming smaller as they retreated behind her neck. Her shoulder-length chestnut hair was fluffy and freshly laundered as usual, shaking as she gave her head that little characteristic jerk that he found so captivating. Surprised and yet not surprised, he noticed that her face was clean of any makeup, and its natural blemishes seemed less noticeable. He longed to touch that clean blemished face and kiss that rosebud mouth that so readily lifted in a cheeky smile. As he approached her the rich aura of her perfume embraced him—an embrace that lingered long after she had left.

All of these details he registered in a moment as she stood there, talking to the neighbour and, turning, smiled at him.

"I went to the wrong hoos," she laughed. "They all look alike, eh! Your neighbour told me, aye, Charrels Haddington's hoos is next door!"

He invited her in and took her coat which he hung carefully over a chair in the dining room just off the entrance hall.

"Coffee?" he smiled nervously. It was like a goddess had come to his house. Instant coffee seemed so banal an offering for this Kennoway deity.

"Aye, that would be niece," she said as she flicked her hair and took a seat in the old-fashioned upholstered chair that used to belong to his grandmother. "You have all these books!" she exclaimed, looking at the tiers of books on the shelves that ran the length of one wall. "I love them wee horsies," she said, looking at two bookends in the shape of horses at either end of the complete works of Dickens.

"Oh those," he smiled. "I picked up the works of Dickens when I was a student in London."

"London?" she said. "I hate cities. I canna abide Glasgow or Edinburgh," she said, flicking her hair. "So much traffic, and people."

"You won't like London then," he smiled.

"London? I've niver been tae London."

Good heavens, he thought. He couldn't imagine anyone growing up in Britain and not ever visiting the capital.

He went into the kitchen and made them both a mug of instant coffee, emptying a tin of biscuits onto a plate. For her mug he chose one that said 'The Boss' on the outside. He smiled to himself—it would upgrade her to a position of control.

He wanted to prolong the visit as long as possible, and to learn more about her, so before going upstairs to introduce her to the laptop he encouraged her to talk generally about her past; this time there was more time for her to talk and he asked her about her various jobs. He was impressed by how relaxed she seemed to be and how easily she laughed and chatted as she recalled moments from her previous bouts of employment. Apart from being a PA to a minister, she had done a lot of shorthand typing, and even worked as an administrator in the local high-security prison.

"You can type, then?" Charles asked. "I mean, do you touch-type, without having to look at the keys?"

"Aye," she said. "My speed was aroond 60 to 80 words a minute—though nae doubt I'll be a wee bitty rusty the noo! But it will come back, I'm sure—one niver forgets, like one niver forgets riding a bike."

He laughed. "You'll have no trouble writing your life story then."

"Oh Charrels," she smiled, "I want to make it just reet. You have given me such confidence. I will write it—I promise."

There was a pause as she helped herself to a second biscuit and took a sip of coffee.

"So you actually worked in the prison down the road," Charles smiled. "Was that a good job?"

"Nae way! I hated it!" she exclaimed. "My office had bars on the windows. I felt trapped like I was in a cell mesel'! My tea was brought in by the 'trusted' prisoners—and I was told niver to make eye contact with them. An' when I went oot home I had to be searched—an' the warders that did this were rough an' uncouth an' made rude suggestions. I stuck it oot till the end of my contract an' niver went back. Couldna wait to get oot of there!"

"Wow," said Charles. Wherever she went, it seemed, she had encountered rough insensitive men. It put him on his guard—no way should he try to hug her or in any way make gestures or a movement that she might interpret as making a pass at her.

When they went upstairs she stopped again at the sight of the rows of laden bookshelves on the landing. "Meer books!" she exclaimed. In his study he was on his best behaviour. He gave her his comfortable leather computer seat while he drew up a wooden chair next to her. He immediately had a sense of being overwhelmed by her seductive perfume. Her long slender fingers went straight to the keyboard, clearly at home there. He was sitting on her left and he was very aware of the ring on her ring finger, and he recalled the belief that a vein in that finger led straight to the heart. That ring was like a padlock on the front door to her heart.

She was quick to catch on to the operating system and the way Microsoft Word and Microsoft Publisher worked. Really, there was very little to show her, or to teach her. As she said again, it's like learning to ride a bicycle—one never forgets. This was a very different Lynsey McCann to the one he had first got to know. She might be shy, but she exuded confidence and competence. Why on earth was she living with an aged alcoholic partner—and she herself succumbed to the demon drink? He had no reason to, but somehow his heart melted, feeling proud of her, seeing her confident and relaxed in front of the computer.

"Lynsey, you're going to be a star!" he said. "Here," he continued, handing her a memory stick. "This is a memory stick. You plug it into a USB port—here—and you can drag your document onto it—then give it back to me and I'll bring it home and edit it."

She smiled, her hands flashing over the keyboard as she gave him one of her sidelong glances. "Charrels, nae bother—ye dinna need to teach me to sook eggs." She touched his hand with her left hand. "Thank you," she smiled.

He took her hand and squeezed it, his stomach somersaulting at the same time. When they stood up together he knew this was the moment—the moment to give her a hug. His heart was racing, palpitating—and he couldn't do it. He took a deep breath and his eyes held hers, and he took her hand instead of embracing her. "Lynsey, you're going to be a great writer!" Then he packed the laptop into a box with the supporting electrical cord and the mouse, and then remembered the copy of *God Calling*, and placed it in the box as well. "This is your copy of the daily reading guide, Lynsey—would you believe it, it arrived this morning. And I was really moved by today's message. Please read it every day, and I will too. I'll pray for you as you pray for me."

She gripped his fingers. "Thank you, Charrels," she said softly.

He walked back with her to her house carrying the laptop in a box. At her front gate he handed the box to her, opening the gate as she went through, carrying the box with the laptop. He waited there and she appeared again in the window of the sitting room, still holding the box and waving to him, a big smile on her face. There was no sign of her partner.

He walked back to his house, disappointed that there had been no hug, but nevertheless feeling like a million dollars. When he reached home his bubble of happiness began to dissolve. He went into the kitchen to make himself a cup of coffee. Next to the sink the mug she had drunk from was still there, the one with 'THE BOSS' written on it. Without hesitation, he lifted the unwashed mug to his lips, merely so that his lips might touch the rim where her lips had touched it. It was the closest physical contact with her that his conscience would allow.

CHAPTER THIRTEEN

CHARLES did not have long to wait to see her again—for the very next day was Sunday, and he was delighted when he entered the church to see her already there, in her isolated place near the back. He slid along the wooden pew to be as close to her as he dared and this time took her hand without delay, aware of the hard lump of the stone in her ring against the soft pressure of his palm.

"Well," he said, "is everything okay? Did the laptop boot up—is it working?"

"Nae bother," she smiled.

"I was worried, because I forgot to give you the password. Though it seemed to boot up without it."

"Well, it didna ask for a password."

He let go her hand, reluctantly, and handed her an envelope. It was a letter from BT offering a deal for broadband. "If ever you want to go on-line, you'll need a broadband package. That BT offer is £5 a month for the first six months—but it will go up after that. You might want to consider it in time." He cherished the idea that he could one day receive an email from her. "Anyway," he said, "I've written the password I chose on that envelope—in case the laptop ever asks for it. It's there—the letters YHWH. Just in case the computer should ever ask for it when booting up."

"Thank you," she smiled.

"You know," he said, "You don't have to have that plain blue background on the laptop's desktop that says ADVENT. I can show you how to change it with a nice seascape or country scene."

"Och, I've done that already," she said, "I went into 'settings' and found a scene with yellow daffodils to put on the desktop. Hamish saw that and said, 'What a lot of pish!'"

"You did!" he said, and took her hand again. "Lynsey, I'm so proud of you!" And he was thrilled to feel her fingers squeeze back. "Will Hamish be able to use the computer too?" he asked with some apprehension.

"I telt him he's no' to touch it! The computer is mines, ken!"

"You know, Lynsey," he said, suddenly giving way to an impulse to bare his soul to her. "The night before you visited I could hardly sleep, thinking tomorrow Lynsey will be in my house!"

That askance smile again. "Ah! Weel, I was excited…"

The organ struck up and cut off her reply as the little red book entered and he and Lynsey stood up with the congregation. Had he heard her right? Her accent was so foreign to his ears and it was too late to say "Pardon?" In a sense it had been easier to talk there in the church because the church protected him (and her) from himself. He had to keep himself in check. There, in the presence of God and the congregation, there was no danger that he would lunge at her and embrace her and jeopardise any chance of anything good coming out of this friendship.

Their conversation was a little more animated than usual during the walk home after church. "Ye ken," she said, "somethin' I found so strange—the minute I walked into yer hoos I felt so completely at home!"

It warmed his heart to hear her say that. "Well, you know where I live now. You're welcome anytime. I'm always there, you know."

"An' anither thing—when I went into the lounge I made straight for that old fashioned chair, eh? It felt like I belonged there."

"You mean the upholstered chair in red? That was my granny's chair! It's where I normally sit."

"Oh, sorry!"

"No, no, you're welcome." He felt touched that she instinctively went for his chair, and had sat where he normally sat. He would treasure that chair all the more in future.

They were using the same reading plan now, and that day's reading (Sunday) said we are to love everyone, even if some are difficult to love: "You *must* love all. Those that fret you and those who do not." Walking home with her, he dared to recall this to her and said, "Well, I have no difficulty loving you, Lynsey!"

"I see I'll have tae watch you!" she said, giving him again that cheeky sidelong look.

"Good," he said with mixed feelings of delight and disappointment, "I'll take a lot of watching."

When they reached the corner where the street branched off to her house, it was the inevitable moment to part again. For a moment they faced each other and the bleak February sun lit up her made-up face. "Charrels," she said, "ye ken what, I really do like you—I do, and it takes a lot fur me tae say that tae anyone." Her eyes held his with sincerity, and as he looked into her brown eyes, looking at her sunlit face too, he saw the blemishes beneath the makeup. Her made-up face in the direct sunlight had the look of pale parchment. He could see the lines, especially around the eyes and the mouth, the creases in the face of 'an older woman', to use her words. And in that moment his heart went out to her more than ever before. How he longed to touch that face, to caress it gently, to place the palms of his hands on those creased cheeks. His eyes went to her earrings, white pearls like teardrops dangling just below the lobes.

"I really like you, too, Lynsey," he said softly. "You must know that by now." He realised this was the moment she had come closer to him than ever before. He wanted to take her into his arms, but he had to abide by the rules—she as well as he belonged to another and, besides, they were in sight of the house where her partner lived, a partner who might even be watching them at that moment from the window. "Lynsey," he smiled, resorting to banality, "you have such lovely earrings."

"These?" she smiled, flicking her hair back on one side and touching her ear to reveal the earring and the delicate ear more clearly. "I like them—my mother gave them tae me."

Her mother had given her so many beautiful things, it seemed. The scarves she wore, the red leather gloves. He had counted three different scarves, for she wore a different one on every church occasion—and he never failed to comment on them.

The moment ended and she walked towards her house. But she turned back again for an instant to wave, saying, "See you Wednesday evening!"

He walked further up the Leven road, keeping to his pretence that he was walking that way anyway to visit the nearby shop for a Mars Bar. 'Lucky old Hamish,' he thought, as his bubble of happiness once again began to dissolve.

When he reached his house he found his mind going back to her words, as his mind always tended to do, mulling over and digesting what she had said. He was thrilled that she had actually said she 'liked' him, and that it took a lot on her part to say that to anyone. He should be privileged, then, and there was no doubt about her sincerity, by the serious way she had looked at him, straight in the eyes, when she said it. What had called forth those words, or triggered her to say it, he wondered? Then, all at once, he remembered Beth's poem! Had Lynsey found it on the laptop? Her words had come out so naturally and sincerely that he had not at the time connected them with the poem. He hugged this possibility to his chest, thinking about it. If she had read the poem, was her comment her way of warning him, telling him that her liking could never turn to love or loving, hence her serious sincerity—or that liking was tantamount to love? It was another puzzle for his mind to feed on.

As the evening wore on he found himself listening to the pathetic words of love songs—songs by the singers he used to listen to when he was young. Mario Lanza singing 'Be My love' strangely touched his heart, while the titles alone of Jim Reeve's songs seemed to echo his situation and his feelings, like 'When two Worlds Collide', 'There's a Heartache Following Me', and especially 'It Hurts So Much To See You Go'—words he always regarded as pathetically trite, sung by some love-sick idiot, yet words that now assumed a new dimension of meaning and pulled at his heartstrings. In 'I missed Me' Jim Reeves sings about how he misses holding hands with his love—God, he hadn't even held her hand like lovers do, or held her tight, but yearned to do so—as the song said.

"You seem to have developed a new taste in music," Sylvia said with a suspicious look. "Are you alright? You're very quiet these days."

"Oh, just a touch of flu, maybe," he lied. "I'll be okay. Nothing a wee dram won't fix."

The following days and nights he was restless and unsettled. It eased the tension in him to take long walks at night, especially through the council estate and past her house. She had warned him that the area was dangerous, that the police visited the area frequently, especially up the road from the corner of her house, that they had drug raids and bashed doors in to arrest the pushers. But he found the area very quiet, and it troubled him that her house never had any lights on. Once he walked by on the opposite side of the road and as he glanced back he thought he saw the blinds moving in the dark window. It made him feel awful—had he been spotted, by Lynsey or her partner? He walked away quickly, away from the street lights, his cap pulled over his eyes. My God, he

71

thought, I've become a stalker! Nevertheless, on more than one occasion, at night, he walked nearly up to her house, near enough to see if any lights were on. They never were. What did it mean? Even on a Sunday evening and as late as 10 p.m., though she had been to church and he had walked her part-way home, the lights remained off. His mind began to race with speculation. After she cooked Hamish's Sunday 'dinner', did they both resort to drink and tumble into a drunken stupor for the rest of the day and night—and during the week, too, apart from the Wednesday evening when she attended the prayer circle, for every other night there were no lights on. If she was working on the laptop, surely there would be some sign of lights? The house was on a corner so he could see around it, on the side and behind it, and there were never any lights on, downstairs or upstairs. It was as though they lived in total darkness. Was it to save electricity—or was there a more disturbing reason?

He had to take control of himself and stop this night prowling. He called it his prayer run, for he would pray for her, and Hamish too, when their house was in sight—but was he just fooling himself to justify a form of stalking? The worst was the three days and nights between Wednesday and Sunday, which were the only two occasions when he saw her each week. It hurt so much, as Jim Reeves might sing, not to see her—never mind to see her go when they parted on Sundays.

He took refuge, to ease his unsettled mind, in the reading from *God Calling* for that day, and he was comforted, knowing how much it meant to the Lord himself to be comforted and loved by his child who longed to be with him just for the sake of being in his presence:

'Comfort Me, awhile, by letting Me know that you would seek Me just to dwell in My Presence, to be near Me, not even for teaching, not for material gain, not even for a message—but for Me.'

Now Charles knew how the Lord felt, what love was really like. His heart longed for Lynsey, just to be near her—and how he would be comforted if she had that same longing for him, just to be near him for his own sake. That must be the true nature of love, and in a sense his love for Lynsey had made him realise it. If the Lord had placed this love for her in his heart, perhaps it was his way of teaching him, of showing him how much he, the Lord, loved and longed for his children. Charles hoped she had read the same passage that day, and was comforted by the thought that she might have, even in the mystery of that dark unlit council house.

CHAPTER FOURTEEN

CHARLES was feeling deeply depressed and unsettled when the phone rang. The whole situation with Lynsey seemed to have come to a dead end. The ball was now firmly in her court and his nocturnal and even daytime wandering near her house brought it home to him that there was nothing he could do to encourage her to move on to the next step—to write, to begin her life story, to activate her mission, and perhaps his in the process as editor and protégé. It was a Friday morning and Sylvia had gone out to the shops and he was alone in his study, sinking deeper into despair as he began to succumb to the pain in his heart, the longing, the ache that could never be assuaged. He bent down with his head in his hands and prayed earnestly, crying out to the Lord. That morning's message in his copy of *God Calling* was at least reassuring: "Remember, trembling heart, that with God, to hear is to answer. Your prayers, and they have been many, are answered." He prayed: "Oh Lord, take away this ache in my heart. Let my love for her in no way cause any pain to others— but if you can, take away this pain that comes with the pressure of my love. Above all, Lord, bless her…"

At that moment the phone rang. He got up and ran down the stairs to answer the phone, desolate but with the crazy thought which he voiced: "Oh, let it be Lynsey!"

His heart stopped when he recognised her voice. She had never phoned him before and though the thought was in his mind, the shock of hearing her voice bowled him over.

"Charrels? This is Lynsey. I was just phoning to see how yer were gettin' along."

"Lynsey, oh my goodness…" He sat down, weak and breathless, on the lower steps of the stairs which were close to the phone. "You know what, I was just thinking of you!" Not surprising because he was thinking of her all the time. "Goodness, Lynsey, I have really missed you!" The undigested thoughts simply poured out, uncensored. But she didn't seem to mind.

"I have managed to write two pages so far, Charrels, of my life story. I even have a title. I've called it *From Darkness to Light*."

He had to admit, it was a brilliant title, and he said so. As he spoke he went up the stairs with the phone to his study and sat down in his computer chair. His heart was racing with the surge of joy speaking to her. "Lynsey," he said, "I hope I'm not suffocating you, with my attention. You know, sitting next to you in church and walking home with you as I do... I really don't want to smother you."

"Charrels Haddington," she laughed, 'I wouldna' have it any other way. You have given me so much help and confidence, eh."

His heart gladdened at her words, at her piquant accent that bordered on the commonplace of Kennoway. If he had not known her and heard that voice for the first time, he would have thought it was the voice of an older local woman, one of many you heard in the local Co-Op.

He took a deep breath. "Lynsey, I have so missed you," he said. "It's such a long time from Wednesday to Sunday."

"Aye weel, I miss you tae," she said. "An' by tomarra I should have three pages doon to give yer."

"I'm looking forward to that, Lynsey—I'm really proud of you."

"I'm reely quite chuffed with mesel', to be honest!" she laughed. "Weel, I'll see yer tomarra then."

As he turned off the phone he was hit by a tidal wave of happiness. Her voice, so strange, so local, so commonplace, yet so welcome, had wrapped around him, tugged at the strings of his heart which beat so fast that the happiness hurt. Still seated at his desk, he put his head in his hands and cried out his heartfelt gratitude to the Lord: "Thank you, Lord! Thank you for lifting me out of the devastating depression I was in a moment ago! You must have engineered that call, prompted her to phone me. Bless her, Lord, please continue to bless her and use me to bless her." All that night the recurring tidal waves of joy kept hitting him, keeping him awake until he dropped into a deep sleep, content with the thought that soon he would be seated beside her again in church.

In the morning he recalled that February the 14th was approaching that week and he was tempted to send her the Valentine card he had designed earlier on-line with a card website that would deliver the card direct. It was personalised with her name: 'Thinking of you Lynsey' with the words 'The Lord bless you and keep you' inside. He signed it simply: 'From Your Guardian Angel.' But in the end he either did not have the courage to give the go ahead to have it sent, or was sensible enough to resist the temptation, aware of the danger it might present to her—for what was to stop her partner from opening the sealed envelope when it arrived? He would have liked to have sent her some yellow roses, which she told him once were her favourite, like the yellow daffodils she placed on the desktop of her laptop. That, too, was out of the question— but then he had a new idea that struck him over breakfast. He would place a 'Love Letter from God' on a memory stick and hand it to her that morning in church. It was a popular letter one could download from the internet, where God tells his child that He cares and loves him or her, having chosen him or her before time began, with various references to scripture in support of these statements. He added one more line towards the end: 'I love you Lynsey—John 3:16'. If she could read between the lines, as it were, she would know how he felt about her.

He was hoping she would have her memory stick containing the beginning of her story with her at church, and he placed his little memory stick with the 'love letter' in his pocket, to give her in exchange. He timed his departure for church so that he would arrive there ten minutes before the service, at which time she was usually in place. He was nervous, all a-flutter as he walked through the door—and she was there! She was there, alone in her usual place by the wall near the back, for him a vision of beauty with her immaculate makeup, the flowing white scarf her mother had given her draped over her black coat. She turned round to greet him with a bright smile. God, she was lovely! He collected his hymn book and slid up to her, perhaps too close, and put out his hand to take hers in a tight squeeze with the words, "I've missed you so." He was looking forward to a corresponding firm grip, if only momentarily, from her slender fingers like an affirmation of her feelings for him. But she seemed to have anticipated his intentions and kept both her hands clasped together on her lap so that all he could do was briefly touch the top of her hand. At no time did she allow her hand to slip into his, or move from her lap unless it was to hold the hymn book while singing. It was as though she were resisting him, letting him know there were boundaries he had to observe. Throughout the service he kept his right hand on the seat beside him, close to her, hoping that a moment would come when she would drop her hand from her lap and touch his. But the moment never came and her hands remained firmly clasped together on her lap. In spite of her encouraging phone call, it was as though she was preventing him from crossing over the Rubicon, saying, in effect, so far and no further. He could only conclude, with a sinking heart, that his galloping feelings had allowed him to misread hers completely.

At the close of the service she delved into her black handbag and handed him her memory stick. "I've written three pages now," she smiled. "You c'n fix them up however you like—I'm sure there will be many mistakes. Change it any way you like."

He was delighted. Through her writing he would get to know her all the better, and by proxy her presence would be with him—in his computer and in his head. His love for her was a spreading infection. He took out his memory stick and gave it to her in exchange. "It's a love letter—for February the 14th," he smiled.

"Och!" she grinned, slipping the little device into her handbag. "Ye must have your wee joke, Charrels, eh!"

He laughed, accepting the gesture as a joke. She probably took it as another document bearing on her writing. Would she be relieved—or disappointed to find it wasn't actually a love letter from him, though in effect it was if she were able, and willing, to read between the lines?

Outside he waited for her to emerge from the church, since he had gone out ahead of her. It had begun to rain with a brisk breeze and when she came abreast with him she opened her small umbrella. "This is a fool-proof umbrella," she smiled as he hesitated to huddle under it with her. "It has double reinforced joints so the wind canna blow it inside oot. Dinna you want to share it with me?"

"I'm okay, Lynsey, it's just a bit of water on my head," he said as he fell into step beside her. After the unavailability of her ungloved hand in church he was careful not to intrude on her preserve. He wanted desperately to draw closer, but feared that he had misread her earlier signals. Like her umbrella, her heart was doubly reinforced against being blown inside out and tumbled by his wayward passion for her. She liked him, for she had said so, but her heart was encased, protected beneath those bands of steel that God's law and the sanctity of a pre-existing partnership dictated.

They walked in silence for a while, and then she asked him a question that blew apart his settled concept of her.

"Do ye like classical music, Charrels? I'm verra fond of Mozart and Beethoven—an' I love Rachmaninoff."

He was stunned. "Lynsey, I never took you for a Radio 3 person! Somehow I thought you would be more into…"

"Pop! Nae way! Hamish canna abide my music an' I have to listen to it when he's away. He likes Country and Western, but most of the time he likes nothing. He calls my music blaring pish! I like ballet, too. I used to take ballet at school, ye ken."

"You like Tchaikovsky then?"

"Swan lake, the Nutcracker Suite—what do ye think, eh!" she laughed. "You've no' said what music you like?"

"Lynsey, I…I'm speechless! You have exactly my taste. I listen to music—classical music—on my iPod, just about all the time. So that's something we have in common—apart from the Lord."

"I ken," she laughed. And he so wanted to hug her at that moment, but there were those unseen bars and the public place they were in—the pavement jostling with pedestrians, in spite of the rain, and they even had to give way to a bicycle on the pavement. This woman was indeed like an onion, he thought— there was always another, unexpected layer beneath the one you peeled away. Clearly his concept of her was wrong. Just because she had been—or was—an alcoholic, and spoke with a regional accent and lived in a drab council estate, didn't mean she lacked breeding and good taste… Look for instance at the way she walked, straight up, regal, he thought, immaculately dressed, like a royal princess. Yet she lived with a rough and ready ex-miner… Had he totally misjudged and mis-classified this woman?

As they walked along he ventured to ask her if she would like him to pick her up for the evening service, and for the

Women's Guild meeting Tuesday night. She seemed reluctant to agree to the evening service so he left it open to her to phone him if she wanted a lift, but she readily accepted his offer to pick her up for the Women's Guild meeting when there was going to be a 'bring and buy' fundraising event after a talk by a prison chaplain. He had a chequered woollen blanket he could take to the 'bring and buy' event. His mind had been casting about for more opportunities to be with her. He was delighted that she agreed to be picked up on Tuesday evening for the Guild Meeting, though he wondered if he had engineered the situation, manipulating her and felt uncomfortable. The rain had stopped now and she took down her umbrella.

"Lynsey," he said, "I do hope I'm not getting too close to you—too close for your comfort?"

This time she did not reply apart from shaking her head and there remained a long period of silence between them on the last stretch of the walk. He felt, especially after the failure to squeeze her hand for a moment in church that she was drifting from him.

At the crossroads he said, "Here's the corner I love because it's on the street where you live, and which I hate because it's where I always have to part from you."

They crossed the road first and then, to his surprise, she stopped and turned to him with her serious face and said, "You know, Charrels, you can always phone me during the week. You don't have tae wait till Sundays and Wednesdays tae speak tae me, eh?" His heart leapt for joy at her words, with the resurgence of hope. Love was so like a squeezebox, an accordion that squeezed and relaxed his heart in succession, vacillating from pain to joy and joy to pain in repeated waves of emotion.

"I will, Lynsey—I would so like to meet your mother, too, you know—and your dad. Would it be possible to invite them to my home, and have tea, with you there too? Do they have a car?"

She nodded. "Aye—she would just love that, and she would smother you with attention!" she smiled. "She likes tae have someone tae fuss over."

"We shall think of a date, then," he smiled. "And… and to discuss your writing, once I've looked at what you've written. You would be so welcome to come, again, to my house next Saturday, say once again at 11 a.m.? Would you like that? Another coffee morning? I can give you some feedback after I have read the start to your story."

"Aye," she readily agreed, smiling. "I really did like coming tae yer hoos, Charrels—as I said before, I felt so much at home there."

He smiled. "You know, Lynsey, I just love the way you say my name—Charrels—like you bounce the word into two syllables with the rr's! Charrrels," he said, accentuating the way she said the name.

"Reely?" she laughed. "You sound verra different from me too. Verra posh!"

On impulse he said, "Before we leave, Lynsey, can I take another photograph of you? You look so lovely!"

"Och, I dinna ken, Charrels, I have a cold…"

She was reluctant but he had already whipped out his little camera. He felt awkward and tried to snap her face quickly, but the camera failed to display her picture in the viewfinder and only presented a blank screen—as though the Lord had disallowed this liberty. He so badly wanted a close-up of her face, which to him was beautiful, cold or no cold—he was not aware that under her immaculate makeup she looked any the worse or less lovely than she had looked before. They were standing at the same location as the last time when she turned her serious face to him, just before the inevitable parting, when the low sun caught and illumined her face with all the weary lines below the coating of pale makeup. Frustrated, he returned the little camera to his pocket. "Well, it didn't work anyway, Lynsey. Must need recharging. So I'll see you on Wednesday then? I'll look forward to that."

"Aye," she smiled, and turned to look up the road. "Look! There's my braw dug Tyson waiting for me at the gate. He kens I am here!"

"Take care, Lynsey," he smiled.

"Take care," she said.

It was another parting. The accordion had squeezed his heart again and as he walked back the raindrops started to land on his head. The thought if her visiting him again in his house, on Saturday, lifted his heart. And she had said he could phone her, too. How he treasured and mulled over everything she said.

CHAPTER FIFTEEN

WHEN CHARLES reached home he could hardly wait to access the memory stick Lynsey had returned to him, to see what she had written. He had expected a fair deal of undisciplined writing, full of concord errors and misspellings, with rambling recollections, and was surprised by the neat appearance of the document, clearly set out with a dedication to her mother and father, to her partner Hamish for his 'continued Love and Patience', and to him, Charles, 'without whose help, support and co-operation' she 'would not have had the courage to write this book.' He was touched, and when he read further he was completely taken by surprise, stunned by the immaculate, educated syntax, the well-constructed, well knitted and perfectly formulated sentences. The diction, solid and concise, was as good as the prose he could write—and she was hopeful of it being improved by his editing skills! Again this woman was like an onion. Her polished writing was not what he had expected. Look closer and deeper under the makeup or sad lines and you found, not a simpleton, or an ugly duckling with some promise, but what she was, through and through—a full grown swan with wings unfurled for flight, bathed in the light of a new awakening.

Her story was well developed, beginning with her earliest memories, her family life with her parents, her love for her grandfather with whom she had been very close and wept when he died, the school (called an 'academy') which she had attended, the good grades she achieved, the tertiary college where she received her formal qualifications in accountancy and secretarial work. And then her impressive array of professional posts, including that of PA to a Church of Scotland minister and research assistant at the University where she helped to develop the study of nutrition in the anatomy of Salmon. It was all very impressive and yet very unpretentious. But then pressure of work and her widening social involvements led to social drinking. As she put it: "Unfortunately, my life was to change quite dramatically. Now I had been introduced to the world of Alcohol." Charles's heart went out to her as he read further:

It was at this point in my life that alcohol, without me actually realising it, was beginning to take a hold on me and my drinking was increasing. Instead of it only being on a Friday or Saturday night, it was now taking place on some week-nights and bar lunches were increasing as well. I had been blaming my drinking on my ex-husband, my mother and father, the rest of my family, the workplace, bosses, but did not stop to realise that it was actually my own fault—that I was the reason for my drinking. I was still able to hold a job at this time, but it was becoming increasingly difficult for me to focus properly on my family and my work. I was physically becoming more ill, sometimes taking dizzy spells at work and having to go home early. Eventually, I was relieved of my position at work because of alcohol abuse. I simply was now becoming unable and unreliable to hold down a job. I could not even trust myself. As well as all this, I had started to experience black-outs, sometimes not even remembering what I had done the night before.

That was as far as her story went to date. Charles wondered what role he could play in her future—which without question was a potential far beyond that which he had previously envisaged. At least for now he could give her as much encouragement as possible, but without allowing himself to become intrusive. He knew he loved her, and that was his burden—to help and encourage but stand back from personal involvement, or the touch of life that lay in his fingertips would be inhibited.

All he could do for now was make some slight adjustments in punctuation, and then, before he saved the file to her memory stick, which he would return to her at the prayer circle, he added his comments:

'Keep it up, Lynsey! You've made an excellent start. Ten out of ten to you, and ten out of ten to your English teacher(s). I love your story and my heart goes out to you. You have been very courageous and strong with tremendous perseverance—but I think your firm faith and wonderful breeding and solid education have stood you in good stead. I have no right to say so, but if I were your father or partner, or teacher, I would be (and am anyway as your sincere friend and editor) very proud of you. Just carry on and write as your feel, as though you were writing a letter to your best friend. Just let it flow and come from the heart. Now you can delete this bit I have highlighted in yellow and proceed with your creativity!'

He would have to wait until Wednesday evening to return the memory stick to her with his editorial adjustments (such as they were) and his comments. In the meantime the waiting was painful. To ease his pain, he took walks, usually round the small lake near her house where she said she sometimes walked her dog. She had said she walked the dog around ten in the morning; it was up to her because Hamish, being disabled and suffering of shortness of breath, found walking difficult. It was always around ten in the mornings, therefore, that he would stroll around the lake in the hope he would run into her "by accident". On one morning he thought he recognised her dog, a lumbering Staffordshire Bull Terrier, but it was being walked by a man. It was clearly not her dog, he thought—but to put his mind at rest he followed the man at a distance. The man crossed the road from the park and walked down her street—and to Charles's dismay he saw the man and the dog disappear into her front door! He was right then—it *was* her dog Tyson—but who was the able-bodied man? He understood that she lived alone in the house with her partner. He pushed this out of his mind, however. He had no right to snoop into her life. But on the Wednesday morning, the day of the prayer meeting, he was back walking around the lake when, just after ten, he saw her! This time there was no mistaking her, with her regal posture and stately appearance, even at a distance. There was no mistaking the dog, either, a lumbering muscular dog. But who was the man with her? His heart gave a twist of agony at the sight of him. They were walking slowly, strolling together, because the dog was old and suffered from arthritis in its back legs. But the man seemingly walked without any difficulty. He appeared to be the same man he had seen on the previous occasion.

Charles turned and walked quickly away in the opposite direction. He didn't know what they would think of him being there.   Had she been alone he would certainly have "accidently" met her. He even had her memory stick in his pocket, ready to give her. This man could be her partner's son, of course, or a neighbour—or a lover. Who knows? But he didn't appear to be disabled.

Charles walked back disconsolately to his house, deeply depressed. The heartache was awful. How could his friendship with her ever be fulfilling if the love he felt for her could never be realised? He swallowed a shot of whisky with an aspirin, looking for any kind of relief. Again he sat down with his head in his hands and cried out to God. "Here I am again, Lord, with this awful pain in my heart, in my brain! Take it away, Lord, just make it go away." He took a deep breath and picked up his copy of *God Calling*. He had not yet read today's reading, and he wondered if she had. The reading, under the heading 'The Difficult Path', seemed strangely pertinent and eased his heart a little:

'Your path is difficult, difficult for you both. There is no work in life so hard as waiting, and yet I say wait. Wait until I show you My Will. Proof it is of My Love and of My certainty of your true discipleship, that I give you both hard tasks. Again I say wait. All motion is more easy than calm waiting.'

Calm waiting! Easier said than realised. But the message, again seemingly addressed to 'both' of them, gave him a measure of peace.

Charles was surprised when out of the blue Sylvia said she would come with him to the next meeting of the prayer circle. "I feel responsible for you," she smiled, "abandoning you to the Church of Scotland while I follow the Lord in Kirkcaldy. I value my worship at the Kirkcaldy church, but the least I can do is come with you to your prayer meetings. You've been restless of late. To tell you the truth, I'm rather anxious about you, Charles."

He did not know if he was pleased or disappointed. On more than one occasion she had accompanied him to the prayer meetings, anyway. She wouldn't be in the way during the prayer meeting that evening since he was never alone, there, with Lynsey. Perhaps her presence would even resolve the conflict in his heart, bring him back to his senses, as it were.

He gave a disconsolate smile. "That would be nice," he said.

CHAPTER SIXTEEN

CHARLES was in a state of combined tension and excitement as he walked into the prayer circle in the company of Sylvia. Naturally his eyes went to Lynsey the minute he walked through the door. His heart lurched at the sight of her. She was gorgeous! The group gave Sylvia a warm welcome, pleased to see her again.

He took his customary place next to Sadie at the far end of the table while Sylvia sat next to him—but his eyes were drawn like a magnet to Lynsey who smiled her usual sweet smile.

"Lynsey," he said, "are you going to a party?" She was in full make-up, immaculate, laundered hair lightly draped over her shoulders and barely concealing the white pearl drops of her earrings. She was wearing the sweeping white scarf that swathed her shoulders and hung over the black top, which was low cut, revealing just a touch of creamy cleavage, suggesting the full liquid breasts just out of sight. God, he thought, she was absolutely stunning, his eyes glued to her.

She was taken aback by his question in front of the rest of the members. "Pardon?" she said, and then, smiling sweetly, continued, "No, this is just the natural me!"

It was the first time since her newfound sobriety that she had come to the prayer circle manifesting such highly charged glamour. Throughout the meeting he was barely able to stop his eyes reverting to her, drinking in her beauty. The red lipstick seemed to accentuate the radiance of her face, presenting a full yet delicate mouth that he longed to kiss. During the Bible readings she put on her ornate spectacles that gave her a schoolmistress appearance that somehow enhanced her grandeur with a touch of sophistication. Their eyes would meet from time to time and she would flash a smile, drawing from him a quick corresponding smile while he dragged his eyes away self-consciously.

The lesson was based on Psalm 51, a psalm of David, and the pitfalls of sin, and somehow the discussion led to temptation and David's akratic relapse the minute he set his eyes on Beersheba bathing on the rooftop. Two of the men were laughingly defending King David, saying the fault lay with Beersheba bathing openly on the rooftop—but the women, Sadie especially, lost no time in laying the guilt squarely at David's door, but pointing out that even his worse sin, engineering the death of Bathsheba's husband by placing him in the "hottest" line of battle, was forgiven by God following David's sincere and abject repentance. She read from the Book of Samuel and seemed to relish the accusing words of the prophet Nathan: "You are that man!"—identifying him with the wicked traveller who had stolen the dear sweet lamb that had belonged to his poor host. All this time Charles was quiet, wilting from guilt yet sneaking peeks at Lynsey who looked so irresistible. Why, of all psalms, was this chosen for the evening's study, he wondered. Was it by sheer chance, or was it providential?

At the conclusion of the meeting when everyone was donning their coats, Charles went up to Lynsey and slipped her the little memory stick that contained her edited piece of writing with his comments. He commended her again for her excellent beginning. "I've given you ten out of ten, Lynsey—your writing is as good as mine!"

She blushed. "I could never write as weel as you, you being a professor an' all, eh!"

This might be an opportunity, he thought, to identify the man he had seen her walking with by the lake. "You know, Lynsey," he said casually, "I thought I had seen you earlier today, by the lake. But if so you were with a man—it was too far to see clearly."

"Och, so it *was* you!" she exclaimed brightly. "I was walking the dug with Hamish and I said to him, 'I think that's Charrels!' I tried to call oot to you, but you were walking away tae fast. I thought it were you because you held your hands behind your back, the way you walk, eh! When we got past the generator I could see doon the rood, but you were away!"

"A pity," he smiled. "I should have waited or turned back but thought it couldn't be you. I thought Hamish was disabled, you see."

"Aye, he can walk but gets breathless, ken..." Just then Sadie, who had been speaking to Sylvia, came up to them buttoning her coat, for she would be taking Lynsey home in her BMW. Lynsey addressed her with her unaltered innocent enthusiasm. "I was just tellin' Charrels, I saw him the day around the Denhead Pond... He were walking that fast Hamish and I couldna ketch oop wi'him!"

"I was taking one of my brisk walks," he smiled self-consciously. "Keeping my weight down."

Why, he asked himself, did he feel guilty and a need to justify his actions to Sadie, who was recently elected a deacon? He did feel guilty, however, for since Lynsey started to come to church regularly he had sat next to her instead of next to Sadie as he had done for the last two years. And, instead of walking back with Sadie, she must be aware, he thought, that he had established a new pattern of walking back with Lynsey—and in the opposite direction to his home. In fact, it troubled him that the whole of the prayer circle, and others in the church, must have surely noticed this change in behaviour. But, he justified himself, no-one else in the church ever took the trouble to sit next to Lynsey—and, bless her, she had actually asked him if he would continue to sit next to her. Sylvia, of course, was unaware of where he sat and with whom he walked back, since she always worshipped at her 'happy-clappy' church in Kirkcaldy.

When they exited the hall Charles reminded Lynsey, before she turned to walk with the other women to Sadie's BMW, that he was picking her up the next evening for the Guild meeting.

"I dinna forget," she smiled with a sweep of her hair as she turned towards him. "I'll be waitin' fer yer, eh."

"Are you coming too?" he asked Sylvia, who had overheard him.

"Mmm," she said with narrowed eyes. "If you want me to."

"That would be lovely," he said, conjuring up an enthusiasm he didn't feel.

You could cut the atmosphere with a knife, Charles thought as he and Sylvia walked back to their house along the narrow pavement. Had she detected his feelings for Lynsey? Because the pavement was so narrow, he fell back behind her, quickening his speed to keep up with his wife's determined pace. Damn, he thought, he had been looking forward to being alone with Lynsey the next evening in the Guild meeting, as well as sitting next to her. Now Sylvia would be there too. Also, he was disappointed that Sadie did not offer, as she usually did, to take him and Sylvia back with her with the other women in her BMW. More's the pity, because it would have meant squeezing up close to Lynsey in the back seat.

The Guild evening really went well and was a surprise to Charles the way things turned out. He was anxious about Sylvia putting up some form of barrier between him and Lynsey and he had to admit she was very shrewd, probably in his best interests, of course. The weather was wet but not the bad stormy snowstorm he had expected from the forecast. He and Sylvia picked up Lynsey on time and proceeded to the church hall where he was able to park the car. The minute Lynsey came on board Sylvia welcomed her like she was her best friend. At the meeting Charles headed for three empty seats together, but hesitated to take a seat hoping Lynsey would sit next to him—so he waited for Sylvia and Lynsey to choose a seat first; but Sylvia, seeing his hesitation and no doubt perceiving his illicit attraction for Lynsey, said firmly, "Come on, take a seat, Charles!" So he had no choice but to take the first seat in the row at the free table, expecting Sylvia to sit next to him so that Lynsey would have to sit next to her with Sylvia between the two of them. But once Charles was seated, to his surprise Sylvia offered Lynsey the seat next to him, so that she was on the other side of Lynsey. And then—one would think Lynsey was Sylvia's best friend because she was all over her, with enthusiastic conversation and questions of interest about her. This meant that Lynsey was in effect turned away from Charles, preoccupied chatting happily to Sylvia. Charles smiled, slightly put out, thinking what a cunning strategy! Forging a sort of bond with Lynsey would make Lynsey more mindful of any attraction she might feel towards her errant husband.

Nevertheless, there were times when Sylvia was obliged to speak to the ladies on her other side so Charles had his fair share of turns to speak to Lynsey too. Lynsey was very soft spoken and with her piquant accent he had to move closer to catch her words—which was nice. She looked wonderful with her flowing laundered hair and gentle honey-brown eyes, her wafting perfume adding to her intoxicating allure. She was wearing her mottled black and red scarf. He noticed for the first time that her hands looked somewhat rough, strong hands, the nails unpainted. It put him in mind of the strenuous work it must take caring for Hamish. She was not made up as brightly and immaculately as the night before at the prayer meeting, and she was wearing black skin-tight slacks and white sneakers.

When Charles asked her if she was able to access his edited copy of her writing with his comments from the memory stick, she turned and with a very meaningful look and soft smile whispered, "*Yes*—thank you." The look and smile lingered long enough to tell him that she was touched by what she had read.

For him that soft whisper and lingering look constituted the highlight of the evening.

CHAPTER SEVENTEEN

THE NEXT TIME Charles saw Lynsey was on the pre-arranged visit to his home the following Saturday, at 11 p.m. This was to give her the opportunity of returning the memory stick with the expanded version of her life story. Sylvia would be at home so he had no other choice but to explain to her that Lynsey would be coming to discuss her writing.

"Is she the member of the prayer circle you gave your old laptop to?" Sylvia asked.

"Yes," he said.

"Mmm, I thought so."

"I thought you knew that," he added.

As on the previous occasion, Charles spent a near sleepless night with the excitement of seeing Lynsey again. He sensed that Sylvia, in the double bed alongside of him, was restless too, for her legs would give a sudden kick or twitch which woke him up just as he thought he was at last falling asleep. He wondered if she was tense because of Lynsey's forthcoming visit. He was certainly aware that she was not comfortable with the woman coming yet again to their house. When he had told her he was surprised at the eloquence and discipline of Lynsey's writing, she had said, "Oh good—then she doesn't need to keep coming here." He had explained that she needed to come since he wanted to guide her about the need to write about certain specifics in her life rather than produce a general factual outline of her life.

The previous Saturday Lynsey had arrived a half hour early, so even as ten-thirty approached he was already a bundle of nerves. He went up to his study and began to jot down various questions he wanted to ask her about her life experiences, since he knew that when she was physically present his nervous tension might cause him to forget the pertinent questions he wanted to ask her. He wanted to know what prompted her to come to the church that day when he met her for the first time, and what prompted her to attend the prayer circle for the first time; above all, he wanted to ask her what had happened between that first visit to the prayer circle, when she was clearly under the influence of alcohol, and the next visit, when she looked so ravaged and careworn. He wanted to establish how the Lord was working in her life, and if she was aware of this—but he wanted to know, too, the extent to which she had noticed him, in those earlier days—and what role he might have played in her attendance and reformation. If the conversation went the way he wanted it to do, it was important that the two of them should be alone together—and he hoped that Sylvia would leave them alone together, and that he might even conduct the interview in the privacy of his study, upstairs, well away from Sylvia whose presence would naturally inhibit Lynsey opening up to him.

That this was unlikely to happen was evident from Sylvia's very obvious presence near his study while he was compiling these questions as the hour of her visit approached. Sylvia was constantly hovering, first very busy with the noisy vacuum cleaner, then folding up laundry, with repeated to-and-fro walking outside the open door of Charles's study. At length it seemed her curiosity got the better of her. She entered and said, "You're very busy—what are you writing about?"

"Um," he hesitated. Her sadden intrusion caught him off guard. "Just compiling a list of questions to ask Lynsey. I want to focus her attention on specifics—to establish the way the Lord has led her to change her life. It's all in the interests of her testimony, which I shall edit afterwards."

Sylvia took a seat on the sofa at the back of the study. "Does that mean she will keep coming here—to answer your questions as they arise from each instalment of her writing?"

He shrugged. "She should be fine once she's launched. My role, really, is to guide her."

"I see. You're giving her a lot more personal attention than you give to your other authors."

He sighed. "Yes, well, the others are far away. And helping Lynsey is like helping people in our own community." He gave an awkward laugh. "Care in the community, as they say."

"So," she said, "what about Bryan Harvey, that atheist science fiction author in Wales—doesn't he need care and guidance, too, even though he's not part of our community?"

"I've preached the Gospel to him many times—but he has a closed mind. And he's not a recovering alcoholic."

"I see," Sylvia sighed as she stood up to resume her housework. "I hope you know what you're doing."

At eleven-thirty Charles was alone in his study and taking deep breaths to control his excitement. Sylvia was back in her study downstairs typing. He would peer at regular intervals out of the window, which overlooked the road in front, to see if there was any sign of Lynsey's arrival. She would be walking, as on the previous occasion that she came. Before making the arrangement for Lynsey's visit he had told Sylvia he could drive over and pick her up, a suggestion that Sylvia immediately crushed. "Her house is just in the next estate—I'm sure she's perfectly capable of walking over here." Sylvia's instinctive resistance to another woman in Charles's life, however her presence might be merited as a result of Christian outreach, was much in evidence—unspoken rather than overt.

When 11 o'clock arrived and went, Charles was in a state of high tension. His chest felt tight and he had to take deep breaths to relieve the pressure. He would walk from the study window to the front bedroom window, seeing if he could catch sight of her coming around the corner. How would he contain his anxiety if she didn't come—and why wouldn't she come? His life seemed to have been divided into two categories—the few bearable moments when he was basking in her presence, and the many unbearable moments when she was out of sight. He went downstairs at length and took a seat in the lounge, turning on the TV, pretending to be nonchalant, trying to cover up his restlessness. He was well aware of the likelihood that Sylvia would detect his restlessness—and being a woman with a woman's instinct, she would know the reason for it.

When the doorbell rang his heart lurched with a burst of joy and relief. He reached the door quickly, before Sylvia responded to it. The door opened to reveal Lynsey, who looked a little apprehensive but fresh and pure in her neatly tied red and black scarf and laundered hair, just a hint of red lipstick on her smiling lips. She was carrying a large NEXT shopping bag as though bearing gifts.

Sylvia emerged from her study and welcomed Lynsey like a long-lost friend, inviting her into the lounge and conducting her to a seat on the sofa near the window, taking a seat further along on the same sofa—which meant Charles, in order to be facing Lynsey, needed to take a seat at the opposite side of the room. Sylvia did not offer to make any coffee so Charles went into the kitchen and prepared the coffee, remembering that Lynsey took two spoons of sugar with milk. This time he did not use 'THE BOSS' mug but a colourful one with a cream egg painted on it. When he returned with the mugs of coffee the two women were engaged in chatter, apparently relaxed, laughing, to all appearances getting along like a house on fire. He realised, after listening, that Sylvia had already begun the interview, if it could be described as such, asking the questions he had planned to use. There was no opportunity to invite Lynsey upstairs for a private discussion in front of the computer, so he made the best of it, listening eagerly to Lynsey's replies about her lapse into drinking, her battle with alcohol, and her bad luck when it came to "males", as she called the men in her life.

"How many were there then, Lynsey?" he put in. "Did you have a partner before Hamish?"

Lynsey laughed. "A partner—there were quite a few! I seem to attract the wrong type of men. I've niver met a man who to me was a real..." She groped for the right word.

"Soul-mate," Charles said softly.

"Aye!" she said, pointing at him in acknowledgement. "Exactly. That's what I mean."

"Well, how did you meet... Hamish, and the others, Lynsey?" Charles asked.

"Bars. Always in a bar."

Well, he thought, that explains it.

"They were all so rough, ye ken," she said. "Like typical Scotsmen, no romance in any of them, eh!"

"But," Sylvia intruded, taking over again, "you're happy with your present partner, surely."

"Aye, if ye can call it that, eh? He gives me a roof over my hid. It seemed to be a suitable arrangement."

"But he loves you—and you him?" pressed Sylvia. "Aren't you close?"

"Well now," she laughed, "if he tried to make love to me, I'm sure it would kill him!" She shook her head. "There's no tenderness between us. I cook fur him, help to bath him an' all. He c'n be so crabbit too. If he complains I telt him to shut it— and ask him if he would prefer being put in a home. He doesna like that!"

This was news to Charles. He could relate to what she said. The lovemaking between him and Sylvia had dried up a long time ago. Though they shared a double bed, they slept curled up facing opposite directions. If he tried to touch her or cuddle up to her, as he tried to occasionally, she never responded. She said she did not like to have her sleep disturbed.

"Does Hamish have a temper, Lynsey?" Charles asked, concerned for her.

"Och aye! But he doesna lose it with me—it's the TV he shouts at! You should hear him—he talks to the box like it was a person!"

"Do you watch TV much together then?" Charles asked.

She shook her head. "We don't like the same programmes. Me—I like a real scary film! I like to be sceered, eh!"

"Charles here has a temper," Sylvia put in. "He has to be treated with kid gloves." She gave him a meaningful look.

"Och, Charrels?" Lynsey laughed, looking at him. "I canna believe it! He seems so helpless, like a pussycat!"

"Looks can be deceiving, Lynsey," Sylvia said.

"Lynsey," Charles said, changing the subject, "I know this is an awkward question, but how serious was your addiction to alcohol? You speak of this in your story."

She was serious now and said softly, "It was real bad, Charrels. It started as social drinking, when I was wurking. But it started to take over—even during the day. Eventually I was taken to hospital. I had delirium tremens. I asked the doctor—am I going mad? I kept seeing things—visions, people that weren't there. Like in that painting up there..." She pointed to a Victorian oil painting on the wall, a mother and child. "I would see more than two people—different people— in a painting like that. The doctor said, 'No, Lynsey, I assure you, you're not going mad. You're having hallucinations. You have to stop drinking.'"

"So, when you came to that first church service last year, Lynsey," Charles said, "what made you come? I think you were still—under the influence?"

"Aye, I was, Charrels," she laughed. "Goodness knows what the people thought of me!" Her voice became serious. "I had some wine when I woke up in the mornin'. Then I felt so rotten—and I thought I must make an effort, I must break the cycle. I looked oot of my bedroom window—and I saw the church spire. I thought, I'm goin' there! That will get me oot of this. So I put on my makeup and put on my best skirt and went! I was brought up in the kirk and I knew God would help me."

A stab of joy pierced Charles's heart. "That was the Sunday I took part in the service. It was about angelic outreach— angels amongst us and messages from angels. Do you remember shaking my hand, Lynsey?"

"Did I shake your hand? I remember being outside afterwards surrounded by a lot of folk. Someone said to come to the prayer meetings. It was a lovely day with a blue sky."

"Well," Charles continued, managing to get more control of the conversation, "there was quite a lapse of time between the first couple of prayer meetings you came to and the next one. We were all praying for you. What happened during that time?"

"I was drying oot, Charrels," she said softly.

Charles remembered how bedraggled and careworn she looked when she came back to the prayer circle. He wanted to reach out and touch her, but she was out of reach. Sylvia threw him a warning look.

"Don't you have drink in your home now, then?" Sylvia asked. "It must be a temptation."

"Oh aye," Lynsey nodded. "Hamish keeps his sherry and lager in the hoos. But I have no trouble keeping away from it. Before that, if I opened a bottle of wine and had some, I would close the lid tight, saying, 'Lynsey, that's enough the noo!' But then I would sneak doon and have another swallow. 'Jus' ccn meer,' I would say, and unscrew the bottle again. Then a wee while later, doon I'd come again… and another wee bittie— and sune the bottle would be empty, ken. But I'm okay now. The prayer meetings have been a lifeline to me. Like the AA meetings I went to. That's what I thought—people there would help me be strong."

Charles stood up. "I'll just take your memory stick up to my computer, Lynsey." He had hoped she would come up with him but she took it as a signal that it was time to leave. She gave him the memory stick from the bag she had with her, but also took out various items she had wrapped up. "Afore I go, I want to give you these," she said. "You have both been so kind tae me, giving me the computer especially." She unwrapped a large parcel to reveal a white scarf and a pair of white gloves. "I thought you might like these, Sylvia," she said, handing them to her.

"Oh, that's nice of you…" Sylvia said, taken aback.

"An' fer you, Charrels, I got you these," she said, handing him a CD of Mozart pieces and a small box containing the Serenity prayer framed with a glass frontage. "I thought you would like that prayer, Charrels," she smiled.

It touched Charles directly, like an arrow to the heart. It was the prayer she had prayed at that first prayer meeting. "Oh Lynsey," he said, "I will treasure this—and place it in my study where I can read it every day. I remember you prayed this prayer at the first prayer circle meeting you attended. You actually knew it off by heart. Where did you learn it?" But he knew the answer before she told him.

"At an AA meeting," she smiled.

He went upstairs alone with the memory stick while Sylvia helped her into her coat. In his study he transferred the updated file of her writing to his hard drive, and on an impulse transferred a WORD file of a chapter from the novel that he had begun to write—a novel he called *Sunset Stirrings* based on Lynsey. The chapter recalled exactly what he had observed and experienced at the last prayer meeting, where he was so stunned by her dazzling appearance and her effect on him. Nothing was left out—the way he longed for her, followed by the details of the Guild meeting where he had sat next to her. His heart was in his mouth as he went back downstairs and handed the memory stick back to her. Whatever would she make if it?

"Would you like me to run you home, Lynsey?" he said to her.

"Oh, that would be greet!" she gushed. "I dinna bring my raincoat, just my hoos coat. I was hoping it wouldna rain on the way over hier."

To his surprise, Sylvia did not invite herself into the car and so he was alone with Lynsey, for the first time that day, on the short journey back.

As they were driving Charles said, "You must feel like you've been grilled in a job interview, with all those questions."

"I really dinna mind, Charrels—it's niece that you care to ask. Sylvia too. She's verra sweet." Then she gave a spontaneous laugh. "Aye, I ken! It were like an interrogation, eh!"

"Well yes," he said, "she certainly got involved." Then he glanced at her and lost no time saying how nice she looked and how much he had enjoyed her company, and thanked her again for the lovely presents. "Did you not remember me at all from that fist Sunday you came to church, Lynsey?" he asked.

"I certainly do, Charrels," she smiled sweetly. "I remember thinkin', what a niece cultured man he looks. I didna want to say that in front of Sylvia, ye ken."

Her words warmed his heart. "You are very sweet, Lynsey." He took a deep breath as he negotiated a corner. "Lynsey, I placed a file on your memory stick. It was a silly thing to do, I guess. Perhaps you shouldn't read it... I just thought, on impulse, that it might encourage you to write fiction as well, perhaps even co-author a book with me..."

"Oh!" she interrupted him. "That reminds me, I read what you said after my last writing... Charrels, it was so niece of you to say such things to me... I never had anyone say that to me before... you're a verra, verra braw man!"

He stretched out his left hand and squeezed her gloved hand, keeping his right hand on the steering wheel. She was wearing red woollen gloves this time. "I appreciate that, Lynsey. You're a very dear girl, too." He took a deep breath. "But as I was saying, I put a rather daring file on your memory stick, and a lot of it is fiction, of course. I created a character like you, but that's not entirely you..."

She laughed. "Oh Charrels, dinna worry, I can read between the lines you ken!"

He put out his hand and squeezed hers again. "Bless you, Lynsey." A wave of happiness lifted his heart as a wave would lift a surfer. "But you must tell me, if I'm going too far, you know..."

"Well, Charrels Haddington," she laughed, throwing him that sidelong look of hers, "that depends on how far you *want* to go—as the actress said to the bishop!"

"Well...," he began.

"Sorry, Charrels," she apologised, still with a twinkle in her eye, "it's that sense of humour of mine again!"

"As I said before, Lynsey," he smiled, "I love your sense of humour." This woman made him feel so alive, the way she kindled a fire of excitement in his belly.

As they drew up in front of her house, he picked up a very large volume that lay on the back seat, and handed it to her. He had secreted it there without Sylvia noticing it. For some reason he sensed his wife would disapprove of him giving Lynsey additional reading material, especially one of his questionable novels. "This is another of my novels, Lynsey—it might familiarise you a little more with my writing style, and even encourage your imagination." He avoided the word 'stimulate' this time. In fact, the rather risqué love scenes might well offer a stimulation of the wrong kind.

"Och, look at the size of it!" she exclaimed, accepting the book. "I'll read it for sure! You're so kind, the way you keep giving me things."

His heart was certainly in his mouth as he drove home. He had been on a plateau with Lynsey for some time now, clearly in love with her and with little indication of how she really felt about him. Not that he had any right to expect her to have feelings for him. Yet if she had the slightest attraction, beyond simply 'liking' him, he would be over the moon! What did she mean by that joking question of how far he wanted to go? Thinking of that certainly made him feel he was on the edge of a plateau, close to falling off—or soaring to new heights.

That evening he was eager to read what she had written in her recent addition to her story. She wrote of how she lost her virginity at 18 to her father's cousin, of the humiliation when it was discovered, and then of how that led to an eating disorder and how she came close to starvation through anorexia. She was tall and lanky and had been terribly thin to begin with, which caused her to be picked on at school. She recorded how she had bad luck with "males", always attracting the wrong type of men. But Charles was deeply touched by what read like a cry of desperation that concluded the new piece she had written—that she still longed for and lived in hope of one day finding a fulfilling relationship, where the right kind of man, loving and kind, would love her for who she is and would satisfy her "both physically and mentally"—and, she said, she had "so much love to give". Yes, Charles thought, his heart going out to her again, she's never had a soul-mate, and that's why she drank.

CHAPTER EIGHTEEN

THE FOLLOWING MORNING was Sunday and Charles walked to the church, slowly, his heart in his mouth. He was carrying another of his novels he wanted to give Lynsey. By now she may have read what he had written on the memory stick which he had dared to share with her. If she had read it, he thought, then one way or another, for better or worse, he would be off this plateau of status quo. It was an ice cold day but the sun was shining. He had donned his sports jacket and abandoned his coat because he wanted to make the most of his good looks, such as they were. He had showered that morning, shampooing his hair, risking alerting the suspicious mind of Sylvia who had commented recently that he seemed to be showering and washing his hair a lot more frequently nowadays. She, as usual, had gone to her own 'happy-clappy' church, taking the car, to be recharged with the Holy Spirit— which left him free to walk to his nearest church, alone, where he knew Lynsey would be.

The cold bit into him. He shivered, but vanity knew no bounds. Then he saw her! She was advancing in the distance, behind some older women. He put up his hand to shield his eyes from the sun to see more clearly. Was it really her? The halo of her long, fresh hair caught the sun. When she waved he knew it was her. His heart beat painfully. At least she had come, and she had waved to him! Promising, he thought—she was still going to speak to him then? Their different approaches came together at the beginning of the short path to the church entrance.

"Are you okay?" he asked. "It's a nice sunny morning so I left my coat. But it's sure cold!"

The trivial exchanges, the small talk about the cold morning as they entered the church covered his tension. In the church she took her usual place near the back and he slid in next to her. There was silence as she removed her coat and settled in. He felt awkward as his eyes turned towards her and caught her sideways smile. She looked so gorgeous, sumptuous even, in her pure white flowing scarf. He dared to break the ice. "Lynsey—are you still speaking to me then?"

She gave that adorable little shake of her head as she flicked her hair away from her eyes and turned to look at him. "Charrels Haddington—now why would I not speak tae you?"

"Well," he hesitated, "I guess you didn't read that sample chapter I put on your memory stick."

"Aye, I did," she smiled. "Everry wurd of it!"

"Oh God," he said aloud, taking her hand and holding it hard. "What… what did you think of it?"

"I loved it!" Her smile broadened, mischief flashing in her eyes.

"Really? Oh God, Lynsey, I'm *so* relieved!" And as they spoke, he continued to grasp her hand, firmly, hard, in his, his heart beating so fast it felt it might explode. He maintained a hold of her hand like it was a lifeline. "I am *so* relieved, Lynsey," he said again, taking a deep breath. "You know, some of it may be fiction, of course… but it's all inspired by you."

"I can read between the lines, Charrels," she smiled. "And I can tell you I was that excited, reading what you wrote. It was last night, and it was wonderful."

He still had her hand imprisoned in his. He recalled how he had described her in that extract, mesmerised by her beauty, smitten by her smiling eyes. "But," he said, "you know I am not free—you are not free—to feel this way… I mean, for me to feel this way…"

"Charrels," she said quietly, still smiling, "I understand. Life is short. You only live once. You have to take what happiness you can while it's there."

"Well," he breathed, luxuriating in the sudden release of the tension within him, "at most I can let my feelings overflow into my writing. I can express it that way, at least."

"Unless I kidnap you in the middle of the night and take you away. Would you resist?"

"No resistance at all, Lynsey—no resistance at all!" He was still holding her hand tightly. God, he loved her.

"You look very niece," she smiled with her sidelong glance.

"It's a nice day—though cold. I knew it wouldn't rain." His sports jacket, the silver tie, lashings of aftershave, braving the cold with no coat—it had all been worthwhile!

Just then Maggie, who ran the Women's Guild, came in and took a seat next to Charles. He immediately let go of Lynsey's hand.

He heard Lynsey give a little giggle and whisper, "You'll have tae watch yourself noo!"

He took a deep breath and chatted to Maggie with exaggerated enthusiasm to disguise his relief and illicit emotions. Then the little red book was carried in and the choir struck up, and soon the hymns and sermon were under way. All the time Charles longed to feel Lynsey's hand in his once again, but he kept his hands on his lap, just as Lynsey was doing with hers. He was in a state of sublime happiness. Mulling over Lynsey's words before the service, he hardly heard the message the minister was giving.

But he forced his mind to listen, to take in the minister's words. He felt uneasy as he registered what he was saying. He was talking about the church's need for discipline, for the need for each member to be self-disciplined and keep to the narrow paths of obedience that God had laid down for each of his recruits. We are all part of the Lord's army, the minister said, and an army must be disciplined. "In difficult times," the minister said, quoting Winston Churchill, "the future of the world is in the hands of disciplined people," adding, "and the future of Scotland depends on disciplined disciples." And here Charles was, sitting next to a woman he loved, a woman who was not his wife and who belonged to another—can you get more undisciplined than that? What did Lynsey say—you only live once, you have to take what happiness you can while it's there? Even at the expense of discipline and the commandments of God? But he brushed the thought from his mind. He knew now without doubt that love can strike like lightning, at any time of one's life. Yes, he thought, we can't always choose who we love—or what happens when we do. In a way we are victims of love. No wonder Cupid wears a blindfold. Love is blind and binding, whatever vows you might have made beforehand.

At the end of the service, after the threefold-amen and a respectable interval of silence, the congregation began to shuffle and gather their coats. Charles stood up and waited to filter into the aisle in the stream of exiting worshippers while Lynsey drew on her coat. He was now in a state of subdued excitement as he returned his hymn book to the shelf and walked out ahead of Lynsey, first shaking the minister's hands and saying, with as much sincerity as he could muster, "Thank you for the sobering message"—though if anything the message had nudged his conscience. He never felt less disciplined, his thoughts centred only on Lynsey.

Outside he loitered on the pavement waiting for her to appear—he felt it wise not to be seen walking out with her. At length she emerged, poised and elegant in her long black coat, and they walked together along the narrow pavement. "Strange," he said, "how Sylvia and I had to walk in single file, usually with me behind, when we walked from the church hall along this pavement—yet both of us fit easily upon it side-by-side."

She flashed her sidelong smile again. He was aware that all this time his pulse was in overdrive. Something had certainly changed during that ten minutes or so while they had sat together before the service and he had for some time gripped her hand. When the pavement widened they gave way to a man walking behind them, allowing him to pass. It was as though there was a constant pressure from behind to get along, the winged chariot of time pressing him, to make use of every passing moment. There was a little awkwardness in their speech, for they had both come very close to lifting the floodgate that separated one soul from another. Charles did not know if she felt the same as he did for her, and could not believe that she, so much younger than he and she so lovely too, could ever do so.

"You know," he said, "I was so touched by what you wrote, in the latest bit of your story—that you longed to find someone to love one day, and that you had so much love to give. It really touched me."

"You read that!" she smiled self-consciously.

He nodded. "I do hope you find that man, Lynsey—and I only wish it could be me. And yet if you do find him, it will break my heart—because it can never be me. If only I were younger, and single—if only I had met you years ago..."

He felt rather than saw her smile. She didn't say anything and they walked on in silence for a while.

"You know," he continued, "I wish we had more opportunities to be with one another—to speak without there being others around us, or pressing us from behind." He was aware of a short elderly lady in a red coat rapidly catching up with them from behind. They were automatically increasing their pace to keep ahead of her.

"Well," Lynsey said, looking thoughtful, "there are times when you can talk to me... during the times Hamish goes out. He goes out at regular times to see his pals. One time is tonight, on Sundays, at nine; then tomorrow, Mondays, from about eight or nine up to midnight when he goes to the Inn; then on Wednesdays, in the morning, about eleven, and again on Friday night when he drinks at the Masonic…"

"Gosh, Lynsey," he smiled, "you mean… I can actually phone you at those times? Wouldn't that be taking a risk? The last thing I want is to make things awkward for you, with Hamish."

She shook her head. "Hamish says I am doing so much better—that I am so much improved, a nicer person… especially, he said, since that chap Charrels has been in my life…"

"Oh gosh, is he okay about that… I mean, doesn't he resent me?"

"No," she laughed, "he means it honestly, eh? He thinks you're having a good influence on me. I'm a much better person, he says, happier, not so moody, bright and cheerful. More patient with him when he grumbles…"

"Well, I promise to be discreet."

The woman in the red coat was gaining on them and he felt flustered, trying to talk and keep ahead of the woman as well. "Lynsey," he said, pulling her over by the arm and making her stop. "Just stop a moment." He drew her to one side to allow the woman in the red coat to overtake them. "I just wanted that old girl to get by—she's been pushing us from behind for quite a while now. Also," he said, taking his small camera out of his jacket pocket, "I want to take your picture, if I may? You know, when your book is published I'll need a picture for the back cover. And today, as always, you look so gorgeous. You really are lovely, Lynsey."

"Och, Charrels, ye always make me feel so much better aboot mesel'." His compliments about her appearance never seemed to fail to amaze her and melt her. "You always say such niece things to me, Charrels."

"I'm surprised the whole world isn't swooning at your feet, Lynsey." He took two close-up photographs of her face, lit by the winter sun. She smiled whimsically, slightly bemused. Then, before he could stop himself, he heard himself say: "Lynsey, you must realise by now that I'm head over heels in love with you. Do you mind me saying that?"

"Of course I dinna mind!" She gave a little laugh. "Yer awful sweet tae say so."

When they reached the crossroads they stopped before parting at the corner. At this point he gave her the novel that he was carrying under his arm. "It's the second novel I published—*A Twist in Time*," he said. "It's about a man in an unhappy marriage but he is given a choice to go back in time and start again. But he makes all the same bad choices because he has no memory of the future. But he does just one small thing differently, because of a girl he fell in love with. He sends her a post card to say he loves her. And that changes everything. When he wakes up from what he thinks is a dream, he finds himself back in the present but this time in the arms of the girl of his dreams—in real life. It's a fantasy, but meeting you has reminded me of my own novel! You know, if only I could wake up from this life and…"

"Och, *shush*, Charrels, you're a real dreamer, eh?" She accepted the book and tucked it under her arm together with her black handbag. "You're so good tae me… so generous… and I still have that thick book you gave me yesterday to read!"

"Just trying to encourage you to write," he grinned.

"Hamish was amazed by how big that book is that you gave me last night! He said, 'Are ye really goin' tae read all of that?!' I told him, 'Yes, I'm going tae read every wurd of it!'"

"Well, this novel will give you more exposure to my style of writing. In case we write a book together one day."

"You give me all these things, your computer and all these books," she smiled.

He wondered what she would make of the novel, if she actually read it, for it had quite a few fruity love scenes. He had been trying to write a best seller and pander to pubic taste, though he was pleased with the quality of his writing and imaginative concepts.

"Lynsey," he said, and she turned her hazel brown eyes upon him. "Lynsey," he said, looking into those eyes, his heart in his mouth. He knew he was going to say something foolish again, but couldn't stop himself. He was on the brink of a precipice and the momentum of his emotions was taking him over. He took a deep breath. "Lynsey, I hope there will be a time when I can take you in my arms—and kiss you on your lips."

Her eyes widened just perceptively, a faint smile barely touching the corners of her mouth.

"I hope I haven't shocked you, Lynsey." He couldn't recall that bolt out of the blue now.

She shook her head, her bemused eyes still on him. "Not shocked—just surprised, Charrrels."

"Well," he said awkwardly, feeling very foolish, "I guess I better leave you now. You have Hamish's dinner to think about."

"Och, we'll just have a sandwich the noo—he usually has his dinner aroond three. But you can call me during those times I gave you, Charrels. Can you remember them?"

"I hope so."

"Do you want me to phone you when you get home to tell you again, so you can write them doon?"

He thought a while. "Better not, Lynsey. I can't say who will answer the phone."

She nodded. "I also walk the dug, as you ken… at ten in the mornings; usually it's just a bit later. It's niece in the summer when one can sit on the bench. But you might find me there, tae…"

"I'll certainly bear that in mind, Lynsey. I like to take my brisk walks in the mornings... I've been in the park before now, as you know, just in case..."

"I ken," she smiled, touching his hand. "Take care now— I'll see yer anyway at the prayer circle Wednesday night." She laughed. "We'll be exchanging sly grins at each other, eh!"

"Yes, Lynsey—take care."

"Take care." And with that she smiled and walked purposefully to her house, her laundered hair swaying as she walked.

As he walked back alone, on cloud-9, he told himself he was definitely off the plateau now—and in free fall. It was intoxicating, exciting, but where would it end? But then he realised, mulling over all her words, that though he had revealed his love for her—he had said as much—she never once said she loved him. She seemed happy to receive his love, even flattered that he should love her. But was his love reciprocated?

Back at home that night, in the privacy of his study, he downloaded the two close-up pictures of Lynsey onto his computer. They were of a high resolution and he could enlarge her face, her eyes and mouth, on the screen, seeing again the look of her bemused brown eyes. Looking at her objectively, for a moment, he wondered if others would see her beauty and not think her plain. Stripped of her living, breathing, sweet and endearing personality, she did look plain, he thought, and he could see the lines, the crow's feet around the eyes, under the makeup. Perhaps, he thought, she was like Becky Sharp in Thackeray's *Vanity Fair*—plain to others, but irresistible to him. Beauty, as always, is in the eye of the beholder.

As he fell under the spell of her eyes on the screen, he could not resist dialling her number on his mobile phone. It was just after nine and within one of the "safe" periods she had given him—and Sylvia was downstairs watching the television in the lounge. He would make it a quick call, just to say goodnight. When he heard her voice, the familiar, strangely familiar accent that could belong to any local Kennoway woman, his voice faltered. He had to clear his throat to get rid of the frog that blocked his voice.

"Charrels?" he heard her say.

He cleared his throat again. He had to speak quickly. "Just wanted to say goodnight, Lynsey, And to tell you how much I liked the additions you made to your story. Especially the new paragraphs to the early part, your holidays, the trip to Blackpool, for instance. And the way you remember feeling the gentle breeze covering your whole body with the warm sunshine! And how during the night you would lie awake in your holiday caravan listening to the sound of the waves sweeping across the shore line. It brings the reader—and brings me too—much closer to you."

"Och," she said, "yer a braw man, Charrels."

"And I think you're terrific," he said. "Good night, my love."

"Good night, Charrels." And so the brief call ended.

Taking a deep breath, he thought of his impulsive words, calling her "my love"—and yet she still did not give any indication that she loved him.

CHAPTER NINETEEN

W HEN CHARLES walked into the prayer circle the following Wednesday his eyes went immediately to where Lynsey normally sat to ensure she was there, and she was. Sylvia was with him—she seemed to make it a permanent routine now, accompanying him to the Church of Scotland prayer circle on Wednesdays although on Sundays she worshiped at the church in Kirkcaldy. He allowed her to walk in ahead of him so that his eyes were unfettered, falling upon Lynsey without delay to soak up the maximum pleasure of her eyes as they met his. She was just so heartbreakingly stunning and her welcome smile thrilled him. As he passed behind her seat he lightly brushed his hand against her hair by way of greeting.

It took a moment for him to register that the table layout was different this time. More tables had been spliced in to make a wider table surface, to provide more seating capacity around the enlarged rectangle that the combined tables provided. When he took his place with Sylvia at the far corner, the distance between him and Lynsey at the opposite corner was greater than usual. He remarked jokingly, addressing Lynsey across the expanse of the enlarged table surface, that he would need binoculars to see her. She looked radiant and everyone was helping themselves from a large box of Black Magic chocolates. "Lynsey brought them," someone said. More people arrived, with the addition of Billy the Church Officer and his wife Moyra, who sat next to Lynsey. The prayer circle was certainly expanding.

As the study got under way, reading from Psalm 103, Charles's eyes were drawn to Lynsey who looked up occasionally to meet his with a knowing smile. These smiles were more meaningful to him now and he recalled her remark at the last parting on Sunday that they would be exchanging glances, mutual peeks that spoke of a mutual love. He luxuriated in these forbidden peeks yet felt the pain of knowing his love was limited to these brief exchanges of recognition that flashed between them. He took in her appearance. What was so different about her tonight? There was a new radiance, a brightness, a sense of confidence he had not seen before. She wore a red cardigan, unbuttoned over a black top with a looped neckline that fell short of her cleavage. He had not before seen the scarf she was wearing tonight—made of a silk material, displaying flowers with varying sizes of red petals on a dark olive background. The scarf was tastefully looped around her neck and clasped neatly in front, leaving the two ends to flow across a bosom that was more ample than he had previously realised. Around her neck was a necklace he had not seen before, more of a choker than a necklace with silver beads that caught the light. But the crowning glory was her hair, falling around her face in sumptuous waves, like gossamer silk caught in a breeze. It occurred to him that she must have used curlers, or tongs, whatever, to get a wavy effect like that. She was going to a lot of trouble to present herself with so much beauty, though it was all understated with excellent taste.

Bert introduced Psalm 103, a psalm of praise and the love of a caring God, and then read out a question for the group: "What's the best thing that's happened to you?" The answer to that came instantly to Charles, as he lifted his eyes to Lynsey. '*You*, Lynsey,' he wanted to say—'unquestionably you, my darling.' Her eyes glanced up at him, briefly, a smile touching her lips. Could she read his thoughts? The others volunteered their own answers to the question, naturally referring to the day, or the moment, when the Lord touched their lives and changed their lives forever. 'Oh my God, Lynsey,' were Charles's unspoken words, 'how you have touched and changed my life!'

Then Bert read out the next task: "Describe your perfect day—who would be with you?" The answer to that was easy, and instant, for Charles. 'You, Lynsey, *you*, every time." He loved her so much it was like a pain in his heart—a pain that he could not be with her. She lifted her eyes from the Bible in front of her and caught his eyes, and smiled. Yes, she knew his answer to that, without doubt. At least he *knew* she knew.

The discussion continued and Sadie spoke of God's deep love for us all, and of the way he has his hand on us, his children. "He is building us in His image," she said, "so we can say, 'I'm a new creature in God.'" Charles glanced again at Lynsey, drinking in her beauty. How, indeed, she has changed, he thought, and become a new creature since that time when she came to the first prayer meeting, tipsy in gaudy makeup, with her pertinent question about the Ghanaian speaker's colour! Oh, how he loved her now—but he realised he had loved her from the very beginning, since that very first day when she appeared in church, a flamboyant tipsy songbird!

Sadie was on a role now. "Yes, God works in mysterious ways his wonders to perform," she quoted. Well, Charles thought, God has certainly worked in mysterious ways with Lynsey, and with him too. Then he glanced at Lynsey whose eyes were now softly resting on her Bible and in his mind he spoke to God: 'Lord, just what are your plans for us? What is this mysterious happening, Lord, that's changed Lynsey and changed me too—this love for her that has pierced my heart? Did YOU plan that? And if so, why, Lord, *why*?'

Lynsey herself spoke up next. "You know when the Lord has touched you—because you feel it here." And she touched her breast. "Ye've got to feel it here, eh? Inside, in your heart, not just outside."

At this point Billy the Church Officer spoke up. "I want to say something about one of our members, and she is present here. I hope she won't mind my saying so. She has been coming to our church and I have seen the wonderful transformation in her. I want to say what a blessing her presence is here, and to the church." He looked at Lynsey who was seated next to Moyra, the Church Officer's wife. "I am speaking about our Lynsey here." Everyone applauded Lynsey.

Charles thought his heart would stop and saw how Lynsey flushed with pleasure, or was it with embarrassment? Oh yes, he thought, she so deserved this praise, this recognition, and he was so proud of her. It gladdened his heart that it was not only he, Charles, who could see the change—but then he knew she was always precious to him, from the beginning, right from the start when he first saw her.

"Och, I won't sleep tonight with all your praises, eh!" she said to Billy and to the group.

It was so wonderful, this recognition of what God had done for the dear girl. And yet Charles felt the pain grow in his heart, for with this recognition the expanse between him and her seemed to have increased, like the size of the table that had expanded and caused them to be further apart. If he tried to express his love, to commit her to a relationship with him, if he imposed his personal love upon her, she could lose all this newfound respectability and recognition. It was as though he had in him the power to destroy her, like alcohol, to unmake the good that had been done—and how could he ever do that? How can you hurt the person you love by loving that person all the more? She had broken her dependence on alcohol, but in a sense if he pressed his love upon her he would be like alcohol to her. The more you love alcohol the more it hates you back, they say—and the more she loved him, if she did, the more that love might destroy her good favour and good standing with the church and the community.

Charles managed a brief encounter with Lynsey after the first part of the meeting with the beginning of the tea break.

The two of them had established a routine to collect the Bibles and return them to a cupboard in the kitchen. They usually coincided their arrival at the cupboard and Charles always 'accidentally on purpose' touched her hand as they were packing away the Bibles. This time she was delayed, holding a stack of Bibles, by Billy who had intercepted her with his apologies, hoping that he hadn't unduly embarrassed her by bringing her superlative progress to the attention of the meeting. This much Charles overheard as he passed them on the way with his pile of Bibles to the kitchen. He lingered at the cupboard and at length she appeared with her Bibles, and he helped her to stack them.

"How are yer, Charrels, are ye okay?" she asked quietly.

"Just missing you like hell," he said with feeling.

"Aye, I ken, me too!" she said.

Her reply lifted his spirits. He took from his pocket a new small memory stick. "Shall I give this to you now, or at the close of the meeting?"

She hesitated. "Wait till the close," she whispered before joining the ladies preparing the tea.

He sat down in his place at the table while the ladies, including Sylvia and Lynsey, served up the tea and coffee. Lynsey was very busy bringing out the tins of biscuits and his heart was lifted by her presence, for she hovered close to him, even brushing against him when reaching over the table to place the tins and jar of milk and bowl of sugar on the table. Was that by accident, he wondered? She looked so wonderful, he thought, noticing how her bosom filled the black top she was wearing. Soon she was back again and placed a saucer with a slice of tart in front of him. He looked up and saw it was her, again. Later he found out that the tart was brought by Nimrod and that there were only six slices to go round, not enough for everyone. Since Lynsey was distributing the slices, had she ensured that one of them went to him? Bless her, he thought.

In the prayer session, the people mentioned by Bert on the list were prayed for. Charles closed his eyes, praying silently for Lynsey while the other prayers were being voiced aloud. Then he prayed silently for himself, too, that whatever he did would not neutralise Lynsey's happiness or favour with the Lord. 'Let my love for her be a blessing, Lord, and in no way hurt her. And please, please, Lord, let me cope with this burden of love I have for her. All things are possible to you—and I am asking that there will be a way to relieve this pain in my heart, the pain that comes from stifling my love for her.'

He felt the tears in his eyes. The others were still praying and he looked up, towards Lynsey. Her eyes were open, looking unseeingly at the table in front of her. He had noticed before that she prayed with her eyes open. What was she thinking, he wondered? Then her eyes shifted and caught his— and they connected briefly, a glimmer of a smile at each end before Charles bowed his head and closed his eyes. He continued to pray earnestly for her.

He prayed earnestly because he had done something very daring again, and it was all on the memory stick in his pocket. There was no point hiding the depth of his feelings for her any longer and he wanted to put all his cards on the table. For some time he had been keeping a diary of his encounters with and feelings for Lynsey in the form of a novel. He had already let her see the sixteenth chapter which, to his relief, she said she loved. So why not let her read everything he had so far written to date? So the memory stick in his pocket contained the file of the entire 'novel' to date. For better or worse, let her read it, he thought. Whatever the consequences, it would be better than this ache in his heart. At least sharing it would put her fully in the picture—the real picture. He had also copied to the memory stick his slightly edited version of her updated story, with his appreciative comments. In his comments he had referred to the 'novel', which she could read if she chose to. "If you read it," he wrote, "remember that it's a novel, about 70% fact and 30% fiction—the main thing being that you are the inspiration behind it." He added: "One important thing—the 'novel' is for your eyes only, dear."

He waited at the close of the meeting by her coat and when she turned up he slipped the memory stick into her hand. He had to do it quickly since Billy the Church Officer was very intrusive, wanting to speak to her again. Lynsey and Charles exchanged a brief farewell glance as they walked away in separate directions. They lived in worlds apart.

That night he lay awake in bed. Sleep eluded him and he fell into prayer, again, silently, in his mind, his head on the pillow. His heart hurt so much, longing for her, and he silently implored God to take away the pain. 'You made me, Lord, you know why I have this love in me. I don't understand. If you put it there, then reveal to me what I am to do about it. I never wanted to hurt anyone—not Sylvia, not Hamish, no one in the prayer circle, especially not Lynsey. It's just that—oh, Lord, you know I love her so much! If only I could hold her in my arms. Please help me, Lord, please help me.' He felt a tear trickle down his cheek onto the pillow. He got up, careful not to wake Sylvia, and went into the en suite bathroom to wipe his face and blow his nose that had become stuffed up with emotion. Where on earth would this end?

He crept out of the bedroom and went downstairs and made some coffee. It was 5 a.m. and he listened to the music on the Mozart CD Lynsey had given him. Then he went up to his study and wrote down what he remembered from the prayer meeting. It was the only form of relief that worked, apart from prayer.

After a while he sat back and thought of the pathetic way he had cried in bed. It struck a memory chord—and he remembered his father. He was a small child at the time, in bed in his bedroom. His father had come into the room and clearly thought his little son was asleep. He had gone into a corner of the room, standing by a bookcase, and wept quietly with his back to the room, which was nearly dark. Charles was aware of this and lay very still, wondering what was happening to his father. Much later he became aware of a tension between his parents, and his mother, with his father present, never lost an opportunity to hold up his infidelity to whoever was being regaled by the story of his lapse. Then Charles's mind travelled to the time he met his first love, at university. He had been invited to the home of a pious lady, a deacon in the church, and he fell in love with her young daughter. They both surrendered their virginity to each other, and when this was discovered their shame was revealed to the whole church. When he was back home for the holidays he confided all this to his mother, and she consoled him, saying bitterly, "Charles, don't be hard on yourself—*any* woman can have *any* man! It was her fault as much as yours."

Why then, he wondered, had his mother been so hard on his father? Thinking back on it all now, his heart went out to his father—especially remembering that time he had wept in a corner of his bedroom. Now he knew what his father had been going through. He wasn't being deliberately unfaithful—he had just fallen in love, properly, probably for the very first time in his life. That thought made him remember some words his father himself had said to him long ago while he, Charles, was still single. "Don't look for a woman," he had said, "let it happen naturally; the right one will come along, and when she does you'll know it." He was indeed his father's son. His heart went out to his father, long since dead, remembering those words.

Finally Charles opened his copy of *God Calling* and read the message for the day. It was printed under the heading 'Endure':

> 'How many of the world's prayers have gone unanswered because my children who prayed did not endure to the end? They thought it was too late, and that they must act for themselves, that I was not going to act for them... Can *you* endure to the end? If so, *you* shall be saved. But endure with courage, with Love and laughter. Oh! My children, is my training too hard?'

"It *is* hard Lord," he prayed. "But I will trust you—for have you not said your servant will not be tempted beyond what he can endure? And that when he is tempted, you will also provide a way out so that he can stand under it?"

CHAPTER TWENTY

WATERSHED I

IT **WAS** with some trepidation that Charles walked to the lake where Lynsey had said she walked the dog around, or just after, ten in the mornings. The night had been emotionally exhausting, with his longing for her, his prayers pouring from his heart to God, and remembering his father who had probably experienced the same agonies of love he was now wrestling with. He had woken early and tried to get it all out of his system as far as possible, writing about his last encounter with her in the small hours of the morning, creating a manuscript that was rapidly developing into a full-length novel. At least thanks to her he was writing again, not just performing the soulless task of editing other people's works. And the inspiration could be fostered by her reading his work too—and what indeed would she make of all the revelations of his heart that came to her in this way? But for that reason his heart was in his mouth as he made his way to the lake. He had been lifted off the plateau, the status quo, in their relationship by her unexpected joyful response to that one chapter he shared with her. But what would be her reaction now, now that she had all of the existing chapters at her disposal in her computer? She had given him some encouragement hitherto by saying she sometimes walked the dog at ten in the mornings—but he had never yet found her there. Would she be there now? It seemed especially unlikely since the rain had been persistent that morning, even beating in his face as he approached Leven road.

He had a good excuse for getting out of the house at that time since he had told his wife Sylvia he had a doctor's appointment for ten. The appointment had actually been for

10:30, which would give him close to half an hour to linger around the lake in case she was there. Having made the appointment and having consulted the appointment card the day before, however, he was surprised, if not delighted, to find he had misunderstood the time of the appointment which was in fact for the same day the following week—but he kept this to himself: it meant he had a good excuse for another potential rendezvous with her the following week. The complaint he had given to the doctor's receptionist was a bogus one, anyway—like the mythical Mars Bars, to give him a reason for walking home with Lynsey. His mind was becoming more and more inventive, if not devious, to manufacture opportunities to meet with her—especially to be alone with her.

It was a bleak outlook with the damp, persistent rain, and the chances that Lynsey would be there seemed hopeless. In spite of his questionable ethical motive for seeing her, he prayed as he walked, pulling his collar up against the rain: "Let her be there, Lord, let her be there, please." His heart lifted as he rounded a corner and the little park with the lake across Leven road came into sight—for at that moment the sun broke through. By the time he had crossed the Leven road the rain had ceased. A touch of excitement came with the thought that she might actually come out to walk the dog, if the weather had thus improved. He reached the path that went round the lake at exactly 10 a.m. His eyes searched the path all the way round the lake and saw two other dog-walkers disappearing in the distance. At least it meant others thought the weather good enough to come out—though clearly she was not there.

He decided he would walk 'withershins' round the lake. It was a new word he had picked up from the radio, which meant an antic-clockwise movement, a movement against the natural movement of the sun, or against one's better judgement—it seemed an appropriate word to describe his present emotional condition, which was inexplicable even to himself. He had been walking round the lake for the second time and had a sinking feeling, for it was five minutes after ten and there was still no sign of her, and he prepared himself for the usual disappointment. The sun was out now and the rain had ceased. He would do two more circuits, he thought, before making his way back. His path at this point was facing the distant entrance of the park and he looked towards where she would appear, if she did, from the crossroads on the other side of the Leven road where they normally parted on a Sunday morning. As he looked his heart missed a beat.

There was a distant figure with a dog, and the figure seemed to wave at him. Surely it was not her, he thought—but the figure waved again. He could not even be sure it was a woman at that distance—surely he was too far away for the person to make him out. But the figure waved for the third time—and he waved back, knowing with quickening pulse that it might be her. Then, his heart in his mouth, he realised it *was* her. "Oh my God!" he breathed a prayer, "Thank you Lord, thank you!" He gave way to a sense of gushing relief. It felt as though he were living in a different dimension. He lingered at the bend of the path where it took a withershins turn to the left, continuing the anti-clockwise direction. The dog, he saw, walked slowly, meandering a bit, and she had to wait for it to catch up before she could continue her approach to him. He still couldn't believe she was coming at last—it was the first time his strategy had worked!

As she came into hearing distance, she said brightly, "Fancy seeing you here, Charrels!"

"Yes, a purely coincidental encounter," he smiled, playing along with the mock conversation. "I just happened to be taking a walk…"

"Probably on your way to buy meer Mars Bars, eh!" They both laughed. "You ken," she said, seriously, "I had a feeling you were here today." As she came up to him she took his arm.

"Look, come this way, further past the lake... from this end Mary MacDonald, from next door, can see us if she looks out of her window. She's a niece lady but a terrible gossip!"

He looked at her. She had no makeup on whatsoever. It was a face scrubbed clean, red and slightly blotchy. He couldn't help thinking, how plain and unremarkable, like any working class Kennoway woman—but somehow he loved her all the more, yet wondered, if he had seen her like this that first day she came to the church, whether he'd still have fallen in love with her. Now without any mask of makeup on her, how plain and worn she really was, he thought. Here was the onion, completely unpeeled.

"Oh heck," she laughed, "I have read all of your story about Charrels and Lynsey, Charrels—what a laugh! I couldna stop readin', and couldna stop laughin'! And Lynsey's accent! I ken I'm Scottish, but do I speak that bad?! Charrels, you are so funny—and loveable!"

"You were not offended by anything I said... about Lynsey's working class background, the drab council house?"

She shook her head. "I loved it all. I ken your writing is fiction, but I can read between the lines, eh. Charrels in yer story is you, through and through, Charrels! And it's true, most of it is true, so true, you awfy man! It's like you've been writing a blow-by-blow account of everything I say, of every moment we've been together! Oh heck, are yer goin' to record what I'm saying the noo? Do yer have a tape recorder in your pocket, eh! But I just love you so much for making me so beautiful! And do you really feel that way about me? Even with my makeup off?"

"Lynsey, you are the loveliest woman I have ever met—a woman to die for. And I love you. I couldn't help falling in love with you—even at my age! That has never happened to me in years. What Charles in the story says is totally true, what he really said to you, as Lynsey in real life—you must know that. Everything I wrote is exactly what happened. Every word you said is exactly as I recorded it. But no," he smiled, "I don't have a tape recorder hidden on me. I don't need one. I cherish every word you say."

"Yes, Charrels, I recognise all my wurds, and yours tae. Oh, I'm sorry, 'every wurrd, Charrels'—is that how Lynsey says it? Everrry wurrd! Oh, you are that funny, Charrels! I don't really speak like that, do I—even though I live 'doon the rood, eh!'" She laughed.

He grinned. "But you do roll your rr's, Lynsey, and it's so cute the way you pronounce my name." He smiled. "Anyway, I'm not that good at conveying a Scottish accent—perhaps I was thinking of the Borders accent, where they say 'ken' and 'een' and 'kirk'! I was thinking that if an international reader read our story, then Lynsey's Scottish identity should be clearer. And to make the story more dramatic I exaggerated Lynsey's drab council house existence."

"Well, it's nice to know... sorry, '*niece* to know!'... that I have a common accent like any Kennoway housewife... *eh*?" She gave him a sidelong glance and punched him playfully on the arm. "It's okay, Charrels," she smiled, "I am no' offended. You didna exaggerate my drab existence—and it's kind of yer to say so. My life with Hamish is as dull and uninspiring as you perceive it. All I am is a live-in carer, and he can be a right scunner! But you know what—I trust you completely... I feel you are the only man I could ever trust..."

As they spoke he touched her face, moved a stray hair away from her eyes. She looked so ragged and careworn, but her honey-brown almond eyes were bright with life.

"Charrels," she said, "I have been up late for two nights reading your story... and I can tell you it has... I mean *you* have turned my life upside doon. Last night standing in a dream thinking of you I burnt two slices of Hamish's toast and he shouted at me: 'What the blazes has got into you, hen!' If

Charrels canna stop thinking of Lynsey, then I can tell you Lynsey Anne McCann canna stop thinking of Charrels! You are some man, Charrels. Whatever do you see in me, eh? No one has ever said all those wonderful things tae me that you have said. You are right—sorry," she smiled, "you are reet—all those compliments of Charrels in the story—they are wurd for wurd the same that you have given me."

They had walked as they spoke and came to a stop at the other end of the lake, the dog wandering close to them. The sun fell full on her naked weatherworn face while her eyes connected with his. Before he could stop himself he bent forward, took her in his arms and kissed her gently but purposefully on the mouth. It was no more than a few seconds but it felt like time had stopped. Her lips were delectably soft, elastic, relaxing, moulding to his in an eternity of bliss. He was reluctant to let go, savouring the joy of two souls uniting at last as one. He stopped to draw breath and whispered, "Lynsey, Lynsey, I love you so much."

"Me too," she sighed, pushing him gently away. "Charrels, do you realise how dangerous this is? There are a thousand Kennoway windows that can see us reet noo. The people here are terrible gossips."

"Sorry," he smiled. "I sort of looked around before I did that… there's no-one else in the park."

"Well," she giggled, "wait until the *Leven Advertiser* comes out next Saturday. Dinna be surprised if we're headline news, ken!" Her laughing eyes held his for a moment longer, her smile almost coy. "You smell niece, Charrels."

"Mm, and you taste nice," he whispered.

They moved a little further along the path, stopping again while the dog ambled up and explored and snuffled through a new patch of grass on the bank of the lake.

"You were so right about the way you described Sylvia at the Guild meeting, Charrels. She was so canny, the way she put me between the two of us. 'Come on,' she said to me, 'the rose between two thorns!' As if I couldna see her strategy." She paused. "Only one thing you really got wrong, Charrels. Hamish is no' an alcoholic. Aye, he likes his sherry and lager when he's with his cronies, but his drinking is no' out of control, like mine was. I dinna ken who telt you that he was an alcoholic—and I think whoever said it was verra unkind—but he is no' an alcoholic. I am, sure—or was—but…" Here she placed her hand on his arm, "I can assure you, Charrels, that that's a thing of the past. There's no way I'm goin' back to that. And you know why—it's because of you. You have turned my life upside doon."

He placed his hand on her cheek and looked into her sincere eyes lovingly. "Lynsey, it was not me… it was the Lord that has given you the courage and the strength."

"But He used you." She smiled gently, then said mischievously, "Yer a verra niece man, Charrels, and I mean it, every bit of it." She laughed. "Did I sound like your Lynsey then?"

He smiled. "I so love the way you say may name, Lynsey. Your accent is more like Lynsey's in the book than you realise. I love it and don't ever change it. Just keep saying Charrels for Charles!" He squeezed her hand. "How do you pronounce the name of Prince Charles, the future King of England?"

"Just like I do your name, Charrels—Prince Charrels," she said, simply.

He laughed. "I do love you, Lynsey." He put his hand on her arm. "How is this to end, Lynsey? Will you help me to plot out the rest of the story? Lynsey must do only what you would do in real life."

"Well, it would have to be a happy ending. I won't have it any other way. Maybe Lynsey should seduce Charrels!" A twinkle appeared in her eye. "I hope he's capable of making love."

"Well, I'm pretty sure he is," he grinned. "Not that he gets his oats with Sylvia anymore. They share a bed but they sleep facing away from each other. You'll know that from the story. But I can assure you he's perfectly okay in that department."

"I am verra glad to hear that!" she smiled mischievously. "As for Lynsey and Hamish, they sleep in different rooms. But you ken that too."

They walked a little further and stopped under the overhanging branches of the adjacent wood. He put his hand up against her cheek. Her skin was smooth and soft to the touch.

She smiled. "It was so strange, trying not to look at you and at the same time peeking at you at the prayer meeting and longing for you!"

"I thought our Church Officer was very kind, to pour all that praise on you openly. You deserved it too! But I felt quite flustered and jealous, him fawning all over you. He was there at the close of the meeting wanting to talk to you again. I couldn't get a word to you in private. All I wanted was to speak to you too. "

She dropped her voice. "To tell you the truth, Charrels, I was feelin' quite irritated by his attention."

"But at least I could gaze at you. You looked so exquisite." He smiled. "Lynsey, you pray with your eyes open!"

"Och, so why were yours open then, eh!" she laughed.

They did not prolong that first meeting by the lake. They were aware of the need to avoid suspicion from their respective partners by not being absent from home for a noticeably longer time than usual. But the rest of the day and throughout the night Charles felt sublimely happy, even resisting the temptation to rush to his study and record the events in the persona of Charles, the protagonist of his story. He felt much too happy to sit down and write. Let the events settle first, he thought... and from now on it would surely be possible for Lynsey to help suggest or dictate the further development of the plot and events that were to overtake the 'fictional' Charles and Lynsey. Up to this point he was seeing Lynsey from the outside, trying to triangulate her character and motives from the various external clues or perspectives that he was able to observe. Instead of writing, he spent the whole of the afternoon on a cloud, reliving in his mind the delicious confirmation that she loved 'Charrels' as much as he loved Lynsey. He lay back on his bed in a world of his own listening to the symphonies of Mozart and Haydn on his iPod, using his earphones. His undisciplined, unfettered mind drifted to Lynsey—the real Lynsey—as he imagined making love to her, and while he did so the iPod, set on shuffle, went on to play Tchaikovsky's 1812 Overture. He realised as he listened to the resounding cannons firing off at the climax and the subsequent rejoicing and fireworks, that the musical piece was a precise representation of a wonderful sexual orgasm; it exactly expressed his imagined relief that had come with the release of his love for Lynsey, in his mind and heart a woman to die for. His whole body and mind was flooded with joyful contentment as he listened.

The next morning at 10 a.m. he made his way to the lake again, not really expecting he would be lucky enough to find her there again. But she was. This time she was waiting for him under the overhanging branches of the small wood on the far side of the lake. His joy knew no bounds. She stood there, the cumbersome dog lumbering around her. She waved as soon as she saw him enter the park from the gate adjacent to the Leven road. He quickened his pace to reach her.

"Another chance meeting, purely by accident, Charrels?" she smiled mischievously.

"Looks that way, Lynsey Anne McCann," he grinned. He slipped his arm around her waist, careful not to draw her too close on account of the Kennoway eyes.

"Not so fast, Charrels Haddington," she said with that sidelong glance of hers. "I've read meer of your story. Now what exactly do you mean, she's no oil painting but a wonderful canvas, eh?" She added: "Yer cheeky bugger!"

He blushed. "I told you, 70% fact and 30% fiction—don't forget it's a novel. One needs verisimilitude."

"Veri-what?!" she laughed. "Never mind, I'm not offended." She went on in a serious tone: "Charrels, did you really walk past my hoos during the nights? And you never saw any lights? I can tell you why—it's because I try not to show any lights in the hoos to avoid any attention and interference from the drug addicts up the rood. I keep a small night light in the lounge and my bedroom, so I can read or write without any light being visible from the street. That's the only reason. Those were probably times, too, when I was alone in the hoos; to think, you could have come in and I would have made you a niece cup of tea, eh! And I can assure you, I was niver rollin' aroond in a drunken stupor!" She laughed. "Charrels Haddington," she slipped her arm around his waist, "I can assure you I have been feeling the same feelings and having the same thoughts as you—the feelings and thoughts that keep you awake at night, troubling you about how I feel fer you. Well, let me speak plainly, you big sumph, I feel the same way about you, ken? I am even prepared to share you with Sylvia—if that's the only way. And what you say about your thoughts about going to church and the prayer circle is true of me tae—I ask myself if I am goin' to worship God, or to see you. My first thoughts are always hoping you will be there, and tae see you—but I go for God too—I ken that should be my priority, and I will make it so—but, Charrels, I dinna think you realise the impact you have had on me. And there you were, torturing yourself about my feelings for you…"

He squeezed her waist. Their backs were to the wood so it would not be apparent from the street and the other side of the lake that their arms were around each other's waists. "Thank you, Lynsey—you are so generous. You don't know how much I am overjoyed at what you have said."

"But Charrels," she laughed again, "The Mars Bar! Heck, what a feeble excuse! Really, Charrels, couldn't you no' think of a better pretext than that! What do you take Lynsey for—a nitwit? Yer really made me laugh!"

"But you were kind enough, all those times we parted, to pretend you accepted my excuse."

"I thought you were so sweet—how could I hurt your feelings when you were saying it for the sake of walking with me as far as you could? Did you no' think that would touch my heart?"

He sighed as he put his hand up to touch her face. "I so wish, Lynsey, that we could meet some place where I can take you in my arms and smother you with kisses."

"There will be times, Charrels." She repeated very sincerely the words she said before: "I want you to know—I am prepared to share you."

"You really mean that?"

"I have no choice, do I? I didna plan this—so what can I do? I love you noo—I've got you under my skin… I need you. I need love … and *you* need love, Charrels. We both need each other."

He squeezed her waist and pulled her a little closer. "The future is in the Lord's hands, Lynsey. We don't know what it holds… but He has a plan for each one of us… Who knows how it will unfold?" He sighed. "The thing is, Sylvia is a good woman—and the last thing I want to do is hurt her. She has always been faithful to me. She doesn't deserve this—but I agree with you… I am trapped in my love for you."

"Do ye regret meetin' me?" she asked.

"Absolutely not, my darling. I have been here for nearly three years, carrying on as usual in my humdrum life—and then this slightly tipsy and gorgeous woman with a sunshine smile and a delicious cleavage comes to the church, like a bolt out of a cloudless blue sky, and shakes my hand. She has shaken my soul."

Her response was a gentle squeeze of his waist.

He continued: "Sylvia packed away your present yesterday—the scarf and the gloves. She said it was very sweet of you to give her those presents—the gloves too. Though she said the gloves are too small to fit her."

"Oh, I have smaller hands... see my wrists?" Lynsey smiled. "They are so narrow I find it difficult to wear a watch."

But oddly enough, looking at her well-shaped hands and her wrist, they did not seem small, but strong—stronger than Sylvia's, in fact. It pained him to think how his love for Lynsey was a threat to Sylvia, how it would hurt her if she found out. But God had placed this love for Lynsey in his heart—of that he was certain. It had taken three years after the Lord had sent him to Kennoway to connect with Lynsey. And now that he had, she was part of his destiny. He could not see ahead to see how their destinies would pan out—only God knew the answer to that—but he would continue to write the story of the fictional Charles and Lynsey, seeking clues as to how that destiny might unfold. A third-person perspective might help him to see their continuing lives a little more objectively, with a little more detachment and help him to understand a little more clearly this strange new phenomenon of being in-love at 71.

PART TWO

CHAPTER TWENTY-ONE

Lynsey Anne McCann

THE NEXT SUNDAY morning in church Charles and Lynsey were like two teenagers in love. Seated in the usual place near the back, alone in the pew against the wall before the beginning of the service, they were barely able to suppress what amounted to giggling and holding hands. They attracted curious glances from two elderly ladies in the pew in front of them while they spoke in hushed voices about the wonder of being in love at their time of life. Lynsey was noticeably animated, her eyes shining as she glanced meaningfully at Charles. He had his hand at times on her leg and under her leg, feeling the soft contours of her thigh. He was so taken with her flawless makeup, the radiance of her beauty, the brightness of her eyes. Something had certainly changed since the last time they had sat together in church. They had to pull themselves together when the little red book was brought in.

The sermon was a sobering message, but one with a strange comfort. The Heavenly father, the minister said, is well aware of the problems we might face if left to our own devices. So, thankfully, He has sent the Gift of the Holy Spirit to enable, to encourage, and to assist us in our lives. In a strange way, Charles thought, the Lord had sent the gift of Lynsey to him, to brighten his life—and yet how could this be from God if the gift tempted him to break His fifth commandment? But the minister continued to say we should be open to the healing touch of Jesus and of the Holy Spirit. This caused Charles to close his eyes and pray silently as he sat there, in a warm glow next to Lynsey: "I know when you touch me, Lord, and it often happens when I am praying for Lynsey or myself, or Sylvia. I feel your touch, like a waterfall of peace that flows through me, calming me. I believe there is a reason for Lynsey being in my life. I know everything is in your hands—that the future is in your hands, and while I do not know the future, I have peace that whatever happens is in your hands. I would not for anything not have had this happen to me."

When the collection plate was brought round the steward inadvertently missed Charles's pew so that he did not have an opportunity of putting in the £5 note he was holding. Never mind, he thought, he would save it for later.

At the close of the service Lynsey delved into her handbag and gave him the little memory stick on which she had saved the recent addition of her testimony. "There's a letter there for you too, Charrels," she smiled. Charles stuck it into his pocket. It was something to look forward to when he reached home.

The two of them walked back in the rain, behind other slow moving members of the prayer circle who all walked under open umbrellas. Charles felt very self-conscious since, walking directly behind Bert, the leader of the prayer circle, he could not conceal his presence from him. Bert at one point turned round and asked Charles where his home was. "Oh, in the adjacent new estate," Charles said vaguely. He felt he needed to say a little more to explain his walk with Lynsey. "Lynsey here is making an excellent job of her testimony. I've been helping her with it and will include it in the next edition of the little book *Touched by Angels*." Bert nodded with an understanding smile. Charles had already published Bert's testimony in the little book—a testimony that spoke of the miraculous touch of God's power when he was healed from a near-fatal tropical disease while away on national service after the war.

When alone on the wider pavement Charles and Lynsey made plans for their next rendezvous. "Come to my house tonight," she said. "Hamish will be away till midnight. He always spends Sunday and Monday nights in the pub with his friends. I'll have a chance to make you that cup of tea!"

"Gosh, Lynsey," he said with a stab of excitement, "is that a good idea? I'll be in a state of nerves if Hamish comes back early!"

"He niver does," she said. "He always comes back in a taxi at midnight, or just before. It's been like that for years."

"Well," he sighed, wondering if this was taking a step too far, "I'll tell you what—I'll give you a quick call on my mobile from outside your house just after nine, to verify that the coast is clear."

"If that will make you feel easier," she smiled. "We can talk with no one else near. And I can make you a cup of tea! That will be so much better than you wanderin' roond in the dark like a lost lamb!"

He looked at her, at her smiling eyes, her hair lifting in the slight breeze. He drew a little closer to her under her umbrella and squeezed her hand. "You are so gorgeous, Lynsey—and so irresistible. I'll see you tonight, then—if I can get away on my own."

As he made his way back to his house in the rain he felt uncomfortable with the arrangement, but the excitement in his belly was like a rushing flow of lava that was too powerful to struggle against.

When he reached home he couldn't wait to read what Lynsey had written on the memory stick she had given him.

First he read the new addition of her story, followed by her letter to him.

* * *

Lynsey's story

It is hard to believe, that for the past 30 years or so, the only objective of my desire came in the form of a wine bottle. This is the way that alcohol affects your body and mind when it is being abused. Your whole way of thinking and reasoning becomes totally distorted and your physical being becomes weak. I was always a quiet person, but towards the end of my alcoholic years, I simply became very withdrawn and tended to stay indoors. I was not looking after myself. I had stopped wearing nice clothes and make-up and just did not care how I looked any more or what people thought of me. Nothing seemed to be of any importance to me anymore. I am positive that the consumption of lots of alcohol gave me the confidence to talk to people, especially men.

In 1997, I decided to go along to my first meeting of Alcoholics Anonymous. I thought I would be nervous, but surprisingly I was calm and looking forward to it. Everybody was seated around a circular table with the Chairperson and the person who was talking about their experience, strength and hope at the top. I remember everyone came and shook my hand and asked me what my first name was. They were very nice people and made me feel very welcome.

The speaker told us about his life with alcohol for about three quarters of an hour, and then we stopped to have tea, coffee and biscuits. After about 15 minutes we all took our seats again and this time the chairperson asked each person in the room if they would like to say anything or maybe want to talk about something that was bothering us. I said nothing. However, I did enjoy my first meeting and met one or two really nice people. I continued to go to the meetings in Kirkgelly every Wednesday morning and Friday night. Eventually, when I became the Secretary of the Group, I would make up sandwiches and rolls for them every Friday night. There was one particular man there who I knew had been sleeping rough for a while and he was so small and thin. I guess I took pity on him and every Friday night, if there were any sandwiches or rolls left over, I would wrap them up for him so that he at least would have something to eat.

I managed to get nine months sobriety under my belt until I started receiving some unwanted attention from a man who ran the group and had actually founded it some 33 years ago. Although I had been sober for some time now, I was still a bit vulnerable and not back to my full physical strength. I have heard it can take a long time for an alcoholic to fully recover. However, this man singled me out for special attention. He knew I was vulnerable at the time and absolutely took advantage of this. You know, I am not usually a person who is easily taken in by someone, but I honestly thought he was only trying to make me feel comfortable and a real part of the group. His house was in the newest part of Kennoway and he always gave me a lift home. For a long time his behaviour seemed normal enough and he would talk about things to do with AA and usually what he was involved in. I remember him telling me that he travelled to Southern Ireland and Spain quite often, to take part in AA Conferences where usually he would be asked to speak. He was well known in different parts of the world due to his extensive knowledge of alcohol abuse. However, if only I had known then what I know now. It transpired that this person had been well known for picking on *newer and younger members of AA, particularly females. He would give them a lift home and then suggest that they stop at a nearby pub for a drink. Once he had managed to help them get drunk, he would then take advantage of them. For a man of his long experience in AA this sort of behaviour was totally unacceptable and quite unbelievable. I suppose you could say he enjoyed collecting trophies. He had started to become far too familiar with me and at one point suggested that it would do me the world of good if I were to have liaisons sexually with him and his partner. That was it! I was disgusted with him and told him I would certainly not take part in sexual activities of that nature. I remember him laughing at me uproariously when I said this and he told me it was high time I relaxed a little and got a life. I am not sure what happened to me after this, but I know I became anxious when the meetings came round and I think I had become a little afraid of him. I started going to different meetings, but everywhere I went he always turned up and I just felt as if I could not get away from him. Eventually, I felt threatened to the point that it might have been perceived he was stalking me. The problem was, I could not actually take action against him for anything; after all, he had not physically tried to hurt me. However, I knew it could have been construed as mental cruelty.*

Anyhow, not long after all this, I turned to the only thing I thought would give me comfort and save me—you've guessed it—the bottle. Oh, what a mess! After having done so well and looking and feeling so much better I went and ruined it all by taking that first drink. I cannot blame this man for me drinking again, but from then on I had nothing more to do with him. As far as I am concerned he is what people would class as a sexual predator and he is well known for this type of behaviour throughout AA. The thing that hurt the most was the fact that the AA members who had known me for a long time did not have the courage and sense of responsibility to take me aside and warn me about this. If only I had known this, things would have been very different. Anyway, I suppose that's life. Sometimes it can hit you with some pretty powerful stuff, as long as you learn from these experiences, or at least become more aware of situations like that. So, that was the end of my time in AA—I never went back but have never forgotten the genuine people I met there and think about them from time to time.

In the midst of this confusion, I was still feeling physically unwell and was advised to have a total hysterectomy by my doctor. I was beginning to lose more blood than I should have when my monthly cycle came around. I was still quite young at the time, probably 40 years old. However, I thought about this long and hard and decided to go through with the operation. I stayed in hospital for three weeks and took around four months to recover.

*   *   *

Lynsey's letter to Charles:

What have you done to me, Charles? You have turned me inside out, but in the nicest possible way.

I read your letters to me every night and they give me such joy. I have never been written to in such a beautiful and sincere way by anyone. It is hard for me to describe to you the true nature of my feelings for you. Anyway, I know, deep down, you feel the same way. Let's face it, we are hardly a couple of youngsters, but I know that we are both mature enough to realise our own true feelings. When I first met you I thought that you seemed to be a really distinguished and kind gentleman and I know now that I was right. I think that I was probably afraid to get too close to you in case you might let me down or get bored with me.

Remember what I said to you earlier. God planned for this to happen. He knew that both of us felt lonely and in need of a hug and he decided to himself, I wonder who I could send to Charles to bring a ray of light into his life, and he chose me.

God bless you Charles and sleep tight.
From your little lamb

Lynsey X

*   *   *

Charles was so touched by what she said, and so impressed by the impeccable style of her writing which, like her makeup, was immaculate. He lost no time in writing a reply, which he saved to the same memory stick. He would give it to her when he made his daring visit to her house that night.

Charles's letter to Lynsey:

My dear Lynsey

Your letter touched me more deeply than I can say. Both your recent update to your writing, about the AA experience and the AA stalker, and what you said in your letter, brought tears to my eyes. I thought again of what you said afterwards, lying on my bed listening to Mozart with my earphones in place, and going over your words, so sincere, and written with such careful and precise discipline, I found my eyes wet with emotion. Oh my dearest Lynsey, my heart goes out to you so much I feel it will burst with love. You have struggled for many years with this problem (arising I am sure from lack of the deep love you deserve), and to have a predator in the AA organisation stalk you like that, in the very organisation to which you went for help, taking advantage of your vulnerable condition, must have been beyond what you could bear. And I feel so privileged, so honoured, that you should feel my role in your life has brought you some solace and help. You come across to me as a very refined and sensitive, incredibly intelligent young woman (to me you certainly are not an 'older' woman!) that has never been allowed to blossom fully and realise the goals in her reach. I know that in the future those goals will come to fruition.

To me there appears to be two Lynseys—the one with makeup and the one without makeup. The one without makeup looks like the girl next door, sweet and sincere, honest to a fault, but bearing the creases, the marks of the battle with life: but which does not prevent the light of her inner spirit shine through. This is probably the Lynsey I love most—and she is not the one I met first.

The other Lynsey, with makeup, is glamorous, totally stunning, amazingly so, who would instantly touch the heart of any man of good taste. This Lynsey is sophisticated, poised, wonderfully dressed, a woman to die for—one I can't keep my eyes off. I love her all the more because of the light of the other Lynsey that shines through.

I have not made any significant 'corrections' to the new addition to your story because it is written so perfectly. (It is saved to this memory stick.)

Keep it up, Lynsey dearest—you're doing great! Keep writing with the same sincerity and honesty. It will touch many hearts.

Charles xxx

P.S. Those novels of mine I gave you—I felt I could be completely honest with you. You may find the content surprising at times, but I felt with you I can be completely honest and expose the real me, nothing held back.

CHAPTER TWENTY-TWO

AS NINE O' CLOCK that Sunday night approached Charles's heart was in his mouth. He used the excuse that he wanted to go out for a walk, to stretch his legs, and hoped Sylvia didn't suggest she would join him, as she sometimes did. But she was absorbed in a guitar lesson on her computer at the time, so Charles was relieved to escape from the house, alone, into the night. He walked quickly through the council estate, following the winding way of the street where Lynsey lived until he stood close to the corner of her house, then turned up the street she said was so dangerous with drug pushers and addicts. He stopped under a street light and dialled her number on his mobile and waited with bated breath.

"Charrels?" she answered in her Kennoway housewife voice.

"Are you alone?" he asked breathlessly, his heartbeat in overdrive.

"Aye," she laughed. "See you in a minute—I'm waitin'."

It felt strange opening her front gate as quietly as possible and stepping up to the front door. The door opened and to his surprise she was in her dressing gown. He slipped inside and drew a deep breath, his eyes feasting on her—a vision of lovely femininity, a sumptuous figure swathed in a red nightgown, showing a tempting acreage of pure white cleavage. "I've come for that cup of tea," he grinned. She helped him take his coat off and hung it in the hallway.

"I'll get it for you," she smiled with the air of an efficient hostess.

"Actually, could I have coffee?" he asked. Coffee would do more to steady his nerves.

She went into the kitchen on the other side of the small hall while he took a seat on the low settee in the sitting room, which was neat and simply furnished. He couldn't believe he was where he was—with the woman of his dreams in another man's house. He was too nervous to sit there and wait and got up and joined her in the kitchen where she was waiting for the kettle to boil.

"So, this is the kitchen," he said, looking round at the shabby wallpapered walls and dated cupboards. "I used to wonder what was behind the window on this side of the house."

"It's an old man's kitchen, really," she said. "You can see it hasna been decorated for years." It had old fifties-style floral wallpaper peeling at the edges, the kitchen units old fashioned, reflecting an earlier, almost pre-war time. "Hamish will no' spend a penny on it. Says it's good enough as it is."

He nodded. "It's perfectly functional, I guess. I'm surprised it's as large as it is." He smiled at her. "I like your dressing gown—and nightdress."

She smiled. "I like to be comfortable when I'm at home. I had a bath a while ago and this is the way I usually spend the evenings." She giggled. "I'm probably the cleanest woman in Kennoway. I have a bath every night."

"Well, you look nice," he said. It had to be the understatement of the year. She looked terrific in a wenchy sort of way, her milky cleavage like a magnet to his eyes and her long hair falling over her shoulders, her face devoid of any makeup.

She poured the coffee into a mug and took it through to the sitting room, where she placed it on the broad low coffee table. He sat down on the settee, nursing the mug in his hands while she sat down next to him. They chatted inconsequently for a while, in what felt like a rather forced conversation—about the house and the dog which snuffled about him with its lugubrious face, coming to rest eventually practically on his feet. He stroked the dog's huge head while he asked about the house.

But he couldn't hold back for long. He sat up and, leaning forward, put the half-full cup back on the coffee table—then drew her into his arms and buried his face in her soft hair and the warm tender skin of her neck. He breathed deeply, taking in the aroma of her fresh femininity that quickened his heart like oxygen.

"Charrels…," she laughed, but he clung to her and she folded her hands around his head, cradling him there like a baby, protectively.

"God, Lynsey, I love you." He was almost close to tears with the relief of being this close to her, breathing in her scent.

"I love you too, Charrels," she crooned like a mother.

He surfaced, looked deep into her eyes that smiled back at him whimsically, then drew her to him in a lingering kiss as their lips searched and explored each other's nerve endings. It was a long time before they broke apart, but in a minute they were lost in another embrace, his hands slipping under her thin nightdress and feeling the soft warm skin beneath, up her arms, down around her waist, along her back, holding her close. He held her really tight, like he never wanted to let her go.

When they stopped and smiled at each other, she laughed, "Well, it was wurth waitin' fur a hug like that!"

He placed his hand on her smooth rounded knees that were visible just below the nightdress. "Goodness, Lynsey," he murmured, "you have such lovely soft knees." Then he drew her close again, his hands exploring once more beneath her nightdress. He was aware of a growing erection as he responded to her silky feminine softness. She drew apart and looked longingly into his eyes. "Charrels," she said softly, smiling, "let's take it slowly. I dinna want to rush anything. Not just yet."

"Of course not, my dearest girl," he smiled, cupping her face gently with the palms of his hands. "But do you mind… I want to kiss your eyes." Her smile softened as she allowed him to draw her face close to him again, his lips gently pressed on each eyelid. Then he looked dreamily into her honey brown eyes. "I love your eyes, Lynsey—they're the loveliest part of you. It's the nearest I can get to seeing the beauty of your soul." He lovingly pushed some of her hair out of her eyes.

"Och Charrels, you sweet man, no one has spoken to me like this before," she laughed. "I dinna understand what you see in me. I'm just from a wurking class background—and you? Were your parents wealthy, of a better class? I think they were."

"They were hard working, certainly. My dad was an accountant and my mother a manager of two or three retail shops. Not wealthy, but what they had was through hard work. I was an only child so I was spoilt, I suppose." He shook his head. "No, I don't think you can make a case for us being worlds apart." But looking at her blemished scrubbed skin, he knew that they were. She came from a world where the hardness of poverty was softened only by alcohol and drugs.

When they stood up he drew her close to him again, to feel the length of her body against his. Against him she was shorter than he had expected, and she commented on this. "I thought I would be taller," she smiled, looking at him, flicking her hair out of her eyes with that little twist of the neck that he loved so much.

On impulse, and not being able to resist it any more, he touched the top of her nightdress that ran across her cleavage. "May I have a peek?" he heard himself say.

She gave him a bemused look that he took for assent. He slipped the top of her nightdress down to expose the full liquid globes of her breasts. His hands slid around them and gently compressed them. They were unspeakably soft. Her nipples were smooth and almost flat in the moulded contours of her breasts. As he looked he forgot to breathe.

Her eyes sought his, the bemused smile still in place. "Charrels," she murmured, "what am I goin' to dae with you, eh? You're an awfy man."

"You're so lovely, so beautiful," he murmured, hypnotised by the full softness of her breasts which he still cupped in his hands. "Are they real? One day I would like to kiss them and put my lips…" He sighed, and gently pulled up the neckline of the nightdress to its original place, which again just revealed the soft swell of her cleavage with the deep valley between them. Then he drew her into his arms again as their lips once again melted together.

"I better be going now, my darling," he murmured as they drew apart.

She giggled. "You better go before you make me lose control! As it is, you've turned my world upside doon."

"I'm so sorry," he smiled, "I didn't mean to lose control."

"Oh," she put one hand on his cheek, "I wouldna have it any other way. What has happened to me feels like a miracle."

He walked back through the night quickly, breathing in the cold damp air, but never felt any of it. He was on cloud nine, intoxicated with happiness. There was a lightness in his step. At 71 he felt he was getting younger by the day.

*   *   *

That night Charles slept like a rock, steeped in his happiness, but woke up at 5 a.m. with the excitement of his newfound love bubbling over.

At 10 in the morning he was back by the lake, at the far end where he could see all the way to her house, hoping she would emerge with her dog. When she did there was no mistaking her in her black coat and a touch of red from her scarf. Even at a long distance he was able to identify her now. He continued to walk anti-clockwise round the lake to coincide his meeting with her. He needed to be near her like an addict needed a drug.

As they spoke standing near the railings that bordered the lake, the familiar figure of Bert, the leader of the prayer circle, walked along an adjacent path, carrying a plastic shopping back. He waved and Lynsey waved back, and Charles waved too with a sheepish smile.

"Oh heck," Charles said quietly. "Now he's seen us here. I think he and his wife live in one of the houses that overlook the lake. I remember he said he had a view of the ducks and swans from his house." He gave an uneasy laugh. "I hope he didn't see us embracing the other day."

"Well," she said, unruffled, "there's no reason why we shouldn't be here chatting, having accidently met. Many people do meet and chat here walking their dugs. And when we kissed," she smiled, "he was probably in his sitting room, or looking the other way—who knows." She was quite unconcerned.

Charles went on to ask her how old Hamish was. She had told him before but he wanted to be sure. "He is 74," she said.

"Hamish is 74!" he exclaimed. "That's only three years older than me."

"Aye," she nodded, "but he is an *old* man. You are young at 71—do you ken what I mean? Some people are old at 60. Age is irrelevant—you're as young as you feel. I'm 54 but I feel like a teenager—with you, Charrels." She giggled. "My heck, Charrels Haddington," she gave him that sidelong glance, "the effect you've had on me, eh! I canna believe you love me—but I am so glad, and I love you back with all my heart!"

"I loved you that first day I saw you, at the church."

"That drunk woman!" she laughed. "You know, when I left the church that day I got lost in the cemetery! I thought there was a shortcut through it. Someone had to come and lead me oot!"

Charles recognised that she had changed a great deal since that first day he had seen her. Yet she still seemed to depend on being a live-in carer for the sake of security. She didn't even drive, she had told him—and had no ambition to do so. He would have thought she would want more independence. Now that through him her life was turned "inside out", as she had said, would she have more ambition, a better inclination to seek a more rewarding life for herself? How he wished he could be part of that new beginning she would be taking. But she was willing to share him, she had said. That was such a comforting thought.

And there would be more comfort tonight, he remembered. "Lynsey," he said, "are you sure it's fine for me to come round to your house again tonight? At the same time?"

"I've been lookin' forward to it!" she smiled.

"Hopefully, I can get away again. I'll phone you from outside your house again."

"I'll understand, Charrels, of ye canna make it. I dinna want you to take any bad chances. I dinna want you to be in trouble—and that would mean seeing less of each other." She smiled. "I think of you all the time, Charrels. Even when I wake up in the mornin'—I think of you first thing. Being alone with you, even for short times, is like a bonus—a gift. Be careful or these gifts will end."

"My love," he said, "you have exactly expressed my thoughts! I think of you *all* the time."

It was not long ago that he wondered if she thought of him as much as he thought of her. Now he had the confirmation that she did. He hugged this knowledge to his chest as he walked back to his house.

He was restless that evening as he sat in the lounge waiting for nine o'clock to approach. At ten to nine he got up and went into the hallway where he put on his coat. "I'm just off for a walk for a while," he announced.

151

"Oh, hang on!" Sylvia called out to him. "I'll come with you."

Oh damn, damn, he thought! There was nothing he could do now to stop her coming out with him. He looked at his watch and fumed inside as Sylvia put on her coat. *Oh bloody hell!* He never felt more frustrated. In ten minutes Lynsey would be expecting him, no doubt in her dressing gown and negligée again—and he would be walking Sylvia like a dog in the opposite direction!

He walked quickly with her, inwardly fuming and giving short responses to her small talk. They went up the hill further into the modern estate and she commented on some of the houses, wondering why so many of them were lit up with unnecessary garden lights. He couldn't care a damn about the lights—all he wanted was to be walking towards Lynsey.

"You're walking ever so fast!" Sylvia said. She had long legs and was a fast walker, and Charles often struggled to keep up with her. But tonight he wanted to get this obligatory walk out of the way as quickly as possible. Perhaps, he thought, there would be enough time left later to take a second walk—to Lynsey's house.

When they got back to the house he lingered outside to put the rubbish bin out for the morning's collection. Once Sylvia was back inside he stood in front of the garage and phoned Lynsey on his mobile. She answered and he spoke quickly: "Lynsey, she wanted to come and walk with me—so I couldn't make it. I'm so sorry."

"It's all reet, Charrels," she said, "I understand. There'll be meer nichts. I kenned when you didna turn up somethin' had happened. I understand, I really do."

"Maybe I can get out again later—how long will Hamish be away for?"

"Till midnight, Charrels—but please dinna tek any risks. I dinna want you to be in trouble."

"Well," he sighed, "I'll play it by ear—I just miss you so."

"And I miss you—but be careful. I understand, Charrels."

He ended the call and took the bin out to the pavement, then went inside and sat down for a while, still churning inside but pretending to relax. Sylvia had gone back to her computer and he pretended to watch TV. *Oh, what the hell*, he thought, and got up and put on his coat again. "I'm off for another walk," he announced as he went by Sylvia's study. "That walk was too quick," he said, "I need more exercise. Got to keep my weight down."

"Goodness," she smiled as she turned round, "You're a glutton for punishment!"

"Well, I'll see you shortly," he smiled back and went out, walking as fast as possible, this time in the direction of the woman of his dreams.

At times he broke into a run, to save time, glancing at his watch. It was almost ten now—close to an hour later. That still left two hours clear before midnight.

This time he didn't phone her from outside her house first but went straight to the front door and knocked gently. After a moment the door opened and she was there, in her dressing gown but wearing a different negligée that was tighter across her chest and revealing barely any cleavage. He slipped in and as soon as the door was shut he took her into his arms. He kissed her, hugging her close and passionately, and when they drew apart his glasses had steamed up; he could see nothing so had to remove them.

Lynsey burst out laughing. "Oh my Lord, your glasses are steamed up! That's the furst time I ever had an effect like that on a man, eh! It's like a funny film! Oh my Lord!"

She offered to make him some tea or coffee but he declined. "I don't want to waste time on coffee this time. Let's just talk a while." They sat down together on the settee as before and he took her hand in his. "The men in your life, Lynsey," he asked, "did they satisfy you?"

"When I was young, I thought they did. But now looking back I know better." She smiled. "None of them were like you."

"And this house," he went on, "Is it owned by Hamish? If he died, would you inherit it?"

She shook her head. "I doubt it. It's owned by him—but I think his sister has an interest in it, too. And she certainly disapproves of me. Also, Hamish has a son."

"You are not very secure then, my love," he said. "Everything depends on Hamish. What if he threw you out? Or died?"

She smiled. "If he dies—well, I'll cross that bridge when and if it comes. But he depends on me," she explained. "He couldna do without me now—I take care of him, cook for him, bath him. He needs me." For the time being she seemed content to carry on as she had done for the last six years—though without the recourse to drink. "My daughter doesna approve of my relationship with Hamish, which is why she never visits. But it's a good enough solution for now."

Perhaps her faith was stronger than his, he thought. On reflection, she *was* in fact as carefree as a bird, something he recalled she had once said when she was in her cups. And did the Lord not say he takes care of the birds—that not even a feather falls without him being aware and that every hair of our heads is numbered?

"If I won the lottery I would buy you a house," he said.

"Och, yer a braw man, Charrels," she said, squeezing his hand. "Do y'ken, Hamish was thrown oot of his wife's hoos because he was a paramour with women? He was a lot younger then."

That was ironic, Charles thought, for he could find himself in the same position if Sylvia found out about his growing love for Lynsey. He drew closer to her and snugged into her neck while she was talking, without his glasses.

"Yer no' listenin' to me, are ye?" she said, placing her hands around his head. He felt like a child in her arms. He had completely abandoned himself to her. "You smell niece," she smiled.

He sighed. "Lynsey, love, I better go. This is supposed to be a short second walk. And it's much later now. But at least I've seen you. It's just so nice being with you." He stood up and pulled her up by the hand, drawing her close to him, tight against his body with his arms around her. "Before I go I want to hold you really close."

Their lips melted together again and they clung together like that, for a while. His hands slipped under her nightdress, scooping up her negligée so that he could feel the soft warm skin over her tight bottom. She didn't seem to mind but relaxed closer against him, her lips parting against his. Then he drew his hand back outside her negligée again but dropped it down, between them and in front of her until he could feel the pubic hairs on her Venus mound through the silk of the negligée.

"Mm—that's my flower," she smiled shyly, glancing up at him. "I call it that because it is a beautiful part of me."

"Oh gosh, Lynsey, I'm getting turned on," he sighed, stopping and forcing himself to stand back from her. He gave an embarrassed laugh. "I guess if I was a honey bee I'd want to pollinate your flower."

She shook her head, her eyes taking on an impish look. "Charrels, ye're an awfy man—you surprise me," she smiled. "You're no' as innocent as you seem, eh? Those novels of yours too—oh dear, dear! You make it hard for a gel to sleep after she's read some of your love scenes!"

He laughed. "Good night, my love."

Walking back to his house he felt his battery had been charged again. It was like he was addicted to her—he needed a shot of her love to keep him going until the next rendezvous, or until the next time he saw her.

CHAPTER TWENTY-THREE

THE NEXT TIME he saw Lynsey was at the Wednesday night prayer meeting. He could not deny that his main reason for going now was to see her, even though he could not speak to her—just gaze at her across the table. She looked lovely and all the two of them could do was smile at each other. He would look up and catch her looking at him, and she would look up and catch him looking at her, and smile. He would try to hide his longing for her as he transformed his sigh into a deep intake of breath. During the prayer time he prayed for her, aloud, in words that only she would recognise—praying for all those afflicted with alcohol and drug addiction in Kennoway who had come 'out of darkness into the light' and for those still on their journey from 'darkness to light'—echoing the title she had chosen for her testimony that she was writing. "Put your loving arms around these people, Lord," he prayed, meaning "put your loving arms around Lynsey, Lord," inasmuch as he was longing to do just that at that moment as he peeked at her, seeing her eyes open and looking ahead of her. He noticed she never seemed to close her eyes during prayer. Looking at her, he admired her profile, her clear, clean sculptured features, a face that would become a Greek goddess—or an Egyptian queen. Nefertiti, he thought, with a sudden realisation that her profile resembled that of the Egyptian queen! He had seen the bust of Nefertiti in the museum in East Berlin, in 1966, when he had ventured into the eastern sector with an American girl on the underground.

With this insight he studied Lynsey with fresh interest. She was dressed in her light white cardigan that was unbuttoned, showing her black top and the same scarf as last time; but this time she was wearing a string of pearls looped down in front of her. They were foregrounded against the black top. She later told him they were real pearls, too, for she loved pearls. Her earrings were droplets of pearls, two pearls just beneath each ear. For Charles it was strange, this time, gazing at her, knowing that just last night he had held her in his arms, had kissed those lips, and kissed those eyes, and the night before had fondled her breasts, the same breasts now concealed under that black top; he recalled how he had brushed aside those silky, wavy strands of hair and buried his face against the soft warm skin of her neck and murmured his love for her, over and over again. What a difference two weeks had made.

The next time they met by the lake in the park it was raining and she wore a hooded black raincoat.

"You look like little Red Riding Hood," he smiled. Then he recalled the way she looked the previous evening in the prayer circle. "Do you know, at the prayer meeting I was looking at you without you realising it, sometimes. I was looking at your profile. You have good sharp features, my love, with a sculptured nose... like Nefertiti. I saw her bust in the museum in East Berlin and I remember it so well. When I saw your profile last night I thought of Nefertiti."

She laughed. "Now Charrels, at this rate my hid will be so big with your compliments I will no' fit through the door when I get back! Anyway, I enjoy reading about the royal Kings and Queens of Ancient Egypt. And fancy you actually saw the bust of Nefertiti—how do I live up to that, eh!"

Just then they saw Bert, the leader of the prayer circle, walking by on the nearby diagonal path across the park towards his home. He waved and both of them waved back.

"Oh dear, that's the second time he's seen us together here," Charles said. "Now the cat's really out of the bag."

She smiled. "He's a niece man, Charrels. It's the women who are awful gossips! Besides, what are we doing, anyway? We are only standing and talking."

"In the rain!" he laughed.

158

"Aye—I have to bring the dug oot whatever the weather."

They walked a little further around the lake until she stopped and made him look into her eyes. "Now I want to telt you something important, Charrels Haddington. Are you listenin' tae me?"

"Yes."

"I love you." She paused, keeping her eyes on his. "Do you understand that? I love you."

It thrilled him to hear her say that.

"Darling," he said, "tell me—if I were to win the lottery and I had enough money to start a new life with you, in a new house, would you be prepared to leave Hamish and live with me for the rest of your life?"

She turned to look at him full in the face, her eyes connecting with his. "Charrels, I will follow you tae the end of the wurld. I will live with you under any circumstances, whether you be rich or poor. Whatever you want of me, is yours to choose. And I will be forever true to you. You can rely on that. You are my dream come true. You have turned me inside oot. You have spoiled me for any other man. I love you. I just told you that."

"Oh God, Lynsey," he smiled, feeling weak with love for her, "if I could just hug you now!"

"Patience, my darlin'," she smiled.

Just then the dog near them squatted in the rain and did its business on the grass next to the footpath.

She smiled. "This is why I have to carry this bag." She went over to the mess the dog had made and scooped it up with a little trowel, dumping it into a small plastic bag.

"I'll take that for you," he said. "I should go now and the path takes me past that little red dog bin by the gate. I'll drop it in there."

"Are you sure? Here—hold it at the top, then you will no' get any of the job on your hands."

He carried the bag gingerly suspended from the tips of his fingers like it was a blessing from heaven as he made his way to the gate that led out of the park.

*   *   *

It was a Thursday evening and not a time when there was any possibility of seeing or meeting Lynsey. But Charles had a letter that needed posting and instead of posting it in the nearest post box up the road in his estate, he decided to post it at the much more distant post box way past Lynsey's house, merely for the sake of feeling he was closer to her. He had just come through the council estate and about to merge with the pavement on Leven road when he saw a woman just ahead of him on the pavement. His heart nearly stopped when he realised it was Lynsey! He saw her look round and their eyes met—two strangers in the night who were no longer strangers.

"Lynsey!" he gasped. He was overwhelmed with disbelief and joy.

"Charrels?" she said. "My goodness—I sensed you were there!"

"I can't believe it, Lynsey—I was just taking a walk to post a letter. There's a post box just beyond the crossroads to your house."

"Charrels Haddington!" she scolded him with that sidelong glance, "I'm worried about ye—I really am!" She shook her head. "A post box? Like the Mars Bar?"

"No, it's true, it's really there. This meeting is by sheer chance."

"It must have been planned then," she laughed. "I was just comin' back from the Women's Guild meeting. A dog-handler was speaking and I was interested. Look, they handed out some magazines." She showed him the glossy magazines she was carrying.

"Oh Lynsey," he said, looking at her and seeing she had her makeup on and was tastefully dressed for the Guild, "You are so lovely—so gorgeous. You've got to be the most beautiful woman I have ever seen."

She looked at him with a sly grin. "You're no' so bad lookin' yoursel', Charrels Haddington." Then she laughed. "Oh, Charrels, I will never forget how your glasses steamed up when you kissed me! I keep thinkin' of that! I was thinkin' of it again last night and Hamish heard me. 'What are ye cackling aboot, hen?' he shouted, and I called back, 'Just a funny thought I had!'" She recovered from her laughter and looked at him seriously. They were standing under a street light so they could see each other's faces clearly. "Charrels, I love you. It does not come easily for me to say somethin' like that to a man. I don't wear my feelings on my sleeve. But to you I can say it and mean it—I love you, Charrels. And do be careful, Charrels. Kennoway is no' a safe place to wander aboot at night."

"I always feel safe though," he said. "By the way," he continued, "you've never mentioned the letter I wrote to you on the memory stick I returned to you. It was my reply to yours. Did you find it?"

"No," she said. "I found your novel about us, which is brilliant. I didn't ken there was a letter, though. I thought the other files were the same ones that were there before."

"It's there—with the title 'Letter to Lynsey'."

"I'll read it tonight, Charrels. As soon as I get back!"

They walked on together for a while before Charles stopped, still a little distance from the crossroads to her house. "I'll say goodnight here, Lynsey. We don't want nosey Mrs MacDonald seeing us walking together."

"Good nicht then, Charrels," she said. "I'll see you in the mornin'—when I walk the dug."

He turned back but soon stopped and turned round again, watching her retreating back as she made her way to the crossroads, turn towards her house and eventually disappear from view. "What a bonus that was, Lord," he prayed. "Did you plan that? If so, thank you, thank you!" He walked back with a rejoicing heart. He had had another, altogether unexpected shot of Lynsey.

* * *

The following morning when they met at the lake they were still brimming over with the joy of that chance meeting.

"To think our different paths came together at exactly that point!" he said.

"And I sensed you," she said, "and looked aroond, to my left, and I *knew* it was you!"

She had read his letter to her and loved it, she said. "I loved what you said about the two Lynseys! Both of us love you, niver fear!" she laughed. "And I ken what you mean when you talk about the lines on my face. I have had a very hard journey, Charrels, and it is a greet comfort to me that ye ken that. But I am getting better."

"Oh, Lynsey, I can see it! I can see it more than ever in the natural Lynsey, the one without the makeup! Your skin, my darling…" He touched her cheeks with his fingers. "…it is so much better already, smooth and without the blotches I remember from the first time you came to the prayer meetings, after that long absence… Just stay away from wine, or anything alcoholic, my love…"

"Ohhh!" she interrupted, "I'm no' ever goin' back to that, niver fear!" She looked at him with her serious eyes. He knew she meant it. She smiled. "Ye ken, Charrels, I have niver been hugged the way you have hugged me. And so hard!" She laughed. "It was lovely! I felt so warm and protected. No man has ever hugged me like that!" She flicked her hair out of her eyes and gave him a bemused look. "Whatever do ye see in me, eh!"

Tears pricked his eyes. "Lynsey, you are the loveliest, the sweetest woman I know! I don't see how any man can live with you and not want to cuddle you all the time, as much as possible." Then he grinned. "And you know what, my love, you have the most perfect breasts I have ever seen or felt. So perfect."

"Och!" she laughed. "And you asked if they were real!" She laughed again. "I would niver have had a surgeon come near them with a knife! And tae think I let you touch and fondle them! I canna believe you did that, and that I let you!"

"Do you mind that I did?" he smiled.

She gazed at him, not speaking. Then she said softly, "No. I dinna mind. Your hands on me were lovely. I loved it. But best was your hugs of my whole body, an' burying your hid in my neck. Charrels, no one has ever loved me like that. And your hugs are so strong, so good!"

"There's more of those if you want them," he smiled.

She smiled: "I read some meer of your *Sunset Stirrings*." She paused. "Charrels, you do have a way with wurds. I canna see how I could ever add to the story."

"You're adding to it all the time, my love. Every time we meet you give me more material. And I no longer want the story to develop in an imaginary or fictional direction. You don't know it, but you're writing the story with me, adding to it every time we meet. It's our story, Lynsey, my dear, wonderful girl. I'm not sure where it's taking us. But as I said, we don't know the future and we've been brought together for a reason." He looked deep into her eyes. "You know, I can't make love to you the way I want to—in private, with you in my arms... but I can make love to you all the time, any time, in words. This story is a way for me to express my feelings... to make love to you. I can pour out my heart in words. And when you read what I've written, you receive those words—that love, not in your body, not in your flower…" He smiled mischievously. "…but in your heart."

She shook her head. "Charrels… what am I goin' tae do with ye!" She looked serious. "An' Sylvia? Has she yet no idea you're meeting me? Has she no' seen the change in you? They say you can see love in a person's eyes, you ken."

"Well now, about that…" He hesitated. "Recently she does seem to have become more… well, loving towards me. A little more attentive, perhaps. Perhaps she detects I'm becoming distant. I don't mean to… but I'm always thinking of you, aren't I? I catch myself sighing and have to change my sighs to yawns!"

She frowned. "In what way is she more lovin'—or is that too personal a question?"

"No—there are just small signals—in bed at night, for instance, she will put her hand on my shoulder, or even find my hand and hold it. As though she feels I might be slipping away."

"Aye…och weel, I dinna want to hurt her, ye ken…"

He grinned. "I love your accent, Lynsey—it's so cute. There are times when I'm hardly aware of it, and then there are times when I sort of stand back and hear it in a detached way… and when you get excited and start 'blethering', as you call it, it's like you go out of phase and you're speaking a different language and I have to keep saying 'Pardon?' But more and more I'm becoming unaware of your accent as we grow closer together." He smiled. "When you write, there's no accent at all—just perfect grammatical English sentences!"

She laughed. "And you sound like you've just stepped out of *Brideshead Revisited* — or *Brideshead Regurgitated* —like Lord Sebastian Flyte!"

He laughed. "They say opposites attract."

"No, we're no' opposites, really," she smiled. "Underneath, we have the same shy spirit. You're my kindred spirit. I'm so completely at home with you."

"Really?"

"Och, ye look awfully niece today, Charrels." She had said it twice, appraising him with a sidelong glance.

"Well, I feel I'm getting younger. The doctor asked me yesterday about my health and I told him I was getting younger! I'm two stone lighter with a new light in my eyes! And it's all thanks to you, Lynsey. You know," he said, stopping to look directly into her eyes, "I adore you, Lynsey—I absolutely adore you."

"Charrels," she smiled, "I adore ye tae. I love you—and I love it when you say these things tae me."

"Can I take your photo again?" he said, slipping his little camera out from his coat pocket.

"My skin feels naked without my makeup, Charrels, but you can if you want to."

He took two close-up photos of her face, then said, "I wouldn't mind seeing the rest of you naked, you know."

"Och, Charles Haddington! You are an awfy bad boy, ye ken that! Just like ye are in your novels!"

"Oh, I'm not that bad really—just when I write. If you came to visit me to discuss your writing, you'll see. I shall treat you with total respect. The only trouble is that if we're alone I might ravish you."

"Charrels!" she shook her head. "My goodness! You're no' the man I first took you fer."

"Which reminds me," he smiled, "that dress you wore to church, that day when I first saw you—I hope you still have it and will never get rid of it."

She smiled. "I ken it's rather low cut. But if it's what caught you, I shall never get rid of it. I'll wear it again in the summer."

"As long as it doesn't catch any competitors for your affections!" he smiled.

"Oh, there will niver be any others, I can assure you of that!"

"Well, that's good to know." He sighed. Time was running out and they had reached the path where they usually parted. "I am so looking forward to cuddling you again—and holding you tight against me. On Sunday night after nine?"

"I'll wear something niece," she smiled.

"To think, Lynsey, when you first came to the church you were drunk with alcohol, and now I'm drunk with you. Who would have thought I would have been infected in this way."

"Weel, we have the same infection, then," she smiled. "Goodbye for now, Charrels."

CHAPTER TWENTY-FOUR

"**NO ONE HAS EVER LOVED ME** for myself, Charrels. No one has ever got to know me first. All the other men wanted just one thing... You're the first man that really cared about me... about who I am and what I want... about my feelings... who cared whether I got hurt or not... who doesna just use me for his own selfish ends..." She paused. "And you ken what? No one has ever sent me a Valentine's card. I saw the card you designed on the memory stick you gave me, and the Love Letter from God." She smiled. "I knew what you were saying—I could read between the lines. You were such a braw man to put that on the memory stick for Valentine's Day. It was the furst time I ever received a Valentine's message—in my life."

"It was the nearest I could get to sending you a card. I designed it on the internet but lacked the courage to have it sent. I was afraid it wouldn't be you that found it when it came through the door. I hated the thought of you getting into trouble—because of a secret admirer!"

She smiled sweetly at him. "You see—even there your kindness to me is shown. No other man would have been as thoughtful or concerned for me."

They were talking standing up together in her sitting room, their arms around each other. It was Friday night—Hamish's night out at the Masons so the coast would be clear for at least two hours.

"Why don't we sit down, Charrels?" she said. "If we can find room next to Tyson!"

Tyson the Staffordshire Bull Terrier had climbed up onto the settee, taking up most of it, leaving only a very cramped space for the two of them; but it meant they were obliged to sit even closer together than they would have had, had the dog not spread himself across most of the settee. Tyson turned his massive head and looked at Charles with wounded eyes when he squeezed in next to Lynsey, as if jealous of his presence there...

She laughed. "Och, *look* our jealous he is!"

But when Charles patted and rubbed the animal on his broad head the dog accepted him, his head sinking down and settling on his paws. Before long he was in a deep sleep, snoring.

Charles and Lynsey kissed each other passionately, their lips intertwining together, their tongues slipping into each other's mouths, relaxing into a long searching embrace of two souls seeking unity.

She sighed. "You smell niece, Charrels—a sharp woody fragrance. Is it the aftershave you wear? I really like it."

"It's called English Leather," he smiled. "It comes from America. The bottle's almost finished—I keep it for special occasions, like this. You smell nice too, sweet and spicy."

"It's called Turkish Rose," she laughed. "I dinna expect you the nicht so as soon as you called I rushed to the bathroom and brushed my teeth—and sprayed on my perfume!"

"Mmm, smells wonderful," he said, snuggling against her cheek and breathing in her scent, "sort of wild spicy, lingering... suits you. You're like a wild rose in Kennoway."

While they spoke his hand had climbed up under her negligée, cupping and fondling her soft well-shaped breasts as they kissed. He drew away to look at the top of her nightie, which was tied together in a loose bow. "What happens when I pull this bit of lace here?" he asked.

"Oh, it comes apart quite easily," she smiled.

He pulled one of the strands and the knot fell apart, allowing him to slip down the nightie to reveal once again, to his gaze, her two full, natural breasts that flowed into his ready hands. He squeezed one breast gently, moulding its supple softness to his hand, kneading it like liquid dough. "Does that hurt?" he asked.

She shook her head, her amused eyes watching him like a protective mother watching a baby suckle at her breasts. "No, it doesna hurt at all," she said. "But you do bewilder me... in the nicest possible way."

It was as though he couldn't get enough of her. Every liberty he took with her made his mind and body desperate for more. He slid off the settee and onto his knees, in front of her, to gain better access to her breasts. He cupped each of them with his hands and put his mouth to each nipple in turn, sucking gently as his hands continued to knead the soft tissue. She was silent as he did this, and he was aware of her amused eyes on him, her hands lightly touching the back of his neck, her fingers playing with his hair.

"You have niece hair," she said softly. "You ken, Charrels, I feel so completely at home with you... so comfortable."

He felt under no pressure at all, not from her... she was being so tolerant, so nice to him, allowing him to work out his passion for her in this intimate way. Eventually he got up and resumed his seat next to her and pulled her to him again in another lingering kiss.

But he wanted more, always more. His left hand was on her soft warm knee and then followed the contours of her leg up to her thigh. "Lynsey," he murmured, looking down at the exposed leg, "Your legs... they are so firm, soft and young. And also somehow so strong." He brushed the loose nightie away from the other leg, exposing them both. They were shapely legs, but not thin—rounded and firm, soft to the touch, giving the impression of great strength. Neither of them said anything as he moved his hand up and down each leg, following the lovely contours of one leg, then running his hand up against the edge of her panties. His fingers yearned for more, almost out of control.

"Lynsey," he murmured, "put your leg over mine."

He wanted to expose her inner thighs so he could run his finger up into the heavenly bliss between them. But she either misunderstood him or perceived his strategy and wished to counter it, and placed her right leg instead of her left leg over his, which closed the access he desired.

"No, I meant…," he began, but seeing how her movement had exposed the broad lush expanse of her right thigh, he said, "No, that's fine, darling," and he was content, for the time being, to run his hand across that lovely thigh, exploring its soft contours, travelling all around it, again diverting his desire for her into another lingering kiss, their lips twisting and savouring each other in a bid to quench an unquenchable fire.

He was under some tension, all the time, in spite of the pleasure of touching her and being in her company, mindful that time was running out; his absence would be noticed if he lingered too long… and what if Hamish returned sooner than expected? Lynsey had said that on Fridays he often came back before midnight, though probably not before the clock struck 11 p.m.

He stood up. "Time to go, my darling—but time for another embrace." He wanted to hold the full length of her body close to him, against him, as he had done before. They stood there, paradoxically, for what felt like an eternity that was rushing to a premature end. His hungry hands slid around her, under her negligée, feeling her full hot body which she willingly pressed against his. He held her close, hard, in a tight hug and she groaned: "Oh, Charrels, your hugs… och…"

"Is that too hard my love?"

"No way," she crooned, "it feels sooo good! No man has ever hugged me like this…, like he really wants me…"

"Oh God, Lynsey, I want you so much…" His hands dropped down easily under her loose fitting panties, feeding on the width of her firm bottom, exploring, cupping and squeezing each cheek, kneading them as they had kneaded her breasts. It was too much... his desire craved more, and he slid his right hand around her warm body to the front, slipping his index finger further down under her furry pussy, along the moist crack. Again their lips melted together as his finger slid slowly to and fro along the length of the sweet moist valley, until it sank deeper into the delicious crevice and gently touched and explored the clitoris.

"You know what," Lynsey sighed, not moving away but with her arms around his broad back, "it's verra hard for me to resist you, eh... to stop myself from tearing off your clothes..."

"*Now* you tell me," he smiled down at her, looking into her brown almond eyes, "now that I really have to go." He was resisting sinking his finger deeper into her cleft and pulled away. "But if I can get away I'll be back here Sunday night..."

"I'll be waitin' for you," she sighed. "And like I said, I'll be wearing something really niece."

"That would be wonderful," he smiled. "You know, I would just love for us to be naked together... I know that's not possible yet... But the more I see you and hold you, the more I want you. I told you before, I just can't get enough of you. How I would love to be together with you, alone and naked, in a hot tub."

She giggled. "I have niver been in a hot tub! To be in one with you would be heaven."

"I have a hot tub on my deck, at home, you know." He kissed her on the forehead. "But heaven only knows when I would ever have the chance of being with you there."

She pulled away and looked at him quizzically. "You really have a hot tub?"

"Yes," he smiled.

"Well then, tonight I'll dream we're together in it. I think and dream of you all the time—so it might as well be in the hot tub, eh!"

He had to find his coat in the hall himself since she seemed so reluctant to let him go. He put on the coat and then they embraced again, searching for each other's lips. It was like she didn't want to let him go when they stood in the hall before he left; when he had his hand on the doorknob she would embrace him again and draw him into another lingering kiss. She had a dreamy smile that spoke of longing and contentment at the same time, as through at last she had found what she wanted in life and was reluctant to let it go... wouldn't let it go.... As though a long-standing deep longing had been rekindled in her...

"Lynsey, I only wish I had met you years ago," he sighed. "I would have been so proud to have had you as my wife, my soul-mate."

Her eyes shone with an inner light, responding to his words. "No man has ever said that tae me," she said, then she put her hands around his neck and hugged him again.

*   *   *

Back at home while he was eating a pear, sitting in the sitting room next to Sylvia, Sylvia sniffed and said, "What's that pungent smell?"

"Pungent?" he said, alarm stabbing his heart. He looked at the pear he was eating. "This, I guess," and he held up the pear.

As soon as Sylvia left the room he went upstairs and washed his face, in case Lynsey's lingering Turkish Rose was still on him. It had probably penetrated his jumper, he thought, and he removed it instantly, changing it for an old tatty jumper he kept in his study.

CHAPTER TWENTY-FIVE

IT WAS BECOMING ROUTINE to watch out for Lynsey as he walked down the road towards the church on Sunday mornings. He would pace himself, leaving the house twenty minutes before the service was due to begin, knowing that allowed the best time to bring them together at the church, at the same time. As he approached the church his eyes would greedily scan the figures approaching from the opposite direction, and he would slow his pace until he thought he recognised her—a tall figure with flowing hair in a black coat, and then she was always the first one to wave and his heart would miss a beat.

"Good morning, Nefertiti," he smiled as their trajectories came together on the pavement next to the path that led to the front of the church door. He liked to call her that because it always made her laugh. They entered the church as a couple, shaking the hands of the doorkeepers who must by now have noticed their increasing friendship. Often Bert, the leader of the prayer circle, served as doorkeeper, and his welcoming smile was always there—though on this occasion he seemed to make a point of asking Charles how Sylvia was keeping.

Charles and Lynsey took their usual places in the pew near the back and their hands automatically found each other with fingers intertwined. When they came together in the church on Sundays it was after a seemingly long interval of deprivation from each other and so their reunion was for those precious ten minutes before the entrance of the little red book, almost feverish in its intensity. "I have missed you *so* much, my darling," Charles whispered, grasping her hand firmly and playing with her fingers.

"And I have missed you, eh," she whispered back, her body turned half towards him as her eyes sought his. "To tell you the truth, Charrels, I think of you *all* the time. What do you see in a Scots lass like me, eh!"

It occurred to him that if the old dears behind them could not read their body language, they must be blind. And that would apply to the doorkeepers as well. The thought was sobering and he tried to curb his enthusiasm and delight at being next to her again. But they continued to hold hands and speak to each other through the pressure of their fingers—this time until they stood up for the first hymn.

When the children filed out of the church to Sunday school after the children's talk, Maggie came to sit next to Charles, who made a conscious effort to attend to the sermon and not seek to touch Lynsey's hand. The minister was making a distinction between a conservative Christian and a radical one. Conservative, he explained, meant traditional, guarded, over-cautious, moderate. "There is a sense of fear of change, fear of failure. Fear of being challenged or moving out of your comfort zone." Radical, on the other hand, he went on to say, meant sweeping changes. "It carries an element of risk-taking, facing potential new dangers with courage, hope."

It was all a question, the minister said, of getting the balance right and moving forward under the guidance of the Holy Spirit. Paradoxically, for Charles, it seemed to apply to his new situation with Lynsey—ironically, though, since it meant moving forward in an illicit way that surely could not have been prompted by the guidance of the Holy Spirit. He had certainly been in a comfort zone before he met Lynsey, such as it was, but having met her it was too late to seek the old security or mediocre comfort of that zone. Like it or not, the change had touched him, he had fallen in love in an impelling irreversible way, a way that had rocketed him into a dizzy realm of happiness that could not be denied. But it was into an uncertain future he was moving now, fraught with risk, and indeed, it felt like walking on quicksand. How could God bless this change, a change governed not only by heights of happiness but desperate lows of depression when the danger threatened to engulf him? If God had engineered their meeting, mapped out their converging paths, he and Lynsey coming together as they did, what in heaven's name had He in mind— for all things work together for good for those who love the Lord and are called according to His purpose for them? Patience and moderation, he thought, were the key words for the imminent future as they walked ahead with care and extra vigilance.

Walking back with her as usual after church along the Leven road, a silver Jaguar travelling in the opposite direction suddenly hooted, and Lynsey waved at the car with exuberant friendliness. "It's Hamish's friend!" she said. "He's taking Hamish to the pub, I guess."

"Oh God," Charles said, ice clutching his heart. "You mean Hamish was in the car—and that he saw us together?"

"Not to worry," she laughed. "I can handle him. Besides, he kens you walk back with me and his fine with that."

"Crumbs," Charles said, "I hope so." But he felt uneasy. This time there was no reason to part at the crossroads and walk up the street a little further for the mythical Mars Bar since Hamish was clearly not at home—and he took his leave of Lynsey at her front gate. When he walked back to his house he was more aware of straying from his comfort zone than ever before… and of the risks that came with the new path ahead that he had inadvertently ventured to take, thanks to the intersecting path of Lynsey Anne McCann.

* * *

"Now just what do you see in a local Scots lass, Charrels? And you having been a professor!" It was the same question she had asked before—one that really seemed to puzzle her.

Clearly, Charles felt, she must have a very low sense of self-worth to keep asking that question. "I don't think you realise how lovely, and how sweet, you are, Lynsey."

She shook her head, the puzzled smile still on her face. "And you, like Lord Sebastian Flyte in *Brideshead Revisited!* Though I thought of Jeremy Irons when I first heard you speak! The minute you opened your mouth I knew you had to have a very important job—and I was reet, you were a professor. How cool is that! And me a plain local Scots gel, eh!"

He was nuzzled up against her, his hand touching her cheek under her flowing laundered hair. She looked especially alluring tonight in her red gown over a black silk negligée and skimpy black panties. It was Sunday night and Hamish's night out at the pub, so one of the safe times to be with her.

He sighed. "I would so like to make love to you, Lynsey—but heaven knows when that will happen."

"Well," she said, looking sincerely into his eyes, "that I will leave entirely up to you, sir."

"But I couldn't do it here—in Hamish's house—I would be too nervous and it would feel so wrong."

"Heavens yes," she laughed. "I would die if he came in and saw us naked together. I would feel so dreadful. Do you ken what I mean, Charles?" She touched his cheek with her slender fingers.

"I certainly do—I feel exactly the same. I would need to be relaxed and under no pressure. But as I said, heaven alone knows when such an opportunity might arise." He smiled. "In any case—we both of us prayed the Lord's Prayer aloud in church this morning—and we both said, 'Lead us not into temptation.' I heard your voice saying it—as I was saying it, too."

"I ken," she sighed. "But it's too late, Charrels, it's too late. I'm already in love."

"Well, the Lord shouldn't have brought us together, should he? I know he brought me here for you—and you for me... but how are we to deal with the pressure of being in love? That was so unexpected."

"Yes, Charrels—and I will no' ever go back tae drinkin' again because of you... it's you that has given me the strength... and given me back my self-respect and confidence. All your compliments tae me... you have no idea how that has strengthened me, renewed my belief in mesel'."

"Well, you deserve all that. I don't think you realise how wonderful, how lovey and sweet you are. I keep saying that, don't I? But it's true. You were drowning all that loveliness and sweetness in drink, floundering because no one appreciated your wonderful qualities. I know this, for a certainty, that you are going to achieve great success—perhaps as a writer, or perhaps in some other field. But you don't deserve to be a housekeeper and a live-in carer for the sake of a roof over your head, Lynsey my darling. You have spent six years in that capacity, almost like a servant. You are not using your God-given talents. I know it's only because of the drink problem that you've resorted to this solution. But there must be a much, much better solution—if only I could find it."

"You are verra sweet, Charrels, for caring that I do. With your help—and the help of the Lord—I will find my calling." Then she laughed. "Oh dear—all those old dears in the kirk—they must be prattling about us, seeing us together like two teenagers in love."

"But how would they know we were holding hands, my darling? They can't see through the wooden back of the pew!"

"Oh, believe me, they ken! They're women!"

"How? Have you heard any rumours about us?"

She shook her head. "No. But I can assure you—the rumours will be going around by now!"

"Well, I was certainly holding your hand very hard, and squeezing it like crazy this morning! And you were squeezing back, my love—it was like a whole new language conveyed through our fingers! I just loved it! And you have such gorgeous hands, such supple expressive fingers!"

They melted together in a lingering kiss. But he felt uneasy and pulled away. "How can we be sure Hamish won't get back early, Lynsey?"

"His times are like clockwork, Charrels. But there are times when he might change his routine. There must be a way I can warn you if the evening is no' right. I canna phone you to warn you because of Sylvia, eh?"

"Well, I'll always phone first on my mobile. But what if Hamish answers? I suppose I could just say I was phoning to let you know your edited bit of writing is ready to collect. And, you know, you can also phone me, even if Sylvia answers— you can say that you have the next piece of writing ready for me—and ask when you can bring it around."

"Okay, that sounds good." She cupped his face in her hands. "You are so nervous tonight, my darling. I can sense it. You were no' this nervous before."

"I know, my love, I know… it's just the worry that Hamish might come back early… since you said he left half an hour earlier than usual… and I have to watch the time since Sylvia will be aware of my 'walk' taking an abnormally long time. We have got to find a better solution—we have *got* to, somehow. And I want you so badly. You are so adorable—at first all I wanted was to hold you in my arms and smother you with kisses… but the more I do that the more I want you… all of you. How will this possibly end, or go on? I know we don't know the future and that God only knows, and holds the future… but I can't see how this is all going to work out for us. I keep saying to myself, 'patience and moderation'—but both of those ingredients are difficult to maintain."

It was just so wonderful holding her in his arms, hugging her really tight, snuggling his face into her lush hair and breathing in her intoxicating scent—yet it wasn't enough. To embrace and hold a delicious woman like Lynsey and feel her holding him back was pure heaven—but it could only be done in small doses.

"I'd love to make you come, you know… even if it was just with my finger in your flower…"

"If I did, you'd know," she said with that secret smile of hers.

* * *

Before he left her that night she gave him a memory stick with more of her story, and with another personal letter for him. Once he was alone in his study he transferred the contents of the memory stick to his computer.

As he said to her before, he couldn't get enough of her— and so readily devoured her words which, as before, impressed him by the solid diction and control of syntax:

Some months after I recovered I started drinking yet again. If I thought my life was bad, it was to become horrendous. I had no friends and my family had simply had enough and washed their hands of me. I was not living life, but just existing. My life was now about to reach rock bottom and at the time I just did not give a damn. Nothing in the world mattered. A stupid thought ran across my mind that I could end it all, but then I realised I probably would not make a good job of that either. I had started to go out at nights to the pub again and with no fear in the world, I would simply find myself in situations that, had I been sober, would never have ended up in. As a drunk woman, I was allowing myself to be taken advantage of and had not realised how dangerous life was becoming. In the meantime, my mother had become a member of Al-Anon, a group that gives support to the family and friends of alcoholics. Somehow or other, she began to learn more about alcoholism and we started to get on better with each other than we ever had. I know she was now beginning to understand my situation much better. After that, other family members seemed to have more time for me and also became more understanding.

Thank God for this—somewhere out there a flicker of hope was wavering for me. My life was not over, at least, not yet. I knew that deep down there was a new Lynsey about to emerge—a much stronger and confident one than I could have possibly imagined. More importantly, a sober one.

A few months after I left my partner Bill, I bumped into a man I had not seen for some years, in the local pub. His name is Hamish and we sat and talked and drank for the rest of the afternoon. By the end of that day both of us were rather drunk and he invited me back to his house. I remember him telling me he had known my parents for a long time and that his wife Beryl had died a few years back.

After a while of getting to know him a bit better, he asked me if I would like to come and live in his home. I had to think about it carefully, but decided it might be alright. Hamish was living in the house rent free as his sister owned it and we both agreed that I could have a roof over my head as long as I kept the house tidy, did the cooking and the washing and ironing. At first, we did not really get along. Hamish is a very kind and gentle man, who in general does not keep well and has been known to lose his temper quite quickly. I found it difficult to get used to this but eventually managed to get my way around him. I am still with Hamish and do the best I can to look after him and make sure he eats his meals. We also have a dog named Tyson, who is a pure bred Staffordshire Bull Terrier. He is a gentle affectionate dog and I absolutely love him to bits. Our house just would not be the same without Tyson in it. He has arthritis in one of his back legs due to his age, but he still loves to get out in the mornings for a walk. I know that both Hamish and Tyson need me and I am just so glad that I am sober and able to do this for them.

* * *

Then Charles read her letter to him:

My Dearest Charles

My heart skipped a beat when the telephone rang. I just knew it would be you. I thought you would be away that night and so I had not been expecting you.

Anyway, I was overjoyed that you came to see me. I am so happy and relaxed in your company and every time you cuddle me I feel a tingling sensation going all over my body. I feel I am getting to know you better now and that I absolutely trust you.

Charles, you have already told me that you love me and I have been trying very hard to tell you what is truly in my heart.

I am in love with you Charles and I have never met a man like you in all my life. I could curl up in your arms forever and I am looking forward to the time that I will be able to show you my love in a sincere and gentle way.

From your darling little lamb
Lynsey XX

P.S. I meant to tell you how handsome you look and I may start calling you Sebastian!! (Remember, *Brideshead Revisited*!)

Charles loved this letter and frequently reread it. It was such a sincere affirmation of her love for him, and he treasured her words.

CHAPTER TWENTY-SIX

TWO WEEKS went by and it became almost routine for Charles to visit her on those 'safe' evenings, each time for under an hour, in Hamish's house. He would always phone from round the corner first, standing under a street light, to check the coast was clear and that she was indeed alone.

Snuggling into her warm body was like heaven. Her soft warm skin felt so feminine, so lush, as he ran his hands up her arms, under her gown, then scooped them under her negligée to feel the feminine warmth, the silky texture of her skin round her waist, up her naked back, then around the back of her neck as his lips joined hers. Each time was like sinking into bliss. Words would stop as their lips worked together, relaxing and parting as their tongues slipped in and out into the damp interior of their mouths, their teeth sometimes clashing as they sought to press their souls together. Their lovemaking, short of actual intercourse, was relaxed yet urgent—relaxed to savour to the full the gentle exquisiteness of each other's presence, and urgent to squeeze in as much as possible into the small amount of time available to them. At other moments they talked as he snuggled against her, one hand around her exposed waist, the other gently kneading her supple breasts, his head in the crux of her neck while he breathed in the exquisite scent of her feminine aroma. The rich flow of her hair would be over his cheek, his face, as he felt her slender fingers caress his neck. Then as time ran out they would stand to kiss goodnight, facing each other, and as they were thus locked together, face to face, his left hand holding her tight against him, his right hand would slip down and delight in her delicate bush, his index finger slipping easily into her soft damp interior, exploring, relishing every fold and contour of her secret garden. That's when her soft brown almond eyes would gaze up at him, a cheeky smile on her lips, conveying a reprimand that was also a consent. "Charrels Haddington," she would sigh, flicking her hair back, "how am I goin' to get tae sleep tonight after this…?"

Parting was the most difficult ordeal in these stolen moments of bliss. She would cling to him, both hands around his neck, her cheeky, smiling eyes holding his, reluctant to release him to the cold night outside. But go he must and he would slip out of the door, and she would stay standing in the half-open door, risking to be seen in her negligée as she waved him goodbye. "Please be careful," she would call after him.

When they met by the lake in the morning—and she was always there with Tyson—they would recall their most recent night meeting.

"I think I was talkin' more than ever," she laughed. "I was that pleased tae see you… I was thinkin' afterwards, 'Lynsey, what were you blethering about all the time!' Och, Charrels Haddington, I do love you!"

It was a thrill to hear her say that. There had been a time when he said it but when she had held back.

"I just adore your eyes, my darling. I love you," he said in return.

"Och, I just love it so much when you say that!" she laughed. "When I wake up in the mornin' I have to pinch myself and ask, is he really in love with *me*!"

"But you're so gorgeous," he smiled.

"You're no' so bad lookin' yoursel', Charrels Haddington," she said mischievously.

On the previous night's rendezvous she had shown him a photograph of herself as a schoolgirl. He was eager to see it, for she had said she was thin and gawky—but the picture showed a lovely girl with a chiselled nose and a coy smile.

"People said I looked Jewish," she said.

"No, not Jewish—Egyptian," he smiled.

That night as he lay in bed recalling all the treasured moments with her, he felt an immense happiness. As his thoughts went over all the things she had said and the way she looked, he prayed for her, that God might bless her and save her for all eternity—and in that moment he was overcome, surprised, by a sudden surge of love through his entire body. It was like a waterfall of love pouring through him, like a baptism of the Holy Spirit. It was a familiar sensation and, thrilled, he remembered when he had first experienced that outpouring of love, when he received the baptism of the Holy Spirit in a small room in London. He remembered how on that occasion the Lord had given him a vision, a mission, presenting in his mind the picture of a lectern that was like a desk, with pen and paper to hand, with the words "Feed my lambs" ringing, not in his ears but in his mind. For months later he had gone about with a great sense of love for everyone. And now he realised that that mission included Lynsey, and that the Lord had heard his prayer to bless her. Did she not even refer to herself as 'your little lamb'?

'Oh, thank you, Lord, thank you,' he said inaudibly, his eyes wet with joyful tears as he cuddled his pillow, wishing it were Lynsey.

CHAPTER TWENTY-SEVEN

WATERSHED II

CHARLES had a brilliant idea! He missed not receiving emails from Lynsey, and she had said Hamish refused to allow her to sign up for broadband because the expense would be a threat to his drinking money. But, Charles thought, what if he gave her his old dongle? Before the phone line was installed when he and Sylvia moved into their new home three years ago, they relied on a dongle to go on-line and collect emails. It was a small device that plugged into the computer and worked like a mobile phone. He scrabbled through a drawer in his study and found the old dongle. Would it work on Lynsey's laptop? After all, it was the same laptop in which the dongle had originally worked, plugged into a USB port. He plugged the device into his present laptop and found he could pre-load it with £15 worth of internet access. Then he plugged the device into his large desktop computer that was not connected to the internet—and to his joy found the dongle worked! Even from the desktop computer that had no broadband connection, he was able to go on-line! It did not take him long, then, to create a Hotmail email account for Lynsey, in her name: Lynsey McCann! He sent an email to this account and saw that it was received. Then he sent a test email from Lynsey's email account, from his desktop computer to himself, and checked his emails in the in-box on his laptop—and was thrilled to see the email appear in bold letters—**Lynsey McCann**! What a joy!

The next 'safe' evening when Hamish was out at the pub, Charles took the dongle with him. "I've found a way to get you on-line to send emails to me," he grinned, producing the little dongle. "It works like a mobile phone, so you can connect to the internet anywhere."

"Really?" she smiled demurely at him.

She looked delicious in a loose-fitting red gown beneath which Charles suspected she had nothing on. But he resisted temptation. He wanted to show her how to go on-line so she could be in contact with him at any time. "Where is your laptop?" he asked.

"It's in my bedroom, upstairs," she giggled. "I canna tak you there—no man has ever been there."

"Can you bring the laptop downstairs then? This is important—it means we can always be in touch." Their time together was limited. He was supposed to be on a walk, and who knew when Hamish would be back!

"Come on then," she smiled sheepishly, and took his hand. "Follow me."

She led him up the winding stairs in the corner of the hallway. She took him into her bedroom which was immaculate, a double bed neatly made and two knotty pine wardrobes at the far end. There was a chest of drawers with an array of dolls and what looked like perfume bottles.

"Oh my goodness!" she exclaimed with a coy smile. "Now you'll see all my wee dolls! Dinna look at all this stuff, Charrels!"

But he only took in the room at a precursory glance. He sat down at the dressing table where the laptop was, open. He pressed the 'on' button and waited for it to boot up. "This will be amazing, Lynsey," he smiled at her as she hovered over him. He was aware of her scent. "I just hope it works. I can't wait to receive the first real email from you."

He had to wait while the dongle's program was installing. He got up and took Lynsey into his arms, and they melted together. She drew her head back and looked at him with her cheeky almond eyes.

"I've no' had a man in this room before, Charrels," she smiled. "I hope ye ken how privileged yer are, eh!"

"Oh, I do, my darling," he sighed, and swept his hands under her gown feeling her smooth warm body beneath. He was right—she had nothing on beneath the gown. He breathed in the scent of her perfume, her hair, and their lips melted together again, with nothing more being said as they savoured and drank in the intoxicating presence of each other. There was something electric about her lips and Charles vaguely recalled an Abba song that sang of kisses of fire. It was like a fire was spreading from her lips, down into his groin, and he had to force himself to pull away.

"The program should be ready now," he sighed with a smile, for a moment lost in the love reflected in her eyes. "Come now, I'll show you how to go on-line and access your email account. I just hope it works!"

It did work. She sat down beside him as he logged into her account, typing in the email address and the password he had created for her.

"Oh, I'll get the hang of it again, Charrels," she smiled. "It will all come back tae me. I used to be a secretary and PA—I'm sure I havna forgotten those skills. Do you ken what I mean? Charrels, you're such a niece man, doing all this for me."

"Look here, Lynsey," he said, "You see—here's an email I sent to you earlier when I was testing the system. All you have to do is click on the reply tab, and type in your message here, in this space..." He typed a sentence: 'Charles, I love you to distraction, you're the greatest!' "There," he said, "that will be your first love-email to me!"

"Oh aye," she smiled cheekily. "Seems you can write love letters to yoursel'—you don't need me, eh!"

"Seriously, though," he said, "you can also attach a WORD document that you wrote in advance. Look, I'll find a document you wrote before on your computer and attach it." He searched for a document and attached one called 'Letter to Charles'—a letter he assumed he had already read, one she had sent him by way of the memory stick. "There you are, now I'll just click the send button." He did so and the message read, 'Sent successful.' "Wow," he smiled, "I'll be able to pick up that email when I get back."

"It looks fine, Charrels—I'm sure I will manage it. My goodness, you're so niece to me, doin' all this."

"It's only because I want your body, my love," he said, feeling her nakedness under his hands once again.

"Oh, you bugger!" she said, giving him a playful slap. "Well, you have a niece bum!" she laughed, flicking her hair as she smiled up to him and putting both hands around him and squeezing his posterior.

Before he left she gave him a new memory stick. "I've written a personal letter to you, Charrels. You'll find it there—a 'Letter to Charrels'. I suppose we won't need to exchange memory sticks anymore!"

He soon left because he was mindful of the time his 'walk' was taking. Sylvia had certainly noticed that his walks out at night were taking longer each time, and he gave the excuse that to get the proper exercise he would walk up the road in their estate, then back through the council estate and back via the church—it was a good round trip, he said, and enabled him to step out energetically.

Sylvia was in the kitchen when he returned so he slipped unnoticed upstairs to his study and checked his emails on his laptop. Sure enough, the test email came through—**Lynsey McCann**—and there was an attachment! He opened the attachment thinking it was a letter from her that he had already read, but as he read it his heart tightened with joy. It was one he did not recognise—probably the same one on the memory stick he still had in his pocket. He devoured the letter greedily:

My Dearest Charles

I have just finished reading the latest three chapters of *Sunset Stirrings*.

You cannot imagine how wonderful and completely humble your words have made me feel. I thank God every night for the gift of such a lovely man. Just the fact that He decided both of us should enter into each other's lives. I know God already knows that you have, somehow or other, been a lonely man for quite some time. I suppose in the same way I have been really lonely. Both of us have been missing an important part of life's jigsaw. It's as if we have been happy enough and secure, I suppose, but lacking that one thing we have both been searching for—true, unconditional love. I feel spiritually at one with you, like two peas in a pod.

I can never get you out of my mind and have never felt as happy as I do now. I do not know what the future holds for us, but I know that I will remain strong and will always be there with you and for you, no matter how tough it gets. It is too late for me to change the way I feel about you now.

Remember I love you Charles and wherever you are I will always be there too.

Until the next time we meet my darling and dinna mak it too long, eh!!!

From your darling little lamb
Lynsey XX

The next morning Sylvia was out shopping and Charles was recording some more of his memories of Lynsey in *Sunset*

Stirrings, waiting for the time to approach a quarter to ten when he would leave to meet Lynsey by the lake, for she was usually there walking the dog by ten or just afterwards, and often feeding the swans. But he got so embroiled in his writing that he forgot the time, and when he looked at his watch it had already gone ten!

He dashed out, not even waiting to put on his 'outside' shoes. Half way there he realised he had not closed the page on the computer screen he was writing—a record of his last meeting with Lynsey at the church, of his delight at sitting next to her, holding and squeezing her hand. What if Sylvia were to return to the house before he got back—would she go up to his study and look at his computer screen? But if he turned back now he would certainly miss seeing Lynsey at the lake—it was a window of opportunity he never wanted to miss. He ran most of the way hoping Lynsey would still be there. When he turned the last corner that brought the lake into view his heart lifted, for he could see her there, a small figure on the far side of the lake. He was getting good at recognising her across a great distance, and even saw her arm raised in a greeting—for she could spot him at a distance too. He ran across the road and instead of following the small macadamised path that led to the lake, he took a shortcut across the wet grass—and before long he was next to her, panting.

"Goodness, Charrels," she laughed, "you were running—I dinna ken you were that keen to see me, eh!"

"I thought I might miss you—I forgot the time," he panted. "Imagine a day going by without talking to you! I'll see you in the prayer circle tonight, but then all I can do is gaze furtively at you."

"Aye," she smiled. "That wee book you gave me, Charrels, *God Calling*, ken? I read it every day. Have you noticed how often the Lord says to be patient?"

"Yes, I noticed that—the message is always never to force anything, but always to wait upon the Lord."

They fell into conversation as they walked slowly around the lake, the dog continuing to snuffle through and explore the undergrowth near their feet. Soon they reached the place where their paths diverged. "See you in the prayer circle tonight, my love," he said as he waved goodbye.

Then he rushed back, hoping to reach the house before Sylvia returned from her shopping expedition. He was mindful of that page still open on his computer screen—had he saved and closed the document? He suspected that in his rush he had forgotten to close it. There were also some photographs Lynsey had given him of herself, from her younger years, in the top inside pocket of his coat in the hall. In his hurry he had rushed out without his coat—and he remembered the photographs were still in his coat pocket. He did recall that he had zipped shut the pocket when Lynsey had given him the photos. He was intending to scan them to his computer. Three of them were taken by her sister, when she was in her twenties—wearing nothing but sexy black lingerie; in one of the pictures she was topless, her well-formed, liquid breasts on display under her cheeky smile. He looked at his watch as he broke into a run. He had to get back before Sylvia returned home.

But when he turned the corner and his house came into view, his heart sank. Sylvia's car was already in the drive. Normally he would be there to help her unpack the shopping and place the items into the kitchen cupboards and refrigerator.

He walked in, his heart beating from the run and the anticipation of what might develop from his absence. Sylvia was in the kitchen with most of the shopping items already stored away, and her greeting was distinctly frosty.

"Off on one of your walks?" she said casually.

"Got to stick to my routine," he said, generating an air of enthusiasm. "My weight's steady at 14 stone now."

She made no response and after stacking a couple of tins of baked beans, he went into the hall and inspected his coat pocket. The pictures of Lynsey were there, but it worried him that the pocket was partially unzipped. He thought he had zipped it shut all the way, but couldn't be sure. He took the pictures out and stuffed them into his trouser pocket and went upstairs to his study. 'Oh hell!' he thought, the minute he looked at his computer screen. The page he had been working on in his story was there, in full view, just as he had left it when he had rushed off. Had Sylvia been up and read it? If so, it would certainly explain her frosty attitude. He couldn't believe how careless he had been!

As the day went on there were certainly signs of strain in Sylvia's disposition. She seemed to be ever watchful of him. But then, he thought, there was nothing new in this—for over the last few weeks he often detected a sense of uneasiness in her. In bed at night she seemed to lie awake for long periods of time, with restless twitches of her limbs. If he got up in the night to make coffee or listen to music, when he returned she would often be awake, the lights on, reading in bed.

That evening Sylvia went with him to the prayer circle, as usual. For Charles it had become an important opportunity to drink in Lynsey's presence, even though contact by way of conversation was limited then. It was an occasion when she always turned up in full glamorous makeup, when his eyes feasted on that other Lynsey that came out on such occasions, like a flower blossoming, dazzling in her beauty and confidence. It was the Lynsey he knew was there, deep down under the plain Lynsey without makeup, whose face bore the lines of her suffering, her alcohol days when she was struggling with depression against the whirlpool of life that threatened to pull her down into an early grave.

When Sylvia and Charles took their usual seats Charles's eyes immediately made contact with Lynsey's eyes. Had anyone detected the fleeting smile that flashed between them, like a spark? It was becoming difficult to conceal his burgeoning love for her, a woman he already knew intimately, whose secret places his fingertips had already explored.

It had become routine to begin the meeting by singing hymns from a popular chorus book, accompanied by Bert's mouth organ. While singing the well-known words of hymns like 'What a Friend we Have in Jesus', or 'How Great Thou Art', Charles sneaked a look at Lynsey who wore her glasses to read from the hymn book. The glasses made her look so sophisticated, and while everyone had their eyes in the hymn books, his eyes were on Lynsey. He felt so proud of her, the way she looked now compared to that first time she turned up, haggard and ragged looking, after pulling herself off alcohol. She had been dry now for what... six months? Her eyes glanced up from the hymn book and again there was that flash of a smile. Then he glanced at Sylvia and saw that she was not singing. She held the hymn book in front of her but her lips were not moving. She looked dispirited and depressed, and somehow he knew the game was up. Surely she had seen that open page on his computer—or found those revealing photos of Lynsey?

At tea break when Charles and Lynsey returned the Bibles to the cupboard in the kitchen, timing their arrival there as was their usual custom, Charles whispered: "Take care—Sylvia surely knows something. She's been acting very strange." Sylvia continued to be very quiet during the prayer time and did not offer up any prayers for those on the prayer list as she usually did. After the close of the meeting she did not join the women in the kitchen with the washing up of the tea things and instead helped Charles stack the chairs, which was his usual job. As they all gathered to leave Sylvia was constantly by Charles's side, making it impossible for him to talk to Lynsey in private.

The next morning when Charles met Lynsey by the lake, she told him there was no need to warn her the previous evening about Sylvia's attitude—it had been clear enough when they prepared the tea in the kitchen.

"She was rude tae me, Charrels," Lynsey said. "She pointedly ignored me if I spoke to her."

They were standing by the lakeside surrounded by the swans that knew her because she always came with a loaf of bread which she broke off and threw to them.

Charles watched the swans fluffing up their feathers as they dared to come close to hoover up pieces of bread. "I was wondering if she had read from the page that was visible on my computer screen, Lynsey," he said. "It was still there, on the screen, when she got back from shopping yesterday."

"Well, that's possible, Charrels," she said as she threw another piece of bread to a nearby swan. "I can tell you as a fact that most women would. But even if she didna, she may have tumbled on it from other signs. You ken, Charrels, women have a kind of sixth sense when it comes to these things, eh? They can read signs in the way people behave. You have already told me she could smell my scent on you, eh? I have tried to use a more subtle scent, ken... but even then, you canna hide being in love, can you? It shows in the eyes, and in small things." She laughed. "Even Hamish has asked me why I'm going round the house singin'! He was verra crabbit. 'You never used to sing—what's the bloody matter with you, hen!' he shouted the other day. And when I'm cooking or ironing I sometimes do stupid things, drop things, because I'm day-dreaming—of you." She paused and turned, looking at Charles full in the face. "Look, Charrels, something will surely happen, if it has not already happened. If it's meant tae happen, it will. And there's never a reet time for you to tell Sylvia—or for me to tell Hamish. Do you ken what I mean, Charrels?"

"Sure," he nodded. "It's just so true, that old trite saying about these things—that 'it just happened'. I never planned for this to happen—falling in love. If I saw it coming maybe I could have stopped it—but when I realised what was happening it was too late. I was already in love. Lynsey, it's the most incredible feeling!"

"I ken, Charrels, I ken!" The bag of bread slices was empty and the swans slid back into the water. She gave a flick of her hair as her eyes sought out his eyes. "Now all I know it's the most wonderful thing that has ever happened tae me. But ye can be sure of this, Charrels—whatever happens I will stick by you. The only thing that will stop me supporting you is if you tell me to stop. Even so, I assure you, there will never be another man in my life, Charrels. You are the only man who has ever loved me for mesel', and who genuinely cares about me."

CHAPTER TWENTY-EIGHT

IN THE WEEK that followed Sylvia stuck to Charles like a leech. He kept up his routine of taking walks every evening just before nine, even if it was not one of the 'safe' nights when he would spend time with Lynsey. The idea was to get her used to his going out every night at that time for his walks, so that when he would actually be with Lynsey, his time away would not seem unusual. Also, if she chose to accompany him for a walk, hopefully it would be on a night that was not one of his scheduled meetings with Lynsey. But Sylvia was clearly suspicious that something was going on. When he said one night that he was popping out for his walk, she said plaintively, "You never ask me to accompany you on your walks anymore!"

It was not a night he was scheduled to meet Lynsey, so he said, "Oh, by all means come along if you wish!"

She did. He made it an exceptionally long walk. Normally with her long legs she walked fast and he struggled to keep up with her—but this time the pattern was reversed. He took a circuitous route through the council estate, coming back via the church, and he walked energetically. By the time he neared their house she was lagging behind, but he did not ease his pace.

"At this point I usually extend the walk," he said, "by going up the hill into our new estate. Are you up for that?"

"Okay," she said—was it with forced enthusiasm?

He walked up the hill even increasing his pace, and she was distinctly struggling to keep up with him. After all, he didn't want to encourage her on his walks—especially if it was to meet Lynsey! He made some observations about the houses they passed, but generally did not encourage conversation. She was too focussed on her breathing to engage in small talk in any case. He felt like a military drill sergeant, injecting energy into the walk—and his heart went out to her, knowing she was doing her best to keep up her surveillance on him. In the past there were times when they enjoyed their walks together. But now he walked with a different agenda. He felt he had developed a streak of cruelty. But Sylvia was like a gaoler, a minder, watching him. At other times there were signs of forced affection from her, a sweetness, as though she were trying to slacken her hold on him, lest her watchfulness should push him further from her. It was a comfort, occasionally, to feel her hand on his shoulder at night, in bed—something she hadn't done for a long time. But the touch acerbated the growing feeling of guilt within him. He didn't want to hurt Sylvia, but the flame of love for Lynsey had been ignited and refused to be dampened. Sylvia and he had not made love for a long time now—more than a year, he thought. She was unresponsive to his touch, and when, long ago it now seemed, they attempted to make love, he found he had lost the power to sustain an erection, something he accepted as being normal for someone his age. Sylvia, though ten years younger than he, seemed to be quite content with the status quo. They had become comfortable with one another, like an old pair of slippers. But Lynsey had sparked and kindled something in him he had thought had been permanently dormant, and the sensation of the renewal was wonderful. He had forgotten what it was like to be in love.

It was a Friday night when Charles told Sylvia he was going out for his walk. She was still halfway through her coffee and did not volunteer to come out with him. The night was wet and blustery, in any case, so he had to take his heavy coat and cap as protection against the fine rain. He was relieved that he had successfully made his escape without Sylvia, for it was a 'safe' night when Hamish would be at the pub until midnight.

198

Because he had made his escape a little earlier than usual, Charles had to lose some time which he did standing in a bus shelter on the Leven road. He waited there for more than ten minutes, glancing at his watch. When it was five to nine he walked off into the drizzle and round the block, coming down the Brae until he was close to the corner where Lynsey's house was. It was routine for him at this point, under a street light, to flip open his mobile phone and select her number. His pulse always raced as he heard the ring and waited for her to answer.

"Yes?" came her now familiar voice.

"All alone?"

"Aye," she giggled.

"See you in a second." And he closed the phone, walked round the corner and lifted the latch on her gate. He always felt so exposed at this point, for it was under a bright street light in full view of the houses on the opposite side of the street.

By the time he rounded the overgrown Camellia japonica bush in the path and mounted the step at the front door, she was there, holding the door open to let him in. She was, as usual, in her red gown and her fragrance embraced him before he could embrace her.

She had said once that she was probably the cleanest woman in Kennoway, for it was part of her routine to have a hot bath every night after supper, and she spent the rest of the evening in her nightgown. Charles could never understand how Hamish could live with such a woman and have no sexual interest in her whatsoever—since, for Charles, she was the ultimate in womanhood, soft, feminine, alluring in her nightgown with very little, if anything, beneath it, her silky flowing hair framing her adorable face and falling across her shoulders.

They stood for a long time in an embrace and he pulled her very tight against him until she groaned.

"Charrels," she purred, "I have never been held so tight! You hold me like you really love me—like you really mean it!"

"I do, my love, I absolutely do," he said, and squeezed her hard again, until she groaned again. He loved to hear her groan under the pressure of his clasp, since she really seemed to revel in it. Had no man ever wanted to hold this adorable woman as tight as he wanted to? He held her like he never wanted to let her go, and she responded by clinging back. Then they fed upon each other's lips again, interrupting only so he could tell her that he loved her. It gave him so much satisfaction to tell her he loved her, and especially when she responded and told him she would never let him go.

His hands swept under her nightgown and luxuriated in the velvet soft texture of her skin. The supple softness of her breasts that he cupped excited him, and he squeezed them gently until he heard her soft groans again. They sank down on the settee and inevitably his fingers began to explore her body while their lips came together in kisses of ecstasy, their tongues flicking and lashing against each other. Before long his hand was in her secret place, the place she called her flower.

"I love it when you have no knickers," he crooned.

She giggled. "We have a saying in Scotland—fur coat an' nae knickers!" She looked at him with those smiling bewitching eyes of hers. "I should come around to your hoos in a fur coat with just a string of pearls beneath, open my coat when you answer the door and say, 'Avon calling!'" She laughed, stroking his hair. "I dinna think Sylvia will be impressed if she opened the door, though!"

"You're so funny," he smiled, "and irresistible." He took a deep breath. "Lynsey, I want you so much—I really want you."

She kept her eyes on his. "Only when you're ready, Charrels. I'll let you choose the time."

He sighed. "I want you now, that's the trouble, my darling." He was exploring her while he spoke.

"You're exploring me—but I've niver explored you," she smiled demurely.

He released his belt and allowed her delicate fingers to find his most sensitive places. The touch of those long, sensitive fingers was beyond ecstasy and his desire for her became urgent.

"Now I'm feeling shy," she said with a coy smile, her eyes still holding his.

"Oh God, Lynsey, I so badly need to make love to you—just to feel myself inside you…"

She continued to survey him with that soft, piquant smile, which he took for consent, and he knelt in front of her while she sat back on the settee. At first his awkward fumbling prevented him from finding his way in—but then she did something amazing. She lifted up her long shapely legs and wrapped them round his neck—something that had certainly never happened to him before and he slipped in easily. It was like heaven laced with chocolate. Making love and staring down at her face, into her laughing eyes in that position while her slender fingers ran over and tickled his stomach, was exquisite, something that was worth dying for.

*   *   *

When he got home, nearly an hour later, Sylvia was in her study seated at her computer. He took off his coat in the hallway and went into the kitchen, where he washed his hands under the running tap of the sink. He hoped all traces of Lynsey were off his hands, and she had said she would not use her Turkish Rose perfume for the time being. His heart was still racing with mixed feelings at what he had just done—and experienced. It was a moment of exhilarating fulfilment, yet frightening, as though he had just jumped from a great height with a very small parachute. Would he get away with the risk he had taken? His heart was still racing, yet he was afraid his face bore the expression of the cat that had got the cream.

"Well, that was a long walk!" said Sylvia as she came into the kitchen.

"It was." He tried to sound casual as he switched on the kettle. "It was raining so I took shelter for some time in a bus shelter."

"Really?" she said frostily. "Did you have a woman with you in the bus shelter?"

"Hardly." He gave a forced laugh, teaspooning some instant coffee into a mug. "Whatever made you say that?"

"Because you're reeking of a woman! You can't miss it—it's filling the whole kitchen!"

His blood froze. Somehow he knew his number was up. But he continued to pour himself a mug of coffee in silence.

"Charles!" she demanded his attention, "For God's sake, tell me the truth! I know you've been out seeing a woman. Just come clean and tell me! I can't go on like this. For days—no, *weeks*, I've sensed it. You go out at regular times and come back reeking of perfume."

"It's just my aftershave," he said lamely, taking a sip of coffee.

"Oh really! When did you put on your aftershave? Just before you went out? Charles, I won't have this—tell me! Why can't you tell me the truth? *Please*, tell me!" Her eyes glared at him, yet were pleading.

He sighed. He knew he was cornered and in that moment he felt his whole world disintegrate. "Very well," he said. "You won't like this, Sylvia—but, I'm afraid I've fallen in love with Lynsey. I am so sorry."

He could see the flame leap in her eyes, yet at the same time there was a reaction of relief. "Oh, thank God!" she said, "Thank God you've told me. And thank you for telling me! Now I can come to terms with it. Charles, for ages I've been feeling sick with suspicion. I couldn't sleep and I've been having heart palpitations." She sighed. "Well, how *nice* for you! I wish *I* were in love! You were in love with me once—I think. What stopped you loving me?"

"Well, we've drifted apart." He didn't know what to say. "You never touch me anymore. Not that that mattered—I was fine—till I met Lynsey. I just couldn't help myself. I am so sorry, Sylvia."

Her eyes narrowed. "It's not just what happens, or doesn't happen, in bed, you know. You stopped touching me, putting your arms around me, in the kitchen or anywhere—the bedroom is one thing…"

"You push me away, Sylvia… or just don't respond. When I try to touch you in bed you never respond."

"Well… you're too hot in bed… I mean, your temperature. But as I said, it's not just in bed that matters… It's all the time. I'm just taken for granted!"

"I'm sorry."

He went into the sitting room with his coffee and Sylvia came in too, taking a seat on the settee near him.

"Well, you'll have to move out," she said. It was like a statement. "I'll give you a few days. I can't have you seeing another woman and staying on in this house with me."

"Yes, I understand," he said meekly. "I'll sleep in my study for the time being. Then find a flat to rent."

She nodded. "Lynsey can move in with you then." She was silent for a moment. "You know, I knew something was up as soon as you gave her your old laptop. That was the start of it, wasn't it? How long has this been going on?"

He shrugged, "A few weeks."

"A few weeks! The laptop was just the tip of the iceberg."

"So what gave the game away then?" he asked. He still wondered if she had seen what he had written on his computer, or if she had seen those pictures of Lynsey.

"Oh, all sorts of things—you've been showering more often, you've been watching your weight, taking regular walks—but most of all coming back reeking of perfume! My God, Charles, you are so naïve—and innocent!" She sighed. "You know, it's interesting—you always seem to fall for needy women, women in trouble, women who have been abused, or been addicted to alcohol! Women with unhappy backgrounds! How strange that you married me—I came from a good background, from a loving family and I've been faithful to you for 35 years. I'm obviously not bad enough, or weak enough, or miserable enough, to be rescued by your love. Well, I'm miserable enough now!"

"I'm sorry. I really am sorry."

"Oh great! That's supposed to fix everything, is it?"

"I won't argue—I know the fault is entirely on my side."

She glared for a moment at the wall across the room. "So Lynsey can leave her partner now and live with you. She can cook and wash for you instead of me."

He sighed. "She can't leave her partner just yet. Hamish is an old man—virtually an invalid, and his lungs are shot to pieces. He depends on her to cook, bath and care for him. I won't put her under any pressure. All this wasn't planned—it just happened, as the trite saying goes."

"Oh great!" she said bitterly. "So now there's someone else I have to feel sorry for!"

*   *   *

When Charles went up to his study to make his bed on the sofa-bed, he sent an email to Lynsey:

My darling Lynsey
    The worst has happened—Sylvia has tumbled to the truth and I have confessed everything to her. She

wants me out of the house ASAP. I will have to look for a council flat. Feeling really depressed and desperate—but I suppose I asked for it. She smelt your scent on me when I got back and would not let it go until I came clean and told her I am in love with you and have been seeing you.

I love you
Charles

It was not the kind of email he wanted to send her—especially after the magical time they had had a few hours earlier when they had consummated their love for each other. He kept checking his email for her reply and just before midnight it came in, short and to the point:

I hope you get this message. Can you please explain everything to me in more detail? Are you sure that you did the right thing by telling her?
Be careful.
Love, Lynsey

He replied immediately:

My dearest
I had no choice. She confronted me as soon as I got back—in the kitchen. "Why were you so long?" she said. I said I took a long walk and sheltered in a bus shelter. "You mean with another woman?" she said. She would not leave it alone. "I can smell the scent of a woman all over you—I have smelt it every time you go out—why don't you just tell me the truth?" she said. It was obvious whatever I said she knew the truth. "Just tell me the truth!" she demanded.

Eventually I gave in and said I was in love with you—that I couldn't help myself.

"Well, thank goodness you told me," she said. "And thank you for telling me." She said she has been in agony for weeks suspecting this, and been close to heart failure. "Well, it's very nice for you—but where does it leave me?" etc etc.

Lynsey, it's obvious she has known all along. "You are very innocent," she said, "and very naïve, and bad at hiding things. You've been taking showers more regularly... is Lynsey also why you've been losing weight?" Lynsey, there was no way I could have kept it all from her, believe me. She said I would have to move out—find a council flat. She will give me a few days.

Please don't let this stress you. I won't expect you to change your situation, though Sylvia said you and I are welcome to live together—but I don't think she understands that you can't just leave Hamish who is dependent on you. So please don't be upset, darling. I need you more than ever now—but this is a lot sooner than you (or I) will have expected. I will have to try and work things out. Finances are also a difficult issue because our income is so limited just now.

I will send this off in the meantime and keep you posted. I love you so much.

Charles

The next evening just before nine Charles went out for his 'walk' as usual—though this time it was without the pretence that it was for the sake of a walk, and there was no reason to conceal from Sylvia that the walk was probably with a view to seeing Lynsey again. It was, for it was another of the 'safe' nights with Hamish out, this time at the Mason's meeting. The two lovers fell into each other's arms as soon as he entered her sitting room, for this time he desperately needed her support and comfort, and reassurance, that whatever happened from now he would at least not lose her. In a sense he had put his whole life on the line for the sake of being with her—and she was worth it.

He did not plan to make love to Lynsey again, and so soon, but the stronger need he now had for her distilled into a repetition of the previous night's intimacy, this time with even greater fulfilment. Her adorable grunts as he thrust into her, with eyes closed, her long legs once again bent over and around his neck, sweetened his desire for her. "You're so strong," she smiled demurely afterwards as her arms clung round his neck. "I love you, Charrels—you've been very brave, staking so much for me."

That night, just before midnight, her email came through to his laptop:

Hello there my darling.

Oh, it was so difficult to let you go tonight. I loved every minute of being with you, but I think you already know this. I have been thinking of you and what has happened all day and, as I said to you tonight, this was going to happen and Sylvia would finally know the truth. There was never going to be a right time to tell her, but in a strange way I am glad that she now knows. I will be thinking of you every day and night and praying that you will find the strength to get through all this. Now please remember I will always be here for you and will never abandon you.

You are the man of my dreams. It has taken me almost a lifetime to find you and I will always be yours. What I said to you tonight I meant sincerely and from my heart. If I cannot spend what is left of my life with you then I will absolutely rather be on my own. There will never be a man in my life that could compare to you and I love you to bits.

You smelled wonderful and when you were inside me what a special feeling I had, like a feeling of being at one with you. I have never had such feelings for a man until I met you. When I look into your eyes I get such a feeling of real love. Sometimes it can be quite overwhelming, but in the nicest possible way. I have to keep pinching myself all the time, wondering if you are real and all of what we are going through is actually happening. It all seems like a dream, but what a wonderful reality it really is.

God bless you my love and sleep tight.

From your loving little lamb

Lynsey XXXXX

Charles replied:

My loving little lamb

I love you to bits too! Tonight was so very special for me, and it was sheer happiness being with you. Thank you, thank you, dearest girl—for I so needed your reassurance tonight. Right now I feel strong and happy to keep going ahead, secure in the knowledge of your love. What a privilege to be loved, and to be in love with, a girl of your striking beauty and gentle, sweet nature. Making love to you was sheer heaven, my darling.

Take care and God bless you—and you are the fruit of my joy. (Yes, I read today's reading in *God Calling*!)

Charles

CHAPTER TWENTY-NINE

IT WAS WEDNESDAY evening, the night of the prayer meeting, and Charles had arranged with a man with a van to collect a few pieces of his furniture the next day to take to their empty house just up the road, which was awaiting a tenant. Sylvia had agreed that he should use the house until a tenant is found, when he would have to find a flat for himself. A flat could be secured for half the rent brought in by the new house, so at the end of the day was the cheaper option.

Charles was looking forward to attending the prayer circle meeting on Wednesday as usual, especially as he knew Lynsey would be there—and Sylvia had said, when he told her about his affair with Lynsey, "Well, that's the end of the prayer meetings!" He had assumed she meant she would no longer be going, but apparently he was wrong, for as the time approached and he asked her if she was going, she said, "I might." He had already told Lynsey when he met her that morning by the lake that Sylvia wouldn't be attending anymore.

Sylvia had come home that day from her shopping with a litre bottle of Grant's whisky and had poured herself as well as Charles a home measure just before supper. "I thought we could both use some fortification," she had said. Indeed, Charles thought she was being very brave and civilised about the new development and she had even helped him to pack a few essential items to take with him to the new house. She had thoughtfully packed a box of groceries, including all the items he usually liked, ranging from fruit and Greek yoghurt to pork pies and oven chips. When she poured herself a generous second home measure of Grant's he felt a little uncomfortable. He would be leaving for the prayer meeting in half an hour, but nevertheless accepted her offer of a second drink. She went into the kitchen and came back with their glasses refreshed, with ice. He did not know what strength her drink was, but his was quite generous. He assumed she had decided not to attend the prayer meeting—thankfully.

Supper over, and he got up to put on his coat. He was surprised, and disturbed, when Sylvia joined him and put on her coat, too. He knew from experience that when she drank she was less able to maintain her sobriety than he was. The church hall was in walking distance, anyway—only 15 minutes away, so driving was not necessary. Perhaps he should change his mind, he thought, and say he wasn't going. But then Sylvia had seemed so civilised and sensible about his affair, and had clearly accepted the inevitable. She had said she would never be able to trust him again, so clearly there was no turning back.

As they walked to the church hall he consoled himself that at least he would be able to enjoy drinking in the sight of Lynsey across the table, as before. When she had her makeup on and wore her favourite scarf and pearls, she looked exquisite. But as they walked he noticed that Sylvia had dramatically increased her pace, walking with energy and determination. He almost had to break into a run to keep up with her.

"You're walking really fast tonight," he said. "We've plenty of time."

"Oh?" she said icily, "You've been walking so fast lately—you should have no trouble keeping up." Her tone was frosty and he began to have a sense of foreboding. She had had two generous home measures of whisky and she could be out of control. Perhaps he should turn back, say he'd changed his mind about attending tonight… but the thought of Lynsey there drove him on.

As they neared the hall her pace seemed to increase. She was walking with deliberate determination, like a woman with a mission. He gave up trying to keep up with her and lagged behind, walking even slower than before. She reached the door of the hall way before him, but turned to see where he was and stood there, waiting for him to catch up. His heart was in his mouth now… a sixth sense told him to turn back.

But she had entered the door while he still hesitated. He paused for a few moments, then took a deep breath and went in. Everyone was there already, seated in their usual places around the table, including Lynsey who looked puzzled and disturbed as he entered. She had been under the impression that Sylvia wasn't coming, and, as she told Charles later, when he didn't immediately follow Sylvia, she thought he wasn't coming. All the others gave them their usual friendly, welcoming greeting.

Charles removed his coat and placed it next to Lynsey's where she usually put it on the edge of the stage. Before Sylvia took her seat she glared across the table at Lynsey and said in a loud voice to her, "*Why? Why?*" Charles was unaware of this and went round the table, passing behind Sylvia where she was already seated, giving Lynsey a look with arched eyebrows that said, 'Something's up.' He sat down in his usual place next to Sylvia who immediately turned to him and said, quite loudly so that everyone could hear, "Why are you sitting here? Why aren't you sitting next to Lynsey?"

He knew then that Sylvia was out of control. "Are you going to behave yourself?" he asked under his breath.

"Oh," she said with a grimace, "who knows? I might behave myself perfectly!"

"Sylvia," he whispered, embarrassment like ice in his veins, "if you carry on like this I shall never forgive you!"

"Oh, so *I'm* the one that has to be forgiven!" she said without modulating the volume of her voice.

Everyone was giving them furtive looks, intrigued or mystified about what was happening.

"Well," Sadie said brightly, trying to set the tone for the Bible study. "Who's done their homework? Who remembers which psalm we are studying tonight? Sylvia?"

Sylvia said stridently: "I don't have a clue!"

"Well," Charles said brightly, looking at the open Bible in front of him, trying to restore normality to the situation, "it's right here in front of us. Psalm 103?"

"Go on!" Sylvia said belligerently to him, "Go and sit next to that woman! That's where you want to be!"

Everyone was now staring at the two of them, and glancing at Lynsey who looked alarmed.

Charles had broken out in a cold sweat. There was only one thing for it—to diffuse the situation, if only for Lynsey's sake. He stood up and walked to where his coat was. He picked it up and said to everyone present, "I'm sorry—but I'm not feeling very well." With that he made for the door and went into the night.

He was halfway along the narrow pavement that went past the church towards his estate when he heard a woman's voice calling from behind: "Charrels! Charrels!"

He turned round, puzzled, and didn't recognise her for a moment—a stylish woman carrying her coat running after him. Then his heart missed a beat as he realised it was Lynsey. It was a moment he would cherish for the rest of his life and never forget. In the midst of his misery there was this angel of light running towards him and calling his name.

She caught up to him, panting. "Charrels... I dinna want you to leave like that... I said I would go and see if you're alright. Sadie asked me if I was comin' back and I said I dinna ken. When I got up to go out Sylvia gave me an angry look."

He embraced her there and then, very tightly. He said: "On no account go back, Lynsey. I am so thrilled that you came out after me. Sylvia is out of control—she has had two double whiskies."

"Och, ye mean she's drunk! No way am I goin' back in there then. Ye canna argue with a drunk woman! Of all people I ken that! It would be a pointless shouting match."

"I've seen her like this before, Lynsey. She doesn't hold her drink very well. But I think she must have planned this—letting off a bomb and leaving us to deal with the fallout. I had a bad feeling about this when we were walking down. Damn! I should have turned back... I should have seen it coming. She probably drank on purpose to give her the Dutch courage, like a suicide bomber."

"Where will we go now, Charrels? I canna go back to Hamish just yet—it's too early."

"Just keep walking. Well go to my house and I'll use the car to take you back. We can find a car park somewhere and sit in the car and talk, to pass the time until the usual time you get back."

They walked to the house and he collected the key to the car and they drove to the local Co-op where they sat in the car park to while away the time. He kept the engine running to keep the interior of the car warm.

He smiled. "I've had a couple of whiskies myself—all I need now is to be caught for drunk-driving."

"Oh Lord, Charrels, do be careful!"

He held her hand. "I'm so sorry I brought this on you, Lynsey. I'm the guilty party. You came to the church seeking help as an alcoholic—and got me, a married man that fell in love with you! But I'm not a wolf in sheep's clothing, you know, like that man in the AA meetings—I'm just a silly old goat!"

"A goat that I love," she giggled. "Oh heck, what a night! This will set all the tongues wagging. There's nothing that the Kennoway women love more than a good scandal! It will be goin' round all the pubs. But you can be sure of one thing, Charrels—it's no' you they'll blame, it will be me. I can just

213

hear them: 'That scarlet woman! She has misled a married man! I telt you she's a real tart!' Do you ken what I mean, Charrels—me with my red lipstick and all!"

He laughed. "Oh my dear, you are funny!"

She laughed. "This is nervous laughter, Charrels!" she said. "Oh my Lord, what a night, eh!"

"But you realise we can't go back to the church or the prayer circle anymore. I'm afraid I won't be going in future. I'll have to find a new church."

She laughed again. "Not prepared to face the music, eh? Well, if you're not going, there's no way I'm going."

"In any case, Lynsey, I'm moving out of the house tomorrow—to our other house, until a tenant is found for it. At least in the meantime we can meet there, whenever you're free to do so. As for me—well, I'm free for you to come whenever you wish now." He smiled at her. "And Lynsey, I want you to know it was a wonderful sight to see you running after me! And to hear you call my name! You don't know how much that means to me. I will always treasure the vision of you calling my name and running towards me, carrying your coat! You didn't even wait to put on your coat!"

"I couldna let you go alone, Charrels—I do care for you. I love you and will always stand by you."

He leant over and kissed her cheek. "Right now you're the only person in the world that cares for me, my love."

"How could I no'?" They were squeezing each other's hands. "You have turned your back on your whole life fur me. Oh Charrels, what have I done, eh!"

"You have done nothing, my love. I just love you—that's all. The rest was just inevitable."

Charles dropped Lynsey off near her house at the usual time she got home, just round the corner from the front door, in case Hamish was watching out for her—for he would have noticed she was not being dropped by Sadie's BMW.

When he reached his house he parked the car in the driveway and went inside, to find that Sylvia had not yet arrived home. He suspected that Sadie would bring her home, as she usually offered her and Charles a lift at the close of the meeting. Sure enough, before long Charles saw Sadie's BMW pull up in the street outside the front door. He expected Sylvia to come in, but she didn't. In fact, twenty minutes went by and she was still there, inside the car, no doubt 'blethering' about him to Sadie, to use a word Lynsey might use.

After half an hour went by Charles decided to go out to tell Sadie that he had seen Lynsey safely home—since Sadie normally took her home and he didn't want her phoning Lynsey's house to see if she had turned up. He went out and stood outside the driver's door of the BMW. The window slid open and Charles said, "Just wanted you to know that I saw Lynsey safely back home, so no need to worry about her."

Sadie said in a strident schoolteacher's voice: "Tell me, Charles, do you *really* think you've done the right thing?"

Charles half expected that question. "I'm sorry," he said, "I do not wish to talk about it."

"Oh, I'm sorry, but I think you should!" Sadie retorted.

"Goodnight," Charles said decisively and walked back into the house, ending any attempt on her part to draw him out. She was a deacon so maybe she felt it was part of her business, he thought. By now all the sympathy—and quite rightly too, he thought—would have flowed towards poor Sylvia, whose suffering had been plainly and very dramatically revealed to the entire prayer circle. It had been like a scene out of East Enders, he thought—no doubt they would all be brimming over with what they had witnessed by now and eagerly replaying the scene to their spouses or partners.

Eventually Sylvia came back into the house alone. "Well," she said, now apparently quite sober but unrepentant, "you'll be interested to know that you have been rumbled! It seems everyone in the prayer circle, and the church, too, have been well aware of your affair for some time."

He sighed. "In any case, you've made sure I'll never be able to show my face in church or in the prayer circle again. And the same applies to Lynsey. Well done, Sylvia. Your bomb went off well. Somehow we'll have to live with the fallout now."

It was almost consolation to him that he would be moving out the next day. By doing what she had done, Sylvia had in effect widened the distance between the two of them and now he was eager to get out from under her feet.

Later that night Charles was in his study, watching out for Lynsey's email. At last it came through:

Hello my darling
   I have just read your e-mail and earlier ones as well.
   Please try to stay strong and focussed, although I know the road ahead is going to be tough. You know that I love you and will always be here for you. I will be right by your side no matter what and will support you through whatever happens next—God forbid. What a night! I do not think it could get any worse— unless Sylvia decides to hire a hit man and have me bumped off. I will be thinking about going to the prayer meeting next week and if I will be at the church on Sunday. But I would rather go to a church that you decide on and be with you. I will leave it to you to decide which one.
   I hope that you are alright tonight and I cannot stop thinking about you. I want to be where you are and spend as much time as I can with you. I will not allow you to be alone in the house you are moving to all the time. I adore you and I know I will never meet

a man like you again. Anyway, I just could not be unfaithful to you—I love you too much and respect you as well. You know the following song—when the going gets tough, the tough gets going.

God bless you and take care. Sleep tight my love.
From your loving little lamb and biggest fan.

Charles immediately sent off a reply:

Oh I do love you my lamb! So good to find your email. You know what, the toughness ahead I can take if I get emails like this! i.e. knowing you are there and love me—you are worth fighting for. No more news to give you—I told Sylvia I am going to bed early so I have closed my study door. I really feel I have lost a lot of respect for her tonight. I have been looking on AutoTrader for good 2nd hand cars. If I am to attend a church further away I will need a car—and I could take you as well, though this might be awkward explaining to Hamish why you are being taxied to a church further away! But we will work something out. After Sadie's attitude to me tonight I don't think I want to stomach sitting in the same church—she addressed me like a schoolteacher to a naughty child! I know my own mind.

God bless you, the sweetest girl I know!
Charles

As he tried to get to sleep on the sofa-bed in his study that night, the thought went through his head: 'I have thrown away the gold for the dross.' But then he realised, no, Lynsey was by no means dross! Had the Lord not put it in his heart to love her—made him fall in love with her, a working class Scots girl enchained by alcoholism, to bring him down, to smash his pride, to let him know that He the Lord had died for the least of his children? The Lord had brought him down, into the potter's field with its broken shards of clay, to know the true nature of God's unconditional love. Charles had despised these people, looked down on them in their council houses, yet here he was, one of them, cuddling to his heart the dearest treasure he ever had, a broken despised pot that had become more precious to him than gold.

PART THREE

CHAPTER THIRTY

Lynsey Anne McCann

WHEN CHARLES moved out of the marital home at 2 p.m. the following day, he had no concept of the extent of the consequences his love affair with Lynsey would have. At first there was a touch of adventure about it. At least it would mean he could go out at will and meet Lynsey whenever she was free to meet him—there would no longer be the need of the pretext of taking a walk. Admittedly his heart was in his mouth when he helped the van man he had engaged to manhandle the sofa bed out of his study and into an upstairs bedroom at the new house. At the forefront of his mind was the excitement of being with Lynsey, even making love to her in his own premises and not in another man's house. The truth is, he had crossed the Rubicon. With this move there was no going back. His past life, the devotion of a faithful wife, the love and respect of his daughters and sons, was forever irretrievable. But all this would only sink in later.

That Lynsey was aware of the enormous significance of his move was clear from the encouragement she gave him in her email which he received in the morning. "I know today is going to be a strange and difficult one," she wrote, "especially when 2 p.m. comes around. Please try not to worry and keep your chin up." He was touched and his resolve was strengthened by her words: "The thought of not seeing you again would devastate me." He could not let her down now and focussed on the prospect of spending a short while with her at the new house that very evening. It was a Guild night in the church hall, and she said she would pretend to Hamish that she was going to the Guild meeting, whereas in fact she would be meeting Charles near the bus stop where they had accidentally met before, and from there they would walk up to the new house to be together for the duration of the Guild meeting—about two hours in all. "Anyway," she wrote, "I hope you get on okay this afternoon and I am so looking forward to seeing you tonight. I love you—Your great big beautiful doll."

It was strange, a new sensation, cuddling up to Lynsey in his own premises. The house, a modern large house with four bedrooms, was eerily empty with just his sofa-bed in one of the bedrooms upstairs, with a table and his laptop in a room below. Lynsey was dressed for the Guild meeting, in tights under her skirt, and with full makeup. With her long flowing hair she looked gorgeous, her hair giving her face a soft look. She wore a string of pearls that looped gracefully just above the slight show of her cleavage. They kept just the one light on in the upstairs hall, so they sat together in the dim light that came through the open door, cuddling together. They did not make love but enjoyed the gentle closeness, Lynsey's head resting on his chest while he played with her hair—the hair he had so stealthily touched in greeting each Wednesday as he walked by her after entering the hall on prayer meeting nights.

Making love was not an option with her tights in place—getting them down would spoil the romantic mood, he thought. But they indulged in long tender kisses instead until he had altogether worn away her lipstick with his lips. She laughed when she saw her lipstick on his lips. But she had come prepared for that, having brought with her, in her handbag, a stick of lipstick to reapply the colour to her lips before she went back to Hamish. Where there was a will, he thought, there was a way, even if it called for a devious way! He wondered about the kind of salutary effect he was having on this vulnerable lady who hadn't touched a drop of alcohol for well-nigh five months now. Instead, they had both become intoxicated with each other, drinking in their love for each other.

The rest of the evening was spent in pleasurable talk. He liked to draw her out, questioning her about her memories of childhood or memories of her busy life when she was a PA, just to hear her pretty patter, or 'blethering', as she called it, laughing in her recollections. When she became excited with her 'blethering' she went out of phase for Charles, who heard the music of her voice without registering the sense of it. She would laugh at her own punch line and he would laugh with her because she was laughing and happy, though he might have totally failed to catch the sense of her words because if her unfamiliar accent. He just loved her so much that the mere fact that she laughed would make him laugh with her. Funny though, he thought, that when she wrote, whether in her testimony or her emails, she wrote, as it were, in perfect English with no trace of accent. When she spoke it was like seeing through an exquisite stained glass window, for you were enchanted by the opaque inflections of light and colour that interrupted and dazzled the view; but when she wrote you saw clearly, into the sunlit fields and vistas beyond the clear glass of her style. Her verbal and written styles were completely different forms of language, he thought, to the unspoken language of love, for then her dancing eyes connected to his, when he made love to her, a connection that made the lovemaking all the more exquisite.

When the two hours were up he walked back with her, only turning back when she was close to her house. Their lives together, it seemed to him, were full of partings. But he had acquired his own dongle for his laptop in the new house, and so was able to receive her late night email:

My darling Charles

I loved seeing you tonight and felt so comfortable and at home with you. I thought you seemed much more relaxed and at ease with yourself. It is a lovely house and as the days go by I am sure you will be able to get things sorted that need it. I do not want you to get lonely and depressed—let's face it, what man would if they had me!! I cannot describe the way I feel when you put your arms around me and squeeze me tightly. I could have fallen asleep that way tonight. I am trying to tell you that for someone like me to feel this way about a man, means that I trust you wholeheartedly and really love you to bits. Yes, I am on your side and never forget this. If no one else wants to give you a bit of support, then you will get it from me unconditionally. I know it is difficult for you to let me go at night, but I assure you I feel the same when I have to say goodnight. I just don't want to.

I will find a way to see you as much as I can and I will send you an e-mail at night always. I know you have said that you will wait for me and just knowing this makes me feel so happy. I am very aware that our arrangements cannot go on like this forever and I need you to know that I will be working hard to get things sorted at my end. You know, Charles, the step you have taken today has been enormous and I admire your courage and conviction to carry this out. It takes a very strong person to be able to do this and you certainly are one. You said tonight that you are very proud of me, but I am so proud of you. I thank God for being blessed that He has guided me to be an important part of your life now. You are not alone; we will both be with you always to look out for you and to help guide you whenever you need it.

I think of you all the time and I will look out for you in the morning.

God bless you. I love you with all my heart and soul.

Love, Lynsey XXXXX

Charles hugged those words to his heart as he fell asleep, curled up on the sofa-bed in the empty house that night: she saying that she admired his courage and convictions to carry out that devastating step of leaving his family for her was a solace to him. Was he a strong person to have done so, or just a poor weak akratic soul that had allowed himself to fall in love and so just let events take their own course? The step he had taken had certainly been devastating—and bless Lynsey's little cotton socks, he thought, for saying he had been brave. Whether he had been brave or just a poor weak fool, only time would tell.

CHAPTER THIRTY-ONE

CHARLES stood by the iron railings next to the Denhead Pond watching the swans race across the water. With the approaching spring they seemed to become more energetic, rushing from one side of the small lake to the other. Charles wondered at the loud energetic flapping of their large wings as they arrowed across the water, necks stretched forward, and lifted majestically into the air only to sink back to the surface in a landing that furrowed the water causing a mighty bow wave as they came to rest at the far end. He turned to see Lynsey approaching with the trailing, snuffling Staffordshire Bull Terrier lumbering behind, her happy smile beaming her greeting ahead of her. It was always a joy to see her, and this time it was a relief, too, after the upheaval of his ejection from the marital home. She was all he had now, all he had to drive him on in his new-found life of isolation, for his existence in the near empty house was little more than the life of a hermit— and even that would be taken away from him when a tenant was found to occupy the house. He had declared himself homeless in his application for a council flat so the prospect was bleak to say the least.

These morning meetings with Lynsey had become a daily routine, and were now a lifeline for him.

"Are ye alright, Charrels?" she said, concern breaking through her smile.

"I can't deny a feeling of being shell-shocked, Lynsey," he said. "I hardly expected our relationship to be brought to a head so quickly, like this. I think I was just so wrapped up with being in love with you, and in the delight of finding you in love with me—I never thought seriously about the consequences. I just thought it was happening for a reason."

Though it was approaching the first day of spring in March, the weather was wet and windy, and Lynsey wore the hood of her coat over her head. It made him think of Little Red Riding Hood though the hood was black, not red. It framed her piquant face which took on a serious look.

"Do ye think you might go back to Sylvia, Charrels?" she said.

"I can't go back now," he said. "She said she would never trust me again." He looked out at the swans as a new pair raced flapping across the water, then fell back in a mighty furrow. "For better or worse, my life has taken a new direction."

"Do you want to go in the new direction, Charrels?" she asked, and added, "With me?"

"Of course I do, my love," he said, still gazing at the swans.

"Charrels, *look* at me," she said, in earnest. "Do you *want* a new life with me by your side? Tell me truthfully."

He turned and looked into her brown eyes and saw a touch of anxiety. His heart leapt towards her and he answered looking fully into her eyes. "My darling, I don't know why you are in love with me, but I know I am in love with you. You are my life and reason for living now. That's what's driving me ahead, living with the woman I love. It's the sudden shock of my new situation that makes me look back, aware of what I've lost—but I will now look to you, steadfastly, as my future. I love you, Lynsey Anne McCann."

Her eyes softened. "Then you have my assurance that I am here for you, by your side. I will no' let you doon. I will wurk hard at freeing myself for you. Just give me time. You'll no' get rid of me that easily now, Charrels Haddington. Do you ken, I keep remembering what you said in *Sunset Stirrings*, that I am not dross but precious gold? Do y'ken how often I have re-read that paragraph? It really touched me, Charrels, and as long as you feel that way about me, I am yours forever, eh.

And remember, there is only one reason why I will let you go—if you ask me to."

"Well, that's not going to happen," he said with a touch of defiance. Then he sighed. "Lynsey, how are we going to see each other now? Apart from these morning meetings and the nights when Hamish is at the pub."

"Well, I have some ideas…," she said hesitantly.

"You could still—for a while—pretend to be going to church or the prayer circle, and then secretly meet up with me."

She smiled. "That's precisely what I had in mind, eh? If you are happy with that?" she added with that sidelong glance of hers.

So instead of going to church on Sunday as usual, they arranged to meet at the bus stop and walked to his house together, hoping Sadie didn't see them walking up the hill. It was a different kind of worship they enjoyed that Sunday morning, not just holding hands furtively but embracing without restraint sitting together on Charles's sofa-bed in his private little bedroom that, in the words of John Donne, made "one little room an everywhere." Charles was mindful that just a few hundred yards away the people were engaged in real worship, in the church, and for this reason he resisted the temptation to pull down Lynsey's tights which, he joked, were like armour plating. It was the Lord's Day and a day for quiet contemplation, perhaps, but Charles's quiet contemplation was relishing the exquisite ecstasy of Lynsey's sensuous and volatile lips as he drank in her kisses. He needed her all the more now that he was banished from his old home and his family. Lynsey was all he had, now, of family and in her he found his comfort.

Walking back after parting from Lynsey on Sunday morning, he saw Sadie's sad crouched figure approaching in the distance, returning from the church service, her handbag nearly touching the ground as she advanced, and he did an abrupt about-turn and chose a different route back to his house. Had she seen him? Still freshly sated with Lynsey's love, he had no stomach for Sadie's bitter self-righteous disapproval.

The times between their meetings dragged and he busied himself as much as he could editing the few books that authors had sent him. It was his job to keep the pot boiling, not just for himself but for Sylvia too, for their finances were still tied together. He never failed to spend time with Lynsey on those 'safe' evenings at her house—or rather, Hamish's house, when Hamish was out at the pub. Fortunately Hamish's routine of going out to drink with his mates was as regular as clockwork. Those times alone were oases of love, and encouragement in his new, very lonely path. He was now swimming upstream, like a salmon, in the face of the opposition or the currents of disapproval from his family, for he received no support from them who only saw the injury done to Sylvia, the faithful and pious wife. It was understandable, he thought, and he was pleased that she was receiving the support she needed, not only from his family, his sons and daughters, but from the prayer circle—for in Sadie Sylvia had clearly found a new and strong ally who Charles now perceived as a powerful enemy, one who threatened to expose his 'sordid' affair with a vulnerable member of the church, a woman who as an alcoholic had come to the church in all her innocence for succour and help. In his 'salmon' struggle against the tide of opposition, Charles felt he was swimming to his inevitable demise—or was it to lay the eggs of a new beginning, to give birth to a new life with Lynsey? At 71, this seemed unlikely, and he wondered how long he could muster the strength to keep swimming upstream.

What kept him going in this struggle were the nightly emails he received from Lynsey, which came in like clockwork every might just before midnight. They were like the refreshing rain to his parched soul.

*   *   *

Lynsey's email to Charles:

My darling Charles

Making love with you tonight was wonderful. It felt so right, even knowing that what we were doing was probably so wrong. I would never be able to have those same feelings with someone else. You have pushed all the right buttons Charles and having you inside me made me feel as if you are the one who should be there. I cannot be with anyone else now, especially in the physical sense. You felt so different inside me tonight and I could really feel you, it was bliss. Oh you big bugger!! What have you done to me? I am all topsy-turvy and you are inside my head all the time. Every time I see you I can feel a great big smile coming on my face and it actually feels as if there are butterflies in my stomach.

I know that I will never lose these feelings for you and I never will.

Now please look after yourself. I am thinking of you always and I know there is a strong bond between us now. I will always be in love with you and I never want you to forget this.

God bless you my love, sleep tight and sweet dreams. I will look forward to seeing you in the morning, but especially at night when I will allow you to ravish me.

Your loving little lamb, Lynsey, XXXX

*   *   *

Charles and Lynsey had agreed to meet up in lieu of going to the prayer circle on Wednesday evening. Hamish, of course would be under the impression that she was going to the prayer circle as usual so wouldn't suspect anything untoward. First they met as usual in the morning at the Denhead Pond and she asked him how she could stop Sadie coming to pick her up as usual.

"Surely she won't anyway," Charles said, "after what happened last week?"

"But she might," Lynsey said, "and then I would be obliged to go with her; and I have already told Hamish she wouldna be comin' because she's in Ireland seeing her relatives, like she did before. Hamish will wonder what's happening and smell a rat—you ken what I mean? And I dinna ken her telephone number so I canna phone her to tell her I'm no' comin'."

"Tell you what," Charles said, "I'll send Sadie an email. I'll tell her you're not going and not to pick you up. If she does she'll spoil our evening together—and you did say I could ravish you!"

She laughed. "Aye, yer an awfy man, Charrels—but I love yer!"

When he got back to his house Charles duly sent Sadie an email:

Dear Sadie

Lynsey has asked me to let you know she will not be attending the prayer circle tonight so there is no need for you to pick her up. She would phone you but does not have your telephone number.

Charles

He was shocked to receive her forthright reply:

Under the circumstances I think this is right but we are very concerned for her. What you are doing is WRONG and you know it. What do you think God thinks about this? He certainly won't be pleased no matter how you justify it. Sadie.

He was even more disturbed to receive her follow-up comment a moment later:

I presume you are not coming either hopefully.

It was like a slap in the face. This was the woman who, as a young girl, had told the Lord she would give her life to him if He helped her find her lost ring in the waves! Was this what one became when giving one's life to the Lord—an outspoken judgemental thrower of stones?

Charles sent an email to Lynsey before he left to meet her, though he realised she would be unlikely to receive it before the end of the evening when she usually checked her emails:

My darling

Nearly time to leave to meet you tonight—so looking forward to it. I wanted to say how sweet you are to assure me of your love at the lake this morning, because I have been feeling very apprehensive, also more aware than before of danger, to you, my love. Beware of Sadie—I believe she has a vicious streak, judging from the responses I received from her: no sign of Christian love there whatsoever. Perhaps she sees herself in the role of the prophet Nathan, one whose mission is to accuse. I will never return to the local church now, but it doesn't mean you can't. But it is clear that "they" (Sadie's words) are very "concerned" for you—in other words they are not seeing you as the scarlet woman but the victim of me. So you have no reason to feel guilty.

As for me—well, I just cannot help loving you and being in love with you. See you later my darling!

Charles

He was at the meeting place near the bus shelter in good time, anxiously awaiting Lynsey's arrival at the agreed time of 7 p.m., so they could walk up to the new house together where they had planned to make love. "In the evening I will let you ravish me," she had joked in her email to him. It was all the more reason to look forward to the evening, though it was sufficient bliss just to be in her company.

His anguish when she did not arrive by quarter past seven was acute. He walked up the pavement along which she would approach, hoping to see her round the corner at any moment. He reached the corner and looked along it, in sight of her house, and there was no sign of her. He had an ominous feeling that something had gone wrong. Had Sadie called on her after all and hijacked her into going to the prayer circle?

He walked back down the road towards the bus shelter, to kill time, but frequently glanced back to see if she was approaching. Still there was no sign of her. The hollow feeling in his stomach told him she was not coming, that he might as well walk back home. But the thought of giving up depressed him even further, for it meant giving up hope. At half past he knew that Sadie had interfered. "That bloody woman!" he cursed. He felt sick in the pit of his stomach with disappointment. He looked up along the empty road again, then went to sit inside the bus shelter and broke down. He held his head in his hands and cried in great big sobs that racked his body. It was as though he would never see her again. "Oh Lord," he cried, "give me a miracle, please—let her appear!"

He got control of himself, stood up and went out of the bus shelter and looked once more up the road. There was no-one there. Dejectedly, he turned and took the first steps back. But his dejection was overbearing and he turned once more to look back.

He thought his heart would burst with relief when he saw a figure in the distance running towards him, her long hair flowing behind her.

It was Lynsey!

He breathed a prayer: "Oh thank you, Lord, thank you!"

*   *   *

Lynsey knew she was hopelessly in love. She was due to meet Charles at 7 p.m. on Wednesday night at their usual meeting place. She had told Hamish she was going to the Prayer Circle as usual and that Sadie would not be picking her up as she was going to Ireland for the next two weeks, so she would be walking to the church hall. Hamish seemed okay with this.

However, just five minutes before Lynsey was due to leave there was a sudden knock at the front door. Lynsey darted to the front window to see who it was. Oh, my God, she thought, it was Sadie! Lynsey had to think quickly and told Hamish who it was and that Sadie must have had a change of plan. When Lynsey answered the door, Sadie blurted out in a loud voice: "Lynsey, we need to talk!" At that moment Sadie tried to push her way into the house but Lynsey flung on her coat and said, "Hamish, I'm away now, I'll see you later!" Both Lynsey and Sadie got into the parked BMW and drove off.

Sadie parked her car just before she arrived at Fiona's house. Sadie turned round and stared at Lynsey and in a strident schoolteacher's voice said, "Lynsey, what on earth is going on? I've had a long talk with Sylvia who tells me that

Charles has been having an affair with you. I just want to hear *your* side of the story and if this is true!"

Lynsey looked straight at Sadie. "Aye, it is," she said.

"Och, Lynsey!" barked Sadie. "Do you know what you have done? And not only that, poor Sylvia is distraught at what has happened."

At that moment Lynsey felt terribly sorry that she had hurt Sylvia and told Sadie she had not planned for this to happen. "It just did and I canna explain why. But what's done is done, eh?"

"But you can undo it, Lynsey, and repent! You know, we all suspected something was going on. You two were seen holding hands in church—and someone said Charles even touched your leg! Can you imagine that—in church!"

"I ken," Lynsey giggled, "it was wonderful!"

Sadie gasped. "Oh Lynsey, really!" She shook her head. "And don't think everyone didn't notice Charles touching your hair when he walked into the prayer meetings! And then the way you two always met up at the cupboard in the kitchen putting back the Bibles. Och Lynsey, how *could* you? But you are very vulnerable! Charles is nothing more than a wolf in sheep's clothing, taking advantage of you. Believe me he will abandon you when he has had what he wants. You do realise he's just after one thing, don't you?"

"I can take care of mesel'!" Lynsey protested. "I'm no' vulnerable. I am a lot stronger than everyone thinks, Sadie!" Lynsey was becoming increasingly annoyed by Sadie's bullying and patronising attitude. All she wanted to do was get out of the car and find Charles. He must be distraught by now, thinking she wasn't coming.

Sadie shrugged and sighed, as if Lynsey was beyond redemption. "He is an *old man*, Lynsey! And you are a lovely woman! Don't throw your life away on the likes of him!"

Sadie went on to say that Sylvia had told her Charles had confessed to the affair and that he was in love with her, Lynsey. Sylvia had informed Charles that she could not live under the same roof as him if he loved another woman. Charles would have to move out. Sadie then asked Lynsey in an aggressive voice, "Do you love Charles, Lynsey?"

"I do," Lynsey said, "I canna lie—I really do, Sadie."

"Well, tell me—have you two had sexual intercourse yet?"

Lynsey was shocked by the blunt question. It was none of her business, anyway. "We havna reached that point in our relationship," she lied. It was a black lie, but it was none of her damn business, she thought.

"Well, thank goodness for that!" Sadie said.

"Anyway," Lynsey said, piqued by Sadie's insensitive probing, "It's no' any of yer business, eh! Even if yer are a deacon! Yer no' *my* deacon, nor my mither. What I do with my life is my choice, no' yours, eh!"

Sadie looked completely bemused by this answer and went on to tell Lynsey that Sylvia had confided in her and had told her that Charles was a selfish man who always liked to get his own way and that she was frightened of him.

"Sylvia told me that you had better watch out, Lynsey, as Charles cannot be trusted. He has simply taken advantage of you. Sylvia also said Charles is a wolf in sheep's clothing—you have no idea what you're getting into!"

Sadie softened her voice and tried to reason with Lynsey. "All of us in the prayer circle are extremely concerned for you, Lynsey. Really, you should end this affair straight away, for your own sake, if not just for Sylvia's sake. It's not right, Lynsey—you know it's wrong."

Lynsey looked at Sadie with growing impatience. "The affair, as ye call it, is between me, Charles and Sylvia, and has nothing to do with you or anyone else. You would be better not to get involved in this, Sadie! I'm my own person, ken, and I ken my own mind! Dinna get involved!"

"I *am* involved!" Sadie said with an outburst of anger. "It's too late—I'm already involved. I am a Deacon of the Church! Lynsey, you must be out of your mind getting involved with an old man, and one who is an ex-professor at that! Don't think I haven't seen him scuttling about at night to see you!"

Lynsey sighed. "Sadie, you have him all wrong—he is gentle and kind. No man has ever loved me for myself and he makes me feel good about myself."

"Oh!" shouted Sadie. "Don't you realise that Charles thinks he is much better than anyone else and that he is only playing with you for a while?" She paused and gave Lynsey a sympathetic look, as one would to a naughty child. "Lynsey my dear, he will go back to his wife and leave you in the lurch once he's had his fling with you."

"I told you," Lynsey replied belligerently, "this is none of your business. I love him and what's done is done, eh!"

Sadie screeched in a high pitched voice: "*God did not mean for the two of you to get together!* In fact, God is very *angry* with you both! And you can take it from me, and from all of us in the prayer circle, that you are not welcome to come back to the prayer circle—unless you end this sordid affair with Charles! Then, when you are repentant, you can come back again."

Lynsey looked at Sadie and thought to herself, my goodness, so this is what a good Christian is like! Surely her new position of Deacon has absolutely gone straight to her head! Lynsey could not believe Sadie was acting on behalf of the whole group. On the contrary, she was scaremongering about Charles and trying to put her off him. But her strategy failed to work and Lynsey's resolve had grown even stronger.

"But just think, Lynsey," Sadie persisted. "Don't you think he will do to you what he has done to Sylvia, leave you for another woman?"

Lynsey gave a wry smile. "It will no' happen—I'll have my finger on his pulse, eh. I ken how to keep a man, Sadie. There's a reason why he's wanderin' now, ken? He's no' gettin' what a man needs, eh? He is not being satisfied. I ken what he's been living with. Believe me—I ken how to make him satisfied, and addicted tae me. I ken how to turn a man on, eh!"

"Hymph!" Sadie smirked, "Sounds like you *have* slept with him!"

Lynsey gave her a sideling smile. "Well, I'll thank you for your concern, Sadie," she said, opening the door of the car prior to getting out. "Charrels and I will deal with the situation ourselves, eh? And that means without any intervention from other people, you included."

Sadie smiled at Lynsey and put her hand on her arm. "Everyone in the church and at the prayer circle is very worried about you, Lynsey, and they only want what is best for you." She sighed. "Lynsey, as I said, you are still very vulnerable as a recovering alcoholic and don't really know what you are getting involved in. Please look after yourself and do what is right for everybody concerned and end this sordid little affair."

Lynsey smiled at Sadie. "Goodnight Sadie, and please take care."

"I suppose you're on your way now to meet Charles?" Sadie asked.

"Yes," Lynsey said with a defiant look.

"Oh, Lynsey, do take care—he is an intellectual. What do the two of you have in common?"

"Goodnight, Sadie," Lynsey said and walked away.

That last statement rang in her ears. What did Sadie mean, saying Charles was an intellectual and they had nothing in common? Was she implying she, Lynsey, was a simpleton, or just a common Scots girl? The implication angered her and made her step more determinedly to meet Charles, who must have been wondering what had delayed her. Please God, she thought, let him still be there at the bus shelter.

*   *   *

Lynsey's email to Charles:

Hello my darling Charles.

I have just been reading the two emails you forwarded from Sadie. The one about her wondering if you are not going to the meeting HOPEFULLY, is very nasty and certainly not Christian behaviour. Oh, and by the way Charles, I certainly do not need to be looked after by Sadie and the prayer circle. I can and am able to look out for myself. When I got home and let Hamish know that I will not be attending the Prayer Circle, he was okay about it and said that it is up to me what church and group I attend.

Charles, I need you to know that I am in love with you and will be right at your side when you need me. I am doing my best to protect us from any more slander and will not stop seeing you unless you want me to. I hope this will not be the case. I know that you are frightened and I do not blame you, so am I. Keep your chin up and remember I think you are a wonderful, very intellectual and kind person. I am not frightened of you and am not prepared to listen to any more nasty comments about you. Sadie has not succeeded in putting me off you; if anything, she has made my resolve much stronger.

Charles, I am comfortable with you and love you inside me and I just cannot give my flower to another man. Please believe me, what I am saying I mean from my heart. I will never meet anyone like you and you cannot blame me for wanting you to be an important part in the rest of my life.

I will love you forever my darling and God bless you, sleep tight and sweet dreams (preferably of me of course)!

Your loving little lamb, Lynsey XXXXX.

P.S. Och Charles, you naughty boy, why could you not just have shagged Sadie, put her out of her misery, then none of this would have happened!

*   *   *

Lynsey to Charles:

Good evening Dr Haddington. Roughly translated this means 'My darling Charles, I hope the rest of your day has been good.'

It always puts a great big smile on my face when I see you at the Denhead Pond in the mornings. I would not change this for the world. I have been thinking about you all day, as usual, and singing to myself as well. Please try not to worry about all the nasty things that are being said about us. I do not believe them anyway. Nothing and no one will change the way I feel about you, especially the love I have for you. You said to me the other night that I was yours—you know that is absolutely true and you could not have put things any better. Always and forever my love, no matter what.

My heart is yours now and that is something I have never said to another man in my life. I cannot wait until the next time we are alone together and I can feel your lovely strong arms holding me tightly. What a feeling that is—the warmth and security is second to none.

From your loving little lamb, Lynsey XXXXX

*　　*　　*

Charles to Lynsey:

My darling Lynsey Lamb

Two emails from you—what a bonus! It was a hard day for me. I felt a little depressed—I suppose the strangeness of this new turn of events was getting to me; but it made me realise how much more I need you now. When I was with you by the Denhead Pond all my uneasiness or unsettledness evaporated, and I was happy—you're like food to me now for you nourish my spirit, which assures me that all this angst at the moment is worthwhile.

I am so privileged and overjoyed that nothing will change the way you feel about me, dearest. That means everything to me. It's not just making love to you that's important—it's just the joy of being close to you, near you. Tonight around eight I took a walk and went close to your house, as far as the Chinese takeaway (no I didn't buy another meal!) just to look at the unlit windows and know that you were there inside, somewhere—and probably thinking of me as I was thinking of you! (I really have you under my skin, haven't I?) Just walking by you and touching your hair when coming into the prayer circle used to give me a thrill, or touching your hand when returning the Bibles to the cupboard! Oh my goodness Lynsey, I am so totally addicted to you! I can just stare into your eyes for ages, and when I hold you it's like I never want to let you go. I used to drink in your eyes when next to you in church, and those stolen moments of holding your hand and feeling your fingers squeezing back—oh Lynsey, you are so precious to me! I am such a wicked Prodigal Husband for straying, falling for another woman—but I cannot imagine how any man could have resisted you. And you know what? You're getting more beautiful, and lovelier, every day. It's like you're blossoming into a new and superlative woman.

Here's a sentence from what I wrote a while ago: "Her verbal and written styles were a completely different form of language, he thought, to the unspoken language of love, for her dancing eyes, when he made love to her, made the lovemaking all the more exquisite."

So your heart is mine, Lynsey? Well, you have mine in exchange. I will press forward in the secure knowledge that I have your heart, even if, as Sadie says, I am an old man. (Which makes her ancient.)

I love holding you tight because it is wonderful having you in my arms. That feeling is second to none—apart from being inside you!

Bless you my darling—and I love it when you call me darling!

I love you—Charles

* * *

Lynsey to Charles:

My darling Charles

It was so good to see you at the Denhead Pond this morning. Every time I see you I feel myself light up and all I want to do is throw my arms around you, give you a great big hug and a kiss. You asked me this morning, "What do you see in me?" What I see in you is a gentle, kind and loving human being. A person who has been needing the company of a woman (that woman being me, of course!), both in the physical and mental sense. A woman who is able to love you the same way you love me. I can tell you that it is a wonderful experience to be in a position to bond with a man, not just any man, the way I have with you. I love the posh and mannerable side of you and the way you laugh at me when I keep telling you my ridiculous jokes. I always seem to talk too much when I am with you. Thank you Charles for guiding me to trust you. You already know that I do not really trust men, but you have somehow managed to gain my complete trust. Now that is a miracle.

Stay strong and focussed, my darling. I already know how difficult this is for you having been in that position myself. I know you feel desperate, lonely and it seems as if your family has abandoned you. Please trust me and believe in what I am saying: your family love you dearly and they are only full of concern for you. In time they will come around. Let's face it, you have been with Sylvia for 35 years and that is a long time. Because you are such a quiet and unassuming person, they are probably still in shock. The thing is, your family probably do not know the exact and intimate details of your marriage to their mother and they do not understand what has happened. You have, like me, been very good at hiding your true feelings and putting a face on things. Inside you feel as if you are crying out for someone to just understand what you are going through. I told you this morning that you are my best friend and I absolutely understand you. Please talk to me and tell me what you are really thinking. I hate not being with you and I would wait for you for the rest of my life. There will never be another Charles in my books and I hope you realise just how deep my feelings are for you. I want you to be happy and free. I will stand by you no matter what happens.

I love you my darling, sleep tight and sweet dreams. I cannot wait to see you tomorrow night and be with you. I am thinking of you constantly and praying that you will find the strength to keep going. What you did in moving out of your home was not the sign of a weak and selfish man, it was the action of a very brave person who showed a lot of guts and backbone to the world. I know you do not feel this, but try not to feel too guilty. Remember the King and Mrs Simpson—everyone said he was stupid to give up the throne for an American divorcee, but I think he showed immense courage to go through with what he did, just like you have.

I adore you my darling and love you so much.

Your darling little lamb, Lynsey XXXX

CHAPTER THIRTY-TWO

AS ONE WEEK merged into another, Charles found his lonely lifestyle in the near-empty house increasingly unbearable. When the Israelites journeyed through the desert wastelands towards the Promised Land they began to yearn for the fleshpots of Egypt from which they had escaped. So it was for Charles who missed his comfortable home, even the companionship of Sylvia with her settled routine of providing his meals, taking care of his washing, and even taking care of the shopping. He began to understand Hamish's dependence on Lynsey, who did much the same for him. Neither woman was appreciated, he thought wryly, by her present partner. He recalled that Sylvia had once said to him, not so long ago, "I don't know what I'd do without you." He felt at the time that she had said that not only because he was the main breadwinner, as editor, but because he was a valued companion to her. Now she was at sea without him, inasmuch as he was rudderless without her. "We need to talk about our finances," she had said after he had moved out of the house, and the week just gone by he went to the old house to have this talk.

"I absolutely can't have you back, living in the house," she said, "not as long as you are seeing Lynsey. But our finances are tied together, and dependent on each other, part of the same business. Now with you apart all the expenses are doubled and we are sinking back into debt. If I did tolerate you back in the house, it would only be for the sake of controlling our outgoings—for the time being, at least. We may be obliged to shack up with each other."

He sighed. "And, if I gave up seeing Lynsey... would you have me back, permanently?" God forbid, he thought, that he could ever stop loving Lynsey. And yet he had shared 35 years with Sylvia, and for most of that time he had been happy with her, united especially in the shared love they had for their children. Going back was a serious temptation, for he was aware that he was not coping with his new lonely lifestyle. He needed a woman by his side, all the time, and as much as he loved and longed for Lynsey, she was committed for years to come, probably, to serving Hamish—for she had a big heart and a genuine concern for him, a concern which he understood and even admired. It was ironic that neither he nor Lynsey was getting the love they yearned for, a love which they were so well suited to provide for each other.

Sylvia hesitated to answer Charles's question, but after a moment she said, "I don't know—maybe."

In the meantime Charles had identified a 16-year-old Mercedes in Glasgow which, for only a thousand pounds, had seemed too good a deal to miss. It had four new tyres and had only 79,000 miles on the clock, which was less than half what a Mercedes was capable of doing. So he went to Glasgow on his bus pass and bought the car on his credit card. Driving it back he felt like a million dollars, assuaged for a while, feeling the smooth power of the car on the motorway. He would need a car if he was going to live apart from Sylvia, but if he gave up Lynsey, then at least, he felt, this comfortable dream machine, however old, was a kind of consolation prize. Driving it, he thought with an amused smile, was almost as good as making love to a woman!

The car gave him the means of picking up Lynsey from their meeting place, on those nights when Hamish thought she was going to the Guild meeting, to take her in comfort, insulated from prying eyes, to his lonely house where invariably they made love with increasing intensity, to wrest as much love as possible from the limited and brief moments of contact they had together. She would be smartly dressed with her makeup on, and it surprised him how quickly she was able to undress, slipping out of her dress and tights to expose her lovely supple body. Once he placed a blanket on the carpet of the empty master bedroom, with two pillows at one end, where they took full advantage of each other's naked bodies. They made love in positions that Charles had never experienced before, with any woman, and they clung to each other as Charles shuddered with relief in her loving arms. Charles loved to make her come and found her little cries of relief as she clutched him close to her intensely endearing. The love they had for each other seemed to overflow into each other as they kissed with passion, then gazed into each other's eyes. There was no way, Charles realised, that he could ever realise this degree of passion and satisfaction with Sylvia, who, compared to Lynsey's soft femininity and generous giving nature, seemed as hard as nails. But in spite of all that, he conceded that Sylvia had loved him with equal dedication, if not more dedication, even a self-sacrificing devotion, that had proven itself through thick and thin over 35 years of marriage.

An added burden was placed on the relationship between Charles and Lynsey when her email stopped working. Her emails to him late at night were a lifeline, and now he waited for them in vain. When they met in the morning she explained that she had repeatedly tried to go on-line but kept getting the message: "No service available." Charles asked a technician to go round to her house and look at the problem, and the technician explained that the laptop was just too old to sustain the contact, and without a virus protection program had become infected with spyware. The only solution, he said, was a new or a refurbished computer. So for the time being they were back to exchanging messages via memory sticks, for Lynsey's laptop was still capable as a basic word processor.

Added to the strain was that Hamish, with the better weather of the approaching Spring, had begun to accompany Lynsey more frequently on her morning walks with the dog around the Denhead Pond. Day after day Charles waited in the distance for Lysney to appear, only to see her in the company of the slow-moving Hamish, or Hamish driving alongside her on his red mobility car. He would sigh and disconsolately turn back to his parked Mercedes and drive back to his empty house.

It was a Saturday morning when he eventually saw her come out alone with her dog, and thankfully he walked towards the end of the lake where their paths merged. He had seen her the previous night and given her a memory stick with the latest chapter of *Sunset Stirrings*—Chapter 31. Since Hamish had been out to the pub the Friday night, Charles thought there would be a good chance that Lynsey would be alone in the morning, for he surmised, correctly, that Hamish would be nursing his usual hangover.

Lynsey greeted him with a smile, but could not hide her concern. "I read your Chapter 31, Charrels." She sighed, and looked at him with love and understanding. "Are ye alright, Charrels?"

"Things are tough, Lynsey, I won't pretend they aren't. I'm not sure how long I can go on like this. It's like living in limbo—but the sunshine breaks through when I am with you."

She looked careworn, her face close to him, her eyes looking full into his. "Tell me truthfully, Charrels, do ye think you'll go back to Sylvia?"

He looked into her eyes. "I…I really don't know, my love. If I do, it's only because of the finances, for a time… and I will never stop loving you. You know that."

"I understand, my darling." She was silent but kept her eyes on him. As he looked into her brown eyes he saw them filling with tears and one tear escaped down her cheek. He put out a finger and touched the tear, wiping it away. "What's this, my darling—a tear?"

"I just want to say," she said with a sincere steady voice, "I understand, Charrels. I understand what yer goin' through.

Whatever you decide, I am here for you… I want you to ken that. There will never be another man in my life. I will always love you. And I will be here for you whenever you need me."

There was an immense sadness in her damp eyes.

"Oh my God, Lynsey, I do love you so," he said. "All I want to do is take you in my arms right now and assure you of my unchanging love. But I can't, here." He sighed. "Lynsey, if I can, I will hang out… but I'm finding it so hard, now, to cope."

They continued slowly around the lake. "I thought you would be alone today," he smiled.

"Oh, aye," she said. "Hamish is verra crabbit this morning. Nursing his hangover. He came back late last night. He was that drunk he couldna get the key in the door. I had to come doon an' let him in. It was past midnight."

Charles smiled. "To think I did not want to risk staying beyond an hour. I could have safely stayed with you for three hours."

"Och I ken," she laughed, "an' yet you had time to ravish me, and I had time to mak you a niece square sausage sandwich afterwards!"

"With a nice sweet cup of tea too," he smiled. "Our times together are very short and sweet—intensely sweet."

"Aye, I ken," she sighed. "If you can just hang in there, Charrels. I will free myel' in time."

As they walked close to the small wood that bordered the lake Charles commented on a tree with outstretched limbs that had been uprooted by the recent winds. Half its roots had been pulled out of the ground so that the large tree was lying at a crazy angle. "That tree," he said, "it's just like me, partly uprooted, part of it still rooted in its old place."

"I ken, Charrels, I ken—but you'll be fine when you're replanted. You will have new roots, eh?"

But he wondered how well one could transplant an old tree.

"How are you bearing up, my love?" he asked. "You saw the doctor last week, didn't you?"

"Aye. He reprimanded me. I had run oot of my beta-blockers and my heart was palpitating, he said. He said I was not to run oot of the tablets again. He gave me a new prescription and I am fine now."

Charles was surprised. "Why do you have to have beta-blockers, Lynsey?"

"Because of my past drinkin', Charrels. My body was under severe stress because of it. The doctor warned me I was drinkin' myself into an early grave. 'You're much too young to die,' he said, 'Dinna throw away your life!' It was Hamish that called the doctor because I had passed oot. But you see how much better I am now?" she smiled. "It's near six months I havna had a drink. Even my mither said on the phone she was proud of me! The doctor has also put me on HRT tablets to stop the stress of coming through the change of life—even though I've had a hysterectomy. An' he's given me vitamin pills too, to help clear my skin. It's all a throwback from the drinkin' days, you ken. I'm so much better now, Charrels—also thanks to you." She smiled. "I have finished writing my testimony, by the way. I will put it on a memory stick for yer. And I will write a letter for yer too—seeing we canna use email for now."

"That's great, Lynsey, I'm looking forward to getting it published." He looked at her and loved her. "It's not just your mother that's proud of you. I'm proud of you too."

The next time they met Lynsey was able to give him the memory stick with her letter, as promised:

My darling Charles

Oh, it is terrible not having my e-mail working at the moment. I feel so cut off from you just now and the days seem to be getting longer. When I read

Chapter 31 of *Sunset Stirrings*, it brought a tear to my eye. For me, it was very touching and I know how lonely and cut off from your family you feel as well.

When we spoke at the Denhead Pond this morning, I already knew what you were going to talk to me about. It is uncanny, I seem to have a sixth sense when it comes to you. I am glad you were able to tell me that you might be going back to stay at the old house. I completely understand that it is a place of comfort for you and that you would not be on your own there. I respect you for this and I know you must do what you think is right at the present time. My only concern just now is for your well-being. I know things are very overwhelming for you and that you are feeling depressed about the situation.

Charles, please do not give up on us. I really feel that our relationship is worth keeping and fighting for. I know that you still love Sylvia, but I also know that you are in love with me and there is a huge difference. I will be in love with you for the rest of my life and am fully prepared to wait for you for as long as it takes. You know that I will be free one day. When that time draws near, I will be waiting for you if you still want me. There is only one man that I want to spend the remainder of my life with and that man is you my darling.

Listen to me Charles, if you do go back to the old house, you may find that things are going to be difficult there as well. Be strong and hang on in there. Please do not let Sylvia boss you around and stand up for yourself. I know you can do this and I have every faith in you. Remember, when the going gets tough, the tough gets going. You know Charles, and I am talking from past experience, it is too easy to give up and go back to your nice, stable and quiet life. Do not settle for second best Charles, you are worth so much more. Spread those wings of yours and really fly, you will not regret it. Even at 71 Charles, your life is not at an end, it is simply just beginning. Mind you I am not surprised especially with a big honey like me dangling on your arm!!!

I love you Charles and absolutely adore you. You are the nicest, kindest and most mannerly gentleman I have ever had the privilege of knowing. I am always with you, wherever you are and you are forever in my thoughts. I will always be here for you my darling and I will be waiting.

With all my love and so much more.

From your great big beautiful doll,

Lynsey XXXX

Charles was eager to read the final part of her testimony. He could never get enough of her so wasted no time to see how she concluded her story:

About five months ago I had my last drunk episode. I had now reached absolute rock bottom and I knew deep in my heart that I did not have much longer to live. I had the worst DTs I have ever experienced. I was not only seeing and hearing things that were not real, but mentally and physically I just could not take any more. I had never felt so lost and lonely and kept thinking to myself, why had I ruined the last 35 years or so? Now, I felt there was nothing more to keep living for and that nobody really cared.

Hamish was lost. I knew he was really concerned about me, but never showed it. He decided to take matters into his own hands and phoned for my doctor to visit me at home. I argued with him at first, telling him I would be okay. But Hamish knew by the pitiful state of me that I had no choice but to let him have his way. My doctor came out and advised me that maybe it would be better if he had me admitted to hospital. I dreaded the thought of this and eventually, after a long talk with him, he let me have my way. There was one condition that I agreed to, which was to take a reducing prescription of Chlordiazepoxide (Librium). This is a drug that you absolutely cannot take alcohol with; to do so would result in a heart attack.

After the doctor left, I was sitting on the floor, alone in my bedroom. I am not sure how long I sat there for, but it seemed a while. I remember thinking how glad I was that Hamish had actually called for my doctor. I knew how ill I had become.

Now I have come to the most important and life-changing part of my story.

From my bedroom window you can clearly see the Church Steeple. I stood there just staring out at it and remembered asking God—please help me. I thought I could cure my alcoholism on my own, but now I really needed his help and knew I could not be saved from the black hole I was in without him. I asked him to take hold of my hand and pull me up. He answered my prayers and did just that. It was a strange yet wonderful feeling and somehow I stopped shaking and felt an inner calmness. After five years my bedroom seemed very quiet and I then became aware of an immense feeling of peace and tranquillity. It is very difficult to explain to another human being what happened next.

After a few days of sobering up and feeling slightly more human, I suddenly announced to Hamish that I was getting myself washed and dressed and going to the Church. He looked at me in utter disbelief and started to laugh. In all honesty though, just after the above took place, I did fall off the wagon and had gone to the church rather intoxicated. I do remember walking through the doors of the church and feeling that I did belong there. I do not have a clue what the members of the kirk must have thought of me. They were, in general, very nice and slightly amused at the sight of this overly painted drunk woman.

There is another reason why I am so glad I joined the Church. I met a gentleman called Charles and I have to say I could never have met a more sincere or kind person. I did not know it then, but he was to become one of the most important parts of my life. At last, I had found what I had been searching for all these years—my soul mate and best friend.

I realised that God had given me a second chance at having a new and much better life than before. The old, inebriated Lynsey had now turned into a new person and a born-again Christian. Although throughout my life I have always had faith in God, I felt my faith was now much stronger than before and, as each day passed, I was becoming more confident and positive. I am now looking forward to the future and have the strength to deal with whatever life flings at me. I am no longer frightened of the dark or of dying.

On reflection, I have a lot of things that I would still like to accomplish in my life and a lot of love to give to whoever needs it. My life up to now has been filled with both good and bad times. Unfortunately, the bad times have far outweighed the good. I have asked myself often, "Is there anything that I would change in my past?" The answer is no. I think God has been testing me all of my life and he only gives me assignments that he knows I can handle. He has been quietly guiding me throughout my life and still is. I feel his presence with me always and, strangely enough, know that I am one of his precious lambs and he will never turn his back on me.

Before I go to sleep at night, I always say my prayers and read passages out of my Bible. When I read different parts of the Bible, I feel as if I already know what has been written. It's as if I had actually lived at that time. What an uncanny feeling to have. I keep a book at my bedside called 'God Calling' which tells you about the power of love and joy that restores faith and serenity in our troubled world. This book is an inspiration to me and helps give me the strength to carry on a day at a time.

Finally, I would like to end with one of the passages written by Reinhold Niebuhr. It is one of my favourites and quite simply says it all:

Living one day at a time,
Enjoying one moment at a time.
Accepting hardship as a pathway to peace.
Taking this world as it is,
Not as I would have it.
Trusting that you
Will make all things right
If I surrender to your will.
So that I may be reasonably happy in this life
And supremely happy with you in the next.

AMEN

CHAPTER THIRTY-THREE

CHARLES WAS BEGINNING to feel the severe effects of the fallout resulting from his new relationship with Lynsey. The intense isolation in the empty house, and being so suddenly cut off from the links with his family, his sons and daughters, and severed from the church and prayer circle that used to be such an important part of his spiritual routine, he felt completely at a loss. His brief meetings with Lynsey and the occasional messages she was able to send him via a memory stick, was all that was left of the tenuous thread that kept him going. The thought of throwing himself off the Forth Road Bridge was beginning to haunt him in his lonely nights and on his solitary walks through the council estate with its drab boxes of family units. He knew that quite a few take this coward's route out of life every year. The captain of the yacht he was training on four years previously said this while he was sailing under the bridge towards the North Sea. The captain said one might survive the fall, but if so it would only be for a few seconds because the impact on the water from such a great height breaks every bone in your body. Usually the body is washed out towards the sea, and it takes a few days in each case to retrieve the body down the estuary. The captain said the authorities try to keep quiet about this to stop others choosing the same option. Charles went so far as to see how many had sought this way out and found that, according to the police, between 20 and 25 people make the same leap from the same spot in the middle of the bridge each year—a total of more than 800 to date. But then—he *might* survive, and that thought terrified him even more than dying—for a woman who threw herself 150 feet from the Forth Road Bridge had recently become the third person to survive the fall since the bridge opened in 1964. No—suicide from the Bridge was not an option, he reflected, even though the thought had recently become his constant companion. Nevertheless, of one thing he was certain—by loving Lynsey he had crossed the Rubicon and there was no way going back. But what was to be the way forward?

Falling in love with another woman and himself now becoming an outcast from the 'norm', he could totally understand where people who were looked down upon by the church and society were coming from, including gay people, for that matter. This thing had blown his mind and he could never be the dogmatic self-righteous person he had been before. Now he viewed life differently and his eyes had been opened to an awareness of beauty where he had never seen it before—in the broken shards of the potting shed. Lynsey, and the people that populated her world, were the people, the poor in spirit, that Jesus loved and was able to mend.

"Whatever happens," he wrote in his emails to his sons and daughters, "and however much my action may have changed the way you feel towards me, I will always love you, the most wonderful and loving sons and daughters a father ever had."

Charles often sought comfort from the words of the Lord, and read in the day's reading from *God Calling*: "I am here… Here to help and bless you… I forgive you. As you have prayed me to, for all neglects of My commands, but start anew from today." That sounded like the Lord was asking him to make a fresh start. But would that involve giving up Lynsey? After all, he thought, after King David had committed his great sin and been forgiven for taking the lamb Bathsheba away from her master—even after he had her master killed—he was nevertheless allowed to keep Bathsheba and even fathered a child with her. And he, Charles, had not gone so far as to have Hamish knocked off!

But something happened that made him think very differently about Hamish. To make a fresh start, Charles had volunteered to take Lynsey to a different Church of Scotland—the one in Buckhaven, her hometown where she had grown up. Lynsey cleared this with Hamish first, being quite open about Charles's invitation. "Aye," Hamish had said, "I dinna care which kirk ye go to!" and he was quite happy for Charles to pick up Lynsey from his front door.

So, on the next Sunday, and not without some trepidation, Charles pulled up in his Mercedes just outside Lynsey's front door. Hamish was in the window and with a smile waved to them both as they pulled off.

"See?" Lynsey said, "I ken how to handle Hamish. Best to be up front with him—that way he will no' suspect anything if someone reports back to him that we were sneaking around together, eh? So dinna worry—Hamish is okay with you picking me up, as long as I clear it with him first."

"I'm causing you to be a devious and deceitful woman," Charles smiled uneasily as they drove to Buckhaven.

"Aye, but only in the niecest possible way," she laughed. "You've got me now, Charrels, an' I'll do anything tae see you and keep you. There was a time when I could have stopped seeing you—but it's too late now. I have fallen in love with ye—do ye ken what I mien?"

Charles nodded. "The die has been cast." He sighed. "The milk has been spilt and the glass broken. Humpty Dumpty can never be put together again."

She frowned as she looked at him askance. "Are ye alright, Charrels?"

He smiled as he looked across at her while driving. "You're looking like a million dollars, Lynsey—you always look so fantastic when you dress up for church, a real knockout! I shall be very proud to be seen with you at your old church today."

And he was. He was delighted to see how she enjoyed and revelled in being seen with him, as the elderly folk who remembered her as a child or young girl recognised her and chatted excitedly about old times, and called forth others to come over and meet "our Lynsey"! In the church they were able to sit together quite openly, without any furtive holding of hands; in fact, they held hands quite unashamedly in the presence of this fresh congregation that was untainted by the disapproving verdict of the Kennoway church. Of course, they were ignorant of the fact that Charles was a married man and that she lived with an elderly partner. The topic of the sermon was God's selection of the young shepherd boy David as King and the rejection of his more likely older brothers—because God does not look upon outward appearances but on the heart. Charles wondered, then, just how acceptable his heart was to God.

It was when Charles returned Lynsey to Hamish that God seemed to pierce his heart. Lynsey had suggested that he come in with her, briefly, to be introduced to Hamish, and when they pulled up at the house Hamish was there, framed by the window waiting for her.

"Lynsey, I'm not so sure about this," Charles said, as he switched off the engine.

"Dinna be afeard, Charrels" she smiled, "I telt you, I ken how to handle Hamish."

So it was with trepidation that Charles went up to the door and was invited in by Hamish, into the very house and the very sitting room where he had on more than one occasion made love to Lynsey. Charles had expected a broad-shouldered man, a rough intimidating man, but the opposite was true. Hamish looked wasted, slightly emaciated with watery eyes and thinning black hair.

Hamish welcomed Charles with a friendly handshake, then stood back with his hands clasped behind his back, clearly

257

feeling awkward and intimidated by Charles, almost cringing, in fact. It had been Mother's Sunday and Lynsey showed Hamish the small wooden crucifix all the mothers had been given at the church. Charles had joked beforehand, "If you show that to Hamish it will prove to him you really were at church—and not at my house making love!"

After a few polite words he and Hamish exchanged views about what their favourite drink was—and Hamish suggested that he might take Charles with him to his local pub! Charles said he was a whisky man—"For whom the Bell tolls! Bells whisky with its peaty undertone goes down a treat!" he laughed—and Hamish surprised him by saying his favourite drink was sherry. "Oh?" Charles said, "Sweet or dry?" To which Hamish replied, still shifting his weight from foot to foot, "Aye well, whatever Croft original sherry is!" When Charles confessed that he liked sweet sherry very much, Hamish said, "Wait! I have a wee bottle fer ye!" And before Charles could protest Hamish disappeared into the back of the house.

"Oh my goodness!" Charles whispered to Lynsey, "I can't let him do that! I feel terrible."

"No, let him," smiled Lynsey. "Let him—he wants to."

Hamish returned with a big smile and a large litre bottle of Croft sherry.

"My goodness, Hamish!" Charles said, really touched and feeling a stab of guilt. It was like the man was heaping coals of fire on his head.

"It will do yer good, Charrels," Hamish said, almost bowing and scraping. "If yer like that, there'll be meer at the Inn."

When Charles saw Lynsey the next day, for Hamish had approved Lynsey's request, if request it was, that he take her to do her weekly shopping in the Mercedes, he said he did not expect Hamish to be so nice, and that he felt awful pretending that he was just a good fiend to his partner.

"Och!" Lynsey exclaimed, "You think his niece! It's just because of your posh accent that he was so accommodating and wanting to impress you! But I ken him! Believe me, he has a wicked temper, eh! Once after he was drinking he stormed into the sitting room where I was, naked as they day he was born and wielding a knife! But I ken how to handle him, eh! I just looked at him with contempt and said, 'Hamish! Yer look ridiculous naked and wi' a knife! Now you just give me that knife an' behave yourself, eh!'"

"Good heavens!" Charles said. "You must have been petrified."

"Oh no," she shook her head, "He just laughed, embarrassed, and handed me the knife—an' I sent him to bed! I told yer—I ken how to handle him."

Charles shook his head. "I still think we are playing with fire—me coming into his house behind his back. You know that he is a Mason—they are dangerous people. They look out for one another."

"True enough," Lynsey said. "His friend Cameron, who is also a Mason, came to see him after kirk yesterday, to tell him I wasna in the kirk! But Hamish already knew I had gone to a different kirk with you, eh? So Hamish was able to put him reet and tell him he knew I wasna in the auld kirk. You see, it's okay if I keep him in the know. Like now—he kens I'm out shopping with you. He's okay with you as long as he kens. He doesna mind!"

"Well," Charles said, "what you have said just goes to prove that the Masons watch out for one another. I still think we're treading on thin ice here. Those Masons are not to be underestimated. You don't know the Master they serve."

"Aye," she nodded. "Hamish has begun to go to special meetings with them on Tuesday evenings now. I asked him what they do, ken? He said it would not be wurth his life if he told me!"

"Well, I rest my case, Lynsey," Charles sighed. "Tread carefully, my dear. We must both tread carefully."

He really felt it was time he stopped these clandestine meetings with Lynsey, especially in Hamish's house. But how could he stop seeing Lynsey now? Ending his affair with her would be like coming to terms with a bereavement. You can't just fall out of love.

"Oh!" she said, putting her hand on his shoulder. "That reminds me! That woman Sadie delivered a handwritten letter to me! She must have slipped it into the letterbox and made away quickly. Fortunately I found it before Hamish did! It was full of warnings with underlined capital letters—telling me God is ANGRY with me and I must REPENT!"

"Oh my Lord!" Charles exclaimed. "That woman thinks she has a direct line to God!"

"Ha!" Lynsey laughed. "Direct line to God my arse! At this rate I'll have to report her to the police for intimidation and stalking! That letter really made my angry! I'm the scarlet woman that has broken up a happy marriage! Direct line to God my back passage!"

"Bloody hell," Charles said. "Lynsey, when you next send me a letter on a memory stick, will you type her letter and save it to the memory stick too? She's not a Mason, but I feel she is just as dangerous to your well-being. I'd like a record of what she has said."

"Verra weel," Lynsey said. "I will no' forget to include it. I'll type it when Hamish is oot, fer I dinna want him tae see the letter—he will go off his hid! You think he's niece, eh—well, that's only because of your refined accent. You don't know him, and his temper, and his swearing! And if Sadie comes around again wi' her nonsense he is likely to be verra crabbit and tell her to f-off—do yer ken what I mien, Charrels!"

"Well, I can imagine," Charles said, a little taken aback by Lynsey's sudden display of wrath. He did not often see her like that but admired her all the more for her downright honesty.

When they met at the Denhead Pond the next morning she gave him the memory stick with her letter, which, as promised, included the typed version of Sadie's note. Charles read the letter as soon as he reached his house, after slotting the memory stick into his laptop. Once again, he was really struck by the contrast between Lynsey's sometimes forthright vernacular and her perfect written style:

My darling Charles

Before I type out the letter Sadie wrote to me I would like to tell you the following:

I feel closer to you now than before. Every time we make love the feelings I have just seem to get more and more precious to me. I know that we have now bonded properly together and I quite simply love you more as each day passes. I know that you want much more of me, but I want so much more of you. I will stand by you no matter what happens and please know that I have never felt this way about another human being in my life. For me it is the most wonderful feeling. The fact is that I am now able to trust another man, and to love him in the way that I have always wanted to. Loving you is not hard, it is so much easier than I thought. You are a complex human being, but a really interesting and loveable one at that. I once said to you that you are the final piece in the jigsaw of my life. The piece that I have been missing all of my life. I never really knew what that piece was until I met you and then it hit me. I think God must have been saving the best until last for me.

Charles, you definitely are the best. You have been worth waiting for and even through all of the heartache and upheaval our feelings have caused other people, I would never change what I have with you for anything or anybody. I will never be sorry for loving you and I do want to be with you in the not too distant future. Please never give up on us because I know that if we did, both of us would be even unhappier and would miss each other terribly. I will do anything it takes to prevent this from happening.

I love you my big darling and always will.

God bless you and sleep tight. Your most precious lamb,

Lynsey XXXX

This was followed by Sadie's letter:

Dear Lynsey

This is what I feel God is saying to you. "Please come back to me." As I said in the car the other day, what you both are doing is WRONG and you both need to REPENT of this. You should know how Sylvia and family are feeling right now. Everyone is sad and I am sure you are too about this wrong relationship. I don't know how it will be resolved, but know God still loves you, but HE IS NOT PLEASED with what you have both done—split up a family and broken a marriage which was a happy one, in spite of what Charles may have led you to believe. It is your relationship with God that is the most important thing and right now you have broken that relationship.

We are all sinful, so don't get me wrong in saying you are too, but Jesus said that if a brother or sister is deliberately doing something we know is wrong, then we must point this out and let them know God is not pleased with then.

Yours
Sadie

The note made Charles angry, too. No wonder, he thought, when Sadie walks she looks weighed down by her heavy handbag that almost seems to touch the ground as her crabbed figure moves along. The handbag is surely full of stones, ready to hurl at any trespassers of God's law. We all live in conceptual prisons, he thought, and that included Sadie with her belief in an angry judgemental God. It made him think of what the philosopher Eckhart Tolle said, that dogmas, whether religious, political or scientific, arise out of the erroneous belief that thought can encapsulate reality or truth. Dogmas are indeed collective conceptual prisons. And the strange thing is that people love their prison cells because they give them a sense of security and a false sense of 'I know'.[1]

---

[1] Eckhart Tolle: *Stillness Speaks*.

PART FOUR

CHAPTER THIRTY-FOUR

Lynsey Anne McCann

C HARLES WAS FEELING shell-shocked when he entered the reception area in the council building. Lynsey was with him and gave him moral support as he entered the modern building of glass and chrome, the wide glass doors swishing open soundlessly as they walked into a spacious foyer. In a reception area a lady encased in glass directed them to another glass door that led to the reception area for homeless people. There was a row of young women and a man who looked like a teenager who sat behind computer screens, tapping keyboards. The teenager looked up with a smile and Charles said awkwardly, "Er, I received a call to… to call in and seek accommodation. I am… well, I am a homeless person."

The man—or teenager—looked across at the nearest woman who had overheard Charles, and she asked, "Were you given a contact name?"

"Well, no… a lady from the council phoned me, asking me to come in. I had sent in an application form for… well, for homeless accommodation. I didn't ask for her name, I'm afraid."

He was aware that his polished English accent was probably at variance with the accents of most homeless people, who were usually from the local council estates, and he was very self-conscious of his request. The young woman detected his nervousness and said with a bright smile: "Never mind, sir... what is your name?"

He gave his name which she tapped into her computer. She looked up with a reassuring smile and told him to take a seat and wait. "Gail will come over shortly and interview you as soon as she is free."

He took a seat next to the large window that overlooked the wide parking area, and Lynsey sat next to him. He noticed some people being interviewed in an adjacent glass cubicle. It reminded him of visits to the dentist. "Oh my goodness," he sighed audibly. What on earth had he got himself into?

"Charrels," Lynsey said softly, sensing his unease and taking his hand, "dinna be afeard. They will find you a place. And mind, whatever happens, you've got me! I will be reet beside you. I will no' let you go, eh!"

He took a deep breath, "Thank you, Lynsey. I'm going to have to depend on you all the more now... It's like I'm a fish out of water flopping about on ice." Or glass, he thought, looking at all the glass partitions around him.

"See you!" she smiled, squeezing his hand, "I love you, eh! An' I'm reet proud of you... You have got this far an' haven't turned back. I have to admit I'm surprised... an' I like surprises! I ken you're doin' this fer me... but you're doin' it fer yourself tac, Charrels. You canna go back to your auld life."

"I know, Lynsey," he smiled at her, looking into her concerned brown eyes. "It would be so easy to turn back... but then I have to renounce you. How can I do that? I'm doing this for you—but for me to... for both of us."

But again, he felt like a salmon, struggling upstream, to whatever fate awaited him. Somehow it was his destiny to persevere. Only God knew what the future held and why he had to keep going. He held on to her hand and took in, again, her steady brown eyes, the auburn hair that fell smoothly around a face free of makeup. She could look so glamorous but this was not a time for glamour. She looked quite plain in her black leggings, sneakers and plain velvet top. He had accepted her invitation to come with him because, as she said, she knew the bad areas and the better areas where he might be offered accommodation.

A smartly dressed young woman appeared in the entrance to the glass cubicle, now empty, and smiled at him. "Charrels Haddington?" she said. Even she had the local accent, yet not as pronounced as Lynsey's.

He stood up and both he and Lynsey entered the cubicle where they were invited to take seats around a glass table. The young woman was joined by another young woman. "This is Lee," she smiled, "she's in training so will sit in on our interview."

Charles introduced Lynsey. "Lynsey came with me because she knows the areas," he explained. "She's from the Church of Scotland and has been very helpful." It was close enough to the truth and he wondered if the women would tumble to the fact that she was the reason for his change of status.

"That's perfectly okay," Gail said with another reassuring smile. "You are entitled to have someone help you. Now tell me—why are you seeking homeless accommodation, Mr Haddington?"

Charles cleared his throat. This was awkward. He would just have to say it as it was. "Well… my marriage has broken down. I have been married for 35 years but… well, I met another woman and had the misfortune to… well, the good fortune in a way…" He smiled self-consciously but avoided looking at Lynsey, "…to fall in love with her. My wife found out and has debarred me from the marital home. So I have nowhere to stay."

He expected a bemused look to be exchanged between the two women but they kept their eyes steadily on him. They must be aware of his accent, he thought… and wondered if in private they would snigger about this. Did they realise Lynsey there beside him was the woman he was referring to? But they both looked kindly at him, and then Gail spoke, softening her voice. "How long have you lived with your wife in Fife?" she asked.

"Three years," he said.

"So then you have a connection with Fife. If you wait a moment, we can have a look to see what might be available for you to move into tonight, as temporary accommodation. At the worst, we can put you in a bed and breakfast, but that's not always the nicest option."

"You are most kind," Charles said. He was aware of a lump growing in his throat and tears coming to his eyes. He didn't expect kindness, somehow. He fought back his tears, embarrassed.

"What I was thinkin'," Lee, the other young woman interjected, "was whether sheltered accommodation wouldn't be better for Mr Haddington." She looked at Gail. "Sometimes we have flats comin' up at St Kenneth Court, for the over-fifties—and that could be on a permanent basis."

"Ohh!" Lynsey immediately responded. "Charrels, that would be perfect, eh! It's in a niece area, an' safe… there would be no druggies or dealers… do y'ken what I mien?"

"No nefarious elements," Charles smiled. "Sounds wonderful."

"Right then," Gail said, "we'll just get you to sign a number of forms, Mr Haddington." She produced a wad of blank forms and Charles was happy to sign them. Gail said she would enter the details afterwards for him—and arrange for a housing benefit. When he had signed the forms Gail stood up and said, "We'll just go and see what's available, then." Both women left and Charles and Lynsey sat alone while they waited.

"Oh Charrels," Lynsey said, "I *ken* the place they spoke of… it's just doon the rood from me… an I could walk over easily. I c'n do your washing and ironing, and your housekeeping…"

"And generally take care of my needs," he smiled at her, squeezing her hand.

"Aye!" she grinned knowingly. "Yer an awfy man, Charrels… but yes, I will do whatever you want me to. Things will wurk out, you'll see. As I said, you've got *me*—as long as you want me. I'm your greatest fan an' I will keep you reet!"

Before long Gail and Lee returned with a young man sporting a white shirt and tie. "We have absolutely nothing available at the moment," the man said kindly. "But we will phone you the minute something comes up."

"And if nothing does, come back in a week," Gail put in. "And we will do a fresh search then."

"And," Lee smiled, "we'll keep an eye out for sheltered accommodation. If that's what you would prefer."

"Oh definitely, Lee," Charles said, standing up. "The two of you have been most kind—I really appreciate your kindness. When a Gail blows I can find shelter in the Leeward side…"

They laughed at his poor attempt at a joke, but their smiles were genuine. Clearly something about his predicament had gone to their hearts. "If you feel you have been unjustly or unfairly treated by us, Mr Haddington," Gail went on, "you have the right to complain. But I assure you we really want to help."

"Why would I ever want to complain?" Charles said. His eyes had really filled with tears now. He had been treated as a sinner, an outcast, by his family and church… and yet here he had found solace, understanding, where he least expected to find it.

That night Charles's sleep was disturbed by a troubling nightmare. He dreamt that the whole world was in depression, people scavenging for food everywhere and his cheque book had been stolen. Everything, everywhere, was lost. He wanted to walk in front of a car and kill himself. Then he said, "I'll move to another country," and a person who overheard his comment said, "No point—it's like this in the whole world, in every country." When he woke up he was full of aches and pains, and the horror of his present condition as a homeless person came home to him. There was no relief! *I might as well have been back in the dream,* he thought. He fell back into an uneasy sleep. This time he dreamt that he fancied a married woman and when he was examining her house he was admiring the way pipes had been used to bind together the sandy fabric of the house; he placed his hand on a section of a pipe and felt that it was hot. Was it more than a structural part of the house? He banged it with his hand and found it loosened slightly. Alarmed, he saw a slight damp patch had appeared at one end of the loosened pipe. He stood back from the house then saw to his horror that the whole side of the house was collapsing under the spreading damp from the leaking pipe. The water was now gushing out, and the plaster was falling away in swathes... "Oh my God, what have I done...!" he lamented. He had destroyed a once happy home...

When he woke up he was in a cold sweat, alone in the empty house. He did not have much longer to live in the house, for recently a prospective tenant had secured it by paying a deposit—and he hoped it would not be long before those nice ladies at the council found somewhere for him to stay. Sylvia needed the rent from the house and let him know that his time in the house was drawing to a close.

When the sun rose it was a pleasant early spring day and he decided to cut the lawn for the first time after the winter, so the new tenants would have a neat lawn when they moved in. But when he tried to start the lawnmower, it refused to start. He tugged and pulled the starting cord until a blister appeared on his hand. He couldn't understand the machine's reluctance to wake up since it had been fully serviced in the autumn and had worked fine before he stored it in the garage for the winter. So he loaded the machine in the car and took it to the service centre, where the problem was immediately diagnosed. "The petrol has gone off!" the mechanic said. "You used old fuel from last year, right?" Yes, he had—the fuel had come from the old Jerri can he had always used.

"I didn't know petrol can go off—like milk!" he said.

"Aye, well, now you know!" the mechanic smiled. The mechanic drained the tank and put some fresh petrol in—and the machine coughed and spluttered and roared into action.

It was a good lesson for Charles. "I've been trying to run on old fuel," he thought, "Fuel that's gone off." He wondered if continuing life with Sylvia would be like that for him—whether his life would never restart. She had certainly gone off him since his affair with Lynsey. When he hugged her she was unresponsive and protested at his firm hard hug.

"You don't like my hugs, do you?" he asked.

"Well," she sighed indifferently, "you're not my favourite person."

His decision seemed clear to him. Jettison the past, dump the old fuel that had gone off, and refuel with the positive energy that radiated in abundance from Lynsey. And what is more, he was *her* favourite person. He knew that because she had said it repeatedly, in her letters and to him personally: "I am your biggest fan, Charrels!" She had said that to him just yesterday after the meeting at the council office. He recalled that Shakespeare had written: 'Sweet lovers love the spring' (in *As You Like It*). Spring was just beginning now, and he knew for a certainly that with Lynsey the spring would be sweet. With Sylvia it would always be sour, remembering only the long lost past springs. What was it he had read on Facebook just that morning? It was a prayer by the Florida evangelist Paula White: 'I pray the Lord will bring you the person you need to accomplish an assignment! New connections and opportunity in Jesus' name!' Well, Charles thought, the Lord had brought him Lynsey. With her there was hope for new horizons, a new life of success. Or was he just rationalizing his dilemma?

A life of success, he mused, was like a three-stage rocket fired into space—you cannot go into orbit unless you release the booster rockets that have pushed you this far. Jettison the past, with its burn out, the lingering negative views, and leap forward with the momentum of new beginnings, with people who appreciate and praise you, fuelling your endeavours into new heights of achievement. If you cling to the past, the old attitudes, you will go about hanging your head in shame in the face of old criticisms, old prejudices, old mind-sets. Jettison all those and look only ahead, to the stars. It was a thought that spurred him on to look ahead and wipe out the memories of those bad dreams in the night.

But the nights in the empty house were always the worst. That night he lay awake, thinking how it was his daughter's birthday and that he hadn't been invited to attend her birthday party. Sylvia had been invited and she was driving down with their son to the Borders to be at the party, but no invitation had been forthcoming for him to join them. It made him think that love, even in families, is not always unconditional. Somehow this seemed to be a significant discovery. His favourite grandson, hitherto a faithful admirer and follower, who belonged to an austere sectarian church with strict rules of obedience, ceased to have anything to do with his grandfather—and ensured that he was never "at home" if Charles were to visit. His own son, hitherto a best and close friend with whom he had shared many joyful moments of adventure and discovery, ceased to send regular emails and share his news with him. Unconditional love, he discovered, is a rare and cherished quality, found in very few people—fewer than most people perceive. If he'd had a heart attack, or a stroke, he supposed, they would all have rallied round, comforted him, helped him to recover. But falling in love with another woman was an act beyond redemption. In the early days of his 'affliction', had his sons, his daughters, rallied round and with kindness and love spoken to him, loved him, he might, then, have still turned back on his course. But their unrelenting coldness, even their avoidance of him, as though he had become a leper, drove him to seek solace in the only place he could find it—in the loving arms of Lynsey McCann, who gave herself to him unconditionally.

The next morning his thinking was clearer, once more. What few people seemed to understand, he thought, was that in falling in love with Lynsey he had embarked on a voyage of discovery. He was beginning to fraternise with the broken shards of the potting shed—the people he used to despise and look down upon. Falling in love with Lynsey had become a doorway, one that led to knowing and loving her people—the people the Lord came to save. These were not your self-righteous Pharisees and Sadducees with their law-abiding rules, but the drunks and the loveable, the down-and-outs, the benefit twilight people who were where they were not by their own fault but because of the circumstances of their lives. These were the people the Lord fraternised with and loved. Out of the dunghill come the roses of success. As the saying went, beauty is in the eye of the beholder, and Lynsey had opened his eyes to that beauty. He was so touched that her 'partner' Hamish had invited him to join him and his Mason cronies in their visits to the local Inn. He would do that very soon, he thought. Also, he would now have the opportunity to write about these people, as Margaret Thompson Davis, a Glaswegian author he admired, did. Lynsey wrote excellent English, he thought, yet she also spoke and understood the brash, rough dialect of these people, and spoke it herself. Perhaps he should encourage her to write about these people herself, to reproduce their lingo, their dialogue, and see where that took her—and him.

Charles felt it was providential that the very next day he received a call from the council: a flat in the sheltered housing establishment at St Kenneth Court had just become vacant, and would he please be there at 11.30 a.m. on Monday to meet a woman from the council to view it? He agreed to be there without hesitation. A strange aura of happiness crept over him at the thought that he would be living with the dregs of society. He would be just where God wanted him to be—that he might be divested of all remaining pride. He praised the Lord for his wisdom and his love. Then he read the day's reading from the little book *God Calling* and was struck by the appropriateness of the message:

Heaven may be in a sordid slum or a palace, and I can make my home in the humblest heart. I can only dwell with the humble. Pride stands sentinel at the door of the heart to shut out the lowly, humble Christ.

CHAPTER THIRTY-FIVE

'I pray divine revelation and insight to you in
the name of Jesus!
Eyes will see, ears will hear—clear visions
of God's plan and instruction!'
—*Paula White*

IN SPITE OF the evangelist Paula White's encouraging
message on Facebook, a deluge of obstacles and challenges
rained down on Charles the following week. The council flat
turned out to be empty, desolate, unfurnished, without carpets,
bare floorboards with exposed carpet grippers nailed into them,
no white goods in the bleak kitchen—and the walls were in an
appalling state, in desperate need of paint or wallpaper. It
seemed it was the Council's policy to strip a flat or house bare
when a tenant left, not even leaving any of the previous
tenant's decorating or built-in modifications like wardrobes or
bathroom cupboards. Even the stove had been stripped out,
leaving a dirty gap like an extracted tooth. Lynsey
accompanied him and saw the way his face fell at the sight of
the desolation. Samantha, the girl from the Council who
showed him the flat, recognised his disappointment, but
reassured him that the Council would make available a
decorating voucher worth £150. All the carpets, white goods
and labour, however, would be up to him—at his own expense.
The only consoling though was that the rent would be as little
as £68 per week—and, Samantha said with an encouraging
smile, there might be the possibility of a housing benefit that
could cover most of the rent.

Charles's disappointment encouraged Lynsey to phone rental companies and she located a private flat he could rent that would cost him just over £100 more per month, thinking that if it did not require decorating, carpets and white goods, then it might be a better solution. She saw his growing depression and urgently wanted to allay it.

Charles was impressed by the private flat in a more prosperous part of the town—a flat that was in walk-in condition, and in his naïve innocence, he easily fell prey to the glib patter of the Irish agent. The Irish agent seduced him out of a £200 non-refundable cash deposit, fully aware that the impoverished evacuated 71-year-old ex-academic was no match for his wily tongue. It wasn't before Charles woke up in the middle of the night, depressed, that he realised his mistake, for that flat would have stretched his finances and was located in an area, however prestigious, that Lynsey would have had difficulty in visiting for it would have required a long bus journey to see him; the realisation of how lonely he would be there dawned on him with the dawn of the coming day. The agent had left him with an application form that required the signature of a guarantor, and the next day Charles realised that no-one was prepared to sign as guarantor—and he was embarrassed to ask any members of his family to do so since in their eyes he had become an outcast; on reflection, he wondered if he himself would be prepared to sign as guarantor for anyone else, unless it was for a son or daughter. With a heavy heart, Charles phoned the agent explaining that in the absence of a willing guarantor he had no choice but to withdraw from the application and requested the return of his £200 cash deposit—to which the agent (his tone now assuming a degree of hardness) refused outright, saying he had explained that the deposit was non-refundable. So Charles had no choice but to accept the loss of his deposit and accept the Council flat that required no deposit and no guarantor. At least his heart felt lightened by this development—it was, he rationalised, clearly what the Lord had planned for him. His pride had to take a tumble. He recalled the blessing of the church minister at the conclusion of the service in Buckhaven: "Love the Lord and serve his people!" The private flat with its upmarket ambience would have insulated him from the Lord's people.

Then, when Charles took his 16-year-old Mercedes that he had acquired for £1000 on his credit card for a service, it appeared that he had been duped again—by the wily Glaswegian dealer that had sold the car to him, for everything he had said about the car appeared to have been barefaced lies. Repairing all the problems, including an oil leak, would require the value of the car being paid again—according to a local garage to which he had taken the car for an inspection. The country seemed to be full of pitfalls for the unwary elderly, the innocent and the trusting naïve—what a nest of vipers inhabited Great Britain, Charles thought!

The £200 loss was an expensive but valuable lesson, and an illumination of the genuine unconditional love that Lynsey had for him. He was deeply humbled and touched by the extent of this love and realised that what he had in Lynsey was a priceless gem. When she said she would love him and care for him even if he had nothing to give and was as poor as a church mouse, he knew her words came straight from the heart. She would live with him and love him anywhere, in whatever flat or hovel he ended up in—as long as she was with him. When he caught sight of his anxious reflection in the mirror while shaving, he would pause and wonder why she loved him at all.

He had prayed desperately and earnestly to God before accepting the Council flat. "This is serious, Lord," he prayed, "do not let me venture on this path if it is not your will. It is a hard road to choose when it would be so easy to turn back and go back to my comfortable home with Sylvia. But what would happen to Lynsey then? And could I ever stop caring for her? Stop me Lord, by whatever means, if I am going against your will." Then he realised that the answer to the prayer was Lynsey herself. Had she not called herself his "earth angel"? She was the answer to all of his prayers. He was happy in the end to accept the pauper flat because it would be close to Lynsey, who pledged herself to help him decorate it and do all his washing. ("You dinna need a washing machine," she said, "you have me!") Compared to Sylvia's heart of stone, Lynsey's heart of loving commitment was an ever-flowing and refreshing spring.

Reaffirmation that the Lord wanted to strip him of all false pride, taking him back to basics, and placed in a situation where challenges and pitfalls beset his path, came when he began to redecorate the flat. It was lonely in the empty rooms as he scraped away some of the old paint from the walls—when the silence was shattered by the loud crying and screaming of a child in the flat below. How was that possible, he wondered—how could there be a baby in a place reserved for old people, in sheltered accommodation? The howling continued unabated, and for one who valued his peace and quiet and enjoyed classical music, the way sound penetrated these walls and floors, let alone the wailing of a child, was a shock. Perhaps once the carpets were in there would be more sound insulation... but the penetrating wailing of babies at his time of life? Never before was the temptation to abandon this madness and return to Sylvia and his detached well-insulated four-bedroomed house in the executive part of the estate stronger. Only one true guide remained to beacon him on— Lynsey who, ironically, was the cause of his plight, for if he had never met her, he would still be in his comfortable middle-class home with his pious and dutiful wife and the silence of a detached executive home where no babies howled and no fishwife voices were raised to reprimand the demanding infants. When, after the second and third day decorating in the flat, the wailing of children continued unabated, he realised that the flat below must be occupied by a grannie who served as a babysitter, or child minder, for her grandchildren. Oh, he thought bitterly, abandon hope all ye that enter here! "Lord," he said aloud while standing on a stepladder with a brush and paint, "you sure know how to turn the screw! Can you bring me any lower than this—to the nitty-gritty edge of raw poverty, amongst the people you want me to love?" However was he going to listen to Mozart, or be able turn up the volume of his music, in this inner circle of hell? For apart from Lynsey, his music was his one remaining solace.

Lynsey nevertheless came to the rescue, helping him with the decorating, lifting his spirits by saying that the babies below were probably only temporary visitors. At least her presence there was a sustaining strength for him—and it was a bonus that now she had more reason to see him, to be with him, for Hamish was sympathetic, approving that she should spend more time with Charles to help him decorate the flat. Her presence caused the clouds of depression and doubt to evaporate, and there was joy when he took her hand and led her into the privacy of the hallway, away from the still uncurtained windows, for a quick cuddle and hug!

Nevertheless, seeing Charles's struggle with this new unwanted situation, Lynsey felt the pangs of guilt, calling herself the scarlet woman that had destroyed a happy marriage. She spoke of the way the blade of guilt had pierced her heart one day as she watched him walk back to his lonely flat, after they had met briefly in the park by the lake, saying to herself, 'There goes that puir man whose life I have ruined!' One night she had a disturbing dream that expressed these anxieties, and when she told Charles about it he asked her to write out the dream. "Dreams are good for expressing the tone and mood of a novel," he smiled, "and I will embed it in *Sunset Stirrings*!"

She promised she would and the very next morning by the lake she handed him a memory stick with her account of the dream:

I am going to try and recollect the dream I had about Sadie and the Church recently. It goes as follows, and I will try and remember as much as I can:

The dream began in the Prayer Circle on a Wednesday night. Everyone was seated in their usual places, with the exception of Charles and Sylvia. However, Billy the Church Officer, as usual, wandered in late and started chatting to us all. We all seemed jovial enough and were catching up on what we had done the week before. About five minutes later, Sylvia came in. She was obviously not in a good mood and spoke to no one. She sat down at her usual place and stared into space. I wondered what was wrong with her, but in my dream she did not know about Charles and I having an affair. I thought she had probably had an argument with Charles before she came to the meeting. A little while later, Charles turned up looking slightly pale. He took his seat as well. I remember the meeting got under way, but was interrupted by the sound of both Charles and Sylvia having words. I could not make out what was being said, but I noticed Sylvia was behaving totally out of character. She suddenly looked across the table at me and shouted: "What is it with you, you little bitch! Can't you just wear jeans and a t-shirt like the rest of us when you come to the meeting? You always have to be dressed up. Are you trying to impress someone or do you just get a kick out of trying to look better than the rest of us?" I was absolutely shocked at this and noticed everyone was sitting staring at me. At that point I think I lost my temper. I shouted back at Sylvia: "You know you are nothing but a stuck up, poe-faced bastard and I never liked the sight of you anyway!" I was shaking with anger. I then had another go at her and screeched: "Well, someone in the group has to look attractive and it most certainly isn't you! Och, I hadn't realised until now just how ugly you really are." At that point I remember feeling ashamed of myself for saying such awful things to Sylvia and I got up, put on my coat and informed the group that I had had enough and was going home.

When I reached the front door of the church hall, I thought I heard footsteps at the back of me. I turned round and I saw Charles walking quickly to try and catch up with me. He grabbed a hold of my arm and said, "Lynsey, I am sorry about what has happened. Please come back and join the meeting—everyone is worried about what has happened." I told him thanks for that, but I was too angry and upset and would have to go home.

The dream seemed to move on at that point and I was in the hall of my house combing my hair and making sure I was tidy before setting off for church. I said goodbye to Hamish and left for the church. When I arrived there Charles was waiting at the door for me. We shook hands with everyone and took our usual seats near the back of the church. I noticed that Sylvia was sitting up at the front of the church with Sadie and other members of the prayer circle. They all turned round and looked at us and threw us the dirtiest of looks! We could not understand why. Sadie then got up to give a reading to the church members. I think the reading was all about sinning and adultery and repenting of our sins before God. I noticed she kept looking at me and Charles during this reading, and both of us were feeling uncomfortable. Suddenly, Sadie shouted out: "Lynsey, you must stand up and repent before God and this Church and confess your sins! We all know you and Charles have been having an affair and you will both be damned forever. Are you out of your mind, Lynsey?" And so she went on: "Charles is a user and has done this sort of thing before. Please come to your senses—you have made Sylvia and her family very unhappy and sad."

I got up and walked straight up the middle of the aisle towards Sadie. I was enraged and felt out of control. I shouted at her: "Sadie, you and the rest of the group are nothing but a bunch of hypocrites and self-centred bastards! You call yourselves Christians—well, I doubt any of you know the real meaning of the word." She shouted back: "The church doesn't want your kind of sinner mixing with us and we never want to see your face at the prayer circle again! That includes Charles. Lynsey, you are nothing but a slut and an adulteress and God will never forgive you!" The next thing I remember is I physically punched Sadie and knocked her out! Charles took my arm and the two of us left the church and went home in his car.

That is as much as I remember Charles. It was a howler of a dream!

Charles replied on the memory stick he would later hand to her:

Wow! Sure is a howler of a dream my darling—shows how much the self-righteous attitudes of Sadie & Co have rubbed off and affected you. Anyway, I'm pleased it ended with the two of us going away together—in my car. (Good thing I had it serviced!) Thank you for taking the trouble to remember all this. It will be a good dramatic moment for the novel.

I love you—and thank you for loving me, sweetheart. By the way, it was exhilarating loving you tonight... I tried to make it last as long as possible because of the delicious sweetness of the sensation and the joy of opening my eyes to drink in the love reflected in your eyes.

In the weeks that followed Charles struggled on at the flat, in his loneliness, clinging on to the realisation that he was doing it all for Lynsey... lest she return to drink... lest she slip... but above all to raise her up to more than she can be, so she can stand on mountains. "Your foot shall not be moved," he had read in Psalm 121, when he lifted his eyes to the mountains, seeing them from his study window three years before when he first came to Fife. But he had moved his foot himself to ensure that Lynsey's foot did not slip, to raise her up, that she might fulfil her destiny... to climb higher... like the winding road upwards in a Scottish glen. And she had said that she was proud to be Scottish... and justifiably so. A year ago Charles had thought his love affair with Scotland had ended... but it had only just begun... with the real Scotland, the heart of Scotland, with the people of Central Scotland... "But I didn't expect this, Lord, not with the crying babies and the shouting woman right below me..." he complained to God.

For some time Charles had noticed that the grey roots of Lynsey's beautiful hair were showing through and growing longer at the crown of her head. "Aye," she smiled, when he commented on it. "It's time I had my hair recoloured, but it costs £50, ken...and Hamish has just sold my gold ring to have more money for his drinking."

"For his drinking?!" Charles exclaimed.

"Aye." She held up her hand with its graceful fingers, the ring no longer in evidence. She laughed. "My hand feels naked without my ring. But it was his late wife's ring, anyway, so it was his property to sell. I just liked wearing it. It's been there for six years... He had run out of money and just came out with the words, 'I've had a good idea...I could sell your ring...' I said to Hamish, 'You *are* serious?... you really want me to give you back the ring so you can drink with your cronies?' He said, 'Aye, we're no' really partners anyway, so why should you care, eh?' So I gave it to him."

Charles recalled the feel of the ring when he had held her hand secretly in church—it was like a lock to her heart. And now it was no longer there—no longer a barrier to her heart. It pleased him, though his heart went out to her. "Perhaps one day you'll wear a ring I'll give you," he smiled. "In the meantime, make an appointment for your hair colorization— I'll take care of it. You know how I always liked to touch your hair—in church and in the prayer circle. I think it's the main thing that gave away my love for you!"

"Oh Charrels," she smiled, "you're always so sweet tae me. You're a dear man, so yer are."

"Well, consider it payment for the help with the decorating—and for doing my washing!"

The next day he went to the bank and drew out £50 which he gave her when they met briefly in the morning by the lake. "That will take care of your roots," he smiled.

She laughed. "As long as it's not fer my body, eh!"

"Of course it is," he said tongue-in-cheek. "It's your body I'm really after. I'm only after one thing, remember?"

"Oh, you dirty bugger!" she laughed. "I ken! I'll have to watch you, eh?" Her smile softened. "You're a verra braw man, Charrels."

At this point they were still exchanging memory sticks as a means of exchanging messages—since his old laptop he had given her had given up the ghost when it came to going online. The situation was ridiculous, he thought, and then he found he could buy a good second-hand reconditioned laptop from Amazon for £112, that was pre-loaded with an anti-virus programme and was capable of going online and sending and receiving emails. Charles bought it and had it delivered direct to Lynsey's house. Hamish was quite happy about this and even stayed in during the day when Lynsey was out, in case it was delivered in her absence. It was delivered very quickly, a Dell Notebook, and Hamish was quite happy for Charles to come round and programme it. The only problem was, Charles could not find the start button and whatever key he pressed the screen remained a blank. At length Lynsey phoned the supplier, finding the telephone number on the receipt. "Do you mind if I ask you a silly question?" she laughed. "Where is the start button?" The man laughed in return and was about to explain. "Wait, you can tell my friend here," she said, and handed the phone to Charles. It was a smaller screen size, more compact than his old laptop, and did not have a start button in the usual place. "It's on the right-hand side, right at the back," the man explained to Charles. Charles looked and pressed a button that he thought was a hinge. The screen instantly lit up!

Charles plugged in the old dongle he had previously given Lynsey and instantly she was back into her email programme! They were both impressed by how fast and efficiently this smaller notebook worked. It was like a lifeline restored! "You know," he said, "you really need to persuade Hamish to let you sign up for broadband. With 'Talk Talk' it only costs £3.50 a month for unlimited broadband above your normal line rental cost.

"Alright," Lynsey smiled, "I'll sort it!"

He was delighted that she was back online—for it was essential that she keep his spirits up as well as her own. Her restored hair colorization was also important to him—for her self-image too. She always looked so stunning when she was made up, in her immaculate outfits and her makeup!

Lynsey, he realised, was a Trinity of parts. Previously he had thought that there were two Lynseys—the smart, dressed up Lynsey in full makeup, the one he first met that sunny day when she appeared like a butterfly of bright colour with her scintillating personality—the one that had originally engaged his attention, and he knew now that it had been love at first sight; then there was the plain, unvarnished, girl-next-door Lynsey that he met in the park walking the dog, face scrubbed clean of varnish… this was the girl that spoke in the vernacular Scots dialect and was able to crack jokes with the most common and ordinary council tenant, the Lynsey who became his best friend, the one that was closest to him and to his heart, and the one that made him laugh and the one he made love to; but then, when she began to write her testimony and he received her emails, he met the third Lynsey—the one who wrote in immaculate English, yet not in a distant way, but in a way that got closer to him than the other two manifestations, for in honest, genuine English she used the same language, the same register, as his, a language that spoke sincerely and truthfully of her love for him, which bolstered him up, sustained his self-belief, and encouraged him to endure and sustain his courage in his new path. It was to this highly literate and loving Lynsey that he opened his heart to when he replied to her emails. "God bless you my lovely friend," he wrote. "You know what, I have really grown to love you—you are so genuine, unlike these whited sepulchres in the churches with their bags of stones, eager to throw accusations at anyone who slips from the straight and narrow."

With his open visits to Lynsey's house, to help with the laptop and to pick up Lynsey for her shopping expeditions, Charles was getting to know Hamish a lot better. He was touched by Hamish's gift of a litre bottle of sherry—soon followed by the gift of a second bottle—and soon thereafter by an invitation by Hamish to join him for a night out: "Dae ye fancy goin' fur a wee swallae doon at the Inn?"

As per his instructions, Charles found Hamish waiting for him at 'the Cross' (the crossroads adjacent to Charles's council flat in the sheltered housing complex), at 8.30 p.m. Hamish was not the stocky well-built man he first thought he was, when he used to see him in the window waving goodbye to Lynsey during those early days when she left for the prayer circle meetings. To Charles he now looked lean and short, if not emaciated, as he stood alone on the pavement waiting for him. An ex-miner who suffered from poor lungs on account of his years working down in the bowels of a coal mine, he looked vulnerable. He was under strict instructions from Lynsey to "look after" Charles and not get "too rough" with him when with his cronies, who liked to engage in raw and crude talk, according to Lynsey. Lynsey, however, had encouraged Charles to accept Hamish's invitation because, as she put it, he needed "a good blow out". (A strange term to be used by a recovering alcoholic, considering Lynsey had been "dry" now for eight months.)

So off to the Inn the two men walked. Charles had observed this forbidding building for the last three years of living in the area, with a fair degree of distaste and superiority, seeing it as a house of ill-repute that he would never be seen dead in. And yet here he was striking up a conversation about mining and working in the depths of the earth as they entered the portal that led into the dark interior of the building. At the top of the portal Charles looked for a sign that read 'Abandon Hope all ye that enter here' but instead saw a sign that said simply,

'Lounge'. In the shadowy interior there was a long varnished bar with high bar stools, for which Hamish made a direct beeline and sat at one of them, inviting Charles to take the stool beside him. In front of them was an avenue of inverted multi-coloured bottles with various prices, and another doorway that led into an inner chamber which Hamish informed him was the snooker room. Behind them were various cubicles with sofas and other comfy seats occupied by couples, including a few stout women who looked like they were permanent parts of the décor and no strangers to a fish supper. In the brightly lit avenue behind the bar strode, back and forth, two very tall Amazonian women (young and well stacked) radiating laughter and bonhomie and dispensing hugs to some of the seasoned drinkers. One of these Amazonian females approached Hamish who immediately introduced Charles as an author and editor. Put on the spot, Charles produced his business card and handed it to her: "If you have a book to publish, I will be happy to be your editor and get you into print. Perhaps you have a life story?" This released an outpouring of mirth: "I'm only 28 and I'm still living my life!" This intimidating response put Charles in his place and he said meekly, "If you write poetry..."— which to his surprise elicited an animated response: "Och, I can write a poem, right enough—aboot a thing or twa that teks place in this Inn!" "Well then," Charles said meekly, "I'm your man."

Hamish looked suitably impressed and gave a seraphic smile. It occurred to Charles that he was where he most liked to be most of the time—in the bar. "What will you have?" Hamish asked.

"Whatever you're having, Hamish," Charles said. Be guided by the expert, he thought. Hamish looked suitably impressed and he turned to the Amazonian: "Two sherries and two half lagers, Vicky." The stately woman who rejoiced under the name of Victoria, but who was known as Vicky by the locals, went straight into action, squeezing off two measures of sherry.

"My God, Hamish, she's tall—and strapping," Charles whispered.

"Aye," Hamish grinned. "She's six foot near enough—the other one tae." He added: "Lynsey's tall tae."

"I know," Charles nodded. "Five foot nine." (Too much information, he thought, but it had slipped out.)

The drinks arrived and Charles had to admit the Tenants lager was really refreshing—the condensation sweating down the outside of the glass. He took his cue from Hamish to see how he combined the two drinks. Charles had already gulped a quarter of the lager. Hamish smiled and sipped the sherry. "I make the lager last," he said.

"I see—so the lager is the chaser, right?"

Hamish nodded. Charles felt he had impressed him. To tell the truth, he felt quite honoured and privileged to be drinking with him in his domain. Before long a smart well-set man took a seat on the other side of Hamish and looked casually at Charles. "I've seen you in church," he remarked.

"This is Cameron," Hamish said. Lynsey had told Charles about Cameron. Loaded, with a big house overlooking the golf course, an expensive Jag. Liked to go on cruises and always had a different woman with him as a companion. Charles remembered Cameron now. He was the man that once gave Lynsey a lift back from church. He had thought of him then as Hamish's guard dog. Not far wrong, perhaps, since he was one of Hamish's Mason friends.

Speaking of the Masons, Hamish informed Charles (between drinks) that his other Mason friend, a mechanic who owned a well-known garage in Kirkcaldy, had found nothing wrong with his Mercedes. Lynsey had mentioned to Hamish that Charles's former garage had found a list of faults that would cost him £1000 to repair, many of them MOT issues, and he had mentioned this to his mechanic friend Greg while drinking at the Masonic—and Greg had said, "Tell him to bring the car in and I'll check it out—and service it for him." Lynsey encouraged Charles to do so, since, she said, they would not overcharge him: the Masons, she said, can be trusted and they look after one another, and their friends. Well, Charles did, and the car was promptly serviced—oil changed with new oil filter, for a mere £88—and Greg reported back to Charles and to Hamish that he could find no faults. Charles had collected the car and it was running like a dream.

"It's much cheaper to drink at the Masonic," Hamish informed Charles, after he had paid for his round of drinks. The Masonic was an old converted church between the council estate and the newer executive estate, with the old arched windows blacked out: windows that let in light but gave out none, so they appeared black. It was a secret place only for the initiated. Lynsey had asked Hamish what went on in there, in their secret meetings, and he had told her it would cost him his life if he told her. But friends and wives were invited to social events—which were drinking events, as far as Charles could make out. Lynsey said a man was always posted at the door when the secret meeting took place, to keep out the uninitiated.

The sherry went down very smoothly and Charles paced his intake of the lager with Hamish's intake. That way it was easier to take his turn to pay. He noticed they had Black Bottle (his favourite blend of whisky—a blend of the Islay malts, which have a pleasant smoky and peaty base), so on the third round he exchanged the sherry for a tot of Black Bottle. Nice, but he missed the sweetness of the sherry, so on the fourth round he substituted the Black Bottle for a tot of Southern Comfort. Nice (Vicky asked: "One or two lumps?"—meaning ice and Charles said he would have a pair) but he seemed to have acquired a yearning for the sweet sherry—so with the fifth round he was back on the sherry, still keeping pace with Hamish.

At this point a man entered with a weary casual disposition and took up a stance next to a very large amplifier and held out a microphone. A stout top-heavy lady moved up and in a bored, casual way, stretched out her beefy arms to take hold of the microphone and looked up at a screen. Words danced on the screen and her stentorian voice cancelled out any attempt at conversation in the room. Rhythmic beats like tremors went through the building while a song of love and betrayal bounced off every wall and penetrated every crevice. It sounded very professional and she frequently took her eyes off the screen, the bored expression on her face unchanged. So, it was a karaoke night, Charles concluded. Conversation, if possible at all, now took the form of intermittent shouting, with hands forming ear trumpets to catch the shouts as they were exchanged. Nodding took the place of words when ordering the next rounds, and sign language to indicate the number of lagers, or lumps—a language the statuesque Vicky was well versed in as she rhythmically bopped up and down to the music, fulfilling the orders. As one set of glasses were emptied, Hamish and Charles pushed them further away on the black towel that ran the length of the bar, and pulled the refreshed glasses closer. The empty glasses were soon collected by Vicky and shortly replaced by the refreshed ones. It was like a regular, well-practised routine, and Hamish's lager seemed to be emptying faster than before so Charles had to accelerate his pace. Various singers from the Bacchanalian congregation came forward to take a turn at the microphone and all sang with the practised air of professional entertainers, with deadpan faces that spoke of the compulsive release of endorphins that were presumably unleashed by this recurring ritual. Some desultory clapping took place after each performance, and Cameron, who suffered from delusions of vocal grandeur, got up on two occasions to contribute his tribute to Frank Sinatra. "Simon Cowell will love you!" Charles shouted to Cameron when he returned to his seat and pint of lager. Cameron looked mildly impressed but Charles wondered why a man of his financial substance found pleasure in this... well, in this rather sterile ritual, he thought. He supposed it was better than drinking at home, on one's own... Not that much conversation was possible here, but there was arguably some camaraderie in the seraphic grins and acquiescent nodding as everyone leaned forward with ear trumpeting gestures to catch the shouted exchanges.

Charles lost count of the number of sherries and the number if lager chasers that had drained down their throats. But it got to the point when he felt compelled to give the "cut off" signal to Hamish, his bladed hand imitating the severing of his throat with a Stanley knife. Hamish understood the signal for he lumbered up and returned shortly with the message that Charlie the Taxi would be ready for them shortly. At this point the pressure in Charles's bladder suddenly manifested itself (it's like that at his age), and he shouted the word "Loo!" to Hamish over the decibels that were still bouncing off the walls. Hamish understood the message again and got up, signalling to Charles that he should follow him.

Charles gave the order to his legs which, however, stubbornly remained in place tucked away under the bar stool. His brain repeated the order and this time with superhuman strength his legs moved, but as soon as the weight of his body was transferred to them they buckled and he was forced to prevent a crash to the floor by his arms taking hold of the bar. In quadruped fashion he managed to propel himself with the combined support of the bar and the floor, his hands clutching the bar for support until he found himself in the snooker area. Hamish indicated the door of the gents across the expanse of the room that provided no support for the upper limbs, so with unparalleled bravely Charles launched himself into a solo flight across the room: it reminded him of the time he did his first solo in a Cessna 150 and got the landing strip nicely positioned just ahead of the nose and the spinning propeller and steadied his speed to just above 60 knots lest the plane should stall and plunge to destruction. Happily Charles made it to the loo door and clutched the handle thankfully, transferring his weight to the door as it swung slowly on its hinges and let him into a room with a long stainless steel urinal. It felt like a mammoth achievement as he relaxed the sphincter muscle and released a golden flow of relief.

Charles had little memory of how he returned to the bar but as he drifted towards it Hamish was there with Charlie the taxi driver. Following them he continued his drift into the open air and sank thankfully into the back seat of a vehicle destined for his house. Charles had not yet moved out of his rental house since the flat was still being decorated. Hamish was telling Charlie how Charles had escaped being fleeced of a thousand pounds by the good office of his Mason friend who had serviced his Mercedes and found no faults in it. "Abtholutely," Charles agreed, "alwathe graceful to you, Hamish," he mumbled, his tongue strangely thick in his mouth. He gathered that Charlie was another Mason and he was sensible of being taken care of by these kindly knights of the night. The taxi pulled up at his door alongside his parked Mercedes and Hamish waved away Charles's hand which held the fare. "I'll tek care of it," he smiled benevolently. Charles didn't know how he must have looked to the pair of them as he drifted to the door, walking like a sailor on a rolling deck with legs wide apart to ensure the centre of gravity of his body fell waveringly between his feet.

Once inside the house it was a whole new ball game. Charles had never before experienced this level of intoxication. Everything began to spin and tilt and walking anywhere required a firm grip on walls and banisters, anything that came to hand. Somehow he managed to make a cup of soup and then sat down at the table and checked his emails. There was one from Lynsey, which he expected. It had just come in and he felt she would like to have confirmation that he had safely reached port, since she had given orders to Hamish to take care of him and to treat him gently in the company of his cronies. It took Charles at least an hour to write the email since each letter somehow shifted away from under his fingers that seemed larger than usual. If it were not for the autocorrect facility the email would have been unintelligible. As it was, it bordered on incoherence—reproduced here only since Lynsey said afterwards that she had enjoyed it immensely and laughed all the way through it. Charles's inebriated fingers kept hitting the 'Caps Lock' key which produced a strange mixture of upper and lower case letters:

Oh my darling Lynsey—I have never EVER been SO DRUNK in my entire Life! I came home in the TAXI with Hamish & He WAS KIND ENOUGH TO PAY—I think he was aware how far gone I am—he is such a loving & kind chap... GOD I AM SO DRUNK—everything is spinning around me—I was trying to keep up with Hamish—GOD I LOVE YOU LYNSEY! You understand me so well... Jeez I am SI FUKIn DRUNK,,, the coffee is in the flat so I made some hot soup (packet of soup) on the gas flame... then found your email—thank GOD!! I need you so much—you are heaven on earth... all i can do is think of you—you are so lovely—god i love you Lynsey—i have resorted to typing with one finger/// .. oh GoD i want TO SLEEP WITH YOU MY DARLING ANGEL/// ,.. YOU ARE HEAVEN ... I HAVE NEVER EVER BEEN SO DRUNK... how does Hamish manage this level of alcohol... he was very caring for me///I really really like him... such a nice man... but i dinna think i can take another evening of booze at this level ... what is the point? All I want is to love you my darling.. GOD I LOVE YOU So MUCH ,,,I just want to be in your arms/... that would be heaven .. no need to be so fucking drunk!! .. the taxi brought me back in a dream ...

Hamish was so nice to me, Lynsey. i REALLY LIKE HIM. which MAKES THINGS complicated eh? I met Cameron who sang two Karaoke songs – VERY good! I told him he should enter for Britain Has Talent! The barmaids were tall and Amazonian— Vicky—kept the booze coming up. Hamish said Lynsey is tall too. I said to Hamish Lynsey is tall and has good posture too. I said I really liked her hair. He smiled and said Aye it was nice of me to pay for it. I thought Hamish was very caring. He invited me to drink with him again but I dinna think my system could take it, All I want is you—the sober you. What is the point of this alcoholic haze! I can't even focus—thanks to the autocorrect function I can just about manage to write this email to my Celtic Goddess

When Charles's head hit the pillow that night he was out for the count—until 5 a.m. when he woke with a blinding headache. Two aspirins and he managed to get back to sleep, waking later with a passable awareness of his surroundings. When he met Lynsey later walking her dog by the lake, she was somewhat 'crabbit' because of the hellish night she had had cleaning up the mess Hamish had made, for he had been sick in bed and was nursing a hangover that made him more crabbit than ever. He had told her about the way Charles had apparently mixed his drinks and she reprimanded him saying, "I thought I told yer to look efter him, eh!" To which Hamish apparently replied: "Well, I didna exactly force it doon his Lordship's throat, ken!" She had not yet read Charles's email of the night before and he urged her to delete it without reading it. This had the effect of reverse psychology. "I canna wait to read it!" she laughed. At least it promised to brighten up her crabbit morning. Also, it appeared to Charles, he had fared better than Hamish! But what amazed him was that Hamish was going to repeat the experience that very night... and on every subsequent Friday, Sunday, Monday, as well as on any other sporadic nights, as long as his funds held out. Maybe his liver was hardened to it, Charles thought. As for him—never again! Unless, he thought, Hamish was to invite him to drink at the Masonic where, he said, it was a lot cheaper to drink. Perhaps, on reflection, he would join him there... just once.

The thought gave him pause and he asked himself the question: was he spiralling into the inner circles of damnation? Not at all, he rationalised—he was just getting to know better some of these nice people that appear to be so at home in these inner circles of the underworld. They were what the church called "the Lost". Surely, he thought, far too many of the church's worthy law-abiding members are all too willing to write them off as "lost", so comfortable and set apart in their smug and cosy humility, self-righteousness and assurance of salvation.

CHAPTER THIRTY-SIX

Eros enmeshed with Agape

IT HAD BEEN a busy few days painting the council flat—the walls, the skirting boards, the kitchen cupboards, the doors, and the ceiling and Lynsey had been very supportive coming every morning around 11 to help and indeed she had done the bulk of the work. Apart from that she had been generous doing Charles's washing, free of charge, and everything was ironed to perfection. She said there was no need for him to install a washing machine since she collected his washing and returned it as required. They had been seeing each other as usual on the nights Hamish was out drinking, and the latest development of the adventure manifested itself when Lynsey took Charles up to her bedroom and into her very comfortable double bed. No man, she said, had ever been in that bed before! Charles was aware of a certain degree of nervous tension in doing this but Lynsey assured him that Hamish was not her partner in the true sense of the word and that they merely lived in the same house, she as his carer, and that there was no sex between them. "He wouldna be able to manage it anyway!" she laughed. "All he cares about is that he gets his meals and his washing done." At 54 Lynsey had a very smooth and still young body with strong shapely legs and well-formed soft breasts, so when Charles climbed under the sheets and wrapped his naked limbs about her he felt he was in his seventh heaven. At first they were giggling like teenagers doing this. For Charles it was wonderful to feel sexually aroused again with the urgent need to enter her, and doing so was exhilarating with nerve endings on fire as his orgasm built up rapidly—then (now here's the problem) suddenly died and without explanation he would go soft, after barely five minutes of wonderful loving. He could only put it to his age—since in all their lovemaking, however wonderful it was, he found it difficult to come inside her. He couldn't explain why and although the intimacy was delightful, it was also frustrating. But Lynsey was very patient and loved having him inside her while it lasted, and said she derived as much pleasure just being with him, cuddling and talking to him, as she did from intercourse. Even when he used Viagra he found it difficult to climax—though the Viagra undeniably helped to keep the hardness going for longer and made it nicer for both of them. Lynsey theorised that his problem was because he was not relaxed enough—and indeed there was always the thought that Hamish might turn up to find the two of them in bed together, both of them in the never-never! There was one alarming incident during this first time they were in Lynsey's bed together. The dog Tyson (the Staffordshire Bull Terrier) was downstairs and just as Charles felt he was about to climax he heard the dog 'speak' from the bottom of the stairs! Charles swore the dog had spoken in a funny squeaky voice: "*Hello! Hello!*" Lynsey said, "Dinna be afeard, it's just Tyson," but Charles panicked and lost his erection immediately, thinking for a moment that Hamish had returned! Then Tyson (who had a gammy back leg due to arthritis) trundled and puffed his way up the stairs and into the bedroom. The dog was overweight and old and sounded like a pig with his grunts and obscene noises—noises that did nothing to add to the ambience of the lovers' lovemaking. Charles tried to ignore Tyson but somehow he could not blank out the dog's presence and the desire to laugh outweighed the desire to climax! With his legs overhanging the bed at times, he also had to lift them like Tower Bridge to allow the puffing trundling animal to pass below like an oversized tugboat. Still, he derived immense pleasure making Lynsey come, by finger and/or tongue, and the way she suddenly tightened her grip and cried out as she climaxed was delicious—and he loved the way she held him so very tight at such moments. At least he knew then that she was satisfied, and in the end the best part of lovemaking was being able to give rather than receive. Other adventures spiced their lovemaking, like the time when Lynsey asked Charles to pick her up in the car and take her to his house while Hamish was out. When Charles pulled up in front of her house she was ready and rushed out in a dark coat and high heels; once in the car she opened her coat to reveal she was wearing nothing but a pink negligée she called 'a baby doll'! Giggling, she said, "I've come oot with nae knickers, ken!" Charles loved her mischievous girlish behaviour. At the house they made blissful love, and when his erection died Lynsey got it back by giving him his first blowjob followed by her making love to him, sitting on him while he fondled her soft, generous breasts.

The two of them began to attend together the church services at the Church of Scotland in her hometown of Buckhaven, since as sinners they felt they had become outcasts at the Kennoway church where they originally met and everyone knew them. He enjoyed seeing her at home in her home church where she recognised old school friends and people who had known her since she was a small girl. One sermon the minister gave, just after Easter, really spoke to Charles's heart. The sermon was based on the Road to Emmaus, with the reading from Luke's Gospel chapter 24. After the reading the minister said: "There is one question that arises from this reading—in fact, it struck me for the first time between the eyes! Anyone know what that question was?" One member of the congregation called out: "Why did Jesus disappear afterwards?" "No!" the minister shook his head. "That's what most people might ask. This was the question that struck me: 'Why did Jesus not reveal himself—and tell the men he was walking with exactly who he was? Why did he not immediately dispel their gloom resulting from his crucifixion and say, 'It's all right, it's me—I'm alive and well and here I am—and I am with you!' Why did he wait until the breaking of bread, when it at last dawned on them who he was?' Now this is the message for us," the minister went on. "It's a question many might ask in times of difficulty, when we feel alone and lost. Why does the Lord at such times sometimes remain unrevealed, distant, at arms' length, when we need his reassurance and strength the most? Now this is an answer that many of you may not want to hear. Is it because he has for a time withdrawn himself from you in your state of need and struggle?" He went on to give the example of a butterfly struggling to release itself from its cocoon. "If you interfered and helped the butterfly, do you know that it would kill the butterfly? No, the butterfly has to struggle on, to grow strong; otherwise its wings would not unfold properly so it can fly! It's like that with us at such times: the Lord stands back so that through struggle and determination we can develop a strong character, to fulfil his purpose for us. If he were to help us too quickly at such times, our new glorious selves would be stillborn."

Charles could relate to this. Falling in love with Lynsey had plunged him into a new set of circumstances full of desolation, struggle and loneliness. Bereft of his comfort zone in his comfortable house, stranded in a desolate council flat with crying babies and a shouting grandmother below, he felt he was on the brink of despair, and he would cry out to the Lord: "Help! I cannot bear this burden—I'm on the brink of giving up..." It was all for the sake of Lynsey that he was going through this agony, and it was indeed a test of his love for her—a test of the depth of his love for her—for if he gave up and went back to Sylvia and his old comfortable life, free of financial anxieties, then he knew it would mean the end of any relationship with Lynsey—the end even of any contact with her, never reading her emails or even seeing her from a distance when she walked the dog in the park. The crying babies and the desperate shouting of the woman below felt like the last straw that breaks the camel's back—but what would his life be like without any shadow or hope of Lynsey in his life again? Would the bond of 35 years of marriage with Sylvia, the restoration of relations with his sons and daughters, with his grandchildren, be enough to cancel out any vestiges of yearning for Lynsey? And what effect would that have on his character—knowing that he had forsaken a woman in need and a woman whose love for him had become the main driving force in her life? Thinking about it as he painted the skirting boards and the crying of the baby and the yells of the reprimanding grandmother assailed his ears, he asked himself: could he abide never seeing her again? For in the few months that they had known each other, made love, laughed together and talked of many things, she had become his best friend, a soul mate, in each of her three manifestations—the elegant woman beside him in church, the girl next door that he made love to and who tickled his back and made him laugh with her rough vernacular humour, and the polished writer who spoke his own language on the most important and intimate of topics. Spider-wise, the tendrils of her web had penetrated and wrapped themselves around his heart. Surely the Lord must have a purpose for this deep bond that had taken place. Yet the Lord remained distant, withdrawn, and so Charles struggled on, always on the brink of giving up, yet hanging on, strengthened by Lynsey herself on those isolated occasions when they were together.

Just how desolate Charles found his position, how acute the crisis was on account of this fork in the road that presented itself in his destiny, was apparent from an email he sent to Beth, his email confidante, one lonely night when, after tossing and turning, he abandoned sleep:

Oh Beth, I do not know how much longer I can persevere in this new lifestyle of mine. Every morning I wake up and it hits me again—the intense depression that I have to go through another day of this nightmare. Thinking about it, the main anxiety is worrying about money, because this new direction is causing me to spiral into debt on my credit card. Little new business is coming in from the editing business, and now all my and Sylvia's expenses and outgoings have doubled—and the flat is forcing me to spend more money like equipping it with cooker and fridge and carpets, and of course there's the rent to pay and the extra utility bills. I cannot see how it will end other than disaster. Then of course there's the emotional issue: (1) the guilt I feel towards Sylvia who has been a faithful and caring wife for 35 years, with the heavy heart of being an outcast from my family (apart from one daughter who really cares although she is disapproving of my 'affair'); and then (2) there's the love that I still have for Sylvia as a wife and a friend,—and on the other hand (3) my love for Lynsey which, while I try to dismiss it as a passing aberration, is very real. She is the only person that builds me up and who loves me unconditionally. If I left her now I would feel awful, and the guilt would be on the other foot.

But how can I continue on the path I have set myself upon without income? Also, there is the added nightmare of the awful, awful noise of babies crying from the flat beneath mine, and the most ghastly, awful, vile shouting of the woman that is constantly disciplining and screaming at the babies. At moments like these I have never ever before felt so close to suicide—and if I had a gun I would surely have blown my brains out by now. I ask myself: what is God doing, is he testing me or punishing me? If so He sure knows how to choose the last straw that breaks the camel's back, or how to tighten the screw. I have thought of suicide many times since Sylvia asked me to leave the house and it is the one thought that gives me some form of bizarre comfort—it will be the shortest route to peace and oblivion.

But what kept Charles going was the encouragement he received from Lynsey's emails. She was aware of his need and never failed to send him an email every night, shortly before midnight, and from these he took his strength, for she had become his lifeline in his journey through the dark night of his soul. He kept checking his emails, every night as the clock approached midnight, for the evidence of her sustaining unconditional love was food and drink to his soul. How could he walk away from a nourishing love like that? When he was with her, and in touch with her through her emails, he was happy; it was only when he was not with her, alone, in the middle of the night especially, that his soul was assailed with doubts and misgivings, when he became aware of and longed for the secure life he once had with Sylvia in the bosom of his family. The adventure with Lynsey had all begun when he saw her that sunny Sunday in the late Autumn, when she appeared before him, in what he now thought of as her butterfly dress, when he was transfixed by her bright smile, her bubbling personality and her creamy cleavage. Had he known what that moment was to lead to, would he have encouraged her that day to attend the prayer circle?

Now with the spring weather, she wore again her floral butterfly dress when he picked her up for the Easter service at the church in Buckhaven. His heart lifted when she flounced into the car, though this time she covered her cleavage with a respectable white scarf. When he emailed her that evening he said how delighted he was to see her once again in that floral dress, but added that he had missed seeing her cleavage. "I'm not sure how Mrs Simpson caught the King," he remarked, "but you certainly caught me with that dress and the cleavage." Knowing how he loved her humour and her use of the vernacular Scots, she freely sprinkled her emails with the local dialect in her endeavour to lift and sustain his spirits. It was this delectable ability of hers to interweave the local dialect and her perfect English that suggested a light at the end of the tunnel for Charles, for he recognised that she could become a successful writer of local colour and he encouraged her to develop this vein of humour.

*   *   *

Emails from Lynsey:

Oh, the next time I wear our Butterfly Dress, I will wear my new white push-up bra just so you can see my 'lovely creamy cleavage' (*your* words!)—as you did that first day you saw me! Och, yae dinnae half hae a one track mind, eh? But I love it. You know Charles you always say such lovely things about me and especially when you tell me I am really intelligent. I appreciate this and you are the only person who tries to build up my confidence and make me feel good about myself. It has been a long time since I ever felt any of these things. I must admit the one thing that you have changed about me is the fact that I feel like a real woman again and I know that I am really loved by you in every way possible. It is a wonderful thing when another human being thinks that much of a person. I said to you tonight that when we first met, I honestly thought that maybe you were just in need of some love and attention (which you were not getting from Sylvia) and you only wanted a fling for a while. Oh Charles, I am so glad you proved me wrong. I know now that I just would not be able to share you with another woman, especially Sylvia. The feelings I have for you are too deep rooted now and I could never turn back or abandon you. The amazing thing is, I would not change these feelings or anything that has happened to us for the world. This is the most important chapter in my life and I am going to work hard at making it right for us both. You will have to be the one to let me go, and I hope you never will.

I love you my big cuddly toy and cannot wait until the next time I see you. That will be tomorrow morning and you can pick me up at 8.45 p.m. tomorrow night. Remember I will be wearing my sexy nightie and a black Halloween wig!!

From your loving little lamb, Lynsey XXXX. Now sleep tight darling, sweet dreams and God bless.

*   *   *

Oh, Charles, you are so handsome. Making love with you tonight was divine and, yes, it felt as if I was in heaven. I cannot describe the way you make me feel, but I just know that it is wonderful. I am your best friend and the love of your life and know I always will be. There certainly will not be another love in my life that compares to you. I am in love with you my darling and adore you and I want you to remember that always. I feel you are going to be very happy in the new flat and it is going to be exciting seeing it eventually take shape. I feel so close to you now, even more than ever.

Charles you have made me so happy and I never want to stop feeling the way that I do now.

Take care my lamb, sleep tight and sweet dreams. I LOVE YOU and I just cannot stop saying this to you.

*   *   *

Och Charles, this has been a bloody long day and I am having severe withdrawal symptoms from not seeing you tonight. How on earth am I going to last until Friday! Just make sure that you drink plenty of Lucozade to give you energy, because I can assure you, you are going to need it on Friday when I sink my crab-like claws into you. Och dear, I'm getting wet just at the thought of it!!!

Oh, I love you my darling and have been thinking about you all day. I hope you have not been too lonely and I will see you at the Denhead Pond in the morning. What changes I am seeing in you as the days go by, Charles! When we first started seeing each other you always looked drawn and worried (naturally), but now you are looking more youthful; you seem to have a spring in your step and you certainly are getting more confident and relaxed. I knew this would happen and that it would just take time. I am so happy for you Charles that you have got where you are today through sheer guts and determination. I admire you so very, very much and you have my total respect. Oh you are absolutely and definitely a man who is worth going to the ends of the earth for and waiting for.

Hello, my darling Charles

I am so glad you were able to get things up and running at the flat later this afternoon. I know you were tired and it says a lot for you to even think about getting started. I already knew that you were slightly absent-minded and you will need quite a bit of looking after. Oh, Charles I cannot think of anyone who would love and be able to look after you more than me. Please do not worry about forgetting things—I will be there to remind you and keep you right. I want you to know that you can rely on me and that you can share any worries you have with me. Remember, there is absolutely no problem in this world that cannot be sorted out. I know things seem daunting just now, but eventually the flat will be sorted into a really nice and habitable home.

I have an abundance of love and patience where you are concerned. I hope that you got on well tonight at the Inn with Hamish and that it was not too noisy for you. I will not distract you by wearing my short skirt tomorrow when I do the roller work at the flat and I cannot wait until later at night when you come to see me. I will wear something nice for you and you can have a try in my bed for a change!

Charles, please never think that you have led me astray. I know my own mind, believe it or not, and I just had the feeling that you would become an important part of my life in the future. I still believe that we came together for a very good reason and I do believe that it was God's will that this should happen. What his reason is for this I still do not know, but only he knows.

Goodnight my darling, sleep tight and God bless you. I hope you did not drink too much at the Inn and, if you have, please try and get a good night's sleep. I LOVE YOU, I LOVE YOU.

Your Loving Celtic Goddess Lynsey XXXX

*   *   *

Email from Charles to Lynsey:

My darling

I can't wait to have a 'try' in your bed for a change! I see I remembered what you said incorrectly—I thought you had said something like "you can try me out in my bed for a change!" That would be even more fun! (Like taking a car for a test drive in a new terrain!) You are so delectable!

Thank you for your wonderful patience and understanding, Lynsey. I feel so comfortable and secure with you. You are also a great calming influence.

When I heard those stout ladies singing professionally in the karaoke at the Inn last night, however impressive they were, I thought how much nicer it would be listening to your melodious voice singing some of the Abba songs. (You know all the right inflections!) There's one song that goes something like "take a chance with me..."—are those the correct words?... well, it made me think of you. That's what I am doing... I'm taking a chance with you! I really enjoyed your company today in the flat, helping me decorate—just having you there was lovely, my world being in your world.

I only got back to the house at 5 p.m. this evening—but I wanted the bedroom ready for the roller work tomorrow. It's all looking pretty good!

Sounds like the woman downstairs is a child minder or baby sitter—second day running with the child there all the time. You're allowed to keep one pet—maybe her pet is the child!

Yes, there is a reason for us being together—Romans 8:28 says 'all things work together for good for those who love the Lord according to his purpose for them'...and he surely has a purpose for us. We have both accepted Jesus as our saviour, Lynsey—and you know that you are saved, don't you? If you have accepted the Lord Jesus as your saviour then he will fulfil his promise to you—and I believe once you have given your life to him he will never let you go. I do want to think of both of us being secure in knowing that we have eternal life and will live forever—not just for the short time we are here in this mortal world. How do you feel about Hamish in this respect—do you see him as lost? He deserves to be saved as much as any of us and the Lord loves him too. Perhaps your example will shine through to him in time. I am so pleased that he read your testimony. You know, even if we have fallen from grace, I do not believe we have fallen out of the Lord's hands. D.H. Lawrence once wrote (in a poem). "It's a terrible thing to fall into the hands of the living God/ But it is a terrible thing to fall OUT OF the hands of the living God."

Now how did I get onto this tack?

I know—because I love you so much, Lynsey precious.

Charles xxxx

Emails from Lynsey:

To my precious Charles:

I loved your company in the flat today as well. It is starting to take shape and the Magnolia emulsion makes the living room look bigger. You wait and see, the flat is going to look lovely when it is finished and I actually think it is not going to take as long as we originally thought. I am glad you enjoyed the pub and Karaoke. I felt that you needed a good night out, as well as a good drink. You are under such a lot of stress at the moment Charles and there will be a lot of things going through your head as well. I really do understand what you are going through my darling and I promise to make the rest of your life as stress-free and happy as I possibly can. A man and human being like you is worth all of this upheaval and stress. It will truly ease off in the long run Charles, as long as you can try to be patient and understanding. I know that you can. I have every faith in you, and God and I are both doing our best to look after you, guide you and protect you.

Having your company in my bed tonight was truly a wonderful experience. I know you really enjoyed yourself and so did I. Och, Charles, it made me realise even more that I just want to cuddle up to you for the rest of my life and be with you. I know now that my life would be completely empty without you—I guess you would call this true, unconditional love—an emotion I have never experienced in my life until now. I would like to thank you Charles, from the bottom of my heart, for being responsible for making me feel this way. I just wish that every man and woman could experience what the two of us have with each other.

Goodnight my love, sweet dreams and sleep tight.

From your very own loving MONA LISA, XXXX

*   *   *

Email from Charles to Lynsey:

See attached picture of the Mona Lisa. No—definitely not nearly as beautiful and lovely as you are, Lynsey. But there was just something when you sat next to me tonight, looking back at me with that secret smile, that made me think of the Mona Lisa. But see the picture—the hair is different, not hanging down the left side in a lovely careless way, and no cleavage to speak of! But you know what that smile tells me—she and da Vinci had just made love! No doubt about it at all. That's what the portrait is all about—to preserve for ever that magical memory!

*   *   *

Emails from Lynsey:

Hello my Darling

Thank you for the picture of the Mona Lisa. You are right, she is not beautiful, but there is something mysterious and alluring about her. Her smile definitely hides a secret—maybe she has just done something she shouldn't have!! I must admit Charles I am enjoying helping you decorate the flat. It really is coming on leaps and bounds and I know it is going to look lovely when it is finished. I had a nice hot bath at about 7.15 p.m. tonight. I really had to and I just lay and soaked in it for a while. My muscles around my hips and thighs were aching. I do not think I have done as much bending over in my entire life. It is all worth it though.

I thoroughly enjoy spending time with you Charles and talking to you as well. You know I was not sure if the two of us would be able to have substantial conversations with each other (you being a professor an all wi an awfy lot o' brains), but we certainly seem to get on very well with each other. You are a complete package Charles (with all the benefits a woman could ask for in a man). Oh, what a man you are Charles—loving, caring, considerate, funny and passionate, with a big helping of romance. No wonder I am in love with you—in my eyes you have it all. I hope you are having a relaxing night and maybe enjoying a wee whisky. You deserve it. Now mind and get a good night's sleep as you will feel better tomorrow morning. I will see you at 10.10 a.m. for church and I will be dressed, with my makeup on as well. I am looking forward to it.

Sleep tight, sweet dreams and God bless you my love.

From Scotland's answer to the MONA LISA, your loving lamb LYNSEY XXXXX

*   *   *

You do not have to thank me for saying all the nice things I have about you—they are absolutely true and I would not say these things unless I truly meant them and thought them. You are a much stronger person than you think and I know you will have surprised quite a lot of people because of this. This is not a bad thing. I can see the changes in you day-by-day and you are becoming a much more secure and better person because of this. Keep going Charles, you should be very proud of yourself in spite of everything that has happened, and I cannot begin to tell you how proud I am of you. I have met the best man I could ever meet in every sense of the word, and you know, I LOVE HIM.

*   *   *

Hello my darling

Thank you for the pictures, they really are lovely. I must say Charles you definitely are looking well in your picture and younger too. You know when I first saw you at church, I thought you looked like a lovely gentleman, but I also felt that you had a slightly haunted and tired look about you. Oh, what a big difference in you and it really shows. To see this change in you over the months has made me feel very happy. You are much more relaxed with me now and you seem to smile an awful lot more. I wonder what has happened to you to transform you into this new human being!! Whatever it is, I want some of it—Oh, silly me, I already have what you have and it is a big helping of you. You seemed really happy at the flat today and it is a pleasure to see. The flat is looking great now and I cannot wait to see it when the carpets are in. I have just had a quick look at the interview from the link you sent me earlier and it looks great (the one with you interviewing one of your authors on Revelation TV). It's really strange to see you on my laptop and to hear you talking as well. I am looking forward to seeing you at 11 a.m. tomorrow and also to have you at my house for some dinner. I hope you will enjoy my cooking.

Och weel Charlie, yae ken that am really in love wae yae an yer such an awfy braw man as weel. I just canna tak my een aff yae.

What I really mean is, I am truly in love with you, you are a handsome man and I just cannot take my eyes off you.

From your loving Celtic lamb, Lynsey XXXXX. Sweet dreams and sleep tight. God bless you. I LOVE YOU.

*   *   *

Hello my darling

Once again, thank you for a wonderful night. I love every minute we spend together, no matter what we do. I must admit though Charles, making love with you is the absolute best. You are looking so well now and I feel so happy seeing you like this.

It was worth it going out in the car this morning. I could not believe the cost of the items you purchased. I felt as if I was in Aladdin's Cave. At least you now know where to go for a good bargain for the flat. Maybe next time they will have a cooker for sale—I hope so.

Oh, Charles, as I explained to you tonight, when I was lying in bed a couple of nights ago I suddenly felt overwhelmed and quite emotional. It was the thought of you giving everything up that you had in your life for me. What a feeling it was—it suddenly hit home to me just how much you must really love me. I feel so thankful to God for this and very, very proud of the fact that you should think that I am worth it. It is the biggest sacrifice a man could ever make for the love of a woman and I certainly never thought that this would ever happen to me. I want to thank you for this gift Charles from the bottom of my heart and I fully understand what this sacrifice has cost you.

I want you to know just how much I love you for this and know that I could never leave you now. You have won my heart Charles and no one in my life has ever been able to achieve this.

I love you my darling, sleep tight, sweet dreams and God bless you.

With all my love and so much more, your beautiful flower of Scotland, Lynsey XXXX. Stay strong and focused my darling and whatever you do from now on, don't ever look back, just forward.

*   *   *

Hello there my big Darling

I hope you got home safely tonight. You know that I worry about you walking up that road all on your own. Och, the flat is starting to look great and I cannot wait until it is finished. I will see you at 11.00 a.m. tomorrow morning.

You know Charles I do not think that I have really let you know just how proud I am of you. You have been putting so much work and effort into fixing up the flat and having to deal with all the upheaval and problems you have inherited since meeting me. I do not know where you got the strength from to put up with all of this, but I have been praying to God every night since we met, asking him to guide you and look after you, and to give you the strength to keep on going. Well Charles my darling, you have done just that. I have watched you going from strength to strength as each day passes and starting to really look to the future now. What a future is in store for you Charles—all you have to do is grab on to it and not let go. I am your guide and I will not allow you to take the wrong turning from now on. I feel very protective of you and would not let anyone harm you. They would have to go through me first, and I must say, that is a pretty daunting prospect.

You should be proud of yourself also Charles and hold your head up high. Meeting me has not made you a bad person; in fact, it has given you a lot of backbone and it is making you a much better person than you already are. You looked great tonight, as well as looking happy and content. It really shows in your face Charles and what a kind and handsome face it is. I love gazing into your eyes when we are making love and feeling you inside me. I love being around you, but I adore it when you show me how much you love me more.

Please take care of yourself my love because you are the most precious person in my life now and I never want to live life without you.

God bless you, sleep tight and sweet dreams, you delicious big bugger—you are so good I could just eat you.

With all my love, your Big Celtic Goddess/ Mona Lisa, Lynsey XXXX.

* * *

Good Evening my darling and how are you? I hope you have not been too lonely today Charles. Well, I have missed you and the rest of my day has been lonely without you. It is strange how you are always on my mind even when you are not there. You know, when I am not with you Charles, I suddenly realise just how much I want to be with you always. What I can tell you is, I now really know that I will always want to be with you and no one else. I do not know just how much more patient I can be not staying with you Charles, but it is getting much harder for me now. I do not know about you, but I feel very lonely here and isolated without you. I live for every moment we can be together and I enjoy being with you so much. Charles, I will never feel guilty about wanting you in my life always and forever. I know I should, but I do not. I ask God to forgive me every night for stealing you away from Sylvia, but I always thank him for sending you to me and I always let him know that I am not sorry for what has happened between us. You are the best thing that has ever happened in my life and oh God I absolutely love you so much Charles that I sometimes find it hard to find the right words to let you know this. Please never give up on us, I know I never will, and I can tell you that everything we have both gone through up until now has been worth every bit of heartache and guilt. You are worth fighting for and I will never give up the fight.

You know how much I am in love with you my handsome, distinguished, big darling and I always will be. Now sleep tight, sweet dreams and God bless you honey. I will see you tomorrow for church. I cannot wait.

*　　*　　*

Yes Charles, it was a beautiful day today in the sunshine with you in Buckhaven. It is always nostalgic going back there, but I certainly do feel at home in Buckhaven and have never lost the love I have always had for my hometown.

Just imagine if I had met you when you were in your early twenties, and I was the same age. My God, our love-making would have been mind-blowing and I do not think we would ever have stopped touching each other. I would have loved you the same then, just as I do now. Let's face it, we are only older now and I hope wiser. I think we are both like a vintage bottle of wine—it has to be savoured and sipped slowly to appreciate its quality and maturity. I love being in your company Charles and today was a bit special for me. I feel proud having you at my side and this feeling will never change.

Talking about Andrew Mackenzie today took me back (his nickname was Beef because he was short and stocky). He was always carrying out practical jokes on his classmates, but he was always cheerful and never had a bad word to say about anyone. I was very sad to hear about his death four weeks ago of a heart attack. You asked me to write out the story I told you, using dialogue and my Scots slang, about the time he pinched my knickers!

Well, it happened like this:

Our class had two periods of swimming lessons from 10 a.m. until 12 noon on a Thursday every week. That particular Thursday everyone was getting changed into their swimsuits and trunks before the lessons began. The girls' changing room and the boys' were both adjacent to one another and there was a slight gap in the door that separated the two changing rooms. My clothes were lying on the floor nearest the door and we all gathered at the swimming pool. However, after the lessons, I suddenly realised that my navy blue knickers were missing and it occurred to me that one of the boys might have stolen them. Anyway, I heard uproarious laughter coming from the boys' changing room and the sound of Andrew's voice telling them "to shut up and keep quiet or she'll ken I've stole her knickers!" That was it—I got dressed and had to go home without my knickers. I was terrified at the thought of telling my mum and explaining things to her. I had nearly got to my house when Andrew ran past me and shouted, "Aw dear, Lynsey's got nae knickers on and guess what, I've got them!" I roared after him: "Just you wait ya wee shit, when ma maw finds oot she'll tell your maw and you'll get an awfy hiding!" Sure enough, when I got home and my mum asked me what had happened to my knickers she lost control. "Reet, that's it, yer comin' wae me and I'm goin' straight roond tae Andrew's hoos to tell his maw what has happened." When we got to Andrew's house his mother answered the door: "Och hiya Isabelle, it's gid tae see yae, and you as well hen. Well, whit can a dae fur yae?" My mother shouted to her: "See yer wee shit o' a son, he's just gone and stolen Lynsey's knickers fae the lassies' changin' room and she's had tae walk doon fae the school withoot them on!" "Right you!" shouts Andrew's mum, "git oor here ya wee shit!" and she grabbed him by the scruff of the neck. "I'm gon tae give you a right tankin for this and one ye'll ne'er furget!" Well, she laid into Andrew until he howled:

"I'm sorry Lynsey, I swear I'll never steel yer knickers again!" At that his mum stopped tankin him and let him go. "Och, Isabelle," she said, "I'm awfy sorry aboot what's happened, but I think he's learned his lesson. He'll no' be able tae sit doon for a couple o' days and a hope his arse is rid raw!"

Well Charles, I hope you can make sense of all that. God bless you my darling, sleep tight and sweet dreams. Until tomorrow morning my love.

From your great big angel,

Lynsey XXXX

*   *   *

Email from Charles to Lynsey:

I am proud of you too, my Lynsey.

Tonight was really a revelation to me—seeing what is possible if you developed your talent to write—for you can really tell a story! Just talk about your life and times like you did tonight, with the focus on being funny and entertaining, and I will be your editor. I can even put a lot of it into dialogue—but you did an excellent job doing that too as you did with your knickers story! In a way writing like this you are a social historian, salvaging and putting to paper real events about real people that are so precious and unique, with all their drunkenness and problems and foibles and loveable traits—people that have gone to an early grave or have simply passed on. Lynsey, you have all this unique vibrant life locked up in you! It means a very rewarding partnership between us—a partnership I could never have had with Sylvia with her different, less colourful 'respectable' background. You can put your finger on the nitty-gritty of life, like the man falling asleep on the loo, and the poor lass falling down the stairs to the loo and crying when being reprimanded by her sister, and then the distinguished lady who turned up as a tart (with no teeth and just in bra and pants). Vickers & Tarts—to think I have never heard of that! This will take discipline, like all writing does, with deadlines, but you have proved to me you can do it, and do it well. You have a wonderful advantage in being capable of writing excellent English and at the same time being able to speak (and write) the vernacular with all the Scots words and blunt swearing! Lynsey, you are in touch with a vein of ore, pure gold, so together we must work it! *Celtic Reflections: The Life and Times of Lynsey McCann*—working title!

I love you, my precious brilliant girl—I am so proud to be in love with a genuine Scots lass, especially the one in the butterfly dress and the cleavage that caught my attention on that first fateful day when you came to church overflowing with spirit!

Charles

*   *   *

Email from Lynsey to Charles:

Hello there my darling

Oh, the pictures you sent me taken at Buckhaven this morning are lovely. You are right, there is definitely something different about me in those pictures. I guess it is the effect of having you in my life that is doing this to me. It is all the love and attention you are giving me that seems to bring out the very best in me. You can see this in those photos.

Well, what a wonderful night in your new flat! I have never felt quite as passionate and loving as I did tonight. I hope you felt the same way Charles and I think you did. It was the best lovemaking we have ever had so far and it would not be a lie if I told you that it felt like sheer ecstasy and I have never had those kinds of feelings in my life for a man. Oh, wow, Charles, the very best is yet to come—I hope you can last the pace. You already know what a man eater I am!!! I cannot wait for the moment when I come with you inside me, it will be sheer bliss. I never really knew what real love was until I met you Charles, and I cannot describe to you just how much you make me feel like a real woman. I want to thank you from the bottom of my heart for this. I did not want to leave this earth never knowing what it was really like to be in love with a man as wonderful as you. You really are Charles and you are my knight in shining armour.

God bless you my love, sweet dreams and sleep tight. I will not forget to type up some of the funny stories I told you about a few nights ago. I will sleep like a log tonight because I feel so content and loved. See you at 10.30 a.m. tomorrow.

From your ever loving lamb, Lynsey XXXXX.

Oh, a nearly forgot, a thot a wid be knackered the nicht wae aw that sex yae cawed oot o me, bit al tell yae somethin, a wis just getin well-oiled and raring tae go tiger—och yer in fur a rare treat fae noo on!

CHAPTER THIRTY-SEVEN

Waiting for Godot

HAVING SETTLED into his council flat, the main social development for Charles was an invitation from Hamish to join him in an evening drinking session on Friday at the Masonic building. Hamish 'collected' him at 8 p.m. and together they ambled their way to the building where a number of cars were already parked. Apparently it was bingo night so there were many women in brightly clad dresses waiting—all clustered about the entrance smoking—and Charles followed Hamish as he wove his way through them into the narrow door that led into a main hall, and then a smaller room with tables and chairs and a bar. On the wall a portrait of Robbie Burns gazed in a superior way at the assembly of geriatric drinkers. Charles expressed surprise that Robbie Burns was overlooking the assembly and Hamish said something to the effect that Burns became a Master Mason to promote his poetry, a clever marketing strategy. It clearly worked, Charles thought, thinking how his love for Lynsey was like a red, red rose.

Hamish ushered Charles to a table nearest the bar where he soon had a glass of cold lager and a smaller glass of sherry in front of him. There were two barmaids, both in their thirties, a dishevelled brunette (Elspeth) and a shorter nonplussed looking blonde (Gina) who had apparently fallen on the last occasion she served (inebriated from drink?) when she grazed both knees. This event was being retold to each old man who entered, to the repeated amusement and laughter that broke out every time the event was regurgitated for the delight of the whole assembly. Gina did not mind and generally concurred that the mishap was an occupational hazard, and then there were some questions about the real reason she found herself on her knees—and some hilarious remark about her knees being grazed on the shag pile of the carpet.

Charles conceded that he was an old man himself at 71, yet found it difficult to identify with the string of old men that came in one by one and sat around him. The first was Billy the Cap (so called because he never removed his Andy Cap cap). He sat next to Charles who asked him what his line was. Billy replied that he had been in the army and from his disgruntled tone it was clear that he nurtured a dislike of the redcaps (military police), a remark which unaccountably led to speculation as to who currently owned the Suez Canal. (One never knew where a topic would lead, Charles realised, and topics were easily changed as the evening wore on and the beer and sherry glasses were emptied, filled, emptied and replaced...) The next to arrive at the table was Cameron who looked remarkably young and well-preserved at 81. He was loaded, Charles recalled, with a four-bedroomed executive house overlooking the Leven golf course (at present for sale at £200,000). He had made his pile as a butler in America, saved his US dollars and wisely invested them and now led an enviable lifestyle of drinking and going on cruises, always with a different female companion. He was well known for shirking his round of drinks—a fact that was loudly bewailed to his face by the group. To this he maintained a calm demeanour that repelled the banter that ran off him like water off a duck's back. Charles had heard him singing in the Inn at the karaoke night and commented on his velvet smooth imitation of Frank Sinatra, a comment that was met by a roar of laughter and drew forth the criticism that his singing was "a load pf pish!" (Cameron's bemused smile deflected the criticism as he urbanely helped himself to another swallow of his lager.) That seemed to be the nature of all of the conversation that went on deep into the night—banter that denigrated the worth of one another, and each gave as good as he got. Being a newcomer, Charles escaped the brunt of their banter. Then there was Ralph who was welcomed into the party as a no-good loafer that knew how to work the benefit system. Ralph had a disconcerting stare that looked through one, since his eyes that were simultaneously glowering and amiable did not seem to focus. "What's your line, then, Ralph?" Charles asked, a question that drew forth another roar of laughter and Hamish's remark: "His line! He hasna done an ounce of wurk in his life! Every year he has a new council hoos, bigger and better, and he does fuck all!" The disconcerting look was unchanged as Ralph, unruffled, helped himself to a fresh pint that materialised in front of him.

The 'f' word was the universal adjective that was freely sprinkled throughout the rejoinders. It allowed for an economy of words and probably saved the bother of seeking the appropriate epithet as the effect of the drink took hold. It was a kind of lingua franca that united the group of old men into a band of brothers. As the conversation and banter proceeded and Charles imbibed more and more of the lagers and sherries that kept materialising in front of him, he grew more and more detached from the group, hearing their words but understanding little of the strange regional accents, yet laughing happily with the group while not having a clue what the joke was. Gina's grazed knees often resurfaced and recirculated in the laughter so it was easy to laugh as it was a recycled joke that did not make any deep demands on the higher intellectual brain cells that in any case were dormant by the third or fourth sherry. Charles's bladder, however, was not dormant and he had to nudge Hamish to know where the toilet was.

Hamish was as helpful in the Masonic building as he was at the Inn, and guided Charles through the labyrinth of passages until Charles found himself isolated in front of a wide stainless steel urinal, hanging on to a pipe above him for support while the pipe between his legs eased the pressure within with an unimpressive trickle. Why, Charles asked himself, does an old man's prostrate swell and hold on to the stream when the bladder is most in need of depressurising? He found himself nearly falling asleep standing there, hanging onto the pipe above him as the floor below him undulated like the deck of a ship, but in time he found his way back to the table where the undecipherable banter was still in full swing with a rich sprinkling of 'fucks' and 'fucking'. In a moment Hamish left and was gone for some time before he made his way back; he had been sick in the toilet, it was reported. When Charles's round came round again he gave Hamish a £10 note that he took to the bar. The drinks were handed out, and then Hamish disappeared again. "Aye, he's being fucking sick again, most like," Billy the Cap put in, looking unconcerned. Charles said, "I'd better go and see if he's okay," and floated up and drifted along the tilting floor of the labyrinth towards the toilet—but found Hamish instead in a corridor feeding £1 coins into a fruit machine. Three lemons came up and a few coins trickled into Hamish's hand, but he immediately fed them back into the machine until they were gone. Charles wondered how many of the coins that went in were part of his change from the ten pound note! Never mind, he thought, as long as Hamish was happy and not being sick!

Charles had to admit that he saw little point in these almost daily (or nightly) drinking bouts that Hamish undertook. Hamish repeatedly disappeared because he was being sick—apparently—though when Charles went to look for him he was again at the fruit machine plugging in coins until his hand was empty. There were certainly some pointless addictions here—to alcohol and gambling, and the fellowship of old men taking the micky out of one another. A pleasurable way of waiting for Godot, perhaps, Charles thought—for in a sense you were waiting for God to call "Time!" and end the pointless burden of Sisyphus rolling kegs of beer down the hill so they could be filled and rolled up again. When at last Hamish announced it was time to go, it was midnight—and Charles thought it wise to stagger back to Hamish's house with him to make sure he reached it. Lynsey had said that he often stumbled and appeared at the door with grazed knees or bleeding fingers. Charles had as much to drink as Hamish, but managed to remain upright as, side by side with Hamish, they staggered along the winding road. They reached the house and went round the back to the kitchen door—Hamish's usual place of entry. He insisted that Charles came in and have another drink with him. Charles objected that they would wake up Lynsey but he did not protest too much thinking it would be nice to see her before their arranged meeting the next day. The two men duly slumped onto the sofa after Hamish produced a couple of tins of lager—and before long Lynsey duly appeared at the foot of the stairs in her nightgown, her hands on her hips and a look of "well, I never!" on her face. Feeling sheepish, Charles poured his beer into a glass and Lynsey exclaimed: "For goodness sake, it's goin' all over your crotch—you look like you've pee'd yoursel'!" Sure enough—Charles had partly missed the glass.

What a state of drunkenness! Charles was not sure if Lynsey was entertained by his summary of the evening with its coterie of old men, but she listened with a bemused expression. It was the first time (and so far the only time) she has seen him completely drunk. She suggested he stay the night on the couch but he insisted he made his way back—which he did, travelling along the fence that lined the pavement down the Leven Road. The fence was useful because he could keep a loose hold of the top rail so that it served a similar purpose as a cable that keeps a cable car in place.

A highlight of the week (such as it was) was when Lynsey invited Charles to join her and Hamish for 'dinner' on Saturday. He arrived with four cans of lager—since the last occasion when he had arrived with a bottle of Californian Rosé he was the only person who partook of it since Hamish immediately introduced his cans of lager, and of course Lynsey had become teetotal. Wine did not do the job for him. On this occasion Hamish produced a litre bottle of sherry and before long that was empty as well as the additional cans of lager that he produced to accompany the ones introduced by Charles. He was offering to open a second bottle of sherry when Charles felt it was wise to say he needed to get back to the flat— otherwise he would never be in a fit condition to reach the flat. Besides, Hamish was about to depart for the pub at the Masonic—and Lord only knew, Charles thought, how he managed to persevere into another night of drinking with his cronies after hitting the cans and sherry with him after 'dinner' (in effect, a late lunch at 3 p.m., a time set by Hamish). What was memorable, apart from the drinking, was the excellent meal of chicken and roast potatoes and succulent vegetables that Lynsey produced. (She said her grandmother had taught her to cook. Thank goodness her grandmother's culinary spirit lived on in her, Charles thought.) Lynsey suggested that he might like to stay on after Hamish left for the pub to share a supper with her and Tyson (the Staffordshire terrier). In his disintegrating mind he felt however that he would be overstaying his welcome, and so used the top of the fence once again as a cable to guide him back to his flat. (Lynsey reprimanded him afterwards: "Why did yer no' take my hint and stay?")

Hamish was eating less and less, failing to make much of a dent in the food Lynsey placed on his plate, but drinking more and more. How much longer can he keep this up before Godot calls him home, Charles wondered? Hamish complained of a 'sair hid' and was very 'crabbit' in the mornings, so went to see the doctor and had a blood test (which actually showed that he was healthy). Charles could take a good guess as to the cause of the sore head, however, thinking the crazy thing was that Hamish didn't seem to have a clue why he was not feeling well, especially in the mornings.

Hamish invited Charles to join him at the Inn again the following evening, but Charles declined, saying he needed to watch his liver and, besides, there was a new book he had to edit and so needed to keep a clear head. ("Fuck your liver," Hamish had exclaimed, "let it pack oop!") The truth is that Charles would rather spend the time with Lynsey—and she was coming to the flat that evening as soon as Hamish left for the Inn. She had promised to bring her massage oils with her and oil his back, then his front, finishing with a more sensitive part of his body. To ensure a successful evening he would swallow a Viagra pill in advance. Ironically it seemed to him that he was addicted to a different way of waiting for Godot and he asked himself, "Am I as lost as the old cronies at the Masonic and the Inn?"

But he knew that above all he was in love with Lynsey, that he loved her so much that, like Orpheus, he was prepared to descend into the underworld and mingle with the lost to bring her back from where she had fallen, poisoned by the adder-bite of alcohol. Eurydice, the love of Orpheus's life, was allowed to follow him out of the underworld, provided he did not look back until they had crossed the threshold to the world of the living. Lynsey had been dry now for nine months and he could see from the many photographs he had taken of her how she had changed, from a girl who looked rough without her makeup to an elegant and beautiful woman with a clear skin. Mingling with Hamish and his cohorts in the dens of iniquity might cause his foot to stumble as he sought a way out of the world of the lost, but he was encouraged by Lynsey's progress and knew that if only for her sake he needed to maintain his course and not be tempted to escape back to his old secure life with Sylvia, and trust that she was following close behind him.

*   *   *

Email from Lynsey to Charles,
just past midnight July 5th 2014:

Well darling, I am now officially 55 years old. I want to thank you for helping me reach this age, because if it had not been for that chance meeting with you in the church that Sunday morning, and then us coming together, I know I would have eventually died through alcohol abuse. It would only have been a matter of a few months. You, more than any living being, Charles, saved my life, and I will never forget this.

With all of my love and gratitude,
Love Lynsey XXXX

CHAPTER THIRTY-EIGHT

Plateau of Paradox

THREE MONTHS had passed and Charles felt he was once again on some kind of plateau—a kind of limbo highlighted with moments of ecstasy when he and Lynsey were together, on those isolated occasions when Lynsey was able to steal away from Hamish and spend an hour or two with Charles in his flat. Those were the occasions, isolated but regular, when Hamish walked to the pub. Hamish's visits to the pub you might say were as regular as clockwork, and Lynsey would always wait for about twenty minutes after his departure before she settled Tyson on the settee and made her way down the road to Charles's flat. It was a life of managed deceit—not, as Lynsey pointed out, a malicious, selfish deceit, but a necessary survival resource, to make her life bearable under Hamish's rough drinking lifestyle where her role was reduced to a household slave, to be at all times on standby to serve his meals, his tea or coffee, his medication, and to wash and iron his clothes, and be there when he came home drunk as a Lord and clean up after him when he wretched up the contents of his stomach in the night. Her love affair with Charles was a light at the end of the tunnel of a bleak existence, a light which burned all the brighter for her when she was gripped firmly in his arms, responding to the waves of pleasure that came from his prolonged and sometimes intense lovemaking. For both of them their periods of lovemaking on his wide firm double bed in the seclusion of his flat were oasis moments that provided the water that nourished their love in what otherwise would have been a desert of drab loneliness. But how long could they maintain this lifestyle of managed deceit? It came close to collapse one Friday evening when Hamish's friend Stevie called at the house while Lynsey was out visiting Charles. He had called to see Hamish and knocked at the door, and when no-one answered he phoned Hamish on his mobile. Hamish was surprised to hear that Lynsey was not at home and left an angry message on the answerphone, which Lynsey picked up on her return to the house. She immediately phoned Hamish at the pub to explain that Charles had contacted her, depressed because his wife Sylvia had become seriously ill, and she had gone to his flat to share a cup of coffee with him. The explanation had a grain of truth in it, for Sylvia had recently been diagnosed with cancer. Hamish accepted this explanation, saying, "Yer shoulda phoned me furst to telt me yer was leavin' the hoos." She apologised, saying she should have done so. "You see, Charrrels," she said to Charles afterwards, "I am able to think on my feet. Dinna be afeard. I am used to being devious in this way because I was so used to covering my tracks when I was drinkin'. It's a feature of the alcoholic mind. I ken how to control Hamish. It has been a year since my last drink now, but my pattern of thought is still well entrenched. I was addicted to the bottle—but now you are my new addiction, and I will move heaven and earth to keep you! I will even lie to keep you and if necessary I will lie for your sake. You see, Charrels, I have become your Angel of Deceit!"

Part of an entrenched routine of the week was Charles joining Hamish and Lynsey for 'dinner' at their house every Thursday at 3 p.m. At first this was an intense drinking session that made the routine acceptable to Hamish, and Charles always arrived with a six-pack of lagers and a litre bottle of Hamish's favourite sherry. In time Hamish drank less with Charles because he picked up a flu bug that caused him to cough uncontrollably, though it did not prevent him from his regular visitations to the pub. Nevertheless, the Thursday dinner routine prevailed, and Charles enjoyed a strange acceptance by Hamish as part of the family; by Tyson, the Staffordshire Bull Terrier, too, who would climb up on the settee after dinner and rest his big heavy head on Charles's lap, while Charles drowsily watched the long hand of the clock visibly creep by, until it was time for Lynsey's bath and eventually for 'supper', which usually entailed a salmon sandwich which Lynsey, dressed in her nightgown, would make for the two men. In the end it was not just Thursdays that Charles came to 'dinner', as Lynsey contrived to make more meetings possible, to alleviate the loneliness of Charles's almost Hermit life. She felt responsible for him, even harbouring feelings of guilt on account of his insular existence—for she understood that it was for her sake that he had given up his safe, secure life in a comfortable executive home with Sylvia and had lost contact with his family. He in turn threw himself into his lovemaking with Lynsey almost with delirious abandon, for it was a form of obliterating his loneliness, guilt and homesickness for his settled, now lost life of security. What it did for Lynsey was to tighten the ties of love, for she had never been loved genuinely or sincerely before. "You are some man," she would smile, "a braw man, a big sumph, so kind and gentle—and so strong!" And she would frequently say it was too late, now, for him to return to Sylvia—for she had become far too fond of him and dependent on his love which gave new purpose to her life. One day she met Maggie, from the old prayer circle, and Maggie told her how much the group had missed her and Charles. Lynsey told Maggie she was surprised that Sylvia had made no effort at all to get Charles back, adding, "Well, if she doesna want him, I do—and so I might as well have him, eh!" To her surprise, Maggy laughed and replied, "Quite right too, hen!" Clearly Maggie and other members of the prayer circle did not reflect the same high-minded condemnatory attitude of the deaconess Sadie. When Lynsey told Maggie of the letter she had received from Sadie, that she could only return to the prayer circle if she publically repented and gave up Charles, Maggie was flabbergasted. "Well, she doesna speak fer the rest of us, hen!" she exclaimed, and added, "It makes a difference that what you have with Charrels is not a one-night stand—that you are both serious about each other, ken?"

In the meantime the guilt harboured both by Charles and Lynsey was acerbated by the altogether new and unexpected development of Sylvia's illness. When Sylvia visited the breast clinic for a routine cancer check, it was found that she had cancer cells in the lymphatic nodes behind one of her breasts. She would require a treatment of chemotherapy infusions followed by a programme of radiotherapy. After the first chemo infusion she developed a serious temperature and was rushed into hospital. Her blood count showed her white blood corpuscles were down to zero and she had to be put on a drip of antibiotics to fight the infection she had developed. When Charles went to see her in hospital, he found her asleep in the ward. She had lost most of her hair, and looking at her through the window from the passage alongside the ward, he felt a stab of remorse, seeing how gaunt and ill she looked. Had he been the cause of this? Later when she was a little better, sitting up and trying to swallow some soup that had been brought to her, he said diffidently, "I have put you through so much stress, Sylvia. I do hope I have not been the cause of your cancer." She did not look at him but stared into her soup. "Who knows what causes cancer," she said softly. "Of course, the stress will not have helped."

His mind frequently went back to the little village church in Yorkshire where he and Sylvia got married just over thirty-five years ago. He could see her again, dressed in white like the habit of a nun, and recalled the vows they had spoken to each other in front of the small congregation, and the deep sincerity in her voice as her eyes held his, promising to remain true and faithful "till death do us part". He had looked into her eyes and said the same words, and had meant them. Yet here he was, looking at her thin wasted body in the hospital bed, knowing he had betrayed those vows. What kind of a man was he? He knew that in giving way to his love for Lynsey he had acted entirely out of character. It was irrational, unforgiveable, yet somehow it had happened. He would still wake up in the empty council flat and find it hard to believe that he was there, away from Sylvia and his comfortable home, an outcast from his family in a kind of limbo where the only joy in his life came from the periodic visits and intimacy with Lynsey. The power of love was irrational, something that swept across borders, across cultures, across class, and didn't make any sense. Lynsey by her own confession had become dependent on him now, having, as she said, found happiness unexpectedly, and beyond her wildest dreams. Thinking of this, he felt obligated to her, and to Sylvia, veritably trapped between two women: was it a trap between two loves, or a pity which he felt for each of them? He was the cause of the misery of one, and the happiness of the other—who, if he left her, would be miserable in turn, for which he would be responsible. And where did God enter into this equation? Was it actually possible that God had put him where he was, in this conflicting situation? Was it the purpose of God, who worked in mysterious ways, to bring about the meeting between himself and Lynsey—at the right time, when she was on the brink of death through her uncontrolled alcoholism?

One night, to pass the loneliness after supper, Charles watched a film called 'Hugo', based on the novel *The Invention of Hugo Cabret* by Brian Selznick. It was about an automaton, a clockwork figure of a man that had a purpose before the figure was broken. One of the characters in the film said that the most important aspect of a human being's life is that it, too, has a purpose, and like the automaton, sometimes people are broken and need fixing so they can fulfil their purpose. It made Charles aware that perhaps he needed fixing—had he lost his sense of purpose in life? And yet... again, that haunting question: had God placed him in this new, lonely place, the council flat, for a purpose? Had he fallen in love with Lynsey, the cause of his agonising lifestyle, for a purpose? What would have happened to Lynsey if he had not been in the church that late summer's day when, tipsy and reckless, she had come to church with a sense of desperation? And, in any case, was his life full of meaningful purpose before the day she came to church, which precipitated the change in his life? The week before that Hamish had called the doctor to see her when, due to her excessive drinking, she was lying on the floor, almost incoherent, hallucinating in the grip of delirium tremens. God works in mysterious ways, his wonders to perform—could that be true in this instance, or was the thought merely a convenient excuse for falling in love and committing adultery? Had he been the instrument of saving Lynsey from death, for the doctor had given her no more than four months to live if she did not change her ways, or had he hijacked a vulnerable woman for his own pleasure? One way or the other, he could not escape the guilt that came with this new lifestyle in the underworld.

His thoughts turned to Oscar Pistorius, the South African athlete who had recently been sentenced to five years in prison for killing his girlfriend. He had been an internationally famous athlete and now, in prison, he had clearly lost his purpose. Did he wake up every morning in his prison cell, wondering that the nightmare was still with him, Charles wondered—inasmuch as he, Charles, still woke up every night in his council flat, with a sense of unreality, of lost purpose? When would he wake up from his nightmare and find himself back in his home, back on track, his purpose and life intact again? That is the way Charles felt, waking every morning, alone, in his council flat.

And yet—was this his new purpose, intended by God—to be placed cheek by jowl with the very folk he wished to avoid, the poor in spirit and the poor in cash, the lost, like the woman that screeched daily at her grandchildren in the flat below him and kept him awake with her TV through half the night? Nevertheless, he conceded that he *was* in love with Lynsey, that he loved her, and if it meant it would cost him his life to save her, so be it.

And yet the sense of guilt prevailed and Charles could not shake off the feeling that he was being punished by God— especially when he heard the raucous voice of the woman below him, or sleep eluded him because of the woman's incessant TV beneath his bedroom. But the alternative point of view surfaced again, one Sunday when, seated next to Lynsey in church, he listened to the words of the minister who gave a sermon on humility and service to God—and Charles recalled the message of an earlier sermon long ago, in Hull, that you are where you are because that is where God has put you. At first his sense of guilt was invoked when the hymn was sung, with the message that while we yearn to see the face of God, he will not hear us if we have deceit in our hearts: 'Who, then, are those who shall ascend the holy hill of God? All those whose hands and hearts are clean, with no room in their mind for worthless vanities or vows of a deceitful kind.' How, then, would God regard him, and Lynsey, who sat next to him in worship, who practiced deceit to maintain their relationship? Lynsey had called herself, in jest, his Angel of Deceit, and yet she was no more than an Angel of Resourcefulness, with no malice in her heart, the deceit merely a contrivance to make both their lives bearable. The minister prayed for "those who suffer" to be restored to the fullness of life. There was no doubt that in this lifestyle of loneliness he was suffering, in so many ways now an outcast from his family who no longer contacted him—and there was little doubt that Lynsey, in her life of slavery under Hamish's demanding and loveless regime, was suffering too—in spite of her having broken free from the bonds of alcoholism and the fostering love that Charles provided for her. In the limbo of the underworld in which they now existed both yearned to be restored to a fullness of life.

The next hymn sung in the church service focussed on service, expressed in the chorus 'This is our God, the Servant King' and in the lines:

> So let us learn how to serve,
> And in our lives enthrone him;
> Each other's needs to prefer,
> For it is Christ we're serving.

This, Charles realised, was the Christian's real purpose—to serve. The minister made the point that by our serving one another we show ourselves to be *distinctive*—like the pink sheep he once saw from a train travelling to Glasgow. "We are different and stand out—not because we seek to vaunt ourselves, but because through service we make ourselves humble," he said. Jesus is greater than any High Priest—but do we seek to be elevated to greatness by serving Him? The way to be great is the way of service, not demanding to be Number One. The trials we experience in life, he explained, are not punishment, but lessons in living the Christian life. "Serving humbly, let us learn how to serve," the minister said, and then went on to voice the very thought that Charles used to justify his present situation in his council flat: "God always puts the right people at the right place at the right time, with the resource that's needed—like the lad with the loaves and fishes, which Jesus used to feed the multitude." Jesus, the minister pointed out, displayed no pomposity, no blowing of his own trumpet. "Because he was humble, God heard him."

In this new lifestyle of near isolation and loneliness, Charles had certainly been humbled. God had divested him of his pride, pruning away all his former self-importance. That day when Lynsey came to church, tipsy and bubbling with Dutch courage, was it God that put him in that line of speakers who held out their hands to her? It was his hand that she had grasped with so much fervour. "You are such an adorable *speugh*!" Lynsey said to him recently, using the Scots term for a pretentious and aloof person. Strange, he thought, that what attracted her to him was the very quality that God was using her to prune away. God certainly moves in mysterious ways.

*   *   *

Email from Lynsey to Charles

Hello my darling. Thank you so much for seeing me safely home tonight. I had the loveliest time this evening, as always. Our times together are now so much more intimate and meaningful. Both of us seem to be much more comfortable with each other now, and our shyness towards each other has now disappeared. My goodness Charles, we have certainly come such a long way since we first met. It just seems like yesterday when I met you in the church, on that beautiful and sunny Sunday. It is a day I will never forget, and I will treasure for the rest of my life. That day is so meaningful to me, as it was the biggest turning point in my life, and I did not know it then, but I was never to look back again. You came into my life at exactly the right time, and I am so glad and grateful for that. It was the day I emerged from the darkness into the light. On that day, you and God saved my life, and I will never be able to thank you both enough for this, especially you Charles. You sacrificed a marriage of 35 years, as well as a comfortable and steady lifestyle to achieve this for me. By going through with what you have my darling, you have more than shown me how great your love for me is. How could I ever repay such a sacrifice, and, God knows, how frightened and unsure you must have felt when all of this was happening to you. All I can do for you now, is love you, cuddle you, comfort you when you need it, and make you the happiest man in the world. I hope you will always be proud of me too, as I am of you.

God bless you my love, sleep tight and sweet dreams.

With all of my love, from your Guardian Angel,
Lynsey XXXXX

CHAPTER THIRTY-NINE

The Winds of Change

Reflections of Lynsey Anne McCann

IT HAD BEEN at least 16 years since I last had a proper holiday. I remember how excited I felt at the prospect of travelling down south to Caister in Norfolk, for a four-day break with Charles. I simply just could not wait. Well, it was everything I had dreamed it would be, and even better. We spent most of our time sitting on the beach, taking pictures of each other, and exploring the local sights. Caister is such a beautiful holiday village, and I remember thinking, how lovely it would be to have a caravan berthed there as a haven for Charles and I to escape to when it was needed. The thought of going home, back to Fife, was slightly depressing, and I was dreading it. Travelling back was a bit easier than it had been on the journey down. Charles decided to take the scenic route home through Jedburgh. I remember thinking to myself, how much I would love to live in such a beautiful and picturesque little town. My thoughts kept drifting back to the four wonderful days and nights we spent in the caravan in Caister. I remember how, on that first night, I felt shy and awkward, especially at the thought of sharing a bed with Charles. It had been so long since I had shared a bed with a man, and I suppose I was a bit apprehensive. Anyhow, my apprehension was short-lived. As soon as Charles joined me, everything just seemed to fit right into place. I felt so at home and content in his arms, as if this was the way things were meant to be. We spent a lovely few days just being in each other's company and getting to know one another even better.

As the car approached Kennoway, my heart just sank. Well, I thought, the holiday is over, and I must now get used to being back in the same old routine again—looking after Hamish and Tyson, as I have always done for the past six years. I have to admit though, when I saw the two of them sitting outside in the sunshine, as the car approached the house, I did feel glad to see them, especially Tyson, my faithful dog. I fetched my suitcase from the boot of the car and said goodbye to Charles. I knew I would not have too long to wait before I would see him again at the flat that same night. For the next few days and nights I was very unsettled, and could not get to sleep without Charles being beside me, and I knew he was feeling the same way too. The holiday with Charles was good for us both, but it actually made me realise just how much I loved him and wanted to be with him.

After a few days of getting myself back into my usual routine, I began to feel empty and alone. Being back at the house somehow seemed different now, as if things had changed and were not the same as they had been. Even the way I felt towards Hamish was no longer the same. Something in me had changed too and I felt it deeply. I now knew my relationship with Charles had moved on, and the feelings of love I had towards him were beginning to intensify, and take on a whole new meaning. It was at this point in our relationship that I realised, there was no turning back, and the strange and exciting thing was, I did not want to. I now felt there was a really good future ahead for the two of us together, and I was not going to waste it by living in the past, or allowing myself to be weighed down any more by overwhelming feelings of guilt and shame, because of what I had put his wife Sylvia through. Anyhow, I knew Charles had spoken to his wife on a few occasions before our holiday, to see if there was any way they could work out their differences and he could go back to live in the house he loved and knew so well. However, it appears he did not get any further forward, and I could not help but feel so disappointed and sad for him. After all, 35 years of marriage must have meant something to Sylvia, surely. Well, I thought, if she is not prepared to have Charles back, then I would do anything I could to keep him.

The months passed quickly and my love for Charles just grew and grew. It was not long before we managed to get away for a long weekend to London. I was so excited at the prospect of going to the Capital, as I had never been before. I would be able to see the sights, with Charles beside me, and the icing on the cake would be our night at the Royal Albert Hall. Well, it was even better than I had imagined. When I entered the Albert Hall, it completely took my breath away, especially the size of it, and I was amazed at how magnificent it looked. The London Symphony Orchestra played the most delightful selection of classical music, and when I heard them playing 'The Pas De Deux' from the Swan Lake Ballet, I could feel the hairs on my neck standing up. It was the most sublime sound I had ever heard. What a night, and it is one I will never forget for the rest of my life. I can never thank Charles enough for treating me to such a special gift. It was certainly a whirlwind visit, but I was surprised how at home I felt in London, as if I had been there before. When Charles and I finally got back to Scotland, both of us were exhausted. We had covered quite a distance in a couple of days, and it took us about a week to recover. It was absolutely worth the exhaustion and sore feet.

It was after this visit that I realised my lovely dog Tyson was getting older and his back legs were failing as he struggled to walk. Also, my dad was admitted to hospital again, and I knew this time he was gravely ill. He was discharged from hospital after a week, and both Charles and I visited him at his home. When we saw him I remember thinking he looked so ill that I felt he did not have much longer on this earth. It was a strange feeling to have, and I felt very uneasy about it afterwards.

Charles and I continued with our relationship, and met each other at every opportunity given to us. Our love for each other was growing from strength to strength, and our intimacy had reached a completely different level. However, it was during this time I noticed Charles seemed rather distant and preoccupied. Deep down I knew what was wrong with him. It was obvious he was missing his family and his old home life. Sometimes we talked about this, but usually he always managed to change the subject. I knew Charles was having a hard time adjusting to his new life and facing up to the fact that he was going to have to sit Sylvia down and really talk to her about his feelings, and try to find out exactly how she felt about him. I remember telling him, that if he really wanted to go back to Sylvia, then I would never stand in his way. You see, the only thing that matters to me is Charles's happiness, and if it meant him leaving me and going back to his wife, then I would have to let him go forever. The prospect of this happening was absolutely heart-breaking, and so very sad.

I have watched Charles grow from a rather shy, quiet and unhappy man, into a strong, and much happier, street-wise human being. I have so much love and admiration for him, especially in what he has achieved so far. For a man like Charles to be able to move on with his life, especially after being cast out of his home after 35 years of marriage, takes such courage and depth of character, which only I knew he had.

It was fast approaching Christmas and the New Year, and I had invited Charles to spend Christmas Day and New Year's Day with Hamish and I. Charles duly accepted my kind invitation, and I am so glad he did. We all had a lovely time and a very nice meal too. The Christmas Tree was nicely decorated and a musical Santa Claus was on display as well. Tyson had a good time too, as he waited patiently to see what leftovers he would get from the dinner table. However, it was during this time that my father was admitted to hospital again, and it would be for the last time. He had taken another bad turn at home and my mother had to phone for an ambulance.

About three days later, I received a telephone call from my sister Heather. It was Sunday, 4th January, and I knew from the way she sounded things were really bad. She told me to be ready within the next hour or so as my brother-in-law, Angus, would be coming straight from the hospital to pick me up. The nurses had told my mother that there was no hope for my father, and it was now just a matter of time until he passed away. The nurse asked my mother to contact any other immediate members of her family who were not already present at the hospital.

I remember getting ready and standing looking out of the living room window. All sorts of strange feelings were running through me, and I began to feel quite sick. I knew when I arrived at the hospital it would be the last time I would ever see my father again. Suddenly, I heard a horn blowing and I knew Angus had arrived in the car for me. When I finally got to the hospital, all of my family were already there. I sat down on the chair beside my father's bed and held his hand. My mother was seated directly opposite me. We all took turns holding his hand and just talked to him. Although he was sleeping, he was still aware of who was in his room. I did not even manage to shed a tear, even though my heart was breaking. I knew he was dying, but the whole thing just seemed like an awful nightmare, and eventually I would soon wake up.

It was getting very late, and my mother and I felt it was time to go home. Angus and my two sisters, Heather and Flora, stayed behind to be with my father. My mother did not want to leave, but we all felt it was best for her to get some rest, as she looked absolutely done in. Reluctantly, she agreed. My mother and I walked out of the back entrance of the hospital, and headed towards her car. The silence all around us that night was so eerie, and as the two of us walked arm-in-arm to the car, all you could hear was the sound of our footsteps echoing all around us.

My mother said she would try to get some rest, and asked me to be ready to be picked up early the next morning, about 5 a.m., to go back to the hospital. I told her I would be waiting for her. However, in the early hours of the morning, about 4 a.m., my mother phoned me and said she was now on her way to the hospital, as she could not sleep. She told me she would ring me later on, as I had a surgery appointment that morning at 9 a.m., which I knew I had to keep. Anyhow, at exactly 6 a.m., my sister Heather phoned me to let me know my father had passed away. She wanted to know if I would like to see him, but I told her no. I wanted to remember him as he was when he was alive. Later that day (Monday, 5th January), I spoke to my mother and she told me he had died at exactly 5:15 a.m.

My family and I went to see my mother regularly that week, just to be with her and give her all the support she needed. It was heart-breaking for me to see the pain and anguish she was going through at the death of my father. I would have given anything to have brought him back, just for her sake. God only knows how she must have really been feeling. My father's forthcoming funeral was hanging around my neck like some unbearable noose. I was dreading it and the whole thing still seemed utterly surreal to me. I know my sisters felt exactly the same way. My daughter, Iona, was so close to her papa, and I knew she was feeling the pain and anguish too, as well as my niece, Isla. All I remember about my father's funeral was shaking hands with a sea of what seemed like strange faces, although most of them I already knew. Our minister conducted the service really well, and my father had a good send-off. It was finally over, but now the biggest test for my family and I was still to come—life after the death of my father.

Exactly one week later, on Monday, 12th January, I had to have my beloved dog Tyson put to sleep because he was no longer able to use his hind legs and was suffering dreadfully. I was, again, to experience the same feelings I had when my father died. The long and painful wait for the VET and his assistant to arrive was horrendous. Eventually they got to the house and came inside. The VET was so very nice to us, and so was his assistant. They talked to Tyson and the two of us for a while before they gave him an injection to put him to sleep. A little while later they gave him the injection that would end his life. While all of this was happening, I was sitting on my couch, with Tyson on my knee, and I was cuddling him hard. Hamish was sitting on the chair at the end of the room breaking his heart. Tyson died in my arms, and I would not have had it any other way. I had just said goodbye to my best friend, who had been beside me, comforting me, through my hellish drinking days, and who saw me get sober. Charles came to visit Hamish and me later that day, and we told him what had happened. I know Charles loved Tyson, too, and was sad at the prospect of not seeing him again. I, on the other hand, had to keep going as I now had to keep a close eye on Hamish, and also try my best to look after Charles too.

My home had become so painfully quiet now, and a huge void had been left in it, as Tyson was no longer there. Charles, in the meantime, had become such a comfort to me and I do not know what I would have done without him. Charles and I had been tested to the limit now. The year gone by was the most awful year for Charles, especially as he had to adjust to a new life without his wife and family, and the new year was the worst start to a year I had ever had in my life. Charles and I were closer than ever now, and our love had grown into something enduring and unbreakable. I know Charles still feels sad and lonely at times, and he really misses his family and part of his old routine. It would be so easy for Charles to go back to his wife and take up his familiar routine again, but, at the end of the day I know he would not be happy, and he would miss me too much.

I have never loved a man the way I love Charles. I do not know what the future holds for the two of us, but I feel it could be a wonderful one. Love only comes round once in a lifetime, and when it does, you have to grab it and hold it tight. I truly believe love is worth taking a chance on, and what Charles and I feel about each other is so special and precious. I will never regret meeting Charles and falling in love with him. What I would regret is allowing him to walk out of my life forever. What would you do?

CHAPTER FORTY

Cold Comfort Sanctuary

IT WAS PERHAPS inevitable that in time the worm would turn. Even before Tyson was put down, Charles felt he was being relentlessly worn down, tested to breaking point. The routine of isolated visits from Lynsey had become an established one, she turning up for an hour and a half on the odd night that Hamish was in the pub. This routine was interspersed with 'dinner' visits to Hamish's house, when Lynsey would be in the kitchen preparing a sumptuous meal for the two men. First she would bring in a cold lager which Charles had supplied, then a tray with the meal. This would be consumed while the overweight Staffordshire terrier (which had already been fed a sumptuous meal of fried square sausage and chicken) would stare at the two men with his lugubrious face, his pink tongue flicking over his chops and nose, until one of them would give in and feed him a titbit—which would only result in the dog "squeaking" (to use Hamish's term) until Hamish gave way and went to the kitchen to bring back a "stinky" (a piece of dried tripe) which the dog would take with gusto and crunch noisily in a corner of the room. Thereafter Lynsey would enter with her 'dinner' which she would quietly eat at the other end of the settee on which Charles sat. The routine was continued, then, by the dog lumbering up onto the settee between them, dropping his huge head on Charles's lap, where he would grunt and fall asleep with Charles tickling his ears. Hamish would finish his meal then, and announce, "I'm away to my bed"—and climb up the stairs to take refuge in sleep. Alone together (apart from the huge mass of the dog between them) Lynsey and Charles would then partake in some disjointed conversation—until Charles went back to his flat to return at 8 p.m. for a supper to be prepared by Lynsey—usually salmon sandwiches. By this time Hamish had resurrected himself from his bed and Lynsey would be in her bath. The two men would sit in silence, Charles watching the clock until Lynsey appeared in her nightgown to bring in another lager prior to making the sandwiches. Charles and Hamish would stare in silence at the TV relaying an everlasting game of football, Charles doing his best to pretend a keen interest in the piece of leather being kicked about from one team member to another, interminably, the score rarely rising above 1-0, and Charles not caring a damn which team won anyway. The dog again would take up his position in front of the two men as they ate their sandwiches, "squeaking" and bouncing from paw to paw to attract attention, expectant, his tongue once again curling over his blunt snout, provoking the delivery of another titbit, or the delivery of another tripe "stinky" which he would crunch, the dry pieces scattering over the carpet. Eventually Charles would make his escape back to the flat and wonder what this was all about.

The final straw however was the incessant daily wails of the babies and toddlers below his flat and the grandmother's raucous screaming at them. Charles would turn up the volume of his music, symphonies by Beethoven, Mozart or Dvorak, to drown out the inharmonious noise. It did not help when the woman went to bed and turned on her TV in her bedroom below Charles's bedroom which made it impossible for him to sleep for two hours after midnight, when the woman would finally turn off her TV and succumb to sleep—at 2 a.m. It was wearing Charles down.

One day, trying to edit a book from a new author, with the babies below screaming blue murder once again, it got too much. He fell on his knees and prayed, desperately:

"Dear God, in the name of Jesus, make this change! Please Lord, I am desperate and I am begging for a miracle! I love Lynsey but I cannot go on living like this. It is an endless, unchanging lifestyle of relentless misery that has no light at the end of the tunnel. Please shine your light, Lord. Let me see your light and take me out of this nightmare!"

Lynsey had told him that he had become her reason for living—for eventually Hamish would die and she would be free from her obligation to care for him. But he could not wait interminably for a man to die. After all, in a sense, he had even grown to like Hamish, in spite of his rough uncouth ways. At heart he was generous, kind to Charles, unquestioningly accepting his invasion into his home. Whether he realised the extent of Charles's love for Lynsey, or was aware that they had consummated their love in the privacy of Charles's flat—even in his own sitting room before Charles had his flat—was a moot point. Charles frequently imagined going back to Sylvia, renouncing Lynsey for ever, for the sake of resuming his old comfortable existence, but feared for Lynsey's future. If he gave up, ceased to hang in for a better outcome, would she not be devastated—and what would become of her? She had become, after all, the love of his life, of his twilight years, and he the love of her life. But he was in limbo—and in a sense so was she, daily subject to Hamish's cantankerous behaviour and demands: Hamish would even insist on being fed omelettes on his return from the pub in the small hours of the morning, even though Lynsey had long since retired to bed.

Charles had now placed his plight in the Lord's hands. He would need faith that the Lord would find a solution, even if he, Charles, could not. What disturbed him however was the thought that surely it was up to him to take the initiative to change his situation. He was struck by what sounded like wisdom in the latest book he was editing, by a woman long since dead, whose daughter had asked him to edit and publish the book: "It's always best to accept what can't be changed but to alter what you can. Don't forget, you're the only one who can do the altering."

If Charles was the only one who could alter his situation, what was in his power to bring about the change—go to Sylvia and humbly beg her forgiveness and ask to have him back in his own home? She had finished receiving her chemotherapy, and was now receiving radiotherapy. She had lost all her hair but showed signs of recovering and renewing her strength. He had probably caused her suffering, pre-empting her cancer through the tension of his misbehaviour, his affair with Lynsey. He would have to go back humbly, like the prodigal son, begging to be taken back—not to his old bedroom he had shared with her, but perhaps to another bedroom, to a single bed, with reassurances to her that he would no longer communicate with Lynsey. He knew he could never stop loving Lynsey. Going back to his old life would be little more than an existence—yet one of peace from raucous noise, the dreary routine, and there would be the welcome freedom from guilt. But it was the thought of what would happen to his beloved Lynsey that paralysed his will to act. Was it not his God-given mission, perhaps, to save her?

Could he expect God to take the initiative? After all, God had taken the initiative in the first place by giving his only begotten Son to save mankind.

Charles's thoughts turned to dreams he had had, more than once, when in his dream one of his small daughters had died. It had happened again when in his dream his small son had died. He did not know it was a dream and in each case he railed against God! "Lord, how could you let such a dreadful thing happen! What kind of God are you? You are a God of love and yet you allowed my child to be taken away from me!" And in each dream, at this point of his wild rant against God, he would suddenly snap awake and be filled simultaneously with sweeping relief and overpowering shame—relief that it was only a dream, and shame that he had wrongfully accused God, even though it was in a dream. And yet the death of his child had seemed so real! It felt almost as though it had really happened, and the relief when he woke up was overpowering. Had God given him those dreams so he could be aware of the cost and pain God experienced by allowing the death of his Son? Or had those dreams really happened and God in his mercy had altered the time line, placing Charles in a different time when everything was restored and back to normal? Could God, who lived outside of time, do something like that? Nothing is impossible for God, he was taught, but there were surely limits to what God would do—and he, Charles, could never deserve a miracle of that magnitude. And yet it was a miracle that he was asking God to perform now.

When he went to sleep that night it was with a sense of deep calm. In the past he had even contemplated suicide, but now he had placed his life and his problem in God's hands. In time there *would* be a solution—even if it were brought about by his death. "Please take me home, Lord," he prayed. He recalled the words of Catherine Marshall in her book *A Man Called Peter*. She said dying would be like going home. You would wake up in the Kingdom of Heaven, she said, and it would be like waking up from a nightmare to find yourself back in your parents' home, safe in your own bed and your own bedroom. One night, he thought as he drifted off to sleep, he would wake up like that to find himself at home in his Father's house. After all, did not the Lord himself say, "In my Father's house there are many mansions, or rooms—I go to prepare a place for you, that when I come again, there you will be with me…"

He felt comforted by the thought as he waited for sleep to take him. Instinctively he imagined Lynsey was asleep beside him, as he always did, his arms in his imagination wrapped around her. He loved to run his hands over her and feel the smooth flawless texture of her skin when they lay together on his bed in the flat, and the tactile memory of her touch, the way she tickled his back, was with him even in his imagination. "I love you, my darling," he mumbled as he drifted off to sleep, "God bless you…"

EPILOGUE

What's Past is Prologue

THE DAWN LIGHT filtered through the curtains and his eyes opened, the dream of a provocative Scots girl still with him. The pressure in his bladder reminded him of the need to visit the toilet. He slid out of bed and lifted himself up, for a moment disoriented as his eyes focussed on the familiar walls of the room. He felt disoriented, slightly dizzy and steadied himself on the door handle to the en suite bathroom beside his bed. Why did he feel disoriented, as though the bathroom should be in a different place, beyond the foot of the bed? He opened the bathroom door and, slipping down his pyjama pants, slumped down on the toilet seat. While the thin stream between his legs trickled into the pan below, his half-awake mind tried to grasp the retreating vestiges of his dream. It was such a weird dream—of a woman, a vital, vibrant Scots girl that laughed and teased him, who tickled his back and seemed so real, yet a woman he could not for the life of him place or recall. Dreams could be like that, he thought, and it was amazing how the unconscious mind can be creative, conjuring up people you have never met yet think you know.

He stood up and flushed the toilet. He liked the comfort of his en suite bathroom, just next to his bed. He liked the way he could just swing out of bed and put his hand on the handle of the bathroom door. At his age, he liked his comfort, and somehow felt especially relieved this morning that he had this comfort. He climbed back into bed and saw that Sylvia had woken, too. She stretched her arm out, resting her hand on his shoulder. It was not often that she touched him, but he liked it when he felt the contact.

"It's time to get up, darling," she yawned. "You said you wanted to go over your part of the sermon the minister gave you to read."

Memory flooded back and clutched his stomach with alarm. "I…," he began. "I can't explain it, but I don't think I should go."

She frowned. "You can't let the minister down—you said you would read your part."

"I'll phone Sadie—she'll read my part," he said. "She's a deaconess… she has a copy of the extract in case something happens to me… I'll say I have a stomach ache."

"That would be a fib!" she laughed. "You're acting out of character. I thought you said the Lord put you in Kennoway because he meant you to go to the nearest church!"

"I just have a feeling… I shouldn't go. I'll come with you this morning—to your happy-clappy church in Kirkcaldy. We should really worship together, you know." He grinned. "It's time I got another hug from Huggy Peter!"

"Well, that would be nice," Sylvia smiled. "We *should* worship together. What God has joined together, you know… Nevertheless, you can't shirk your responsibilities. Go to the Church of Scotland this one last time, then next week we'll go back to the routine of worshipping together at the Kirkcaldy Full Gospel Church."

"Okay," he said. He felt uneasy—but then succumbed to an overwhelming sense of comfort.

It was right that he and Sylvia should do things together. After all, they belonged to each other, like a comfortable pair of slippers.

He got out of bed to go to his study and practice the sermon extract he had agreed to read, but he hesitated: a disquieting thought crossed his mind. "Did you have that annual cancer scan at the hospital?" he asked.

"Yes, darling," she smiled, sitting up. "I've been given the all clear—nothing to worry about."

www.ingramcontent.com/pod-product-compliance
Lightning Source LLC
Chambersburg PA
CBHW071515260626
47170CB00002B/379